The Game Begins . . .

Danica stepped off the platform and walked across the pavilion. The shield hummed on her arm, warm to the touch.

Bellasteros rose to his feet, fists clenched, dark eyes blazing. "Danica!" he shouted. She stopped but did not look around. "Danica! I did not give you leave to go!"

Slowly she rounded on him. Her shield flamed with a rivulet of pale starlight and Ashtar's voice pealed through her mind. "Bellasteros," Danica said, "may have the mastery of man and beast, but I am neither, and he does not master me!"

"A richly colored tapestry of character."
—Patricia C. Wrede
author of <u>The Seven Towers</u>

SABAZEL

LILLIAN STEWART CARL

ACE FANTASY BOOKS
NEW YORK

For my parents,
Robert E. and Bonnie N. Stewart,
who taught me to read.

SABAZEL

An Ace Fantasy Book / published by arrangement with
the author

PRINTING HISTORY
Ace Original / March 1985

ISBN: 0-441-74522-9

Ace Fantasy Books are published by The Berkley Publishing Group,
200 Madison Avenue, New York, New York 10016.
PRINTED IN THE UNITED STATES OF AMERICA

Chapter One

AT DAYBREAK THEY crossed the borders of Sabazel, riding down from the high plains and mountains sacred to Ashtar. At noon of the second day they came to the edge of an escarpment; the land fell away into a thick forest that edged a glistening rim of the sea. The Sardian encampment lay there, on the sea strand, in a clearing hacked from the wood. The purples and scarlets of its pennons were muted by a haze of sun-gilded smoke.

Danica gazed narrowly at the tall cloth-of-gold pavilion that dominated the camp; Bellasteros of Sardis, the conqueror, rested there. "The oracle," she commented to the woman at her side, "told him that a victory would be won beyond the borders of Sabazel."

"He threatens to throw down Ashtar's high altar," returned Atalia. "But Sabazel is small pickings compared to those provinces of the Empire he has already won."

"Perhaps the victory to be won here is not his." Danica glanced back at her Companions, a hundred warriors ranged in good order behind her, breastplates gleaming and crested helmets spilling sunlight onto spear and shield. She nodded in satisfaction. Her shield rested securely on her arm, its emblazoned star humming with a latent power.

"Look," said Ilanit, Danica's daughter. She thrust her chin toward a slight disturbance in the brush nearby. "His sentinels grow clumsy. It would be great sport to flush that one."

1

Danica exchanged a smile with Atalia over the young woman's eagerness. "Our gambit must be more subtle," she said. "We play for more than our own lives." She urged her horse on down the path and the company was engulfed by the moist stillness of the lowlands.

Then a wind purled down from the mountains, stirring the trees with a distant melody of chimes. Danica's mind stirred with the words of the goddess; her thought rippled like the surface of a pool disturbed by a touch. *Bring him to me, daughter. When he pays the debt he owes me, redeeming the bones of his mother, then shall Sabazel be secured.*

The camp was encircled by a palisade of sharpened logs and a deep ditch. The horses' hooves clattered on the drawbridge, and the guards waiting in the gateway stepped aside, their weapons at rest. Their plumed helmets swiveled curiously after the company as it passed. The Sabazians were expected, if hardly honored, guests.

White waterbirds wheeled overhead, their screeches blending with the cacophony of voices that rose and crashed against the riders like waves against the shore. "I'll be damned," cried one ill-shaven soldier, starting up and dropping the scarred armor he mended. "Sabazians!"

"So they do exist," exclaimed another. "I never quite believed the stories."

A third called, loudly and pointedly, "Are they truly women?"

And someone answered him, "Only women worship Ashtar."

Danica looked neither left nor right but guided her horse up the main street of the encampment toward the gold pavilion. The Sardian legionnaries closed around the company and the man-scent overwhelmed them. Ilanit's nostrils flared. Atalia leaned to the side and muttered, "Some of these men must have followed Gerlac even before he was husband to the conqueror's mother, before her child was born."

Bellasteros doubtlessly believed that these same men would desert him with derisive laughter if they knew the truth of his birth. Why else would he threaten Sabazel? Danica's brows tightened; she remembered well the imperial princess, Viridis, who had been secretly consecrated in Ashtar's rites before her marriage to Gerlac. She had died not in childbirth as rumored, but at Gerlac's hand, for delivering in seven months a full-term babe conceived in Sabazel. *Bring him to me,* sighed the Goddess in Danica's mind.

Danica spat a command and Atalia, with an oath, thrust her horse ahead. She pushed a way through the crowd with the toes of her boots and the butt end of her javelin, and the Companions drew closer about their queen.

In the shadow of the pavilion an orderly group of soldiers surrounded the Sabazians, throwing back the mob. Officers shouted orders and the crowd dispersed. Danica leaped to the ground. Ignoring a pageboy who ran forward, she threw the reins of her horse to one of her own warriors. The others ranged themselves in a line before the tent, weapons to hand.

The doorway was flanked by standards bearing the bronze falcons of Sardis, symbols of Harus, the godling said to be the conqueror's true sire. Danica paid them no obeisance as she strode into the shadowed interior of the tent. Ilanit and Atalia followed closely.

An official of some kind, dressed in imperial robes, came fluttering up to the women, but Danica brushed by him, directing her steps to a group of men gathered before a low platform. Over the dais hung a tapestry, threads of scarlet and of gold depicting a great battle, Sardian cavalry overrunning imperial chariots and Sardian phalanxes deflecting the arrows of imperial archers. Above the silent battle floated the widespread wings of another falcon.

The group of men parted as Danica approached. She passed through without slackening her pace, glancing from side to side. Sardians stood there, and imperial and other peoples as well. None of the faces showed the sycophancy Danica had seen at the imperial court.

The two men at the edge of the platform she identified immediately: General Mardoc, grizzled veteran of many Sardian wars; and Patros, childhood friend and chief companion of his king.

And seated in a chair placed at the center of the platform, under the protective wings of the embroidered falcon, was Bellasteros himself.

Danica stopped at the platform's edge, braced one foot on the step, and removed her helmet. She tucked it under her arm and shook free her fair hair. Her shield she set before her; as it left her grasp it shimmered in a quick murmur of light. Ilanit and Atalia paused a decent two paces behind her, young face and old equally impassive. Behind them the Sardians closed their ranks.

The game begins, sighed Ashtar. Above the pavilion the scarlet pennons of Sardis whipped in a wind that whispered of distant chimes.

Bellasteros leveled his dark eyes at the tall woman standing before him. He was indeed young, she noted, but his body was lean and hard-muscled with rigorous campaigning. His mouth might have hinted at boyish caprice if it hadn't been so tightly closed, set firm with the habit of command. He was short-haired, clean-shaven, and dressed in a short tunic, carrying the customs of Sardis with him into the heart of the Empire. If he felt any discomfiture at the appearance of the daughters of Ashtar, he concealed it well.

She had waited long enough. His gaze had not wavered. Danica sketched a brief salute with her hand. "Greeting," she said. "I am Danica, queen of Sabazel. These are Atalia, my weapons master, and Ilanit, my squire and my daughter."

"Greeting," Bellasteros returned in a mild but formal voice. "I am intrigued to find that we rest near legendary Sabazel." He made no effort to repeat the salute.

"Felicitations on your defeat of Kallidar's imperial armies before Farsahn," she went on.

His mouth twitched and settled into an amused smile. "My thanks, but I am told that you were Kallidar's ally."

"Then you were told wrongly. He sought to hold us in fief, but he failed. We, too, would welcome his death." Danica's smile did not even attempt amusement.

"Ah." Bellasteros nodded. He leaned back in his chair and allowed his fingers to tap a lazy pattern on the curved armrests. "I had thought to visit your capital; the oracle did suggest that I placate all the gods at the end of the world."

"Had you thought to come alone?" she replied. "At the turn of the year, when men are allowed across the borders of Sabazel to celebrate the rites of Ashtar? Or had you thought to come with your armies, at your pleasure?"

His fingers stopped dead on the armrests. "But you sent a message to me, asking for this meeting," he continued smoothly. "May I hope for your allegiance?"

Atalia made a growling sound in her throat and Ilanit grimaced. Danica said, "My Companions and I come to offer you a gift."

"Ah," he said again. "A bribe, you mean, to turn my attention from your barbarous ways and leave you . . . "

"Free." She swallowed the insult and clamped her teeth on it. So that was to be his excuse for invading Sabazel. What of the barbarisms of Sardis? The shield hissed, a spark swirling against Danica's thigh. Several officers started, exchanged wary glances. Danica lowered her head and gazed at the conqueror from under her brows.

His hands clenched on the arms of his chair but his voice remained light, almost bantering, as if he were indulging a precocious child. "And what gift do you bring me?"

"The fortress of Azervinah."

One of the Sardian officers gasped. Others muttered among themselves. "Kallidar himself hides there," one of them said.

"Our victory is incomplete while he yet lives," said another.

Patros frowned. "It would be the work of years to starve him out, and our soldiers grow restless. Azervinah guards the pass to the southern provinces of the Empire and the summer capital Iksandarun."

Bellasteros slapped the arms of his chair and leaped to his feet. He strode forward, his indolence discarded and replaced with the vigilance of his falcons. "Azervinah is impregnable," he said. "My scouts surround it now, but Kallidar only looks down and laughs."

"He told you, I believe," commented Danica, "to grow wings."

Again the officers muttered to one another. Mardoc thrust forward. "She knows too much, my lord," he asserted, but Bellasteros waved him away.

"And how do you suppose to deliver the fortress to me?" the conqueror demanded.

She let him wait a few moments; she dropped her jade-green eyes and looked curiously around the pavilion. When she looked back at Bellasteros he hadn't blinked. "Sabazel is a land of mountain as well as plain," she told him. "The rock of Azervinah can hold no mystery for us." Our spies are indeed most efficient, she told herself.

"But you would not be able to take it alone," he shot back.

Very good, Danica thought. Aloud, she said, "No, I fear you would have to contribute a few of your warriors to gain your gift."

Again the king scrutinized the queen before him, searching

the planes of her face and the smoothly muscled angles of her body as if he could read her thoughts. Danica suffered his inspection calmly. Only Ashtar was privy to her mind.

At last Bellasteros sighed, settled his hands on his hips, and tilted his head to the side. "And in exchange for Azervinah I must bypass Sabazel, leaving you and your people unharmed?"

"Yes," Danica answered. "I am told that Bellasteros of Sardis is a man of honor and keeps his bargains."

He released a sudden grin then, as if pleased by a game well played. "Agreed," he announced. "Sabazel is little price to pay for the Empire."

Danica sensed that the women behind her breathed only a little more easily. She bent to slip her shield onto her arm. "Agreed," she said, and permitted herself to return the smile with which Bellasteros had favored her. He had, it seemed, an interesting humor. . . .

Ashtar whispered, *First game for Sabazel and for me.*

The first day of the journey up the Jorniyeh River to the mountain foothills of Azervinah passed in silence, Sabazian and Sardian not mingling but riding separately. Danica said nothing to the conqueror, warned away by the set of his jaw. Jests flew behind his back—good-natured jests, if they concerned Bellasteros himself—but he would tolerate none in his presence. Jest was too close to hate, and if it came to hatred, Bellasteros would himself choose its target.

The second day of the journey began in a silence even tighter than that of the day before. But at midmorning a Sardian scout burst out of the tangled woodland that filled the river valley and cried that a herd of deer had been sighted.

"I am told that Sabazians are great huntresses," Bellasteros called to Danica.

"And so we are," she replied, pressing her heels into her horse's flanks as she spoke. The animal lunged forward.

"Hail, Bellasteros!" shouted Patros. "He has the mastery of man and beast!"

Ah, murmured Ashtar. *The game is joined again.*

The chase led over the tumbled roots of the great trees, through thick stands of fern and thistle and over hidden ravines. Some of the Sardian chargers stumbled and fell, but the lighter Sabazian horses leaped over concealed vines and potholes, seeming to spend as much time in the air as on the ground. The Companions shouted encouragement to each other as they rose in their stirrups to cast their javelins.

The hunters, like the deer, scattered to the winds. Ilanit led a group of Sabazians and Sardians in a plunge through the forest. Her breastplate and shield sparked as she flicked from viridescent shadow to sunlight and back, like a gleaming exotic bird in headlong flight through the wood. Her voice, raised in an exultant paean, echoed through the branches until it sounded like the cries of an army. Atalia rode at her side, watching her proudly.

Danica found herself riding flank to flank with Bellasteros, her mare keeping pace with his great warhorse as they crashed through the underbrush after a stag. She noted that the rest of the hunters had gone another way; she could no longer hear the shouts and cries, the rhythm of hoofbeats and the wail of Sardian hunting horns. But the golden-brown body of the stag flicked through the trees before her and the muscles of her horse flexed and loosed between her thighs. The goddess laughed in her ear, the leaves of the forest chimed with melody.

She glanced to the side and saw the conqueror grinning like a child, his eyes gleaming as he leaned low over the neck of his horse. The scarlet horsehair plume of his helmet streamed behind him.

The deer hurled itself across a brook, the froth that dripped from its mouth mingling with the water droplets stirred up by its hooves. On the other side it plunged into a thicket. For just an instant it vanished into shadow. Then the hand of Ashtar touched the forest, and the stag catapulted back out of the bushes. The hunters, storming across the stream, had but a glimpse of the rough hide of the boar and of the glint of sunlight along the curve of its tusks before those tusks buried themselves in the deer's flank. The stag thudded to the ground in a melee of legs. The boar stood over its shuddering body, tusks dripping blood, black points of eyes fixed angrily on the approaching horses.

"By Harus!" cried Bellasteros. He reined in his horse so abruptly that it reared.

"Ashtar, my thanks," Danica hissed under her breath. The shield thrilled against her skin. But in her eagerness she urged her horse onto a patch of mud at the edge of the stream; even as she raised her javelin the horse lost its footing. With a squeal it fell sideways into the water.

Danica threw herself clear, rolling over and over on the greensward with her javelin held at arm's length. She sprang to her feet, inhaling sharply, as her horse scrambled up with a questioning whinny. She heard clearly the man's delighted laugh.

The boar's tiny, red-rimmed eyes glared at her and she matched its stare. The bristles heaved along its sides, scattering the sunlight. Then it jumped, tusks lowered, straight toward her. Danica grounded the butt of her spear on a rock, braced her body against it, and raised her shield.

Then the boar was on her. She leaned on the javelin as the beast's impetus carried it onto the sharp point. The point struck deep into its body and it screamed. Blood gushed, burning, over Danica's hand and arm; where it touched the shield it steamed. The huge body of the boar carried her backward, but in its killing frenzy it only impaled itself more deeply on the spear. Danica fell beneath it, her shield protecting her throat from the slice of the tusks. She released the spear to draw her sword. Even as her slender blade turned and bit, another blade flashed with fire before her eyes. The boar screamed again, grating the forest with its death cry; then it collapsed, a reeking hulk that oozed blood and foam over her shield.

Danica exhaled, slowly, and pulled her sword from the animal's throat. For a moment she rested beneath the sheltering circle of the shield, considering the falcon-headed sword that protruded from the boar's breast. The image remained branded in her mind; Bellasteros, feet braced wide apart, hewed the boar with a two-handed stroke. His eyes blazed and his teeth were bared in a killing frenzy as strong as the beast's.

A shadow came between her and the sun. She looked up. Bellasteros extracted his sword from the body, drove it into the ground beside the carcass, and levered the animal away from her. "Foolish," he commented, "to turn your horse on the mud. Even the most sure-footed beast would slip." He was breathing hard but his expression was of casual interest.

"My thanks for your assistance," Danica said politely. She ignored his proffered hand and clambered to her feet The sun-dappled surface of the stream beckoned and she made no effort to resist. She laid the quiescent shield down, stripped off her armor, boots, and the softer garments beneath, and cleaned them as best she could. Naked, she threw herself into a pool to wash away the blood and sweat of the hunt.

Bellasteros watched with great interest, not even pretending to avert his eyes. At last he, too, laid aside his bronze armor to bathe in the stream. "What did you think?" she asked him, catching one of his glances. "Did you believe the tales that we Sabazians mutilate ourselves, cutting away our womanhood to better draw our weapons?" He dropped his eyes then, and she laughed. "How could we nourish our infants?"

Bellasteros splashed out of the water, laid himself on the bank of the stream, and regained his composure. "Indeed," he said, with a sly sideways gleam, "a people that did not bear offspring would soon perish."

"Truly," she replied. She seated herself some paces away, drying the golden waves of her hair in the sun and in the breeze that rang through the forest. The water murmured to itself, singing a half-remembered song of ancient heroes and their deeds.

After a time Danica said, "We are not the barbarians you name us."

"You take many lovers and marry none," he told her by way of evidence. "How do you know your child's father?"

"We accept those men who wish to make offering to Ashtar," she returned. "I know well my child's mother. Your marriages have not prevented your taking lovers."

Bellasteros opened his mouth, shut it, frowned slightly, and tried again. "We bury our dead according to the rites of the true gods."

Danica smoothed her hair over her shoulders and picked up her trousers. "Ashtar, the true goddess, requires that we burn our dead."

"And you give away your sons."

"To be cherished by our neighbors. You expose your daughters, to die at the mercy of the cold and the wolves that prowl the garbage middens of your cities."

"Harus," muttered Bellasteros. He grabbed his tunic. Danica settled her breastplate over her chest and slipped her sword into its scabbard, making no further comment but watching him through her lashes.

He buckled his cuirass and strolled across the grass to stroke his horse's nose. "Bellasteros," he mumbled, "the master of man and beast." The horse nickered against his shoulder.

Danica surprised herself with a smile. When the conqueror turned back to her their eyes met and held, exchanging not challenge but wary respect.

Game and set, sighed Ashtar. *Bring him to me, daughter, in Sabazel.*

Chapter Two

THE FORTRESS OF AZERVINAH, a titanic block cast off from the neighboring mountains, did, indeed, appear to be impregnable. Danica craned her neck to see the distant points of light along the shadowed walls at the top of the rock. It was difficult to tell which lights were torches and which were stars spread lavishly by Ashtar's hand across an indigo sky.

"How did Kallidar build a fortress up there?" asked Ilanit. Her helmet threatened to slide off her head as she looked up and she steadied it with her hand.

Atalia shrugged. "They say he ferried up the stones on the wings of giant eagles."

"A block and tackle would have served as well," Danica said. "And the slaves of the Empire."

Bellasteros materialized out of the darkness, the small watchfires gleaming in his burnished armor. "I am told there are secret passages in the rock," he said, "but in the two moons since the siege began no one has entered or left."

"And you've set no more fires than usual?" she asked. "The watchers on the rock have no cause to think this night different from those before?"

"Mardoc gave the order," he responded with some acerbity. "As I ordered him."

As I ordered you, Danica added to herself. But she said nothing. He had lost five trusted men trying the same move she and her Companions were now attempting. The game still hung in the balance, and Azervinah was only a piece on the board.

She tested the weight of her sword and shield, strapped securely across her back. Her body felt oddly light without its armor, and the soft slippers on her feet made only a disconcerting patter across the stone.

"I await your signal," said Bellasteros. "Show Kallidar that we have grown wings." His hand fell on Danica's shoulder in an expression of polite encouragement.

A few moments later she and six chosen Companions were wedging the first of the tent pegs into head-high crevices in the darkest shadows at the base of the rock. From peg to peg they crawled like patient spiders, straight up the face of the precipice, clinging, reaching, grasping. Their breaths mingled with the night wind and their bodies became blots of shadow against the rock.

Danica drove a peg into a crack, tested it, pulled herself up onto it, and reached over to steady a nearby Companion. She paused a moment to let the pain in her chest and shoulders subside, gazing out over the tumbled hills at the base of the fortress and at the three tiny campfires like fireflies. The wind chilled the sweat on her body even as it whispered strength. She felt she'd been clinging to the cold stone all night, through dark day and on into eternity; the man-made walls above her had grown so close she could pick out the pattern of cyclopean blocks.

Danica inhaled, squatted, and yanked loose a peg beside her. Then, slowly, she rose and began to pound the peg into another crack just opposite her face.

"We are almost there," she hissed to the weary woman beside her, but her words were caught up and blown away by the wind that purled through the night. The other woman reached, grimacing, and grasped the peg just above her head. She put her weight on it. With a patter of gravel the stake pulled loose from the rock.

The wind stopped still. Danica held her breath. For one long second the woman hung suspended between earth and sky, cradled in the hands of the goddess. A small cry escaped her throat. Then, gently, Ashtar released her. The Companion's eyes were glazed with a merciful death before her body fell, a dark crumpled shape, into the night. Danica heard no impact; it was as if the woman had been snatched away from the plane of existence on a breath of wind that was Ashtar's sigh.

Danica leaned her face against the cold roughness of the stone and whispered a prayer. On her other side someone made a short comment, part curse, part supplication. A dissonance of jangling chimes sounded faintly around the rock.

Above the serrated mountaintops appeared an aureole of pale gold, presaging the rising of the moon. Was there not peace in death? Danica asked herself. The jangled chimes smoothed into distant melody. "Come," she called quietly.

Soon the crescent horns of a waning moon gleamed in a pool of light several handsbreadths above the horizon. Dark shapes clambered over the parapet at the crest of the rock and dropped to the paving stones with a faint ring of weapons.

Danica set her star-shield on her arm; it caught the luminescence of the sky, a cloud of light motes centered on the now pulsing star. Her form glimmered in and out of soft-silvered darkness, slipping ahead of the Companions like a will-o'-the-wisp.

A guard dozing in a puddle of torchlight had no time to wake but fell with a clash of armor, taken from behind by Danica's sword. The arched doorway he had guarded was closed by a metal grille; beyond it steps disappeared downward into the heart of the rock. Danica wrenched open the grille and a woman started cat-footed down the steps to open the outer gates to the warriors of both Sardis and Sabazel.

Danica ordered her Companions to pull the body of the guard into a place of concealment, but no one came to investigate the quick noise of his collapse. Her lip wrinkled in scorn.

The Sabazians crept through the shadows of the fortress, avoiding other sentries, until they found themselves before the carved doors of the most choice apartments of the fortress, guarded by two sleepy soldiers.

A rumor of violence, Sardian war cries, and the answering yells of soldiers awakened roughly from sleep echoed in the corridors. Sparks shimmered across Danica's shield. "Now!" she cried. "Sabazel!" She and her Companions leaped forward. The guards before the door pulled themselves to attention, but Sabazian swords struck them down. Danica kicked open the doors. They flew back against the stone walls with a crash.

The large room was richly furnished; tapestries and chests of ornaments lay along the walls, glittering in the torchlight. The emperor had brought his treasures with him in his flight only to find them useless in Azervinah. But Danica had no interest in the assembled wealth. On a canopied bed at the far corner of the room a brawny dark-bearded man sat upright, rubbing sleep from his eyes, his florid face twisted with incomprehension. Beside him a tousled woman clutched the bedclothes to her breast and screamed.

"Emperor Kallidar," Danica purred, advancing with sword and shield ready. "King of kings, god-king. Long have I waited to avenge your insults to me and mine."

The man's face grew even redder as uncertainty was swept away by rage. He leaped from the bed and plucked a huge scimitar from the wall. "Sabazian bitch!" he stated. "You would always demand the right to bear your weapons in my audience hall, believing yourself better than my subjects, who would gladly lay down their arms for the Empire."

An altercation began in the doorway as Kallidar's soldiers tried to force their way into the room. But the Companions stood shoulder to shoulder just inside the aperture, their shields ringing as they parried the swords of the imperial troops. They bent and swayed in unison, lunging again and again. The thrill of Ilanit's paean reverberated through the fortress as the doorway filled with dead and wounded. Then the fighting was over. A bronze helmet rippling with scarlet horsehair appeared in the door.

Danica's eye flicked for an instant to that figure in the doorway and to the forms gathered behind it. Kallidar saw his chance. Spitting a curse, he leaped, surprisingly quick for his bulk. The scimitar whistled through the air just where Danica's head had been. But she had thrown herself to the side, spinning on her feet; her narrow blade flashed and her shield glimmered with an aureole of pale fire.

"The Empire is no longer yours," she told her opponent. "Bellasteros rides with me."

Kallidar's face contorted and he looked curiously down at the oozing red furrow across his upper arm. Danica smiled at him, her green eyes cold. "Strike, emperor," she murmured. "Strike again." She lowered her sword mockingly.

The man's eyes bulged. He lunged and Danica danced aside, her weapon glancing up under his extended arm and gashing the muscles there. Even as he bellowed in pain he laid his other hand on the hilt of his giant sword, slashing the air so close to Danica's body that she sensed the wind of the blade's passage like gooseflesh on her throat.

Again she leaped, faster than he could turn to follow, evading the scimitar. She thrust her shield into the emperor's face as if it were a flaming brand. He winced as the light of the star-shield glanced off his features, draining his skin of color so that he seemed to already be a grinning death's-head.

Danica lunged, following the gleaming path of her shield with the blade of her sword. It struck deep into Kallidar's chest. For an instant the two stood frozen, face-to-face, as Danica's blade held the man impaled. The scimitar fell from his grasp and clattered across the flagstones. Then, in one smooth movement, she pulled her scarlet sword away. Kallidar crashed to the floor like a sacrificial ox. She regarded his corpse with narrow-eyed disdain and pushed at it with her foot.

A motion in the corner of her eye became Bellasteros. He lifted the emperor's great sword and weighed it in his hand. His voice vibrated with barely controlled anger. "I had thought to kill him myself," he informed Danica. "I am the son of Harus, I am to be emperor, and I had thought to kill him myself."

Danica rested the tip of her sword on the floor, catching her breath. The light in her shield was undimmed. "Long live the emperor," she said with a shrug. His eyes, their flame hooded, didn't leave hers. Behind him Patros frowned at Ilanit and Ilanit met his frown with studied indifference.

Weapons clashed in the corridor and Atalia burst into the room. She was pursued by several imperial soldiers, who leaped through the doorway and then realized their mistake. The Companions closed around them, aided by the Sardians who had stayed at the conqueror's side, and Bellasteros and Danica turned together to the attackers.

They stood shoulder to shoulder, their swords pealing. Danica beat back the attack of a soldier hardly more than a youth and was just turning to aid Ilanit when the shield spat a warning, jarring her arm. "My thanks," she gasped as she spun to face the upraised dagger of the woman who had shared Kallidar's bed. She batted the knife away with the flat of her sword but the woman struck again.

The woman's dagger hit the star engraved on the shield and shattered in a burst of light. She cried out in terror and shrank back, her hands before her eyes. With a sweep of his sword Bellasteros disposed of one of the soldiers he faced; the other threw down his weapon and fled. The conqueror turned, saw the cowering woman, and raised his sword.

Danica's blade flashed up underneath his and they met with a clang. "The woman belongs to Ashtar," she said.

Bellasteros stared at the queen who stayed his hand. His body quivered; his mouth was only a tight line across his face. And yet the flame ebbed from his dark eyes even as he stared at her.

Kallidar's partner scrabbled away across the floor. Her eyes were widely dilated, transfixed by the pulsing star on Danica's shield. Like a puppet dangled by the flare of light, she rose, opened a narrow casement on the far wall, eased herself onto the sill, and fell backward into the night. The gust of wind that shrieked around the fortress and carried her body away jangled with muted chimes.

The silence was absolute. Danica heard her own heartbeat within her breast and the ragged, awestruck breaths of the warriors behind her. With part of her mind she noted that one of the tapestries illustrated the legend of the deified hero-king Daimion, the tree and the sword—the beginnings of the Empire.

Then Bellasteros lowered his sword and released a pent-up breath. He bowed, stiffly, to Danica and summoned up a wry smile. "You have kept the bargain. Should I come to your capital at the turn of the year and make my offering to Ashtar, in gratitude for victory?"

"Would such rites please the gods at the edge of the world?" she asked. Her shield ceased humming and she sheathed the sword.

He gestured expansively, gracious in defeat and victory mingled. "I am told that all gods must be placated in turn. And your goddess seems to be no exception."

"Then you will be welcome in Sabazel," she said. She laid her fingertips on his face just long enough to kindle his eyes with a different kind of fire.

When she turned away her fingers retained the warmth of his skin. She met Atalia's quizzical expression with a thoughtful smile.

Ashtar murmured, *Not yet, daughter. You have not yet won the game.*

The interior of the pavilion was illuminated bright as noontide by countless torches, the flames doubled and redoubled by cloth of gold, gleaming utensils, and burnished bronze armor. The falcons of Sardis preened themselves in the vortex of light, watching unblinking as a Sabazian woman feasted beside Bellasteros.

Danica eyed the dishes of larks' tongues and sugared roses before her, next to bowls of chickpeas, salt fish, and olives, standard army fare. She permitted herself one more sip of wine. The Sardians drank their wine unwatered, and she had no wish to lose control of her faculties. But the liquid was blood-red, blood-warm, and delicious, stroking her body into an insidious lassitude while drawing her mind tighter and tighter.

Bellasteros reclined beside her, a respectful handsbreadth away. The scent of his body was strong in her nostrils and it was almost a pleasant sensation. If he did come to the summer rites of Ashtar, crossing the borders of Sabazel, then she might think that sensation very pleasant indeed.

His officers passed before the platform, weaponless, bowing to him. Some of the older ones, such as Mardoc, made of their bows perfunctory inclinations, but the imperial officials in the conqueror's employ made the deep obeisances due an emperor, and more than one of them murmured the name of Daimion. Bellasteros's deification nad begun.

Bellasteros called for more wine as he watched his officers take their places on their own couches. A boy filled his rhyton, dodging around the bored guard just behind him, and the conqueror drank deeply.

He realized then that Danica was watching him and favored her with a salute of his drinking horn. The wine slopped over the ram's head carved on its base. "Bellasteros rides with me," he mimicked. "I might have argued with such words, but now . . ." He drank again. The smile he turned on her was complacent.

She was somehow disappointed that he thought the game over. The voice of the goddess sang in the flame of the torches and the conqueror waited for a placatory answer.

"What would you have me say?" she asked him.

"I would have you and your warriors as allies, to secure the southern provinces of the Empire." His smile now was less complacent than proprietary.

She shook her head. "I want only Sabazel."

"And if I come to you, Danica, in the rites of Ashtar?" He reached out to touch her arm.

The caress sparked her body. The hair on the back of her neck shivered and she stiffened, drawing away. "Then you will make your offering," she replied, more harshly than she had intended. "I bargained for freedom, my own as well as Sabazel's."

He dropped his hand and his smile faded. "Then perhaps I shall not offer to Ashtar after all. She seems only a minor deity, served by barbaric rites in the outlands of the world. Only women worship Ashtar." One corner of his mouth wavered, not in jest but in renewed challenge.

The voice of the goddess cascaded off Danica's tongue. "Men and women together worship Ashtar," she stated quietly. "Women such as Viridis, your mother, and men such as those who fathered you under Ashtar's eye."

The sharp intake of his breath made the torches flicker. "You know too much," he hissed. His head snapped around, his eyes a dark tempest of horror and anger mixed. "So that is your game. That has been your game all along."

Her own eyes were opaque. The wine turned to vinegar in her mouth and she set her rhyton, very carefully, on the table.

He scowled. "You would hold my birth over my head and name me bastard. You would sever me from my kingship, from the rule of the Empire. You would mock my god."

"I would bring you back to your mother, Ashtar. When you pay the debt you owe her you will no longer be bastard."

His reply was short and ugly.

Danica turned, stood, and plucked her sword and shield from where they rested beneath the couch. "I weary of this game," she said so that none but he could hear. "I shall return to Sabazel, and there shall I await your coming, for your debt is long unpaid. Bellasteros is, after all, a man of honor." Her voice shook and she clamped her jaw against the tremble.

She stepped down off the platform and walked across the pavilion. The shield hummed on her arm, warm to the touch. The light it reflected was not that of Sardian bronze.

Atalia leaped up to follow, shooting a sharp glance of

triumph at the bowed head and shaking shoulders of the conqueror. Ilanit rolled off the couch she'd been sharing with Patros and stood, uncertain. Every voice in the pavilion stopped between one word and the next.

Bellasteros rose to his feet, his fists clenched. "Danica!" he shouted. She stopped but she did not look around. "Danica! I did not give you leave to go!"

Slowly she rounded on him. Her shield flamed with a rivulet of pale starlight and Ashtar's voice pealed through her mind. "Bellasteros," she said, "may have the mastery of man and beast, but I am neither, and he does not master me!"

And there, she said to the goddess. There.

No one spoke. No one moved. The conqueror's teeth glistened between his drawn-back lips. Danica stared him down. She refused to remember for even one moment the discomforting touch of his hand or the disturbing scent of his body.

Then Mardoc stretched, grinned drunkenly, and snickered under his breath. The chuckle echoed through the silence of the pavilion. Bellasteros snapped. His face flushed scarlet and his eyes fired in a mindless frenzy. In one motion, faster than the eye could follow, he snatched the spear from the hand of the guard behind him and threw. The iron point of the weapon ignited, slicing the air into tatters of light, singing as it sought Danica's heart. The bronze falcons flapped on their perches, ready to take wing after their prey.

Ashtar's shield sprang up, wrenching Danica's arm, and the spear burst against the emblazoned star. Burning shards singed the rugs covering the floor and fouled the air. Danica fell back against Atalia, her forearm beneath the shield bruised and numb. Ilanit shivered as she cradled arm and shield together in her hands.

Those men who had leaped to their feet settled down again, shrugging, and reached for their wine.

Bellasteros braced himself on the table, his face as deathly pale as the surface of the moon. Patros went up to him and laid a hand on his shoulder, but the conqueror shook it away. "Danica," he croaked, "by Harus, I meant not to dishonor the bargain." He was suddenly, desperately sick, his body rejecting the blood-red Sardian wine that had fueled his frenzy.

Danica turned away, sparing him that indignity. "And there, Mother," she whispered. But she felt only pain. Atalia pushed aside the cloth covering the door of the pavilion and

Ilanit lent her shoulder to her mother's arm. The cool darkness blinded them. The still shapes of the waiting Companions seemed like ghosts.

"Come," said Danica. "We must seek the borders of Sabazel."

She knew without looking that the conqueror's eyes followed her. "Danica," he called quietly, in a voice that seemed to enter her mind without passing through her ears, "Danica, I shall come at the turn of the year. I swear, by Harus and by Ashtar, I shall come to Sabazel."

She did not reply. The stars appeared out of a pool of shadow and she blinked. The night wind caressed her face, cooling it and soothing it with the faint melody of chimes. The shield on her arm lightened, drawn toward the sky.

He will come, sighed the goddess. *He will come, Sabazel.* But only Danica could hear.

Above the encampment, over the high plains and mountains sacred to the goddess, the moon hung suspended in a shining arc, Ashtar's implacable smile.

Chapter Three

NIGHT FILLED THE mountain hollow. A wind purled through the shadows, stirring them with the melody of distant chimes. Starlight gathered like cool, crystalline fire in the wide basin of water on the flagstones.

Danica knelt an arm's length from the polished rim of the basin, bowed over her scarred and dented shield. Starshine caressed the high planes of her face and flickered green in her eyes. Her hair fell like spun electrum down her back.

She raised her head, lips parted in a taut eagerness, searching the night sky beyond the mountain peak. There, yes, the eerie glimmer of the rising moon. Tomorrow night would be the full moon of midsummer.

She leaned forward and brushed her fingertips over the water. The mirror of its surface shattered. A slow, pale flare stirred in its depths, molding the light of the stars and moon into a luminescent mist.

Danica, sighed the melody of the chimes, and the light in the basin wavered.

"Mother," responded Danica. "I am here, at your service."

Starfire sparked in the shadows. *He comes tomorrow for the rites. He comes to you and to me. He will be mine.*

"Yes, Mother. Yours." But Danica's brows tightened as she spoke, and her fingers flexed over the basin.

What do you fear? Him?

21

"No. Not him. Never him."

The water in the basin rippled with swirling flecks of light, splashing over the rim. Star motes fell gently on the shield, and it sparked in a sudden flare of gold. The dents smoothed themselves, the metal buckling silently into place, and the scars shrank and disappeared. The many pointed star shone out bright and clear, humming with one high, sustained note of power. Then the luminescence faded, the music of the star died, and the shield lay mute against Danica's knees. She laid her hand on its warm curve and her face smoothed.

You are my morning star, daughter. You bear my shield, and you will be true to me.

"Mother . . ." She looked up. Only a flutter on the water remained, as if a wind stirred waves in molten light. Only a flutter remained in her mind. "Mother," she sighed, her shoulders heaving. "My thanks." The waves stilled themselves, slowly, so that her reflection took shape on the surface of the water like a distant memory called into conscious image.

Danica lifted the shield and set it thoughtfully on her arm. As she turned from the basin a figure stepped briskly up the flight of rock-hewn steps leading to the hollow. "Danica?"

"Shandir. Do you need me?"

The healer was a plump turtledove of a woman; her bright eyes missed nothing, and their glance held compassion for everything they saw. "No matter. The preparations are in good order. He will bring twelve men with him, the message said."

"And Atalia?"

"She will stand guard this midsummer's eve; she does not trust the Sardians."

Danica laughed shortly. "And I do? Vigilance, Shandir, now more than ever."

The woman did not so much as smile. "And you also, my queen. Be wary."

Danica did not reply. She lifted the shield, turned, and hurried down the steps, Shandir close behind. Rounding a buttress of the mountain, they came out into the courtyard of the queen's own chambers. There Danica paused and looked with a sigh over the parapet to the walled city of Sabazel.

The city lay at the end of a steep-sided valley. The wood and stone buildings lapped at the precipices on either side. Beyond

the Horn Gate were the farming and grazing lands, the trees
and streams of the small country that was Sabazel. Danica
heard the fruit trees sighing in the breeze, the delicate notes of
a harp, a woman's song soothing her child into sleep. On the
walk above the closed gate was the quick, even sparkle of
spear points. The sentries posted farther down the valley and
across the high plain did not show themselves as readily.

Danica lowered herself onto a bench against the parapet, set
the shield beside her, and looked away from the city. Before
her rose the bulk of Cylandra, the moon's passage, Ashtar's
sacred mountain. Even in the summer the snows of its summit
glinted in the moonlight, cloth of silver against the stars.
"Many times," she said quietly to Shandir, "the moon has
completed its journey from the underworld up the flank of
Cylandra into the heavens. Many times the seasons have
turned, since I climbed the mountain alone and slept in the
cavern in the snows, waiting for the touch of the goddess's
hand, the visions that would sanctify me a warrior. The walls
of the cave are painted with the exploits of our ancestors,
when we rode free over the plains and did not huddle like
frightened sheep close to Ashtar's womb."

Shandir's skilled fingers closed over Danica's shoulders,
rubbing the tightness from them. "So speaks the high
priestess, the queen, who bears the star-shield and hears the
voice of the goddess, who is troubled by the changing world."

"It used to be that the priestess-queen did not have to be a
warrior as well," Danica said. "Long before my mother's
time. . . . She died defending Sabazel from change, and still it
comes. My daughter returns from initiation, our future resting
in her hands, and still it comes. The Empire fails and Sardis
reigns. Bellasteros comes to Sabazel." She shifted, not
angrily, but in a weariness so taut it would not let her rest.
"The world changes, but Sabazel shall remain free. As I live,
Sabazel shall be free."

Shandir sighed. "Atalia wishes that you let Bellasteros
make his offering with another, that you keep your distance
from him."

"So she has said to me more than once, calling upon the
shade of my martyred mother with whom, after all, she was
paired. She fears his strength—and well she should. But he is a
consecrated king and, thanks to Ashtar, claims the name of
emperor. He is destined for me."

"Then I shall attach myself to as many of his men as possible, to learn their temper."

"Shandir," Danica murmured, "my pair, you are as surely my shield as this." The star-shield beside her rang gently as she touched it.

"I? I never even attempted initiation, fearing the nightmares that come to those unsuited."

"So you heal those of us who are suited to the savageries of survival. Swordplay is not the only courage."

"But do I have the courage to fail?"

Danica shot a keen glance upward. "You, fail? No, love, failure is my greatest fear, a chancre eating at my soul—"

"Shh. I should not have spoken." Shandir stroked Danica's hair, soothing her, and laid a gentle kiss upon her brow.

The moon mounted inexorably into the sky. The city grew silent, fires banked. Danica at last relaxed in Shandir's embrace. "I cannot prevent change; I can only try to turn it to our advantage. Bellasteros is strong indeed, but it is his weakness that could be our undoing." Or mine, she added to herself.

"We are in Ashtar's hand," Shandir said.

The queen, her bright eyes focused on the horizon, did not respond.

Bellasteros's movements were abrupt. He might as well have been putting hapless enemies to death as packing a change of clothing in a saddlebag. "I made a vow," he told Mardoc, who followed him, scowling, from chest to chest. "I must fulfill that vow or lose the favor of the gods."

"My lord," protested Mardoc, "that vow was extracted from you by deceit. Harus will absolve you of any promise made to Ashtar and her whores. The gods could only rest more easily knowing that Sabazel had been conquered."

Bellasteros glanced at his general, making a quick, calculating appraisal of the man's mottled face and burning eyes. It would never do to turn Mardoc against him. His kingship rested on a sword's edge. His strength was tested in the flame of Danica's green eyes. . . . He shook himself. "I should not forswear any god," he said, as smoothly as the knotted muscles in his jaw would allow. "Ashtar is not without power; witness the power in Danica's shield. If our campaign into the southern provinces is to be successful, if we are at last to win

Iksandarun and the Empire, then we need a strong Sabazel to
guard our flank.''

"You trust *her* to guard our flank? She would as soon
plunge a knife into your back when you bow to her wiles.''

"I did not say I trusted her. I said I needed her as an ally in
the campaign—as she needs me to secure her borders. She,
too, made a bargain.''

Mardoc spat eloquently on the ground. "The witch-shield
glows with the sickly sheen of black sorcery. Ashtar's meager
powers can never approach the glory of Harus.''

Bellasteros closed the bag, flung it to a pageboy, reached for
his cloak and his helmet. "True," he said. "But power is
power.'' More acerbity than he would have wished crept into
his voice, and he paused to swallow. "Mardoc, I trust you to
stay here and ready the troops to move out on my return.
Trouble brews in the south, and we have waited too long. Let
me dispose of these warrior-women with soft words and with
honey; we have no blades to spare for them now, and Sabazel
would not fall without great loss.''

Mardoc's mouth tightened and his eyes fell. "As you say,
my lord. I will respect your decision.''

The conqueror grasped the older man's arm in an encouraging gesture and nodded. But as he turned out the door of the
pavilion his smile grew tighter, stretching his lips until his teeth
showed between them in a grimace. Mardoc had once been a
father to him; now, increasingly, he was an adversary. This
woman took too much—more, perhaps, than she offered.
Soft words, indeed; it had not been soft words that had won
him the Empire.

But it might, he thought suddenly, be soft words that kept
it.

He strode to his horse, leaving his dilemma behind him in
the shadowed tent. He snatched the reins from Patros's hand
and leaped onto the animal's back. The standard-bearer raised
the bronze falcon in invocation toward the sky, and the company set forth.

Bellasteros glanced sideways at Patros, glanced again,
frowned. "You look like a cream-filled cat," he snapped.
"Perhaps you anticipate disporting yourself with that girl—
what was her name?''

"Ilanit," Patros replied, quickly rearranging his features
into sterner lines. "I follow your lead.''

You do indeed. Harus, she is only another woman. . . .
Bellasteros growled some epithet and spurred his horse to the
head of the procession. He acknowledged the salutes of the
men he passed, but his gaze was turned inward, his eyes
clouded with storm and doubt. The great horse pounded over
the drawbridge; white waterbirds screamed overhead.

Patros bit his lip, hard, and tossed his head to throw away
some thought. The short plume in his helmet shivered.

Behind them Mardoc saluted and held the salute until the
company had left the encampment. Then, decisively, he
dropped his hand and turned back into the pavilion. Within a
moment he sat at the conqueror's writing table, armed with
quill and tablet, penning a letter cut with slashing upstrokes
and violent crosses:

To His Eminence, Adrastes Falco, the Talon of Harus,
Inquisitor of the Kingdom of Sardis; to be delivered into
his hand only.

Reverential greeting.

Our lord has been bewitched by the Sabazians; he does
not waver in his resolve to consort himself with their
Queen. I fear the consequences of his actions, even as I
assure myself that he acts as always in that temper which
has proven him superior to other men. Please to send to
the oracle, questioning her closely about the campaign to
come, for my mind is troubled.

And please to send to my daughter Chryse, the First
Wife of the King, my assurances of our lord's devotion.

I am, Your Eminence, the most respectful and obedient
servant of the God; signed, Mardoc, General of the
armies of Sardis.

The dust of the conqueror's company still lingered in the
air, veiling the rising sun, when the courier took the road to
the east. Mardoc stood for a long time in the doorway of the
pavilion, until at last the hoofbeats, east and west, were swept
away by a gentle breeze that had in it the sound of chimes.

The Sardians came at midday, riding up the valley in a panoply of jangling saddle buckles and clashing armor. The sun
flashed on the bronze of the falcon standard.

The red horsehair plume was in the lead. Bellasteros sat his warhorse as tensely as if he expected any moment to receive an arrow in his back. Beside him Patros shot glance after dubious glance at his king but did not speak.

The Horn Gate opened before them. The sentries there leaned on their spears. With many ribald mutterings, the Sardians entered the capital of Sabazel.

Atalia stood armed on the steps of the temple, watching, letting no expression touch the frozen creases of her face. The soldiers passed through the agora, looking with unconcealed interest at the women gathered there; but many of the women were also armed, and the men's comments died on their lips. Other men—local peasants, traveling minstrels and tradesmen, several warriors of the Empire—stood gathered in a hot, dusty group to one side. The looks they bent on the panoply of the Sardians were not friendly, but neither did they dare to speak.

Bellasteros reined in his horse, leaped off, and strode up the steps. He threw back his crimson cloak and laid his hand on the hilt of his sword. "Greeting," he said to Atalia.

She offered no salute. "Greeting," she returned, in tones as cold as Cylandra's ice-crown.

Beside the conqueror stood Patros, gazing about him eagerly, searching for one certain face.

Atalia turned on her heel and led the Sardians under the portico, into the sanctuary of the goddess. There, by the reflecting pool under the skylight, Danica waited. She wore a long shift of linen, belted with silver, and her hair was bound with a silver fillet. Ilanit stood at her right, and Shandir at her left; the youngest woman brightened, not imperceptibly, when she saw the tall form of Patros. Shandir saw her expression, and one corner of her mouth twitched.

Bellasteros made a great show of removing his gleaming helmet, tucking it under his arm, folding back his cloak. He looked about him as if seeking some statue or other representation of the goddess, like the great image of Harus in the citadel of his temple in Sardis; there was none, and his nostrils flared in disdain of the plastered walls, the vases of barley and millet, the small pool.

His bow to Danica was perfunctory, his voice brittle. "I have come, as I vowed, to make offering to your goddess for her help in my victory."

Danica looked not at him but through him. Their last meeting had been shameful for both. The pool rippled, the mosaic on its bottom shifted, and the small tiles rearranged themselves: the star-shield, a bronze falcon, a spear exploding into motes of golden light. "You are welcome. You shall remain welcome, if you and your people respect the laws the goddess has set for the conduct of these rites."

For we have only this rite, Danica added to herself, to share with outsiders, and that of initiation into the warrior band for ourselves alone. Only these rites for such an ancient worship. And our lives.

Bellasteros stood with his chin high, his back straight, holding his arrogance like a shield before him; his dark eyes glinted over a concealed turbulence as if moved by Danica's thought. But all he said was, "Set forth the laws."

"Three days and three days only are men allowed within the fortress of Sabazel. During that time they may approach only those women who wear the asphodel; the others have chosen not to participate, or have babes that cannot be left, or carry the fruit of earlier rites within their wombs.

"During these three days a man may not approach a woman with other than a polite request; if refused, he will go his way; if accepted, he will respect her wishes in all matters. A woman may choose her partner as well, but the man has the right to refuse.

"Any man who forces himself upon a woman who does not accept him, or who shows violence to a woman who does accept him, will be repaid in kind. As will be repaid any man who seeks to cross the borders of Sabazel at other than the solstices and the equinoxes, the designated rites of Ashtar."

"Repaid with death?" demanded Bellasteros.

"Or," Danica replied, "with what might, for a man, be worse than death."

He did not flinch. "Very well, then. You ask only the courtesy that comes naturally to us; with it we shall respect your laws." And he added, quietly, for Danica's ears, "Have we a choice?"

She released a quick, tight smile. Courtesy? she asked herself. But to him she said simply, "No."

The surface of the pool stirred as if touched by an unseen hand. From shadowed doorways on either side came hooded forms, shuffling forward with the uncertain steps of age. They bore garlands of white and yellow asphodel. Danica took one;

with a look almost of defiance toward the conqueror, she placed it around her own neck. The petals fluttered on her breast. "As you are king," she said, "so I am queen, and the goddess destines us one for the other. But your polite request is still necessary."

For one brief moment the opacity of his dark eyes flickered, and sparks whirled deep within them. Then he blinked, restoring his composure. "Indeed," he murmured, as if hardly interested.

The mosaic in the pool shifted again. *He plays the game well, daughter.*

I would wish the game over, Danica thought. She took another garland and set it about Ilanit's neck, caressing her daughter's warm cheek as she did so. She took Ilanit's hand and, leading her past the taut form of the conqueror, approached Patros.

The young man stiffened, and his cloak rippled as if brushed by a wind. With a start, in response to Danica's nod, he extended his hand. Danica laid her daughter's fingertips in his. "Her preference has been stated; she is the heir to Sabazel, and would choose the companion of the king. Will you respect her wishes? Or would you prefer another?"

Patros's sun-burnished face crumpled in a moment of uncertainty. His eyes sought Bellasteros's, but the conqueror had noticed the change in the mosaic at the bottom of the pool and was staring transfixed at it. Inhaling, Patros said, "Yes. I would respect her wishes, and her person as well, and I prefer no other." And, directly to Ilanit, "I am honored."

Ilanit flushed and covered her sudden color by offering a salute with her free hand. Danica turned away; the look the two shared discomfited her—too much of desire, too much of trust. Beside her Bellasteros moved impatiently, turning his back on the mysterious pool. They collided, the cheekpieces of his helmet ringing against his cuirass, and leaped apart as if burned.

Danica set her teeth, lowered her head, and targeted Patros with a steady look. "You shall indeed respect her person. She was only this spring initiated, and these rites shall be her first. Respect her youth and the goddess shall smile upon you both. If not—"

"You do not," Bellasteros cut in, so loudly that the doves preening themselves in the rafters exploded upward through the skylight, "you do not need to instruct him in courtesy. He is a Sardian noble and my companion."

"Yes," Danica told him. "Quite." Her eyes met the conqueror's with a clash, steel blades crossing.

Patros and Ilanit stepped hurriedly apart. Shandir settled the asphodel on her breast and stepped forward, her hands outspread. "The games," she murmured. The softness of her voice smoothed the harsh words; Danica and Bellasteros exchanged another look, angry, resentful, yet resigned.

The aged priestesses scurried between the columns of the portico, bearing more garlands to the women waiting outside. Atalia, waiting in the doorway, pointedly did not take one. She executed an abrupt about-face and grounded her spear beside the door.

Danica's teeth were clamped together so tightly that her jaw and throat ached. She set her hand on the conqueror's arm. His muscles were as hard as the metal of his armor. His scent came to her, a breath of spice and sweat, and she inhaled with a shudder. And yet, and yet, there was something pleasant in it.

They walked together, in a false amity, out of the temple, and they stood side by side at the top of the steps, wincing in the sudden glare of the sun.

The Sardian troops cheered their king; the Sabazians took up the sound, cheering their queen, and their voices overwhelmed the thin sound made by the men. At the conqueror's gesture the bronze falcon standard was placed carefully at the entrance of the temple; Patros set a guard on it. Danica pretended not to notice.

The other men moved irritably and muttered among themselves, shooting jealous frowns at the Sardians. But then the Sabazian warriors began to clear the central space of the agora, and the men, seeing the rites begin, brightened.

"You would join in the games?" Danica asked Bellasteros from the corner of her mouth.

"Need I prove my prowess like one of those peasants?"

"That is for you to say."

He glanced sharply around and caught the ironic resonance in her look. "Would it make of me a worthy offering to your goddess?"

Her green eyes mirrored his face. "Indeed, he who does well

in the games is favored of Ashtar. We would have the strong
father our children.''

With a savage jerk he reclaimed his arm. He thrust his
helmet into a startled Patros's hand and began to unbuckle his
cuirass. At his gesture the other Sardians began to lay aside
their armor. The hooded priestesses moved slowly down the
steps and set themselves as judges along the course of the
track. Sistrums rattled in the sanctuary, a quick, subtle heartbeat drawing the people in the agora into one equal tension.

Danica regarded the set lines of the conqueror's face; one
corner of her mouth flickered in what might have been a smile.
Of course he would prove himself. He had won his kingship
proving himself, answering to a herd of fickle followers, a boy
playing a man's game. No. That was unfair. A man playing
the most dangerous game of all. And she had made of herself
a piece on the board.

Ilanit watched Patros lay down both his and his king's
armor. The short tunic he wore beneath revealed the lines of
his body, and her lips parted in bemused anticipation.

''The games in the honor of most revered Ashtar . . .''
Danica began, stilling the bustle in the square with the clear
tones of her voice. The wind stirred her hair, tugging at the
fillet, and the goddess murmured in her ear, *You also, daughter, play well*.

Danica's cool, ironic expression didn't alter.

Chapter Four

DANICA WALKED SLOWLY up the rock-cut steps that led from the dim street to the moonlit courtyard and garden of her quarters. Thanks be to Ashtar—the fight had been only rough words between a Sardian farmer and one of the conqueror's warriors. Atalia had summarily ejected the civilian from the city, and the soldier, with a grudging acquiescence worthy of Bellasteros himself, had taken up the guardianship of the falcon standard. It might have been worse; blood would have called for blood, and the king would have rushed to defend his soldier.

She shook herself, forgetting the incident, and paused to contemplate the night around her. Torches gleamed before the temple doors, brazen below the radiance of the moon. The city echoed with a decorous murmur of voices, music, and celebration. In the garden the pale moonlight spilled from olive leaf to fig to fragile anemone. Danica reached out to lift a handful of the sheen, but it ran through her fingers and drifted away. The sistrums had fallen silent; it was her blood that pulsed quickly, insistently, through her senses. The wind was still, the goddess holding her breath.

Through the open shutters of her chambers, in the feeble light of an oil lamp, she saw him waiting. Not patiently, never patiently; he paced across the room, from doors to curtained bed and back again, marching in as strict a cadence as if he led his troops to war.

Danica inhaled deeply. He had won some games and placed high in others, careful to assert his strength, careful not to earn the resentment of his followers. Then his body had shone, sun-gilded, moving with the grace of an antique figure; now he was naked, washed and scraped and gleaming with oil. His arms and thighs were laced with the scars of a dozen battles.

His quick ears had heard her sigh, and he stood at the door. His eyes were the darkness of a moonless night, smoldering with anger and lust. The clear line of his chin was as sharp as a steel blade.

If she had hoped that the exercise of the games would dampen his energy, her hope was in vain. The sight of her alone seemed to strengthen, tighten, the lean muscles of his body. "There was no need for veiled threats," he said. "There was no need to so insult my companions."

"Veiled threats?" she repeated, gauging the exact timbre of her voice. "I would not have thought they were at all veiled." She brushed by him into the room. A taboret held olives and flat bread, quince jelly, pomegranates, and cheese. Her stomach rejected them all and she chose instead a cup of thin pink wine.

He followed her, reaching for his own cup. "Hardly more than water," he scoffed.

And have you drunk the thick wine of Sardis, blood-red, blood-warm, since that night you tried to kill me? But she knew not to say that aloud. "The grapes we grow are delicate," she said instead, "as is our place in the world."

"I am not here now to speak of your place in the world." He gulped the drink and dropped the cup onto the table. With thumb and forefinger he snuffed the guttering wick of the oil lamp. Moonlight flooded the room and draped his form with silver.

She turned away from him. Slowly she untied the fillet from her hair, letting the golden waves fall free. Slowly she unclasped the belt from her waist and folded the linen dress into a nearby chest. The breadth of his shoulders, she noted in a sideways glance, trembled.

His armor lay neatly in the corner, piled upon the crimson cloak; hers rested in its rack across the room. Their empty helmets regarded each other expressionlessly, and the star-shield lay mute.

"Did you examine the frescoes?" she asked, gesturing toward the murals on the wall. She found a comb and ran it with painstaking care through her hair. "There is Mari, an ancient queen, my ancestor, who aided Daimion in his quest for the tree and the sword. There is Ashtar's daughter Ataliana, the foremost warrior of her generation. She played in the games in Farsahn, it is said—you burned Farsahn, winter capital of the Empire, sending Kallidar scuttling to Azervinah. Is it true that the pyre turned night to day, that the owls hooted in confusion? . . ."

The painted figures shifted uneasily, eyes glinting, bodies tensing. Bellasteros snatched the comb from Danica's hand and sent it dancing across the planks of the floor. "You mock me," he said hoarsely. "You goad me. You said you were destined for me."

"I said," she returned, spinning away from his grasping hands, "that a polite request is necessary."

For one quick moment he coiled, and she thought he was going to strike her. She braced herself; that would give her an excuse to cast him out, that would destroy her hold on him. And that would betray the goddess.

But Bellasteros clenched his fists at his sides, stood to attention, and spoke, spitting each word between his lips as if tinged with acid. "Danica, queen of Sabazel, if you would please to celebrate the rites of Ashtar with me, your humble Sardian servant."

"Enough," she told him as she strangled the brief laugh that had tickled her throat. "Your point is made. Humble you are not, nor have you ever been, I think; and never would you be my servant."

One corner of his mouth shivered, as if he choked down some echo of her laugh. "We understand each other," he said. He extended his hand.

Danica laid her fingertips on his palm; his skin was as hot as hers. It was she who drew him toward the bed at one side of the room, who pulled aside the gauzy hangings and admitted him to its pillowed depths.

"Such luxury for a warrior," he commented lightly, but his hand tore away the garland of asphodel and scattered the blossoms across the coverlet.

"And your cloth-of-gold pavilion is not luxury?" she returned. He did not reply. Slowly he bore her backward, and for one long minute she did not resist. His face was a hands-breadth from hers; his exhalation was the warm odor of sandalwood in her nostrils.

Mother, she prayed, if ever I have needed your aid, now, lend me your strength, lend me your resolve.

The laugh excaped him then, a short bark of triumph. Deliberately he released the rage he had for so long held in check. He fell on her and started to pry her legs apart.

No triumph, Danica told him silently. The victory is for Ashtar. She tensed, gathering her strength, and threw him to one side.

She could have punished him with impassivity but she knew her own body, her own desires, would make that impossible. This was a contest to be won, fought with angry passion; they struggled, speaking only in sharp intakes of breath and muttered imprecation.

Bellasteros would have broken a weaker woman, despising her weakness even as he used it. But Danica held him back, twisting around him so that he could not pinion her beneath him, and at last, with only a token reluctance, he served her with the attentions she demanded.

He was not unskilled; his touch, rough and direct, suited her well. She grew drunk on the scent of his skin and the taste of his mouth, and his lithe, feline strength, so like her own, excited her.

He sensed her pleasure, the fevered pounding of her blood. He smiled. He closed for the kill.

And it was she who pinioned him, holding his shoulders against the pillows, kneeling on his thighs. Her body strained toward his, aching, but she ignored its sudden pain. She fixed his face with a hard, clear emerald gaze. "A polite request," she whispered. Louder, and her words might have trembled.

His chest heaved with his breath; his teeth glinted, set, between his lips. His narrowed eyes considered the expression on her face. "You jest," he hissed. "Still you jest with me."

She grimaced in what might have been a smile. "A polite request, my lord of Sardis, and I shall make you Ashtar's own."

His body shuddered, struggling to cool its own fever. "No," he said, hoarsely but steadily. "It is you who will now request of me. I have attempted to fulfill my vow; it is on you now, my lady of Sabazel." His hands closed on her arms like talons, tightening as if to push her away from him.

And he would push her away. He would throw her down, get up, and walk away, just to spite her, just to spite the goddess. Just to spite his own birth.

A wind sprang up, rattling the shutters, ringing through the shadowed room. Danica winced as it smote her mind: *Checkmate, daughter. Take him.*

And it will be you, Mother, who wins.

Her voice did tremble. "I would ask, with all due respect, if I may receive your vow."

His mouth relaxed into a lopsided grin. "Indeed." His right hand released her arm and stroked her cheek in a gesture that was too close to a caress.

She fell on him, enclosing his body with hers so firmly that his breath caught in a cry. It was a sword thrust into her own vitals and she, too, cried out, sobbing the ancient litany, "Ashtar, in your name, in your honor. . . ." His hand against her face closed on her hair, wrenching her head back; his body arched and she tightened her thighs on his hips, riding him as she would ride a wild stallion.

Then it was over. He lay quietly beneath her, his tension ebbing quickly, his body shivering as if chilled by a cold wind. He released her and laid his arm across his face, concealing its expression; she could see only the dark strands of his hair blotted across the dampness of his forehead. Their bodies were locked together, and yet he was as distant as if he lay alone in the echoing halls of his stepfather's Sardian palace.

Danica threw herself away from him, rolled over, and lay with her limbs spread wide to the night air, to the moon's rays that slanted in pale strands across the chamber. Her muscles sang, straining tighter and tighter toward a conclusion that would not come, not now—that much she could deny him. That much she could spite him, and herself as well for using him so.

Mother, she sighed, I have won for you, and in that my will is yours I am pleased; Mother, have pity.

The wind calmed itself, purling through the shadows like a rumor of distant, gentle chimes. *Your will is mine, and I am pleased. Pity, then.* Her body cooled, forgetting that she had cheated it.

"Danica," Bellasteros said. Her name plummeted into the darkness.

She scooped the tangle of her hair away from her face and

stretched, groaning. "Yes?"

He sat up. His neck was bowed, his back curved, his head hung almost to his knees. "You would take my substance from me, my will, my strength; you would have me give you everything, but you give me nothing in return. Do I deserve so little? You name me Ashtar's son, born into her hands as surely as you, but you show me nothing but scorn."

She raised her hand and with her forefinger lightly traced the line of his spine. When she reached the curve of his hips she rolled to her side and placed both her palms against his flank. His back and shoulders were scored with the red marks of her nails and teeth.

"If you are Ashtar's son," she asked, "why do you punish me for my devotion to her?"

Silence. Then, quietly, "I fear her. Her power touches me too closely."

Pity, Mother. "Have we served each other badly, Bellasteros?"

"Perhaps."

She rose and looked into his face—chagrin, pain, and the dignity of acceptance. Her tension snapped and she found herself chuckling. "Bellasteros. Have you another name? Such a mouthful, that."

His surprise disarmed him; he turned to her. "My mother, they say, named me Marcos. It was not the name I would have chosen at maturity. My father"—he paused, continued smoothly—"Gerlac named me Bellasteros, intending to make of me a warrior."

"Marcos, then, if I may call you such in confidence."

His smile was faint but composed. "A polite request, my lady of Sabazel."

"A polite request, yes, but I am not the lady of Sabazel. Come." She led him from the bed, across the room, through the shutters into the whispering darkness of a midsummer's night. The breeze was cold against Danica's moist skin. The chill was welcome, scouring her senses clean.

The moon hung low beyond the Horn Gate, drawing its train of stars across the sky. Stars, too, were the spear points that glittered in the dimness of the pass.

The water in the bronze basin shimmered in motes of silver, retaining the light of the moon. Danica passed her hand across the surface, swirling it. "This basin collects the mountain freshets, Ashtar's tears," she told Bellasteros. "The mountain binds the earth to the sky, and our lady lays her embrace over both."

He nodded. "In Sardis we must build our own mountains to bind us to the gods."

"And do their artificial heights please them?"

He grimaced. "The gods favor Sardis, it seems, even if they use Sardis's king for sport." She glanced sharply up at him, but he did not speak in bitterness.

She scooped up a double handful of the water and sprinkled it across his chest and shoulders. The bright droplets left shining trails across his skin. Another handful, and the silver rivulets cascaded down his back.

The water in the basin stirred, dissolving into luminescent mist, which flowed upward from its boundaries. It wavered on the wind, shaping itself into a form that was perhaps human, perhaps not human at all. The light it emanated was so bright that the shadows of Danica and Bellasteros stretched behind them across the flagstones.

The conqueror did not stir. His upturned face was set, calm stretched tightly over pain, his hands opened in supplication over the water. A tendril of the shining mist brushed his lips, strayed around his throat, coiled between his fingers.

My son, you have been long in coming.

He sighed deeply, the breath torn from the depths of his being, but pride kept his lips sealed.

Your brow is stained with your mother's blood. Your worship of me, so long delayed, will erase that stain.

And pride kept his back straight, his chin high, acknowledging his nemesis at last.

You will preserve Sabazel, and Sabazel will guard your back. You will make obeisance to me, and I shall lay the world before you.

The mist again touched his face and he blinked, quickly, as if loath to lose the vision. But the light disintegrated, distant sparkles drifting away down the wind. Muted chimes rang in the shadows. The basin of water darkened.

Danica slumped, exhausted, beside the still form of the conqueror, watching for his reaction. But for a long time he did not stir. His profile was the image of an archaic god chiseled in Sardian granite.

Is the game truly over? Danica thought. Or do its rules

change? And she thought, If I cannot have faith in Ashtar, I can have faith in nothing.

She reached out and lightly pressed her fingertips against Bellasteros's forearm. He started at her touch, then crumpled onto the stones. His hands closed into fists in his lap. "Here," he said faintly, "here within her borders, I can listen. But beyond . . ." He turned to Danica, allowing her to glimpse the struggle in his eyes. "With all respect to the goddess, I am not solely her son. My mother's death I shall repay—that much I owe. But I am caught in the nets of my life, and not even Ashtar can free me."

His mouth had softened; after only a moment's hesitation Danica leaned forward to kiss it. "Here, at least, you will know peace. And after . . . We shall trust in the goddess. She moves in subtle ways, and her paths are many. She holds us both securely in her hands."

But still he frowned, troubled. Again he set his hand against Danica's cheek, and, tentatively, he returned her kiss.

They rose and walked arm in arm down the steps to the garden. But his eyes looked beyond the city of Sabazel to the invisible lines of its borders; beyond those borders to the Empire and to Sardis itself. "Here?" he asked.

"Marcos," she returned confidently, "here you will begin a new life."

His body was warm against hers, his voice an echo of the wind. "Show me, then," he murmured, "how the bastard son of Harus can honor his sister in Ashtar."

So she led him back to her chambers, laid him on her bed, drew the curtains around them. And they made love with a tenderness that surprised them both. Not that she would trust him, Danica assured herself. He could yet betray her. But his strength was great, his surrender graceful, and his smile showed wry amusement at her, at his own confusion, at the gods themselves. Never before had she known a man of his complexity—and his beauty.

But even as she lay in his arms, satiated with what might have been her own surrender, she knew that neither could she be freed from the nets of her life.

The wind stilled itself that dawn, and the day broke in a silent rush of pink and amber. The morning star glittered above

Cylandra's crown, drawing the shadow of the mountain from the high plains and the tiered buildings of the city. Ashtar inhaled the night.

Atalia dozed in the guardroom beside the gate, her eyes glinting between half-closed lids, her hand clasped around a javelin. A cock crowed, and she started to attention, but the only living creatures she saw were the contentedly clucking chickens that paced the street and the bees that coasted on cool air toward the honeysuckle on the walls.

Shandir lay wakeful between two Sardian soldiers—Aveyron, tall and fair, young, fresh from a provincial town in the shadow of Sardis; Hern, stocky and dark, older, grown weathered in Gerlac's and now Bellasteros's service. Her chestnut hair lay tangled over them all, and her cheeks were still flushed with the night's efforts. But her expression was somber, and her lips moved in silent prayer.

Patros glanced between the shutters; only the leaves of the pomegranate trees moved in the garden. In the street, nothing stirred. He smiled. He closed the shutters, plunging the room back into night, and walked with quiet steps back to the bed. For a time he stood, watching Ilanit as she slept, flushed with an ethereal rosiness, her lips still parted from his kisses. Then he knelt over her and awakened her with a gentle murmur. "You have ravished my heart." She opened her arms to him.

Danica slept dreamlessly, and beside her Bellasteros lay as if struck down by an avenging deity; the rhythms of their breathing were the same.

The days passed in a honeyed slowness, and the nights were velvet soft beneath the stars. But the dwindling moon rose later and later each evening, and Atalia, at least, was pleased.

Danica set a small incense burner in the ruins of the meal, crusts and seeds strewn across the taboret. "Here," she said, "you might find this of interest. The smoldering leaves of lethenderum induce visions in some."

Bellasteros watched, one brow cocked in skepticism. "I have heard of the juice of the poppy, and of the drug taken by the mad hashishin of the northern wastes. But I have not heard of this. Is it a soporific?"

She sat down beside him, chuckling. "No, Marcos, it will not dull your . . . faculties. I have already told you, you need not prove your prowess to me.''

"Have I not already proved it?'' he asked, mocking his own arrogance.

She groaned. "Amply.''

His grin was that of a small, innocent boy, drawing an echoing laugh from her. She tickled his side where the ribs curved just under the skin, and he leaped on her, bearing her down onto the bed with an upheaval of the coverlet. For a moment they wrestled, laughing, until their lips met.

After a time Bellasteros raised his head. The spout of the incense burner emitted a tail of dark smoke, and a blue haze had gathered over the bed. He sniffed at it. "Coriander, perhaps; saffron and sandalwood.''

"Lethenderum,'' she informed him. She inhaled deeply of the fragrance; it sparked across her mind, tickling her senses, and her nerves sang. *Pleasure yourself, daughter. Pleasure, and no tomorrow.* "Come,'' Danica said to the man she held, "we shall talk later.''

Strange, she thought after a few moments, how quickly they had learned the peculiar melodies of each other's bodies, how quickly they had learned to play those separate melodies and blend them into one that blotted out all memory, all dread.

And, she thought after a few more moments, it was also strange how quickly they had learned to crave that duet, so that sleeping and eating and bathing became only chords in it, so that their greatest need was the touching, the clinging and straining one against the other, the sweet contentment after.

Then for a long time she thought nothing at all but listened bemusedly to the squeaks and sighs of her voice as she circled him, clasping him tight inside her. "Mother, in your honor. . . .'' And he, too, let the words of the litany be torn from him, in one long gasp of pleasure and submission.

"Marcos Bellasteros,'' Danica murmured, making of the name a caress. Strange, that she should so crave the body of a man. . . .

He lay sprawled among the bedclothes, blowing small whorls in the haze that covered them, holding her against his side. "Tell me of Sardis, the city of the two rivers. Tell me of the boy Marcos.'' She propped her chin on her hand to watch the expressions, exaggerated by lethenderum, range across his face.

Thoughtfulness, and a brief frown of painful memory, and the tightness at the corners of his mouth that was resignation. "Marcos, the nurses called me, as a boy in the great halls of the palace. But soon I was given to Patros's father, to be raised as his brother, and I was known as Gerlac's and Harus's son.

"My mother Viridis was a name on an insignificant monument in the necropolis, to be remembered with a handful of beans on Hallow's Eve; once I saw a faded scroll picturing the procession that carried her across the eastern river and laid her to what must have been an uneasy sleep in a rock-cut tomb. Must have been uneasy, until now."

The black pupils of his eyes dilated and his voice slurred as the drug worked its changes on his mind. Danica's head grew heavy and fell forward to rest on his shoulder. "Are these the visions you would choose?" she whispered.

"No, they are not; I think you have given me the elixir of truth." But his voice continued, and the images blossomed before her.

"I thought the rumors of my birth were jealousy of the king's son. But as I grew Gerlac declined; he himself began to make the sideways remarks, the quick sneers, that told me the rumors were true. And my old nurse confirmed it before she died—dying, she no longer feared Gerlac's wrath.

"The old king died violently, in an apoplectic fit, and I was pleased. He was a fool, never having learned to rule; in him, temper was a weakness. I was but twenty, but the troops cheered me in the citadel, and the generals offered me their fealty.

"My first wife was Chryse, Mardoc's daughter; we were wedded at fourteen, for Gerlac would not have me waste my substance—too proud to admit that that substance was not his. She was dull, she remains dull, and my other wives taken in diplomacy are likewise placid cows. Chryse bore me two daughters; Mardoc, shamed by the second, exposed it outside the city walls. The others? I did my duty by them. But always there was Patros, the company of men, and the military camp."

His voice faded and died, but the thoughts remained, molding the blue mist of the chamber into phantoms, ziggurats rising above the rivers of Sardis, the meek faces of women, Gerlac's poisoned pride; and over all the outspread wings of the falcon god.

He did not taste only his dutiful wives. After Gerlac's watchful eye had closed, Bellasteros haunted the taverns and the gleaming brothels by the river wall. All he had to do was lower the hood of his cloak, revealing the dark, even features of the young king, and the women flocked to him. If he found a courtesan who could not only play games with him, or entertain him with song and dance, but who could converse about politics and geography and the doings of the gods, he chose her. And he descended upon her like a falcon upon its prey, leaving her whimpering; the next time she no longer met his eyes, and he pronounced her dull and forgot her.

Under Gerlac, and then under his stepson, the power of Sardis grew—by conquest if necessary, by alliance, by the tribute of the lesser states about the Great Sea. The legions accepted provincials as soldiers and rewarded them with citizenship. Roads for couriers and merchants were driven through hills, across swamps, along the coastline; aqueducts spanned the valleys, and ships plied the sea in trade. Sardis was one tautly knit body, strongest of all the world—except the Empire.

The Empire, facing Sardis across an uncertain border, a border marred by years of dispute. The Empire, waning as Sardis waxed strong. . . .

And the Empire was a goal held before Bellasteros by the old king whose respect he could never earn. The Empire was a chance to earn his own name and forget the whispers of bastardy that echoed in the citadel of Sardis. The Empire had spawned the woman Viridis, who had branded him at birth and left him motherless.

So Bellasteros led an army of fifty thousand boldly across that uncertain border. It had taken him two years to defeat Kallidar and win Farsahn, two years to conclude the conquest of the known world and draw near the end. By the gods, there must be an ending. . . .

Danica heard his thought as if he spoke it, carried by the spiced smoke of lethenderum from his body to hers, circling and returning so that their minds were one—it was you I sought, only you; you have ravished my heart, my sister, my spouse.

But he would never say the words or acknowledge she had heard them, and she would pretend ignorance of his thought.

This man, of all in the world, had the power to draw love from her, and to draw fear.

The mist shimmered. The vision of Sardis became only light motes in the mist, fading, winking out. And the king and the queen who lay so tightly together smiled in other, better dreams; peace, and a world where peace was possible.

On the morning of the fourth day Danica and Bellasteros arose, and in silence they dressed again in their armor. Warily they regarded each other from the shadows of their helmets. "You will fight at my side in the campaign to come?" he asked.

"No. I want only Sabazel. I shall guard your back, and Ashtar will ride by your side."

His nostrils flared. "I would have thought—"

"Spare me," she told him. "The rites are over."

So he turned and paced from the room, leaving the tumbled bed and the ashes of incense cold behind him. Danica bent to lift her shield onto her arm; the metal chilled her, reflecting nothing from a gray sky.

A taut Patros glanced from the grim expression of his king to the gates of the city that closed behind them; he hid his face and did not speak.

"So much for that," Atalia said with satisfaction. "May they never trouble us again."

But Danica shook her head wearily and turned away from Shandir's outstretched arms to walk alone up the mountainside. Ilanit hid in her chambers and wept, too young for the burden laid upon her.

Bellasteros led his men over the borders of Sabazel. He sat tall on his horse, his mouth set, arrogant; his gaze was fixed on the standard carried before him, as if pleading release from some enchantment.

From Cylandra's flank Danica watched them, tiny horsemen creeping down the valley and across the plain. If I cannot have faith in Ashtar, she repeated, again and again, I can have faith in nothing. The wind whispered, *Sorrow, daughter, for a game that cannot be won. But a new game begins, and you will play again.* Weariness overcame her, the weight of her shield bore her to her knees, and she crumpled over its edge.

A falcon floated on the mountain's updraft, its talons curved beneath its belly, its eye sharp.

Chapter Five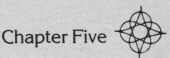

THE SARDIAN ENCAMPMENT resembled an anthill; workers streamed out purposefully from the central pavilion, carrying weapons and orders. The tents fell and were folded, the palisade was torn down and its planks transformed into carts; horses milled in temporary pens, whinnying indignantly. Camp followers gathered their children, and shrieking arguments broke out over cooking pots and bedrolls. Smoke and dust shrouded the sky, so that its clear blue arch faded to gray. The wind was still, and the scarlet and purple pennons hung lank until they, too, were furled and packed away.

The Sardians left behind a new town, a community of veterans wounded or grown old, of tradesmen and artisans who had gathered at the gates of the great encampment, of weary imperial soldiers. And, always, of women and children seeking the protection of men.

The soldiers Aveyron and Hern guarded the opening of the pavilion, watching with interest as pages carried tables and couches and rolled tapestries to waiting carts. "Good," Hern said. "Action again. No more of this consorting with barbarian gods."

"It looked to me," commented Aveyron, his blue eyes wide and wary, "as if you quite enjoyed consorting with barbarian gods."

"Now, lad, a soldier takes his pleasure where he finds it.

But those Sabazians—they would as soon slit your throat as spread their legs."

"So would most of the women in this camp, if they thought they could escape punishment."

Hern spat and ground the spittle into mud with the butt of his spear. "The Sabazian women know not their place, and we are well rid of them. Our young king is at times too courteous, I think, to the strange gods in these outlands of the world."

"He is a man of honor," Aveyron said. "And we are far from Sardis."

"Too far—" began Hern, but a horse came plunging up the avenue of the camp, scattering people before it, and the two soldiers snapped smartly to attention.

The messenger reined in, leaped off his mount, hurried inside the pavilion. "Dispatches from the garrison at Azervinah!" he shouted.

Hern glanced from the corners of his eyes at his companion. "May Harus lead us to a speedy victory in the south, and a return to Sardis before the snow flies."

Aveyron did not reply, but his hand tightened around the shaft of his spear.

Bellasteros slumped in his chair. From his hand dangled the dispatch tablet, switching back and forth as if to time the tumbling of his thoughts. His opaque eyes were focused on the middle distance. For the last two days, since his return from Sabazel, he had brooded over maps and messages, and not even Mardoc had dared to disturb him. But now Mardoc waited, his body poised in expectant impatience, polite but never subservient. "A dispatch," he said, prompting the conqueror into speech. "A dispatch from the garrison—"

"At Azervinah," Bellasteros interrupted, waking.

Mardoc nodded, waited, exhaled in frustration. "What does the dispatch say?" he asked.

His tone was much too acid. The king's chin thrust upward, and his eyes held Mardoc's unblinking. The older man gritted his teeth, nodded again, added, "My lord."

Bellasteros stood and with a gracious gesture presented the tablet to his general.

Patros, seated at the writing table nearby, shook his head with a smile that was partly aggravated, partly amused. He looked at what he had written:

To Danica, Queen of Sabazel. Greetings.

Bellasteros of Sardis, King of Kings, presents his compliments and his thanks for hospitality rendered.

Somehow his hand, of its own accord, had begun to write, *Ilan* . . . Quickly, with a guilty glance over his shoulder, he blotted the letters out.

"By the tailfeathers of the god!" Mardoc exclaimed. "I thought the satrap Bogazkar had died in the battle before Farsahn."

Bellasteros smiled humorlessly. "So did we all. But as military governor of the south, he may not even have been there."

"And now he has declared himself Kallidar's successor, forcing the southern provinces under his standard!"

"I wonder how many of the refugees declaring fealty to Sardis are really in his pay?" Patros inquired from the side.

"We shall never know," growled Bellasteros. He set his hands against his hips. "I would have thought the Empire weary of this never-ending war. I would have thought it drained of men and weapons. . . . It is the nobles with their private armies, surely, who seek to expand their power by fighting on. As if they were not powerful enough. The emperor and his lords owned everything, the people were so many serfs, bodies to be sacrificed at need."

Mardoc blinked. "Thanks be to Harus that the pass at Azervinah is ours," he stated heartily, establishing one fact in the morass of imperial politics.

"Thanks be to Ashtar," said Bellasteros. Go on, some ironic part of his mind muttered. Goad him. Goad him into spitting it out and ridding himself of it.

And Mardoc snapped around like a cobra prodded from its den. "You say that name here? Have you so easily forgotten your father Harus?"

I know well my child's mother, Danica said somewhere in the conqueror's memory. He turned abruptly and threw himself back into the chair, set his elbows on the arms, clasped his hands before his chest stubbornly.

"Bellasteros," Mardoc said, his voice rising, "has that slut bewitched you, stolen your soul from you so that you no longer have the stomach to be king?"

"Enough, Mardoc," Bellasteros growled. "I have bought

and paid for an alliance, no different from wedding a chieftain's daughter."

"Your wives, from Chryse to the last, wait upon your word, and you do not bow to them."

Bellasteros bit his own tongue, viciously, to stop the words that would have flown from it.

Patros frowned, laying down his pen. He jumped up and advanced to the side of the conqueror's chair. "An alliance," he asserted.

Mardoc turned on him. "And you, Patros, acting like a sick calf, not a warrior. The whores in this camp offer better sport than that scrawny Sabazian girl."

Patros scowled, coiled, tensed for the leap. The king's right hand shot out and seized his friend's forearm in a grasp of steel. "Mardoc," he said, in a voice so soft that the general had to step forward to hear, "it does not become our courtesy to mock the rites of another land. It is said that even the ancient hero Daimion had the help of such a warrior-woman. My vow is fulfilled, my bargain complete, and the episode is over. If you wish to test my stomach for the kingship, General, you will get this army ready to move into battle—through the pass of Azervinah which my efforts won for us!"

Mardoc's features resembled nothing so much as the mottled face of a rocky escarpment. Slowly he drew himself up, and slowly the flush drained from his cheeks. "My apologies, lord. My concern was only for you, and for the future of Sardis which rests in your hands."

Bellasteros ducked his head in polite acknowledgment. "You have long been my most trusted mentor, and I respect your concern, for it is always mine as well. But my soul is safe, thank you, and Sabazel lies behind us."

Mardoc bowed. "You comfort me greatly. Now, with your permission, I will see to the breaking of the camp." He offered the dispatch tablet and Bellasteros released Patros to take it.

"Continue, General, with my compliments."

The two men waited stiffly as Mardoc marched across the now empty pavilion, bowed once again in the doorway, disappeared into sunlight. They exhaled as one. The conqueror's right eyebrow arched upward questioningly.

"Forgive me," Patros said. "I have been on edge of late."

"Like a sick calf," returned Bellasteros.

Patros tried to smile but did not succeed. "No longer a cream-filled cat?"

"No longer."

They shared a long, reflective look, each daring the other to speak. At last Patros stepped close to the chair and said, in a husky conspiratorial whisper, "Do you suppose they did indeed steal our souls?"

"Perhaps our souls were freely given." Bellasteros sighed. "Perhaps they never belonged to us at all." He paused. The shouts of a centurion bullying a work squad echoed in the sudden silence. Hoofbeats trotted past. The wind was still.

Bellasteros closed his eyes. The sunlight failed, and the moon-silvered form of a woman stood before him. She was not beautiful, not by the standards of a Sardian brothel; her beauty was in her strength, in her reluctant smile, in the boundaries she held so carefully about her own soul. He looked quickly up and shook himself, but Danica's clear green eyes were still fixed on him; spare me, the rites are over.

Patros touched his hand. "I count myself very fortunate that my parents are mere mortals, that I know them both. I have brought troubles enough upon my own head without the help of gods."

Bellasteros flushed. "What?"

"I have brought enough troubles—"

"No, no. About your parents."

"Mortals. Not gods." Patros's gaze was open, honest, his hand quite steady.

"My father Harus," ventured Bellasteros.

"And your mother Ashtar."

The centurion shouted again, loudly enough to make the pavilion tremble. Bellasteros had a sudden impulse to leap up, stalk outside, and offer the man evisceration at the very least. No; unworthy of a king, to turn the issue and make a subordinate suffer for it. Or a friend.

The blood drained from his face, leaving it tingling, icy. "How long have you known?" he croaked. "Did Ilanit tell you?"

"With all due respect, my lord, Ilanit and I did not speak of you. It was earlier, when the old king watched you with hatred in his eyes, that I knew. How could I know you, and not sense your secret?"

"But you never told me you knew. . . ."

"My lord . . . Marcos." Patros's voice dropped even further. "You are my brother, and I would protect my brother from pain, whether it be in the field or in his mind. You rule in your own right, and not because your birth was the battleground of deities."

Bellasteros swallowed his panic. "How do you always know what to say, my brother, and when to say it, and how? I do not deserve such loyalty."

Patros shook his head. A rueful half grin touched his face. "You can understand what I left behind in Sabazel. The next time Mardoc insults Ilanit—"

Mardoc. Bellasteros held up his hand warningly, stopping Patros in midbreath. "So my secret is not a secret after all. Does he know the truth as well? He was, I am told, among the first to hail my divine paternity; was it only a political move to preserve the one strong prince born to Sardis before he could fall like his mother to Gerlac's wrath?"

"No, Mardoc is neither so subtle nor so crass. His faith is a simple one. He dreads the power of a barbarian goddess over the king he loves. If you forswear the falcon, he thinks Sardis will lose the Empire."

"And if I forswear the goddess?"

Patros had no answer for that. "I can only counsel caution," he said. "It was Mardoc who razed the temple of Ashtar in Sardis, not knowing that he avenged Gerlac's pride; he thought to prove his obedience to Harus. He must be convinced of your obedience, also."

"As always, I tread a narrow path." Decisively, Bellasteros rose to his feet. He stretched so that his sinews cracked. "Enough of this. I must busy myself with the campaign. It cost us two years to take half the Empire, for we had to struggle with Kallidar's armies every step of the way; Iksandarun is as distant from Farsahn as Farsahn is from Sardis, but I daresay we shall travel much more quickly now. Bogazkar commands only the dregs of an army, and we still have fifty thousand."

"Not the same fifty thousand with which we started," Patros reminded him. "New legionaries from the provinces replace those veterans killed—how many have we lost, one in ten? And the number of camp followers grows daily as the impoverished of the Empire claim your protection."

"One in ten." Bellasteros sighed. "An ending soon, I pray. . . ." He raised his chin. "Onward. No calves, or cats, or any creature but the falcon of victory. Sabazel is behind us, Patros. Do you not agree?"

His mouth settled again into the tight line of command; reluctantly, Patros agreed. But the constraint between them was gone, and the conqueror's hand fell in an affectionate gesture on his friend's shoulder. "I thank you. . . ."

Spears glinted in the doorway. A page hurried across the carpets. "My lord, a messenger from General Mardoc."

The rounded figure of a woman stood dark against the glare of the sun. At Bellasteros's gesture Hern and Aveyron stepped back, raising their weapons. "Not quite a messenger, my lord," called a rich, fruity voice.

"Ah," Patros said faintly. "Theara." He turned aside and busied himself again at the writing table.

Bellasteros flashed a quick, wry smile at Patros's back and then allowed his features to shade into annoyance. "If not a messenger, then what?"

Theara glided into the shade of the pavilion; ebony ringlets bounced above the soft curve of an exposed shoulder, silk rustled, bracelets jangled. She raised a small square of linen and dabbed at the sweat streaking her powdered forehead. "My lord, your pages tell me that I may not place my poor belongings with your goods, that I must walk with the—the trulls populating this camp." Her full red lips pouted.

"Poor belongings?" Patros mumbled into his quill. "The gold and the brocade we draped over you at Farsahn?"

Bellasteros cleared his throat harshly. "And the general sends you to ask if you may move as part of my household?"

"Yes, my lord," the courtesan returned. Her trembling kohl-rimmed lashes seemed about to take wing from her eyes. "My lord could not so soon forget—"

"Pack your belongings with mine," Bellasteros interrupted, exasperated. "And tell the general that I have better things to do than dispose of the baubles paid to painted . . ." He stopped. And my price is the Empire, he thought. He dismissed Theara with a brisk nod.

She curtsied, murmured her thanks, turned. Patros glanced over his shoulder at her swaying progress to the doorway; her last meaningful glance backward was directed at him as well.

"Mardoc sends our follies to haunt us," he said.

"Harus!" Bellasteros sighed. "He is as subtle as a rampaging bull. I believe you are right; he knows nothing. Would that I enjoyed his ignorance." And the conqueror stood, silent, his hands on his hips and head cocked back, listening for some distant sound beyond the cacophony of the camp.

Theara stepped delicately across the gutter that edged the avenue; a soldier shouted a question after her and she cut him dead with a stare. "Ashtar," she whispered under her breath, "your will, not mine, be done."

A wind stirred the haze that shrouded the camp, tearing it into rivulets of cloud. A murmur of chimes echoed in the vault of the sky.

Patros looked up, startled. Bellasteros set his teeth deep into his lower lip, as if the distant bells were a torture almost too painful to be borne.

Four figures emerged from the dim tunnel of the avenue. The two soldiers, dressed in the black-and-bronze livery of the palace, stopped with a clash of weapons beside the gateway pylon. The cloaked women hurried on, across wide dark tiles that only faintly reflected the starlight. A thin curl of smoke rose from the altar in the center of the courtyard, reaching upward until it smudged the face of the full moon. The scent of burning flesh hung heavy on the air.

The women started up the steps of the great ziggurat of Harus. They looked neither to the right nor the left, ignoring the mounds of lesser gods that were ranged in obeisance at the falcon god's feet. In the shadows at the far corner of the courtyard was a patch of scarred tile, overgrown with nettles and fireweed; once it had been the shrine of Ashtar, the twin of that in Iksandarun, but the soldiers of Gerlac had long ago looted it, burning and smashing, and had pried up its blocks of stone to add to Harus's mountain. The blood of the priestesses, it was said, stained scarlet the anemones that blossomed there in the full of the moon.

Halfway up the steep staircase of the great ziggurat was a doorway. The women stopped there, huddling together, frightened by a sudden rush of invisible wings in the darkness. Below them lay the city of Sardis, a black velvet drape displaying the lamps of the night like so many jewels; the braziers in the temple courtyard flared a sullen red, the street lamps glittered yellow, the torches set about the palace citadel burned with a steady white light.

The lamps stopped at the banks of the two rivers, the red and muddy Sar Cinnabran, the clear Sar Azurac, that embraced the city with their confluence. Beyond them, on the west, was the flat farmland that fed half the known world; on the east was the necropolis, a vast city of the dead where no lamps burned.

The doorway opened noiselessly on its hinges. One woman emitted a short squeak; the other raised a hand as if to soothe her. Adrastes Falco, the Grand Inquisitor of Sardis, the Talon of Harus, waited in the opening.

"Welcome," he said with a courteous nod. His black eyes were hooded by their lashes. "Please, come into my chambers."

The women stepped through the doorway into a low columned hall. An acolyte filled an oil lamp that danced above a table strewn with tablets and scrolls. The suggestion of a great statue stood lost in guttering shadow and a distant ripple of wings.

Adrastes indicated a cushioned chair. "Please, my lady, be seated. May I offer you refreshment?" He turned to a stand holding an amphora. Over his shoulder to the acolyte, he said, "Declan, you may go." The young man hurried out.

"No thank you, Your Eminence," said the woman who sat in the chair. Her voice was breathless, with the climb perhaps, or perhaps with some emotion. When she drew back her veil her face was as pretty as a child's, her eyes large and guileless, her chin soft. A gold chain sparked at her throat.

"It is a pleasure," Adrastes said, "to receive the first wife of the king in the precinct of Harus." He arranged himself and his feather-patterned robes in a chair opposite and set his long, tapering fingertips against the winged pectoral on his breast. His face was ageless, frozen in sharp, sly maturity; his hair and beard were a glossy black. It was the thinness of his lips and the shielded glitter of his eyes that betrayed his fanaticism.

Chryse regarded him as a rabbit would regard a snake; respectfully, but with caution. "While I would prefer to remain within the walls of the palace, paying my devotions at our private shrine, your summons must be obeyed."

The black eyes flicked to the form of the serving-woman. It

was the one he had noticed at the palace: slender, fair, with the pale eyes of the northern barbarians. "Lyris can be trusted," Chryse rushed to say.

"Of course," Adrastes said smoothly. His hand moved forward, choosing a tablet from those on the table, shoving it toward her. "A message from your honored father."

"Not bad news?" Chryse asked as she picked up the tablet.

"That remains to be seen," the priest replied. He waited patiently while she spelled out the words, her brow furrowed, her small mouth repeating the letters. Over her head Lyris watched, not stolidly, but with a well-trained alertness.

Chryse spoke at last. "Sabazel. The oracle said that a victory would be won beyond the borders of Sabazel—my lord's victory, surely."

"That, lady, is what we must assure."

"We? I am named regent only by my lord's courtesy and my father's rank; you are the ruler of Sardis in the absence of the king. I am but a woman."

"Indeed," murmured Andrastes. "But you are the first wife—unless the king begets a son on some other woman, a son to inherit the Empire he has won. Your position is secure."

She flushed and looked down into her lap where her hands lay clasped. "I have given him only daughters, true, and he will not return to my bed. He spent only a moment by my side this last spring, when he came so quickly to visit the oracle and then returned to battle." Her voice grew almost inaudible. "I would gladly forego my rank, Your Eminence, if my lord could only have his heir."

Adrastes favored her with a bow. "May your virtue be a model for all the women of Sardis."

"Thank you." Chryse fluttered in confusion, her cheeks blushing even rosier.

Adrastes glanced again at the serving-woman. Her eyes widened at his scrutiny and she straightened self-consciously.

"Now, my lady," the priest said, turning back to Chryse, "as I said, we must assure the king's victory and safe return. You saw the letter; I have sent to the oracle as the general requested, but she speaks in riddles of a hooded falcon, its jesses tied to Ashtar's wrist."

"Ashtar," Chryse repeated. Her mouth shaped the word awkwardly. "The goddess of Sabazel, on the outlands of the world. And the king—surely he has not been bewitched. Surely it is as my father says, only his courageous temperament, as fine and free as Harus his sire."

Adrastes smiled reassuringly. "You are correct, my lady; he has always been a soaring falcon. But remember the riddle of the oracle."

"Oh," Chryse gasped. Her hands flew to her mouth.

"But we can help him. I can make an amulet, sending the power of the god to free him from the wiles of this unwomanly woman. You must give me your permission to intervene, and some talisman that the king has touched, and you must give to me as well your serving-woman to carry the charm to the king."

Lyris started, glancing quickly from Adrastes to Chryse and back, bewildered. But Chryse set her chin and reached to her throat. "Whatever you direct me to do to aid my lord, Your Eminence, I shall do." She removed the gold chain from her neck and held it under the lamp so that it spilled like sunshine from her fingertips. "My lord gave this to me as a token of his respect, seven years ago when he became king and I stood beside him on the dais. I—I hate to part with it, but . . ."

Adrastes touched her hand gently and took the necklace. "I will care for it. Remember that with the amulet I make from it you assure the king's victory."

"Yes," she said. "Yes, I shall remember. Lyris." She turned with a sigh to the other woman. "His Eminence will instruct you. May your journey be easy, and may you soon return to me."

Lyris opened her mouth as if to protest, but the priest raised his head and his glittering gaze pierced her. She swallowed and nodded meekly.

Chryse rose and drew her veil again over her face. She extended her hand to the priest and he bowed over it. "My thanks, Your Eminence," she said. "I shall make an extra offering at the god's shrine this night."

Adrastes's mouth smiled, but his eyes remained shuttered. "So gracious a lady as yourself," he purred, "brings the favor of Harus upon Sardis."

She flushed again and hurried with small steps to the door. There she paused and with a rustle of her cloak cast one last regretful look at Lyris. "Give my lord my respects," she called. Lyris jerked forward, as if she would follow, but the movement became a curtsy and she stayed behind.

The priest watched as Chryse picked her way down the steps and rejoined the waiting guards. Only once did she hesitate, glancing fearfully back over her shoulder to the patch of scarred tile, to where scarlet anemones nodded as if touched by a breeze.

"My blessing, child," Adrastes hissed under his breath. "If Bellasteros is a bird of prey, then you are surely a sparrow, scratching contentedly in its yard, uncaring of the world beyond its walls. If your lord is indeed enamored of this warrior queen, then you will need the favor of the god to turn his wrath. Despite Gerlac's suspicions, Bellasteros is his son."

Chryse was gone. Only a few lights continued to burn in the city. The Azurac and the Cinnabran murmured along the base of the river wall, rushed between the pilings of the docks, mated to make the mighty stream of the Sar that carried its mingled pigments to the sea. A lateen sail tacked up the river, and the necropolis lay silent.

Adrastes turned. "Come," he called to the waiting servant. "Come with me."

Lyris started, as if waked from a sleep, and she walked toward the door. "Your Eminence," she said, her words somewhat slurred, "How may I assist you?"

"Are you not a daughter of the northern nomads?"

"Captured young, and raised by the hands of the lady Chryse."

"But you will remember your barbarian ways, I wager. Are you confirmed in the eye of Harus?"

"Yes, certainly; my lady herself taught me the catechism."

"The lady's piety is to be commended." He took Lyris's arm in a strong grip and guided her up the steps, higher and higher to the sanctuary of Harus at the very peak of the temple mount. At the colonnade she stopped, staring around with glazed eyes. It was as if the world lay at the feet of the god; to the north a silver glint of the sea, to the south a smudge hinted at mountains. To the east hung the moon, round and rich, straining toward the earth. A shaft of cool light sliced deep into the sanctuary.

Adrastes frowned and brandished the gold chain into the face of the goddess. "From this shall I make jesses for your queen; what you witnessed at your midsummer's fullness you will not see again. Harus rules, and with him Bellasteros!"

The pupils of Lyris's eyes dwindled suddenly to pinpricks. With a moan she crumpled to her knees. "Your Eminence," she whispered, "please, I am unworthy of your trust."

"Be quiet," he ordered. He still held her arm, and he pulled her swiftly into the thick shadow of the columns. There he left her, huddled at the base of the obsidian slab that was Harus's high altar.

The acolyte Declan stood, hesitating, on the steps outside, his narrow face somber, his hands tightly clasped.

Quickly Adrastes hung a tapestry at the eastern side of the temple, blotting out the rays of the moon. Embroidered soldiers fought under the outspread wings of a giant falcon, and its curved beak dripped the blood of Sardis's enemies. A puff of wind stirred the cloth; as it moved the soldiers writhed.

Red flames leaped from a brazier. Faint war cries echoed in the depths of the tapestry. The priest laid out the elements: colored sand; a vial of water from the Sar; a sharp, gleaming blade. He arranged the gold chain along the ancient carvings of the altar, in the arcs of the god's talons. As he worked he sang, quietly and clearly, and the incantation stilled the wind.

The wavering melody fell on Lyris where she lay, and slowly she looked up. Her eyes dilated, the blue irises disappearing as the pupils opened wide on flickering red firelight. Adrastes smiled, cruelly complacent; he gestured, and she stood and slipped her clothing from her body.

Invisible wings beat about the temple. The tapestry shifted, its threads rippling; soldiers shouted and died. The priest mixed water with sand and painted Lyris's body, outlining her breasts and loins with the sweeping curves of feathers. "Harus," she whispered. "Harus, I await your envoy." Her voice did not come from her throat, but from an undertone in Adrastes's incantation.

He arranged her on the altar, pillowing her head on the fair curls of her hair, settling her hips upon the chain. He paused, turned, paced to the eastern door of the temple. Arms outstretched, head thrown back, he stood. A murky blue flame sprang up among the dark shapes of the tombs across the river.

Declan turned and fled into the night.

The flame wavered, tossed by a sudden gust of wind, but the incantation lay heavy across the city and the wind died. The fire grew stronger, leaping into the air; it was a falcon, burning in a blue heat yet not consumed, beating its wings in powerful strokes, gliding upward on the updraft beside the temple and landing at Adrastes's feet.

The priest bowed deeply. His long-fingered hands crawled like spiders down the sides of his robes and seized the blade. Slowly he backed away from the bright shape of the bird. Slowly he rose beside the black altar. The knife flashed, blue fire and red mingled; the whorls of paint on the woman's body became patterns of blood. She caught her breath in pain and pleasure mingled.

The falcon walked in stately tread forward. Adrastes stepped back, the dark glitter of his eyes watching both demon and woman.

The blue flame shimmered. The falcon grew taller, its brightness fading as it took human form. The image of a man stood over the altar, insubstantial but defined in every detail: stocky, middle-aged, strong but twisted in its strength. Its eyes were whirlpools of madness—a poisoned pride, a hatred stronger than death. It looked about and its lips parted in a vulpine smile, revealing sharp, white teeth. "Adrastes Falco. My thanks, priest. My thanks."

Adrastes bowed. "My lord Gerlac. Amusement for your shade. Revenge, if you will."

The demon stretched, throwing off its grave-wrappings, and an odor of unguents, natron, and decay emanated from its form. Its churning eyes raked the form of the woman on the altar.

She reached up to it stiffly, as if her arms moved against her will. Her face went from blankness to horror and she opened her mouth, inhaled to scream— Adrastes raised his hand and her expression faded, her breath expelled in a moan.

The demon fell on her. The priest laughed, delighted in his power. Wings cracked the night over Sardis.

Behind the tapestry the moon mounted higher, but its light was shadowed, and Lyris's choked cries rent the sky in vain.

Chapter Six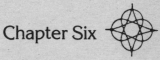

THE COUNCIL CHAMBER was stifling; hardly a breath of air stirred through the open shutters. Outside the late summer sun lay in shimmering waves across the agora.

Danica's head slumped forward into her breast; with a start she caught herself and pulled herself awake. Fortunately the council meeting was over, and only her immediate advisors sat scattered about the curved benches of the chamber. It seemed to her as if every pair of eyes were focused on her, disapproving her lack of attention; even Atalia, who stood beside her bearing the star-shield, cast more than one quizzical look at her queen.

But she had already worried so much about the subject under discussion that she seemed incapable of spending any more emotion on it; her mind moved slowly, laboriously, through the same patterns it had traced a hundred times.

Theara's most recent message, smuggled out of the Sardian camp via a traveling merchant, confirmed the rumors that had already reached Sabazel. The campaign that had started so bravely two months before had bogged down; the newly revived imperial troops under Bogazkar had proved much tougher than Mardoc had estimated, slowing Bellasteros's march toward Iksandarun. The satrap knew better than to stand and fight a pitched battle, as Kallidar had before Farsahn. He skirmished and ran, skirmished and ran, training his army at the Sardians' expense.

As Bellasteros moved away from the sea, following the ancient caravan route along the Royal Road, his lengthening supply lines were exposed to frequent raids. This half of the Empire was not only poorer but had already been stripped; it offered little sustenance. And the Sardian baggage train grew more and more unwieldy as refugees flocked to the falcon standards.

Some of those refugees were no doubt spies; Bogazkar seemed to anticipate every Sardian move. The morale of the legions, so far from home, failed.

But the voice of the goddess counseled patience: *Soon, daughter, shall I set the pieces in motion. Remind him of the lay of Daimion. . . .*

Danica wrenched her attention back to the meeting.

"The subjects of the Empire," aged councilor Neferet was saying, "would greet in joy anyone who came to liberate them from imperial tax collectors, and press gangs, and slavers."

"I would not wish to be 'liberated' by the Sardians," said Atalia. "They burned Farsahn."

"It was an accident," Danica cut in. "Drunken soldiers upset the sacred fire in the temple, and the oil stored there set fire to the hangings." Her stomach heaved, flopping loosely around a pocket of warm air, and she stopped to swallow. Perspiration gathered on her forehead. "The Sardians have never enslaved their conquests. . . ."

"You hear only one side of the story," Atalia stated. Her meaning was clear.

"A pity," said Neferet, "that the marriage of Viridis and Gerlac proved a tragedy, the opposite of its intent. She went willingly, I remember, thinking to stop the everlasting war between the Empire and the kingdom of Sardis. Her mistake was in trusting the Sardians to behave with common decency toward her."

"Her mistake," Atalia said dryly, "was in believing that a woman could make a difference in the wars of men. That a woman could retain her dignity in the world of men."

"She must have been very brave." Ilanit sighed.

Danica leaned back and closed her eyes. She had been only five years old, standing at her mother's side on the temple steps holding a garland of asphodel for the princess; the young woman's grave smile, the quiet conviction in her eyes, had remained branded on Danica's memory. Yes, Bellasteros would now be all of twenty-seven. . . . She had indeed had courage, had Viridis, to prove her love for Ashtar and then go on to Sardis. She had indeed been foolish.

She was not the only foolish one. Danica's blood seemed to be draining slowly from her head to her abdomen, so that her stomach pulsed more strongly than her heart, pumping waves of nausea through her body. She swallowed again. Her skin prickled cold, but still the sweat coursed down her back and between her breasts so that her linen shirt and pleated trousers were soaked with it.

"Mother?" Ilanit knelt by her side, her wide green eyes, so like Danica's own, filled with concern. And with something else, a shy decisiveness.

"Yes, love," Danica responded. She raised a hand that was by itself as heavy as her shield and stroked her daughter's hair.

"Mother, may I ask permission—forgive me, but the next turning of the moon will bring the autumnal rites, and . . ." She stammered, looking away from her mother's face.

Danica grasped Ilanit's chin and forced her eyes to again meet hers. "You would wish," she said quietly, "to stand guard during the rites, not to participate. Am I correct?"

"Yes." The words were only a whisper. "I—I was so sore, I would have more time to heal. A man's touch is not like a woman's."

"Though each has its pleasures," Danica said ruefully. "But I wager that your true reason is less than a handsbreadth taller than you, with the dark eyes and hair of a son of the Sar."

"Mother, please. . . ." Pain muted the brightness of Ilanit's eyes, and Danica felt the shadow of it touch her own heart.

A sudden crash made them both start. They looked around to see Atalia picking up the shield. "I beg your pardon," she said smoothly. "It seemed to leap from my hands."

Oh, my daughter, Danica thought. But it was a scowl that she summoned to her features. "No. You are bound to the rites, and glad participation at that. You behave like a meek peasant woman, believing herself excluded from all other men when touched by one."

The pain spilled from Ilanit's eyes; she bit her lip in an effort to show no emotion. "Yes, Mother," she whispered. "Your forgiveness, Mother."

Oh, my daughter, I ache as surely as you do, and I am old

enough not to be caught in such a trap. But the sound of her voice continued, short and sharp. "I want to hear no more about it. A daughter of Ashtar, indeed."

The room was stifling, she couldn't breathe, and her clothing was drenched, it seemed, with her own salt sweat. Better sweat than tears, she told herself.

Danica's stomach twisted, like a fish pulled helplessly from water to land; she lurched to her feet and vacated the council chamber; and managed to gain her own garden before the inevitable occurred.

Ilanit called for Shandir, and they assisted Danica to her bed, while Atalia watched in resigned concern from the doorway, the shield glowing in her hands. "Ashtar's will be done," the weapons master murmured with a sigh; she laid the shield on its stand, caressed it with her fingertips, crossed the room to kiss Danica's damp brow. "I shall attend to the training of the acolytes," she said, and she walked from the room as if bearing the entire weight of Cylandra on her back.

Danica lay, cold and trembling, while Shandir found a wet cloth to clean her face. "Your forgiveness, Mother," Ilanit said. "I upset you."

"I was already upset," Danica told her. "Your forgiveness, for speaking so harshly to you."

Ilanit smiled and shook her head. "I had wished that Ashtar had filled my womb at the midsummer rites; now I think I am pleased she did not."

"Your time will come," Danica told her darkly. "And I think I shall soon take a vow of celibacy, after this my fourth babe." Her mouth tasted like the bottom of the cattle byre and gratefully she accepted Shandir's offer of fresh water.

The healer seated herself on the edge of the bed and clasped Danica's hand. "I have thought you pale and melancholy of late. Why did you not tell me?"

"Perhaps I hoped to wake and find it a dream," Danica replied. "Think; Ilanit was my first child, and all the time she grew within me I was never sick. But my other two babies were male, and my stomach revolted against me for three turnings of the moon. I have good cause for melancholy, Shandir."

"You think this one, too, is male."

"It is," Danica said, "Bellasteros's only son." She closed her eyes on another wave of nausea.

Ilanit and Shandir exchanged a cautious glance. "And if

you gave this infant to the neighboring peasants," the healer asked, "as the others were given in exchange for female babes?"

"No. This child has but one sire; if Bellasteros did not find him, then his enemies would."

"Will you tell him, then? He will not be pleased, I think, to find himself entangled even further with a goddess his followers despise; I spoke with his soldiers, remember, and not all of them would even accord Sabazel respect, let alone trust and the honor of a king's son."

"In time. In time he will have to know. But not yet. Mother . . ."

A soft breeze whispered through the garden and the shutters clicked together. Ashtar's hand touched Danica's face, and she was soothed. *Sabazel yet hangs in the balance, daughter, but you play well, and you will win. Remind him of the sword of Daimion.*

"Ashtar moves in subtle ways," Danica murmured. "If I am to bear the heir to Sardis and the Empire, so be it."

Ilanit sat down on the floor, clasped her arms about her knees, and bent her face onto them. Shandir continued to stroke Danica's face, so gently that her touch was a kiss of butterfly wings. And Danica let herself float downward into dream-haunted sleep; a great ziggurat thrust itself into the stars, the moon set, and the blade of a sword gleamed amid gathering darkness.

By the time the message came that evening, she was feeling much better and had managed to eat the broth and bread Ilanit had prepared as a peace offering. She had even written the reply to Theara's message, sending the courtesan Ashtar's instructions and a packet of lethenderum.

"This woman, Lyris—she seeks sanctuary?" Danica asked Atalia as she folded the parchment.

"Neferet has spoken with her; she has been a slave in Sardis, she says, and escapes a gang of prostitutes sent to the army. She does indeed carry a horror about her."

"So should she." Danica took Atalia's arm, stood, and found that her knees were steady. "I will speak with her. Perhaps she can tell me how Sardis takes the news of the king's dalliance with . . . what do they call me, do you suppose?"

"I would rather not," Atalia grimaced. "Shall I come with you?"

"You can wait outside; she will be more comfortable with one inquisitor, I think."

The sun had just dipped over the horizon, and a lilac glow still hung in the western sky. The streets were quiet, children called inside for their suppers, and the guards at the Horn Gate leaned reflectively on their spears. Cylandra wore an aureole of silver as the full moon climbed her eastern flank.

Two of the old priestesses met Danica and Atalia on the steps of the temple. "She was weary, having walked for weeks on end," one said. "We gave her food and a pallet in the small room yonder," said the other.

Danica nodded her thanks. She entered the dimly lit temple alone and paused as a movement caught the corner of her eye. A mist lay over the pool, shadows streaming upward from the water, phantom wings. The mosaic shifted, the tiles tumbling themselves every which way in some frantic effort to form a picture. Danica walked warily to the edge of the pool and knelt on its coping. The mist was dark and thick—no, there. A figure. A grave smile and eyes bright with a quiet conviction. Hands open and filled with asphodel as dry and brown as a funeral wreath.

Viridis. Of course, Danica had been speaking of her; of course she would see her. But the back of her neck prickled in warning. Slowly she stood, cursing the lassitude with which her pregnancy had afflicted her, and she pulled her nerves and muscles into the singing tautness that alertness demanded.

The woman Lyris lay on the pallet, flat on her back, her arm over her eyes, reminding Danica of the way Bellasteros had lain defeated. Something about the posture disturbed her; it was unfeminine, wrong. She stepped inside the room and lifted the feeble oil lamp from its niche by the door. "Greeting," she said quietly. "You have come safely to Sabazel, sanctuary and a new life. I am Danica, ruler."

Lyris's hand twitched, her fingers crawling like spiders across the coverlet. Her arm dropped from her face and for a moment her oddly translucent eyes rolled in their sockets. Then the pupils dilated, the irises steadied, and the woman sat up. She was pitifully thin, her chin and cheekbones as sharp as the beak of a bird of prey. Her hair straggled tangled and dirty over her shoulders; her garments clung like tattered grave-wrappings to her bones. Yet there was the spark of gold at her throat.

Despite her misgivings Danica extended her hand in welcome. Atalia was right, a horror hung about this woman, some deep and mortal fear, as if her spirit were buried alive in a rockcut tomb and only her shade walked the waking world.

"Danica," Lyris said. Her voice was weak, distant. She staggered to her feet, faltered, began to fall.

Danica reached out to help her. Lyris's body closed around itself, regaining control; deliberately she fell against Danica's knees. The lamp went flying, landing on the pallet with a splash of oil and fire, and blue flames leaped instantly upward.

Danica's taut body did not crumple but hit the floor and bounced up again, crouched for battle. But Lyris was strong—too strong for her emaciated condition—and her elbow struck Danica's midriff in a vicious blow.

Danica's breath hissed from her lungs in a gasp, and her queasy stomach surged into her throat. Even as she fell she ordered herself to roll, ready to rise again, but Lyris's hands closed like talons around her arms and Lyris's eyes glittered darkly a handsbreadth from her face. The look was a stiletto thrust deep into her mind, and with a gasp of pain she collapsed backward.

It should have been a simple matter to toss her assailant away from her, but Danica's body no longer responded to her thought; her finely honed muscles were as limp as spun flax. The odor of unguents, natron, and decay emanated from Lyris's form, choking her, and she could not regain the breath she had lost. Atalia—Atalia was outside. Her voice was only a faint gurgle in her throat. The glittering eyes laughed at her, reflecting the blue flame that leaped and hissed but did not consume the pallet.

Lyris drew back, and still Danica could not move. Mother, what—? But it was an effort just to remember her own name, where she was, what office she held; her thoughts crawled through a putrefying ooze, seeking air and light. The stranger's voice no longer hesitated but was deep and resonant. "Queen of Sabazel, Ashtar's daughter, who dares dispute the power of almight Harus . . ."

Mother! Lyris reached to her throat and removed the gold chain that hung there. She bent and wrapped the chain securely around Danica's ankles. "Golden jesses, my queen. A gift from the falcon."

Mother, no! Lyris was dragging her inert form away from the coldly blazing fire. "No, you will not burn, though that is the preferred death for witches. You will die like a rat before the eyes of your false goddess."

How shameful. No—such thoughts were not hers. Danica closed her eyes, spiraling downward into her own mind, tracing the threads of her thought. Her head bumped over the doorsill but she hardly felt it. It was a spell that held her, and a spell could be broken; desperately she searched through the nerves and tendons of her own body, summoning at least some small measure of her former strength. She managed to writhe feebly against the chain.

Lyris smiled, cruelly complacent, and jerked the chain so sharply that pain exploded in Danica's legs. The pain cut through the ooze clogging her mind; Mother, as you sent the princess Viridis to warn me, send her now to help me!

Lyris jerked Danica to the edge of the pool, seized her arm, and pulled her onto the coping. The shadowy mist engulfed her and she struggled again. It was too late. Lyris pushed, and Danica fell helplessly into the water. Her mouth and nose and eyes filled; she seemed to fall down, down into some dark crevasse, suffocating. Viridis—the falcon must not kill again—this time to kill your own grandchild, Viridis.

Even as her breath rattled in her lungs the tiles shifted beneath her cheek. From the skylight above her fell a pale luminescence, moonlight and yet not the normal light of the moon. A wind rippled through the shadows and the mist dissipated. The transparent form of a woman floated above the pool, bending, her pale hands reaching out and scattering dried leaves of asphodel upon the drowning woman. With a crack the chain shattered, its individual links piercing the surface of the water and pattering down like a golden shower on the edges of the pool.

And Danica surged upward, her strength restored in one sudden flood of light. Without pausing for a deep breath she threw herself at the still form of Lyris. The woman fell back, her mouth dropping open in a wail of dismay. Her eyes went blank. Danica bore her onto the floor but she did not resist; her body was as limp as Danica's had been a few moments before.

"Atalia!" Danica shouted, and she spat water from her mouth. "Atalia!" Her second cry had hardly left her mouth before Atalia was there, and the dagger that marked her weapons master pressed against Lyris's throat.

"What—" she began, but Danica signed her to silence. The two priestesses fell to their knees in the doorway.

The moon-silvered figure of Viridis still hovered above the pool. The distant lights that were her eyes sparked. Her hand beckoned, and Lyris moaned, the sound wrenched not from her throat but from her soul. Her body trembled and her eyes rolled back in their sockets.

A phosphorescence gathered about her, shaping itself to her form and then shifting. A man, strong, twisted. . . . Viridis beckoned again, and the man-shape struggled against her, its teeth slashing around it, its form flickering with hellfire. Atalia removed her knife from Lyris's throat and cut at the demon, but her blade moved with harmless sparklings through its shape.

Danica's grasp of Lyris's body gentled into an embrace, trying to protect the young woman as she thrashed in agony. It must be Gerlac, she told herself; a hatred from beyond the grave. Again her stomach heaved, and she forced it down.

The man-shape grew larger, its sickly glow touching the faces that watched it with a pale miasma of death.

Viridis beckoned a third time, peremptorily, her eyes flashing. The demon shrieked as its limbs shredded from its torso, as its face peeled away. Like a guttering candle flame the demon flicked in and out of this world, not here, not gone. . . . Its form winked out. A cool wind, fresh with the scent of Cylandra's ice-crown, scoured the temple clean of the stench of the demon's tomb. The water of the pool surged briefly over the rim, gathering in the separate golden links.

Yet the demon still existed, though weakened, on some distant plane. Danica frowned, not liking what she sensed, not liking her ability to sense it. . . . At this moment she could do nothing more. She bowed, numb, over the girl's head.

Lyris sobbed against Danica's breast. The two priestesses stumbled to their feet and hurried to the small room; the fire was the small yellow flame of a spilled oil lamp, quickly extinguished.

"Sanctuary," Danica murmured to Lyris. "Sanctuary, here, in Sabazel." She raised her eyes to the shining form of the martyred princess. "My thanks. A thousand times, my thanks."

Viridis raised her hands upward, toward the bright roundness of the moon. Her image wavered, grew fainter, vanished. Only the soft, clear tones of her voice remained, drifting down the distant chimes of the wind: "Danica, to you I commend my child and his line."

Atalia exhaled and reclaimed her dagger. The mosaic at the bottom of the pool sighed, shifting quietly into a pattern of linked gold wires—the chain, knit together once again, gleamed softly beneath water that danced with moonlight and starshine.

The talons of Harus were strong indeed, Danica told herself. Stronger than she had seen in her worst nightmare. She was seized by a fit of shivering, her wet clothes and hair like ice against her body, her thoughts echoing hollowly through her mind. She slumped to the floor beside Lyris. She would cry, too, but she was much too tired and much too frightened for tears to help.

Atalia was calling for Shandir, and lamps, and hot wine, but to Danica her voice was as faint as the buzz of an insect. The goddess whispered, *The game is joined again. A worthy opponent, daughter, but you have checked his move. The next is ours.* And it seemed as if a warm breath drove away the chill.

A gale blasted Sardis, howling down from the west as the moon mounted higher into an indigo sky. Adrastes Falco stood on the uppermost terrace of Harus's ziggurat, his robes whipping around him, Declan crouching pale at his side; although the wind pushed at him, as if it would throw him down from his own mountain, he stood steady and defiant. "You are strong, Ashtar," he shouted, "but almighty Harus will yet prevail!"

The gleaming circle of the full moon winked in and out of scudding cloud; the moon, Ashtar's implacable gaze.

Chapter Seven

BELLASTEROS KNEW HE was dreaming. This particular dream had caught him more than once of late. But, struggle as he might, he could not escape it.

He walked, naked, cold, alone, through a dark passageway. He was shamed somehow, smarting and frightened. What had happened to bring him to this pass? He could not remember. He had lost the Empire, perhaps; perhaps his followers had discovered the secret of his birth. Each step he took was like a sword thrust deep into his vitals . . . but something chased him, and he could not stop to rest.

Chittering shapes swooped by him, brushing his face with leathery wings. The ground underfoot crawled with a living slime that grasped at his ankles. The cave, the tomb—whatever it was—the passageway stretched darkly on into infinity.

But no—a light shone, feebly, far ahead of him. He summoned the last of his strength and struggled toward it. The light brightened, shaping itself into an arched doorway. Beyond it Bellasteros glimpsed the spreading limbs of a tree. Something shone among the dancing green leaves; the tree was green and gold and supple, like Danica. Danica.

He reached the doorway. his hands reached out to the open air, to freedom. And strong arms seized him, pulling him back into darkness. He was choking, his mouth and nostrils filled with the stench of the grave, of funeral unguents, natron, and decay. Desperately he tried to throw off the grasp of the

demon, turning. . . . The twisted face of Gerlac watched him,
its mouth gaping in silent laughter.

His own mouth opened in a scream. The hands of his stepfather, talons, cut into his arms, forcing him down. The face
closed with him, as if to merge with his own. The stench overwhelmed him.

No, it was not a bad smell, but a tantalizingly familiar odor,
spices tickling his nostrils. Cool hands touched his face and he
grasped them, pulling himself from the nightmare. His
scream, he realized, had been only a sickly whimper in his
throat.

Bellasteros blinked stupidly around him. The sullen glow of
a brazier illuminated his tent, the hangings of his bed, and his
armor laid ready at its foot. Theara cradled his head, stroking
the perspiration from his face with a cool cloth. He tried to
speak, could not, cleared his throat, and muttered, "I thought
I dismissed you."

Her eyes, smudged with kohl and sleep, did not waver from
his. "I stayed. I thought you might have need of me."

As a nursemaid, to wake a child from a bad dream? He was
no man, it seemed; she had already discovered that, earlier
that night. The first woman he had attempted since his return
from Sabazel, and his skill even in that had been taken from
him. If I cannot have Danica, I shall have no one. . . . "I told
you," he snapped, finding his voice. "I have need of no one."

She calmly continued stroking his face and he wrenched
himself away. "But I shall overlook your disobedience this
time," he added lamely. No stomach even to punish a painted
whore, it seemed. But then, it was unbecoming in a king to
punish others for his own folly.

"My lord," she said, her voice as soft as the cooing of a
dove, "your duties trouble you. Such happens to every man,
and is nothing shameful. I have failed to ease your mind in the
one way, so let me try another. Let me sing to you."

My duties, yes, he thought. They troubled him more than
anyone could know. His army's brave march through the Empire had become an awkward scramble from fortified position
to fortified position. His Sardian troops were allowing themselves open mutters of discontent, and they suffered for it at
Mardoc's hand. His imperial followers grew lax in their
obeisances to his divinity, and a troubled Patros set only a
halfhearted example. But why, Bellasteros asked himself with

a curl of his lip, should they have any more reason to think him divine? The satrap Bogazkar laughed at him. Conqueror, indeed.

Mardoc would say that Bellasteros had been unmanned by the Sabazian witch Danica. . . . Danica. Her name was an open wound.

"My lord," Theara murmured. "Let me sing for you." She slipped off the bed and padded in alluring dishabille across the tent. He realized he had liked her hands on his neck and shoulders, but he would not call her back.

She picked up a lyre and tested its strings with one flowing trill. Harus, the wind through Danica's garden . . . Ashtar.

And he had quarreled with Patros, responding with ridicule when his friend had asked to return to Sabazel for the autumn rites. He hurt everyone he touched, it seemed.

"My lord?"

"Yes, yes, sing for me." He threw himself down among the tangled bedclothes, trying vainly to find a comfortable position. A song, to turn his mind from the doubts, the dreams, the curse of his stepfather Gerlac.

Her voice was a clear soprano, delicate and yet forceful enough to stir the air. Bellasteros watched bemusedly as the shadows shifted in brief subtle movements just at the edge of his vision. The coals in the brazier sprang into flame, sparking into an iridescent mist that blurred the outlines of Theara's body and suggested those of the gods and demons of her song.

It was the ancient lay of Daimion, the hero who with his sword Solifrax had carved out the Empire. The god-king who had ruled most of the known world, ages ago when Sardis was only a village of mud huts. But even then Solifrax had been an ancient weapon, forged in the time of the gods' awakening. When Daimion in his pride refused to relinquish the enchanted sword, he was struck with madness and his descendents cursed.

And Daimion in his pride also had repudiated his companion, the Sabazian priestess-queen Mari. Even her name had long been expurgated from the Sardian version of the story. But Bellasteros had heard it—not only from Danica, he realized now, but earlier, in the songs sung to an infant prince by his nurse, the last of Viridis's imperial retinue.

Theara sang, and images formed themselves from song and shadow like those called from burning lethenderum—lethenderum, Bellasteros told himself in a weary resignation. That's what that scent was, coriander, saffron, and sandalwood. He did not wonder where Theara had obtained the Sabazian drug. He had, after all, been encompassed since birth by the borders of Sabazel.

He glanced at Theara and she smiled at him above the arch of the lyre. Her eyes counseled rest and sleep, and her voice led him from his body into the midst of the wavering images.

He stood beneath a great tree. Its trunk was gnarled with age, but still it sent forth fresh shoots, and the branches were heavy laden with golden fruit. The blue vault of the sky winked and sparkled behind cascading green leaves.

Thick grass welled up between the writhen roots of the tree, and there, driven deep into the turf, was a sword. It trembled, as if it had just that moment been set there, an unseen hand plucking it from the sunlight and carving for it a sheath from the earth itself. The blade was of a steel so highly polished it seemed crystalline, curving in a gentle arc, not like the straight stabbing swords of Sardis, but resembling rather an imperial scimitar—or the slender saber that Danica carried.

It seemed she was there, watching him. Her shield hummed with a pale light, not that of the sun but of the moon. Her green eyes were shuttered and cool, her lips tight in a secret, inward smile. He wanted to shake her from her complacency. He wanted to see her as troubled as he.

But the sword glistened, and she nodded toward it, and his hand moved to set itself on the golden filigree of the hilt. It was warm to his touch. It might have been made for him, so well did it fit his hand. Light flared around his fingers, so that his flesh seemed to burn, but he would not release it. He pulled, slowly and steadily, and the turf yielded the blade to his grasp.

Bellasteros raised the sword to the sky. The sunlight flashed along its length, leaped across the grass, gleamed in rippling refractions from Danica's shield. She threw back her head, smiling, raising the star-shield in reply.

Beyond the branches of the tree a falcon floated, its sharp eye glittering in the light of day.

The oracle was partly concealed by the pungent smoke that welled from a hissing firepot set before her. She swayed back and forth, muttering, her wizened hands outstretched, shredding the smoke between her fingers. She wore a loose robe and hood of an indeterminate color, perhaps gray, perhaps blue—the color of dawn on a hazy, rainy day. Within the hood only her eyes could be seen, glinting oddly pale, reflecting not the crimson fire but some internal light of their own.

Adrastes tightened his clasp of Chryse's arm. But she made no move to flee; she stood upright, her back stiff, her chin high. Her body quivered like a plucked lyre string.

The smoke coiled upward, snaking around the rough-carved columns, dimming them to shadows. Some small creature cheeped, high in the rafters, and was quickly stilled. Through a fissure in the ceiling a sliver of star-studded sky wavered and disappeared, scummed with smoke as the walls of the oracle's chamber had been scummed by centuries of soot.

The oracle bent forward and inhaled deeply of the smoke, her lungs laboring in deep, rasping wheezes. Chryse blinked, the whites of her eyes glinting above her veil. Adrastes stood as still as a statue, his sharply angled nose and bearded chin as fresh and cold as from a sculptor's tool.

The oracle spoke. Her voice was high-pitched, uninflected, vibrating in the smoke rather than in the old woman's body. "The hand that draws the sword of Daimion will carve with it an empire, even as did Daimion's hand in the dawn of time. A new god-king, a new empire."

The voice trailed away into a sigh. The smoke thinned, eddying upward in trailing wraiths among the pillars. "Where?" Adrastes demanded, so harshly that Chryse started away from him. "Where is the sword?"

The oracle inhaled again, shuddering. For a moment it seemed as if the woman's frail form would slip from the stool where it perched. But she reached out, and the smoke buoyed her up. "In the tree at the world's edge. Guarded by . . ."

Adrastes leaned forward, his black eyes brilliant adamant in the shade of his brows. "Guarded by the eye of Harus," he stated.

"Guarded by Sabazel." The oracle slumped from her stool, a crumpled bundle on the stained flagstones, and the smoke whirled away and was gone.

"Sabazel," hissed Adrastes. His hand crushed Chryse's arm and she squeaked in pain. In a moment he regained his cool demeanor, released her, bowed graciously. "My apologies, lady. I was taken aback, to hear that name spoken here beneath Harus's wing."

Chryse tried to speak, failed, swallowed. "My lord will draw the sword," she whispered. "Surely it is he who will take for Sardis Daimion's ancient Empire. And if the witch-queen can aid him . . ."

"Can she?" Adrastes murmured. "Is that why my spell went awry; Harus saves her for another fate? But the hooded falcon on Ashtar's wrist— I like not this talk of Sabazel. I like not that he should see her again."

Chryse looked up at him, as bewildered by his words as if he spoke in a foreign tongue. "What can I do, Your Eminence, to help him in his quest, and to help free him from . . . that woman?"

Adrastes smiled, thinly, slyly. He took Chryse's elbow and guided her away from the ashes of the firepot and the blue cloak covering the still form of the oracle. "I fear, lady, that I must summon you from your devotions. Prepare yourself for a journey."

Chryse opened her mouth as if to protest, thought better of it, bowed her head dutifully. Her clasped hands trembled on her breast.

The door closed behind the inquisitor and the reluctant wife. The dark shapes of priestesses moved to gather up the fallen oracle. As their hands touched the cloak it shredded into mist and dissipated with a faint shimmer upward, a star shadow reabsorbed into the sky. Where it had lain only a faint soft-silvered shape marked the stones. The priestesses glanced hurriedly around, but no one else was there. They fell to their knees before the signature of the goddess.

A gust of wind chimed through the columns, and then all was silent.

It was late afternoon when Danica turned away from the shimmering basin of water, left the hollow in the mountainside, and started up Cylandra's flank. The valley that sheltered Sabazel narrowed here to the merest cleft, a rocky defile impassable to those who did not bear the ancient knowledge of foothold and handhold and balancing point.

Danica's only companion was Lyris, the Sardian servant freed from the evil spell that had bound her. Shandir's attentions had healed the young woman physically and Atalia had taught her the use of weapons as she had once taught Danica herself. But Lyris's spirit was still weak, her faith in Harus torn from her, her faith in herself sorely wounded. She followed Danica up the mountain as she followed her every day in the streets of Sabazel, tight-lipped, silent, guarding the woman she had tried to kill with the same dogged desperation with which she guarded her own sanity.

Danica glanced back as the young woman leaped gamely over a deep fissure. She made an encouraging sound and turned to the next stretch of the path that circled Cylandra. Lyris more than deserved this initiation into the ranks of her Companions—she needed it to survive. Faith in Ashtar would sustain her.

And my own faith, Danica thought, suffering a trial by ordeal. . . . It was time to renew her own initiatory vows, she told herself. It was time to see the cavern once again. Although this time she had not fasted beforehand, and she had not required it of Lyris. The Sardian woman was still emaciated from her solitary journey, and Danica would not starve her babe—by the gods, she told herself, the agitation of our minds should bring visions enough.

Slow but surefooted they left behind the olive and asphodel of the lower slopes, emerging at last on a tumbled scree at the base of a cliff. Rivulets of ice glinted down the face of the rock, strands of crystal reflecting the pale pinks and ambers of the setting sun. Above the grey stone a rim of snow stood stark and white against the darkening sky.

Danica wrapped her cloak more tightly around her body and inhaled deeply of the cold, clear air. Lyris stood just to the side and behind her, in her usual position, her chin thrown back and her hands raised as if in supplication. Before them the high plains stretched to a shadowed horizon smudged with a hint of mountains; clouds like smoke barred the livid face of the sun. The slender horns of the ripening moon drifted high above, borne upward by the high, clear song of the wind.

"There," Danica said quietly. "There is the edge of the world. Sardis lies behind you."

Lyris said nothing. Her hands dropped to her sides.

In her mind's eye Danica saw scarlet Sardian pennons ranged as watchfires around Sabazel, shedding a thick smoke into the sky, closing Ashtar's alert eye. She saw the gold pavilion glinting blood-red, blood-warm in the light of the fires. She saw the flame in the conqueror's dark eyes, a deep unquenchable flicker of ambition and of arrogance. She wanted to shake him from his complacency. She wanted to see him as troubled as she.

The sun disappeared into darkness, engulfed by streaming night. Danica turned, picking her way across the scree, and Lyris followed. They ducked into an opening in the cliff.

Danica found an oil lamp set ready on a shelf, lit it with the waiting flint and tinder, and held it before her as she led Lyris down the tunnel. The tiny light showed the marks of ancient axes on the arching ceiling and the smooth floor. The women emerged onto a promontory like one end of a broken bridge, overlooking a gentle blue darkness filled with the murmur of running water, water singing half-remembered legends. A distant tongue of flame stood up bright and clear in the shadows.

Here the marks of the axes stopped. This was a great natural cavern, carved by a rushing underground river in some early age of the world. The dome of the roof was supported by pillars of living rock.

Danica smiled. It was a comfort to come here, to the very heart of Cylandra, within the warm womb of the earth itself. Ashtar's womb, she thought. Once she had come here as an acolyte, a young and untried sprig of her present self. Long ago, it seemed, like a faintly remembered legend garbled by the telling and the retelling. She had dreamed of battle, of enemies hemming Sabazel; she had dreamed of a man's dark, even features. She had awakened bathed in sweat, her heart pounding, knowing that her dream was not the nightmare of an acolyte unsuited to be a warrior, knowing that her dream was true. And that was more frightening than any nightmare.

She had emerged from the cavern her mother's squire. She had borne her arms in the presence of the emperor Kallidar, on that fatal embassy a decade before; Kallidar, blaming the Sabazians for the death of his cousin Viridis, had closed the ancient temple of Ashtar and treacherously attacked them. Danica had received the star-shield from her mother's dying grasp, beneath the walls of imperial Iksandarun. And now she was herself Sabazel.

'I ask for your counsel, Mother,'' she murmured. "Your counsel, and peace for this my friend."

And peace for yourself, daughter?

"Peace for Sabazel. For myself—if I have earned it."
Danica stepped carefully down the rock-cut staircase at the
side of the promontory, finding the path that stretched across
the floor of the cavern toward the solitary flame. Pale, blind
snakes whisked silently away from her feet and she clucked to
them as she would to a pet parrot or hyrax.

The fire had burned in its carved basin for uncounted
generations, fueled by some seepage in the rock. Behind it was
a wide doorway in the wall of the cavern; Danica led Lyris
through into a small round grotto that echoed to the trill of a
waterfall. She bent over the ancient water channel, bathed her
face and hands, and drank. The stream was ice-cold, like a
sparkling wine on her tongue. At her signal Lyris drank also
and ducked her head into the water as if she sought to drown
herself.

"Yes," Danica told her. "The water will cleanse you of the
past. Take heart."

Lyris emerged shaking her head, drops flying upward like
jewels in the firelight. "I—I would believe that, lady."

"Believe it." Danica set the lamp in a niche and stretched
herself on a rush-strewn bench. Lyris crouched at her feet,
arms wrapped around her bent legs, her face hidden.

The nausea and lassitude of Danica's early pregnancy had
indeed spent itself by the third month; for the last two turns of
the moon she had felt almost her old self. Five months, she
thought, since we . . . loved. She would never be her old self
again. As for what she would be—the uncertainty of the
future gnawed at her. She would be leaving Sabazel soon,
after the next full moon, when she should be waiting quietly
for the birth of the child. She would be leaving her sanctuary
on a quest. *This night I shall show to you your path. And I
shall lend you my power, to smooth your way.*

"And his way, Mother."

Yes. This game is his as well.

Danica glanced at Lyris. Something in the young woman's
attitude reminded her of Ilanit. They were the same age, after
all, a taut sixteen. Her daughter had made no more mention of
Patros but had participated in the autumn rites, gracefully ac-
cepting the embraces of a young minstrel. Had the young man
wondered, Danica asked herself wryly, why Ilanit asked again
and again for the songs of Sardis and the lay of Daimion?

Daimion, yes. There was the key to this new gambit.

Theara's latest message reported that she had indeed been singing the legends to Bellasteros, and that his conversation was beginning to turn on the whereabouts of the sword Solifrax. He had only to ask for Sabazian assistance, and it would begin. Danica had no doubt that he would, for whatever reason of his own, ask.

The oracle, probably. If the Sardians ever discovered that their sibyl, ancient when the city was founded, spoke with the voice of Ashtar . . .

The thought made her shift uneasily. She folded a corner of her cloak into a pillow. The grotto was scented with laurel, she noted; Atalia, no doubt, had mixed the leaves with the fresh rushes on the bench, preparing the shrine for Danica. Atalia, who thought little of Bellasteros, and less of the coming quest, but who nonetheless trusted implicitly in her queen and her goddess. As I trust, Danica said to herself. She reached out and stroked Lyris's damp hair. The woman's shoulders trembled.

Atalia had seen the soldier Hern among those men gathered for the autumn rites. Shandir had drawn him away, skillfully plucking information from his lips. He had been patrolling the supply lines along the Royal Road, he said, when he passed close by Sabazel; remembering the pleasures of the summer, he had ventured in. Shandir had smiled and nodded and said nothing. A spy, Atalia had said. Sent by Bellasteros.

Sent by Mardoc, I would think, Danica had replied. What could he see? Let him report that life in Sabazel proceeds unaltered, turning to the rhythms of the year.

And the queen of Sabazel, Atalia had retorted, who did not join in the rites of autumn?

Too overwhelmed by the embraces of a god to accept those of a mere mortal. Now let the matter rest.

Her reply had been perhaps too close to the truth, Danica thought. Even Shandir's gentle attentions no longer aroused her, and the thought of any other man's touch repulsed her. If I cannot have Marcos Bellasteros, I will have no one. And she shuddered, rejecting that thought, too, before it could sink its talons into her mind.

Lyris looked up. Their eyes met. Wordlessly Danica opened her arms, and Lyris came into them, resting her head on Danica's shoulder. "Your troubles, lady, are so much greater than mine."

"Are they? Say instead that my duties are greater, and that greater disaster may result from my failure. . . ."

Lyris waited a moment and, when Danica did not continue, said quietly, "You? How could you fail?"

Danica wished she could laugh. "So many ways, Lyris. So many ways. Our fate is netted with that of Bellasteros; if he fails, returning to Sardis like a whipped cur, Sabazel will be left at the mercy of a vengeful Empire. If he wins, and his followers learn of the child I carry . . . what then? What?"

Lyris had no reply.

The tiny flame in the lamp guttered, suddenly, as if in a long exhaled breath. Sistrums rattled in the dimness of the outer cavern. The walls of the grotto flickered in the dancing light, and Lyris looked up, startled. But she was reassured by Danica's calm demeanor. "Are those paintings, on that wall there?" she asked.

"Yes," answered Danica. "Old ones, from the dawn of time." A crescent moon overlooked stick figures of men and bison and deer. A male form wearing the antlers of a stag lay supine, surrounded by female figures bearing knives. "The winter king," Danica explained, "sacrificed at the turning of the sun."

"Is that the way it used to be here?" Lyris asked. Her widely dilated eyes gleamed.

"Not here. In kingdoms ruined even before Daimion lived. Ashtar no longer craves such sacrifice." She smiled. "Can you see Bellasteros baring his throat to my knife, as docilely as a bullock on butchering day?"

"No, I cannot."

"I would not want that of him." The fire guttered shards of flame into the darkness. Danica raised on one elbow and pointed toward a ledge below the paintings. A clay female figure, still fresh in the dampness of the cave, lay there. Its elongated neck and head were bent shyly over pendulous breasts and swelling stomach; its tiny arms, just strips of clay, cradled its sex. The fingerprints of its maker remained on its belly and flank. "She who made it is long since dust, scattered by the wind," said Danica, "but her vision remains. The goddess, when she ruled alone, worshipped by men and women alike, omnipresent."

Next to that figure was a more recent one, a baked clay statuette of a young man, slender and elegant in a pleated kilt, its arms upraised in an attitude of devotion. "The consort of the goddess," Danica went on. "Men long ago discovered their own role in the creation of children; fittingly they were accorded worship in the role of helpmate and companion to the mother. And still Ashtar ruled the world."

Danica's outstretched hand clenched into a fist. "Now men seek to carve their offspring with swords from the body of their mother; they seek to cut her into little pieces and sow her in the fields and forget her. They accord more respect to their brood mares and heifers than to their wives. They forget they ever had a mother-goddess, and worship only a harsh, jealous father-god. They turn their faces away from us, a reminder of their past, calling us barbarians and threatening to destroy us.

"The Empire worships many different gods; it was not unusual even three decades ago for a noblewoman such as Viridis to discreetly bow to Ashtar. But when she went to Sardis, carrying the fruit of the rites within her . . . Sardis bows only to Harus, repudiating their own history. They did not have to admit Viridis's supposed infidelity to excuse their destruction of Ashtar's temple there. They needed no excuse to once again attack the Empire, as the Empire hardly needed Viridis's death to excuse their renewed attack on Sardis. And to attack us, who had once been the friends of all." She sighed. "And the future . . . ?"

The lamp went out. The solitary flame flared up. Beyond it, in the blue depths of the cavern, something stirred. A faint, shimmering mist, a suggestion that shifted and moved and formed—nothing.

Lyris exhaled shakily. "Mother," she whispered. "I have seen how other gods treat their servants, and it is you I would serve."

Danica shook her head. "A god's follower does not always do the work of the god." And she wondered suddenly what caused such strange words to spring to her tongue. Mother, I no longer know my own mind. . . .

She composed herself on the bench, clasping Lyris close beside her. *Sleep,* murmured the goddess. *Sleep, and your path shall be shown to you.* And within moments the exhausted Lyris was breathing gently in sleep.

Danica gazed up into darkness, her eyes forming pinwheels of light that spun and collided in patterns she was almost ready to understand. She closed her eyes, and the patterns continued behind her lids.

Her free hand rested lightly on the mound of her belly. Under her fingertips the child moved, a faint flutter that was no more than the flexing of a butterfly's wings when first it tries the walls of its cocoon. Her hand caressed her skin, reaching in vain for the baby. So small as yet. So vulnerable.

She slept, and the pinwheels of light entered her, filling her, so that her body gleamed with them. In a vision so clear it was like a map sketched on parchment she saw a wasteland, a tree, Bellasteros impaling the sun on the blade Solifrax. And her own hands held not only the star-shield, but the vouchsafed power of the goddess.

She moaned in her sleep, "I, carry your power—I am unworthy. . . ."

When morning came, a lavender hush in the depths of the cavern, Danica woke. Lyris sat beside her, wiping her hair from her face. "I dreamed of battle, and your shield lighting the way beyond battle, to peace. Am I . . . favored?"

"Yes," Danica told her. "You have been accepted."

Lyris smiled proudly. "And may I ride at your side?"

"Soon," Danica replied. "Soon." Her own dream still thrilled in her body, like the fever of battle, like the fever of love. She inhaled and calmed the passionate beating of her heart. Strength, beyond any strength she had ever known. . . . Truly I am honored, she thought. No queen since Mari has been given such a gift.

With a snap of her fingers she lit the lamp. She parted the waterfall with a wave of her hand. With eyes as wide as a child's she led Lyris through a narrow concealed passage; they emerged onto Cylandra's eastern snowfield in time to see the sun break free of the horizon. Through a silvery mist, far below, Sabazel nestled in the mountain's embrace. Its houses were as small and fragile as beads of amber on a string. Danica spread her blessing over them, spilling sparks from her upraised hands. Yes, it was power, and a welcome renewal; she looked to the sunrise and laughed.

The goddess spoke in the dawn breeze. *This is my gift, to aid you in your quest, to be reclaimed in time.*

"My thanks," Danica said, and her voice wavered and died. The power—she was swollen with it, like a ripe fruit ready to burst, pained and yet thrilled. Oh, Mother, she thought suddenly, would you give me power in exchange for your counsel, would you have me decide my own course? Oh, Mother, I am more vulnerable now than ever.

Lyris's eyes were wide with worship, as if she had known all along that her queen was a goddess as well.

So then, Danica told herself, I must be strong. I shall be strong, for you and for the others and for Sabazel itself. She set her chin and summoned a smile. And, indeed, there was a pleasure in it. . . . "My thanks," she murmured.

Arm in arm the women picked their way down the path, toward home and the morning meal.

Chryse knelt before the image of the god, lighting taper after taper on his small altar. Behind her, in the brightly lit bedchamber, her servants packed her clothing. Her daughter clung to her mother's skirts and wept.

"If I may help my lord," Chryse murmured, "I will leave, I will journey to his side—Harus aid me, for I am frightened—the world beyond the walls of Sardis is so wide."

The tapers burned with a steady light, yellow pinpricks of fire reflected in the adamantine eyes of the image, and the eyes did not blink.

Bellasteros was more bemused than surprised to receive the message from Adrastes. "I never thought to see the inquisitor of Harus commending me to the queen of Sabazel," he said to Patros.

Patros fingered the broken seal, rolled the parchment, returned it to his king. "I doubt if his plan is quite that simple."

"True," Bellasteros said. One corner of his mouth crimped in annoyance. "Adrastes has always taken too much upon himself, and his pride is limitless."

Patros nodded. "Shall I send a message to Sabazel, then?"

"Yes," said Bellasteros. "Ask for a meeting." And his lips smoothed unbidden into a smile.

Mardoc stood behind the tent flap, listening, frowning, his own private message from the high priest clasped tightly in his hand.

Chapter Eight

BELLASTEROS LED A CENTURY of Sardians three days' journey from their camp beside the Royal Road, along a watercourse that crawled painfully through a stony wilderness; they stopped on the shores of a marsh, as the message from Sabazel had directed. His army was two-thirds of the way to Iksandarun, but he was not the only Sardian beginning to wonder if the imperial capital was, after all, unattainable.

Danica led her Companions ten days' journey from Sabazel to the rendezvous set by the goddess. The company made camp on a low hill, across from another hill where the Sardian camp bristled, and sentries nodded polite but cold greetings in the wasteland between.

It was late evening when the king and the queen met again. The pale sun that swam uncertainly on the horizon was too weak to warm the chill slime of the marsh, and no life stirred. The gutted shell of a village, charred sticks and stones and bare-limbed trees, stood nearby; the hooves of the two horses stirred the bones of the dead to a choking dust. Ravens fluttered nearby, satiated.

Danica reined in, leaned on her saddle, looked directly into his eyes. "So your army has been here," she said.

Bellasteros's gaze did not waver. "Not my army. That of Bogazkar, my enemy."

"There are those who say that you find your enemies where your caprice takes you."

"There are those who set themselves as my enemies when friendship would serve them better."

"Friendship," she repeated. She was surprised that she could look at him so calmly. But his face was a mirror of her own, polite, casual, closed.

"Yes, my lady of Sabazel. Friendship."

"We need each other, it seems," she murmured. For just a moment the corner of his mouth indented, a smile beginning and quickly suppressed. A smile of triumph? Or of relief? "And I have told you," she continued, "I am not the lady of Sabazel."

"Indeed? I think you are."

Perhaps, she thought. Perhaps. . . . She had been given power, some of the goddess's own. Ashtar's voice no longer spoke to her, and yet there was no emptiness in her mind, but a fullness, a second heartbeat complementing hers. It is now my decision, she thought. My will, how the game is played.

She wondered again how much of her will was her own. She exhaled slowly, and a light wind stirred the putrid dust of the ruins into a rising spiral of smoke, bearing the ravens away.

He was watching her, his dark eyes steady. "The oracle says that you can guide me to the sword of Daimion. The oracle says that I shall conquer the Empire. If the Empire belongs to me, then shall not Sabazel be secure?"

"Shall I have bought its safety?" returned Danica.

"Of course," he said, almost impatiently. "I thought the bargain had already been made." His great warhorse shifted restively in the breeze, and his crimson cloak swirled around him.

"Ah, yes," she murmured, "Bellasteros is a man of honor. But even Daimion failed in the end."

He scowled. His lips began to form an epithet. But she met his eyes evenly, and his mouth softened. "I shall not fail, Danica. With you by my side. . . ." He jerked the horse's head around and galloped back to the Sardian camp.

Danica watched. It was as if she watched from two perspectives, with the eyes of a woman on horseback, with the omnipresent sight of a god. She winced; the sensation was akin to that of being torn limb from limb. Was this the way it was to Ashtar, watching as the pieces of her game moved slowly across the board? But then, Danica thought, why did Ashtar play at all? Why could the goddess not simply set the pieces as she wished?

Danica shook her head. She knew only that the plume of Bellasteros's helmet streamed behind him, and the hoofbeats of his horse reverberated in the depths of the earth. No, she thought, he would not fail. The set of his shoulders, the angle of his jaw, the firmness of his hands—he was chosen by the gods to shape the world, and it was his very weakness that made him strong.

The breeze was chill. She drew her bulky cloak more tightly around her and walked her horse back to her own camp.

"No," Danica told her daughter firmly, "he did not bring Patros with him. He had to leave his most trustworthy friend to assist General Mardoc in ruling the main Sardian encampment."

Ilanit nodded. "I see."

"And if he were just over there, separated from you by only some uncertain boundary?"

"I would stay here, Mother, and keep the Companions until your return."

Shandir sat unobtrusively in the corner, checking over her parcels of herbs and her rolls of bandages; at Ilanit's words she smiled gently to herself. Danica opened her arms to her daughter and embraced her, nuzzling into the fresh tousle of her hair. "You tell me what I want to hear. Is it truly what you would do?"

"I do not know," Ilanit replied, muffled against her mother's shoulder. "But fortunately I shall have no opportunity to commit folly."

"Fortunately."

The tent flap opened, and the angular form of Atalia stood in the doorway. "I have set Lyris at guard here," she said. "Ilanit, you are detailed to watch the horses."

"I am there already," the girl said, and she hurried out. Danica's eye held her daughter's image even after she vanished into the night shadows. There was yet another resolution postponed; too soon, now, the Sabazians would be again in the Sardian encampment.

The resonance in Danica's mind, the lingering touch of the goddess, stirred. Cylandra and the city of Sabazel, the remaining warriors sleeplessly guarding their families . . .

Her vision faded. Atalia was still there, watching the thoughts move silently behind her queen's jade-green eyes. "Must you go with him?" she asked bluntly.

"Yes. The game continues, Atalia."

"And will the conclusion be the destruction of Sabazel?"

Danica stepped forward to take Atalia's arm. Sparks seemed to leap from her flesh. "My mentor, my friend, please . . . if you cannot have faith in me, then can you at least trust in our mother's love for us?"

Atalia grimaced, shaking her head as if she would throw away the entire problem. "You know that I trust you with my life. And I know you do not mean to insult me by questioning my devotion to the goddess. But I fear . . . change. The changes that this game, as you call it, has already brought to you, to Ilanit, to Sabazel."

Danica sighed. She had no answer to give, and yet she had to give one. "Ashtar moves in subtle ways," she said at last. "She will not abandon Sabazel." It seemed a lame reply, but Atalia accepted it. Perhaps she felt the power of the goddess in Danica's touch.

With a nod and a salute the warrior was gone.

Shandir padded softly across the tent and set her hands on Danica's shoulders, her fingers pressing away the tension. "She, too, is a worry to you?"

"I wish she would not trust me. If I fail, I will destroy her."

"But you will not fail. And her trust sustains you."

"Shandir, my shield. . . . Ah, yes, that feels good." Danica stretched like a cat and let the healer lay her on her bedroll. The soft hands comforted and asked nothing in return. "But if I do fail, my pair . . . ?"

"Shh. Rest now, and stop thinking so much."

Ashtar's trust sustains me, too, Danica thought later, after the healer had slipped understandingly away. Surely the goddess foresees the end of the game.

She stared wide-eyed into darkness; a faint doubt touched her, a chill shivering the back of her neck. Bellasteros had perhaps reason to doubt the power of his own deity, the falcon, who was served by such an evil minion. But surely Ashtar was omnipotent—even if she shared her power with her daughter. If I bear power, Danica thought, then am I a demigod like Bellasteros? Is he a god simply because he thinks himself one?

What then; who truly orders the world? . . .

It was dark, dark and cold. But I cannot doubt Ashtar's love for Sabazel, Danica thought at last. The goddess will love the king of Sardis, too, if he would permit it.

Perhaps she sensed the tumbling thoughts of Bellasteros, so close to her, so far away across that uncertain boundary. She slept, and her sleep was fitful. The child tossed inside her as if it, too, both feared and anticipated the morrow.

The wind jangled amid rushing cloud, emitting spasms of sunlight that did little to warm a gray, cold day. Danica thanked the chill; she arranged her cloak carefully about her thickened waist and the chain mail corselet she had had to substitute for her breastplate, and she held the star-shield before her.

Bellasteros strode to her side and greeted her with a courteous, cautious nod. "Did you sleep well?" he asked.

"No," she replied. "Did you?"

He glanced back over his shoulder, at the Sardian camp glinting with armor, at the Sabazian camp glistening with weapons. "Do you want an answer?" he asked.

"I think not."

As one they turned and trudged off, across the dry stubble of what had once been broad wheat fields. Bellasteros stumbled and cursed under his breath. "What kind of quest is this, that we cannot go horseback like warriors?"

"Horses cannot go where we are going," Danica told him.

"And how do you know where we are going?"

"I dreamed it, and it shades my mind like a map."

"Ah. . . ." He started to speak again, thought better of it, said nothing.

They mounted a low rise and paused. The ruined fields and tumbled, blackened walls of the village smudged the land behind them. The two hillocks where their respective followers camped were twin blots of darkness on a lowering horizon. One tiny figure stood outside the Sabazian camp, her armor reflecting a quick gleam of sunlight. Ilanit. Danica waved. Ilanit waved in return. Danica's throat closed and she turned away, her teeth set into her lip.

They plunged down the far side of the rise and were suddenly alone in a barren world.

Bellasteros took a deep breath, as if relieved to no longer have the eyes of his soldiers on his back. "Mardoc wants me to wet Solifrax first with your blood," he said.

"Atalia, I think, wishes me to take Solifrax for myself."

They paused to look at each other, in the first open gaze they had shared since Sabazel. Slowly they raised their right hands and clasped them together. "Allies?" Bellasteros asked.

His eyes, Danica noted, were just as she remembered them, dark and deep, lit by a smoldering fire. "Allies," she said, and she wrenched herself away. She had the impression that he was smiling at her, but she did not want to see. She might smile back. The pace she set was a quick, impatient one. "What do you suppose was the crime of that village, to be so destroyed?"

Bellasteros fell into step beside her. "My crime, I would say. Bogazkar needed soldiers, so he took them. And he would deny me food and shelter within the borders of the Empire."

"He has little regard for his own people."

"Indeed. They come streaming to me, as if I could feed them. . . . At least I do not enslave them." He gestured toward the rolling hills before them; abandoned farmland, perhaps, for the traces of walls and terraces still lingered, outlined in sedge and thorn bushes. "I have never seen so many impoverished towns, ruined villages, desert farms, as along the Road. The Empire was dying before we ever broached its borders, overburdened by the dregs of Daimion's dynasty. Why should it not be my turn?"

"Why, indeed?" she replied. "But can you rule what you have conquered at such cost?"

"Yes," he said, with a quick sideways glance. "Yes, I can."

They walked on in silence, down the flank of a hill, up the opposite slope, over the crest and down again. The hills seemed to be mounting slowly toward a cloud-mottled horizon and the suggestion of a solitary steep-sided peak. They paused only once, for rest and a bit of food; by evening the peak stood out hard and dark against the turbulent sky. On its top was an upthrust spire of rock.

The sun was swallowed by the western horizon, and murky winter's dusk overtook them just as they gained the base of the peak. The wind grew stronger and colder, scouring the rolling lands behind them and dashing itself against the rocky slopes. They found a sheltered place to make camp, just where a weathered path started upward. In the last thin gleam of the sun they saw that the spire of rock was really a man-made tower.

Danica gathered brush and Bellasteros lit a small fire. For a time they debated about whether the prominence at whose base they sat was a hill or a mountain. Finally Danica offered a vision of majestic Cylandra, and Bellasteros, a son of the Sar's flood plain, had to admit that this peak was only a high hill.

They stood guard in turn, and in turn slept on opposite sides of the glowing embers, each wrapped in well-learned reserve. And yet, Danica thought drowsily, when they were alone together that reserve softened into a kind of . . . comradeship. She would name it nothing else.

The morning dawned damp and chill. Mist hugged the ground, like a cloud too heavy to grace the sky; the sun was a faint, watery luminescence on an immeasurably distant horizon, chasing the sliver of a dying moon. Danica and Bellasteros stood at the end of the path and gazed upward. Ancient olive trees climbed the mountain slopes between rocks that now, in the hazy light, seemed to bear traces of carving. Faces peered from the twisted roots; winter-withered vines concealed sprawled bodies. There was no breeze, no song of bird or insect, and the silence itself was a litany to the tumbled figures. . . .

Danica blinked. It was just an illusion, a trick of the sun, her own god-haunted mind. She set her shield on her arm; beside her Bellasteros loosened his sword in its sheath. "Shall we go?" he asked. They began the ascent.

Beneath Danica's feet the ground rang hollowly. Her shield was heavy, borne downward, reflecting no light from the hidden sky.

Bellasteros's voice almost made her start. He was looking around him, at the stones and the gnarled trees, beyond to the mist and smoke-wreathed folds of the deserted lands. "My scouts have ridden here," he said, half to himself. "They would have seen this tower, certainly."

"Perhaps it hid itself from them," offered Danica. "We draw the edge of the world close to us."

His eyes widened, darkening. "I would rather fight a pitched battle with Bogazkar, in the open, under the light of the sun I know. . . ."

"That, too, will come. Would you have the sword Solifrax in that battle?"

"Yes," he hissed. His lips tightened to a slit and he plodded on.

Danica nodded. "It is receding as we approach. Some things cannot be confronted directly. . . ." She led him off the path, through a thicket of brambles into the midst of the olives. Vines coiled about their feet; pebbles chased them with little puffs of dust. Through the silver-green of the olive leaves the silver sky diffused with blue.

They clambered down the side of a narrow ravine, and the tower disappeared from view. Up the opposite side, Danica's foot sought leverage on a rock and it turned beneath her. Bellasteros seized an overhanging branch with one hand, her arm with the other, and heaved her to safety. Her shield struck his cuirass; the clang shivered through the hillside and the ground seemed to shrug like a great beast stirred from sleep. They both looked cautiously around them, but the ensuing silence was heavier than before.

He released her. "My thanks," she said, flexing her arm, and he nodded politely.

They burst from the underbrush, dry stalks of marigold and thyme, to find themselves on the crest of the hill. The tower was only a few paces away.

"Harus!" Bellasteros exclaimed.

The tower could well have been a natural spire of rock, so well did it blend with the hilltop. It was built of cyclopean masonry, great hewn stones weathered by centuries of wind and rain, settled solidly together and immovable. A patch of darkness at its base was a door.

A tentative ray of sun struck through the clouds. The olives rustled. The doorway grew even darker.

Danica hesitated. Yes, she had seen this in her dream. But this was not image but reality, solid, consuming. . . .

Bellasteros drew his sword and advanced on the shadows. "We must go in, I suppose," he said from the corner of his mouth.

"Yes." Danica sighed. She joined him in the doorway. The darkness was impenetrable, like a wall between this world and . . .

"The underworld?" he asked. "The seat of the dead? Shall I take Solifrax from Daimion's skeletal fingers?"

"Say, rather, the otherworld. The passage to the tree of the gods." She raised her shield, running it through the edge of the darkness so that shadow flowed over its edge. The deep, secret pulse beneath her own quickened at the touch; a shimmer lit her mind, starlight and moonlight gathered in the wide bronze basin below Cylandra's shining snowfield. The memory tightened her thoughts, twisting them into a taut expulsive thrust like an all-consuming birth pang.

The shield sparked, guttered, flared with light. The darkness fled tattered into the tower. Danica inhaled, stilling a sudden tremble of mind and body, and she smiled with pleasure. Well, this power could be most intriguing. . . . "Shall I lead?"

Bellasteros, his sword dangling unheeded by his side, stared at her. "And when did you truly become a witch?" he asked.

"A favor of the goddess," she told him, "that I may aid you."

He looked hastily around, as if Ashtar herself stood just behind him and had leaned forward to tap him on the shoulder. "Ah," he said faintly and, with an elaborate shrug, "Yes. Lead on."

The interior of the tower was empty. A wooden staircase had once led upward but now lay in splintered heaps along the wall. Bats murmured uneasily in the high shadows, wings fluttering. Stone-carved steps led downward through a gaping hole in the flagged floor.

They picked their way through debris and brush to the stair. A spray of dried asphodel clung to Danica's foot and she kicked it away. Bellasteros probed the still, dank air with his sword, reminding Danica that she should draw her own. She did, and its curved edge flowed with phosphorescence.

She held her shield over the stair, revealing warped, uncertain treads hollowed in the center as if by multitudes of feet. But now the dust lay thick on them, and they spiraled down, down into a well of darkness.

With another inhalation Danica started to descend. Bellasteros moved just at her back, a warm presence stirring the chill air. The light of the glowing shield flickered along walls of rough-hewn stone that soon gave way to walls carved of living rock. And still the steps went on.

The darkness sighed with a rumor of voices, faint and faraway cries and pleas. Strain her heightened senses as she might, Danica could make out no words. She began to see shapes moving in the blackness, wisps of form like the dim afterimages left behind one's own eyes. Her eyes were dazzled by the light of the shield, she told herself.

Bellasteros muttered something under his breath, a prayer or an imprecation, and she knew that the phantoms were real. Ancient memories, she thought; the fears and hates and loves of a thousand generations. . . . Her foot slipped on an exceptionally narrow step. She teetered for a long breathless moment over the brink of nothingness, held only by the light of her shield—the light was tangible, a quicksilver bubble lifting her upward. Once again Bellasteros seized her arm and pulled her back. She turned and saw his wide eyes, his clenched teeth glinting. "My thanks," she murmured.

"And you so surefooted," commented Bellasteros. His voice croaked and he stopped to swallow. "You have become clumsy of late."

"Mm," she responded, not trusting her own voice. She collected her wits and turned again to the stair.

The steps ended at last on a breadth of scarred rock. Danica held the shield as high as she could, sweeping the light about her; there were no walls anywhere, no indication of a passage.

Bellasteros paced back and forth at the boundaries of the star-gleam, making sallies into a blackness denser than the darkest cloud-ridden night. The voices, the dim shapes, followed him. "Shall I lead?" he asked at last, returning to her side, and he swallowed again, convulsively.

He was frightened, she realized. He had been here in a nightmare, and the reality of it was more frightening than any number of imperial troops. Such fear might well make him foolhardy. "We shall go side by side," she replied. "We shall go . . ."

She closed her eyes; the darkness, the drifting phantoms, looked just the same behind her lids. She cast her thought into the depths of the caverns, into the depths of her dream, slipping through the blackness like one ghost among many. The constant murmur of voices seemed for just a moment to take on meaning, like words in an old language seldom spoken, often sensed. A pinprick of light appeared in her mind, a distant flicker just beyond her grasp.

And the dream ended at the mouth of a passage, a passage leading into more than one kind of darkness. . . . Onward.

She opened her eyes. Bellasteros was not watching her; his sword swished about him like the tail of a hunting cat. "Your new weapon is almost within your grasp," she said. "This way."

And you are not frightened? she asked herself. She began the litany: If I cannot trust in Ashtar . . . They walked into the darkness.

After a time walls materialized around them; they had indeed found a passageway. Danica heard more than one dry slither at her feet, and she clucked for the blind snakes as she did for those in Cylandra's cavern. A faint, sickly light began to glow from somewhere ahead.

Danica glanced at Bellasteros. His chin was up, his jaw set. His features were as sternly carved as those of some archaic statue. His eyes did not reflect the pale light but glinted with an internal fire. In a few strides he had gained the doorway of a large illuminated chamber, leaving Danica to follow.

She followed. Before them was a cavern hewn from the rock of the mountain. The sides, the central pillars, swarmed with carved gargoyles, a twisting, tortured mass of sharp teeth, pointed wings, glaring eyes. Was that shape . . . ? No, it was a trick of the light, surely, that made the forms in the corner of her eyes seem to be turning toward her, grimacing, reaching with talons extended.

The floor of the chamber was slabs of dark, glistening rock, set as closely together as a reptile's scales. There was dust here, yes—a thick acrid dust shaped around pieces of stained armor. Shaped like human hands grasping futilely at rusted blades; shaped like human faces peering eyelessly upward from crumpled helmets.

Bellasteros stepped out into the room, walking warily toward a great flat rock at the far end. The greenish light that emanated from the walls, the ceiling, the forms of the gargoyles, wavered and gathered about him.

"Ashtar," Danica breathed. She sensed danger here, but it was a resonance of danger long past. The gibbering ghosts swooped at her back, urging her on. "Marcos," she called softly, and the name echoed down the chamber. Again invisible wings fluttered in the shadows.

He paused, waiting for her, his alert look focused not on her progress to his side but darting suspiciously to every corner of the room. Together they advanced to the rock—the altar,

Danica realized. On it were the mortal remains of yet another warrior.

The bones were brown and brittle, honeycombed by the withered egg cases of worms, unencumbered by any shreds of clothing or armor. The eye sockets of the skull were pools of nothingness. No memory, no identity; he had been laid naked on the slab, and naked he remained.

"Who—" Bellasteros began, but Danica pointed to one hand. The finger bones, outspread like a scuttling spider's legs, held a disk of silver emblazoned with a tiny, many pointed star—a miniature star-shield. The amulet alone of everything in the chamber remained untouched by decay.

"Ashtar's sign," said Danica. The back of her neck shivered. "Mari gave to Daimion such an amulet to bind his faith; still he betrayed her and the gods as well. He paid with his death."

"Daimion?" Bellasteros's voice ranged upward an octave. "Daimion, cursed, hounded from his kingship—and his guard could not save him from the sacrifice. . . ." The pale light of the chamber swirled, palpable motes of putrescence, about his form. The gargoyles murmured among themselves, and the ghosts howled.

Mother! Why threaten him, your own son! Danica lifted her shield. The pale shimmer, starlight and moonlight mingled, fell around Bellasteros like a cloak. The shimmer touched the ancient bones and, with the faintest, most distant sigh, they crumbled into an uneasily shifting dust. The amulet glinted, the star flashing out so brightly that shadows streamed confused into the farthest corners. Then it, too, dissolved. Silence fell on the chamber, the dust quieted, the voices stilled.

Bellasteros closed his eyes. A quick shudder shook his body, a shudder echoed in Danica's. "And will you," he whispered, "give to me such an amulet, to call me to my death?"

"Can you be bound by any other than your word, freely given?"

His eyes opened; he turned to her, mouth tight, shoulders square, eyes opaque. "So I choose to be bound, then. As I told you, I shall not fail."

Ah, Marcos, she thought, as they walked side by side from the cold, quiet chamber. Daimion's day is long gone, and I could not bind you even if I wished. Not even Ashtar could force you to her will; the circle of time carries us away from the ancient gods and their cruel strengths, and together we forge new allegiances. . . . She frowned. Her thoughts bewildered her, concepts flowing through her mind like water between her fingers, ungraspable.

If Bellasteros's thoughts were as difficult, he gave no sign; he strode in silence at her side. A faint scraping of scales against rock, wings in the darkness, and another faint luminescence touched the passageway.

A chasm cut across the tunnel. Its sides were sheer, a knife slash in the rock, black obsidian reflecting the sullen red glow of fire. Bellasteros knelt on the edge of the crevasse, Danica leaning over his shoulder, and scanned the depths with narrow eyes. Tongues of flame licked upward from some great subterranean pit, shading rock and flesh alike with garish crimson.

Danica exhaled through pursed lips, letting her breath caress the surface of the shield. She blew the golden gleam out like a lamp, and the shield, too, shone red. Her shoulder blades prickled; she looked around, her sword raised. Nothing, nothing but a creeping unease.

Wordlessly they followed the passageway down the side of the chasm. A few steps away, around a buttress of rock, they saw a bridge. It, too, was of black obsidian, rising from a smoothly carved coil of rock, spanning the crevasse in one long arch, anchoring itself with another coil. Beneath it the flames danced, swirling upward in greedy leaps and spirals.

Bellasteros started forward, placing one foot on the coiled step. Danica held him back. "No." And, forcing calmness, "I am the guide. I shall lead."

His brows shot up his forehead. With a mocking bow he turned aside and stood with exaggerated patience, leaning on his sword.

She stepped reluctantly onto the coil of rock, wondering why, indeed, she had not let him go first. The sole of her foot thrilled. She stepped onto the arch of the bridge. Her legs tautened like bowstrings. The heat of the fire hit her, a gust of searing wind, and she almost lost her balance. "Take care," Bellasteros called. "I am not close enough to catch you."

Another cautious step, and another . . . It was not the hot breath of the chasm that pushed her. It was the bridge itself, shifting beneath her feet. Mother, what . . . ? She fell to her knees, scrabbling desperately for purchase on the slick rock, her heart beating against her ribs. . . . It was not rock. The anchoring step on the far side of the abyss uncoiled itself, and the great plumed head of a basilisk rose swaying into blood-tinted shadow.

Bellasteros shouted something—just what, Danica could not tell. The eyes of the basilisk were glittering, incandescent gemstones, holding her own eyes fascinated. A fiery mist gathered about them. . . .

No! She grasped at the last trailing tendril of her thought, following it deep, deep; she cast it into her shield, threw the shield upward. Her body flamed hot with the effort and her face burned. The mist shot forward as fast and deadly as a spear thrust.

The shield flared, turning and dissipating the mist into scin-tillants of quicksilver, and the silver sparks reflected them-selves in the creature's eyes. The gemstones shattered, dull lightless shards rained down onto the rock. The basilisk screamed. Its body lurched, throwing Danica onto her back. It heaved again, head coiling back over its body, and she was falling, falling into the fiery chasm. . . .

Mother, why give me such power only to let it end here? My will, my own will, to live or die—I almost fell on the stair, and the bubble of light sustained me. . . .

She clenched her teeth until her jaw ached, searching for the thought, shaping it, spinning it out. I must be strong, I must be . . . Her body was borne up like a feather on the wind, floating in the warm blush of the fire. She twisted, falling back onto the basilisk's body. Now! And her slender blade flashed scarlet. Scarlet from the light. Scarlet from the thick blood welling around it as she drove it to half its length through the smooth black scales.

The creature shrieked. The sound was repeated, over and over, echoing down the rocky galleries. It thrashed from side to side, but Danica held grimly to her blade and could not be dislodged. She realized, with some small part of her mind, that a man's voice was calling her name, urgently, desper-ately, even as her own voice prayed aloud, Power, enough power. . . . She spared one glance, and saw Bellasteros's face flushed in a frenzied rage.

He raised his sword, brought it down in a swift two-handed thrust. Its point drove deep into a crevice in the rock, pinion-ing the basilisk by its tail.

The creature was coiling backward on itself, the head questing for its prey, the great blind eyes oozing scarlet tears. Bellasteros, unarmed now, threw himself full-length onto its back and grasped a fold of Danica's cloak. The basilisk reared upward, Danica's sword at last lost hold, and she and Bellasteros tumbled together down the expanse of shining obsidian scales onto the ledge.

The plumed head crashed like a battering ram against the wall above them; the tail jerked convulsively, and Bellasteros's sword snapped in two. The huge body of the basilisk fell toward them, its crushing weight driving a gust of hot air before it.

In one concerted movement Danica and Bellasteros rolled away from each other. The creature's body struck where they had lain, and the rock of the mountain trembled. As it writhed upward again Danica heard her own voice screaming the paean. Her shield ignited, the emblazoned star burning with a clear light. Her strength twisted within her, her body coiled —she struck, her sword glancing into the creature's throat.

Again it shrieked, but the scream was strangled in blood. The huge body heaved, knocking Danica to the side; her sword slipped from her grasp and went spinning across the wet, blood-slick rock, under the creature's belly and directly into Bellasteros's hand. He plucked it up. He shouted the incoherent name of some god, lunged forward, struck with a berserk strength. The basilisk's head, sliced cleanly from its body, bounced across the rock and over the brink into the crevasse. A gout of fire leaped upward, hissing.

The heat drained from Danica's face. Suddenly nauseated, she turned her back on the final jerks and thrashings of the creature's body. She staggered around the buttress of rock to hide herself in the rose-tinted gloom of the passageway. She rested the shield against her knees and bent over it, stilling the trembling of her limbs; the child stretched against the suddenly slack muscles of her abdomen, and she tucked her cloak around it.

The tide of power she had summoned ebbed from her. Mother, how could I let myself be taken by surprise? Do I think myself invincible?

A scraping noise from the edge of the crevasse, and the sickening thuds and bumps of a falling body. The fire snapped. Bellasteros's slow steps came around the corner and his shadow fell lightly across the shield. She looked up.

He offered her sword hilt first. "It is just as well," he said, "that I will soon have a new one."

She took the weapon, noting that he had cleaned it well. "My thanks yet again," she said. She was hoarse, but she could barely remember shouting.

"No. I thank you." He settled down beside her, removed his helmet, leaned his crisp dark hair against the rock, and closed his eyes. Beads of sweat stood like drops of pale blood on his brow. "I would," he said plaintively, "much rather face the army of Bogazkar under the sun I know...."

His voice shook and he stopped it in his throat. She touched his arm. "We shall soon be there."

His eyes rested on her face, her hand on his arm. The walls of rock flickered with firelight, with the light shared by their eyes, with the words unspoken that hummed in their throats.

At last Danica returned to herself. She gathered up the shield, and her strength, and rose to her feet. Beside her Bellasteros replaced his helmet, smoothed the plume, stood. "We seem to have destroyed our bridge," he said.

"Then we shall spin a new one." She laughed, briefly, and drew a smooth breath. The murk of the passageway thickened. She inhaled again, and the darkness gathered on the face of the shield. She drew it from the tunnel and across to the edge of the chasm, a rope of shadow reflecting the dancing crimson light of the fire. Well, this power does have its pleasures....

Bellasteros followed, his head cocked to the side, disbelieving.

The rope grew dense. Carefully Danica stepped onto it; the darkness bore her weight. She guided the shield over the crevasse, spinning the rope around and behind her. She stood in midair, supported by shadow and flame, and glanced back over her shoulder. "Are you coming?"

With a grimace Bellasteros stepped up beside her. She walked on across the crevasse and he followed, taking great care to set his feet only where her feet had been. Their footsteps were small whorls of smoke.

Then they were across. Danica tugged at the shield, and the shadow rope broke, springing back into the darkness of the tunnel from whence it had come. A small gray cloud lingered around the shield; Danica blew it away. She turned to

Bellasteros with the smile of a conjuror whose trick is well done.

He bowed. "I am impressed. Do you enjoy being a demi-god, my lady?"

"It is not at all what I would have thought," she told him. "The power is too much, it seems, or not enough. A beguiling confidence that could well be misplaced."

"I know, Danica. My power is, after all, only illusion."

"Is it?" she asked. "Are you sure?" But he had no answer.

Side by side they turned down the passageway; in just a moment a point of light, of blessed daylight, appeared far ahead. Bellasteros hurried forward.

He was frightened, suddenly and uncontrollably frightened. Danica's heart leaped into her throat. A faint odor of hatred filled the passage—not from him, but around him. . . . She sprinted to catch up, but the floor here crawled with the living slime of a bat cave, lichens, droppings, half-digested prey, tiny scuttling creatures. For a moment her feet could find no purchase and she slipped back, sliding into a nightmare. His nightmare, she realized with a pang of horror, his evil dream come upon him at last.

Bellasteros was at the clear, dry rock before the doorway, reaching out for the sunlight, when the demon seized him.

It was a wan shape, a pale suggestion of a man, but it was twisted and malevolent still. Gerlac. Danica remembered only too well the hatred that had possessed Lyris. She swallowed her heart and lunged forward, shouting imprecations.

Bellasteros turned, paled, went down with one brief cry of dismay. The demon's hands tightened on his throat, and the stench of unguents and decay filled the tunnel.

Danica pelted up, raised her sword, struck. The weapon passed cleanly through the wraith. It was only a wisp of form and motion, wasted and feeble. "It is but a sour, spiteful memory," she called. "It has no more power. . . ." But even as she spoke she realized that over Bellasteros it had great and deadly power. Her nostrils flared at the smell of it.

Bellasteros was choking, his face mottled red. The tunnel echoed to distant, howling laughter, channeled from hell. The demon's face shifted, gaining substance, decaying to a skull with a gaping jaw which bent forward as if to consume the living man. . . .

"Gerlac, no! You will not have him!" Danica shouted. She threw herself down beside Bellasteros, clasped him to her, laid her shield over them both. And the shield began to glow, not with the nearby daylight, but with the light of moon and stars. The light leaped upward, shaping itself into the form of a woman with arms outstretched.

Bellasteros looked up, and his glazed eyes filled with the light. "Mother," he croaked, "Ashtar, Viridis, help me. . . ."

A breeze chimed down the tunnel. The laughter stopped suddenly and invisible wings beat the air, fading, gone. Bellasteros threw the wormlike fingers from his throat. "No!" he cried, to the empty eyes, the hollow mouth. "You have no claim on me; I have none of your blood and I deny you!"

The demon moaned, growing transparent; the gleaming female form lowered her arms and the last of Gerlac's hatred shredded like smoke into nothingness and was dissipated by the wind.

Bellasteros collapsed in Danica's arms. "Mother"—he sighed—"save me from myself." But she, too, was gone. The shield faded, humming gently, and grew inert.

Bellasteros rested, ordering his breath, and for a time Danica rested at his side. At last, the demon defeated at last. . . . But soon she thought, Enough of this . . . comfort, and she commented, "Foolish, to rush ahead of your guide."

He gave her an exasperated look, cleared his throat, and sat up, pulling his brisk and confident manner like a cloak around him. His eyes, though, were haunted, dark with the shadow of hate. "How did you know who that was?" he asked, too casually.

"Adrastes sent him in the body of your wife's serving-woman to kill me in Sabazel." And in a few clipped words she told the tale.

He understood, and his reply was an epithet. Mouth tight, jaw stern, he struggled to his feet and offered Danica his hand. She took it. Together they walked into the light of another world.

Chapter Nine

THE VALLEY WAS a verdant bowl lidded by a shining blue sky. Sheer precipices closed the horizon in three directions; in the fourth was the craggy mountain slope and the dim mouth of the tunnel where Danica and Bellasteros stood.

He looked about him. "Would it be usless to point out," he said, "that this is not the same hill or peak or mountain that we entered?"

"Quite uscless," returned Danica. She turned her face toward the sun and cleansed her nostrils with the warm scented breeze. "This is the garden of the gods."

"And we are permitted to trespass?"

"I certainly hope so."

Shimmering groves of olive, orange, and almond dotted the floor of the valley, and spring and fall flowers intermingled were strewn in bright patches, red, yellow, purple, across the grass. Doves murmured in the shade and the bees were busy, humming in drunken ecstasy from bloom to bloom.

On a prominence in the midst of the valley was one great tree, gnarled with age and yet laden heavily with golden fruit. "There," breathed Bellasteros, "there. . . ." He started off, then stopped and glanced around for Danica. "Are you still my guide?"

She shrugged. "I am not sure. But I will walk with you, gladly."

They moved through the shade of the groves as through

an airy liquid, sunlight and shadow shifting and whispering around them, dancing to the music of the wind. Danica realized she was smiling, enspelled. She did not even start when some small furry animal, alarmed by their footsteps, dashed away in an upheaval of iris blossoms. Was this, then, what it was to be a god? Peace, and beauty, and the senses soothed. . . . But even the gods had duties in the world of men.

The tree was above them, the blue vault of the sky winking through its lacy green canopy. The smooth brown branches twined downward, offering lush handfuls of golden fruit. They had only to walk up a rough stairway of granite boulders half-buried in the swelling grass. Bellasteros took the first steps with a bound, and sparks flew from his boot.

Someone waited. A hooded figure waited in the fluid shadow of the tree. It had not been there a moment before. Bellasteros stopped abruptly between two rocks and braced himself. His hand fell to his side, groping futilely for the hilt of a sword that was not there.

Danica leaped up beside him and placed a restraining hand on his arm. The figure was that of an old woman, bent and wrinkled with age, leaning on a staff; her eyes, as clear and blue as the sky, were piercing, looking through the warriors who stood before her as if their armor, their flesh, were no more substantial than the sunlight. As if even sunlight were a substance to be molded by her glance into whatever flesh she chose.

Danica knelt, raising her palms. A laugh escaped her throat, the pleasure of a lost child found again. "Mother," she began, but she was interrupted.

A fluttering in the sky, a hoarse cry, and a falcon spiraled between the branches of the tree to land trustingly on the woman's outstretched arm. It settled its wings, preening itself, and turned its gaze on the warriors. Its eyes, too, were the clear blue of the sky.

Bellasteros gasped and fell to his knees at Danica's side. His mouth dropped open, his eyes glinted, shocked, awestruck, even pleased. . . .

Perhaps the woman spoke; perhaps it was only the wind and the rustling of the leaves. Danica felt the sound like a note of music in her mind, a strand of melody filling her senses and straining at her consciousness as if she were a ripe piece of fruit, ready to burst. The baby leaped within her, and at her side Bellasteros caught his breath in a sob.

Then the moment of harmony was gone, leaving only a humming aftertone in her thoughts. No—it was her shield that was humming. She glanced at it, at the glowing star, at Bellasteros beyond. His eyes were closed, his face drawn and pale. Did you think it would be easy, she thought, to be one with the gods?

The woman and the falcon were gone. Only the staff was left, driven upright into the thick grass between the roots of the tree. A serpent coiled around it, swaying gently, its hood spread and casting an iridescent shadow down the steps.

"Ah," said Danica, understanding. "The staff, Marcos, take the staff. . . ."

The color returned to his face. He rose. He stepped forward, into the shadow cast by the serpent, and the snake withered away, leaving only the gleaming scales of its shed skin wrapped about the staff.

Bellasteros set his hand on the staff. Light flared around his fingers, so that his flesh seemed to burn; light flashed in his hand, so bright that the staff, the tree, the rocky knoll itself disappeared.

Danica blinked, shook her head to clear it, and looked up. Bellasteros held in his hand the gold filigreed hilt of a sword, protruding from a smooth serpent-skin scabbard. It was Solifrax, the sword of Daimion. It might have been made for Bellasteros, so well did it fit his grasp.

He drew it, raised its gleaming arc above his head; steel so highly polished that it seemed like carved crystal. "Danica," he cried, "look, it came to my hand." His voice vibrated with a fierce joy. The blade caught the sunlight, snapping lightning from its tip, and the light sparkled in rippling refractions from Danica's shield. Sunlight, not moonlight. . . .

His eyes, midnight dark, sought the green radiance of hers, opening to it, reflecting a fleeting viridescent glimmer. He lowered the sword in salute. And, suddenly, he grinned, his teeth flashing in his bronze face. The plume on his helmet rippled in a whispering wind.

Danica raised the shield in return, laughing with him, at one with his pleasure and with the beauty of Solifrax.

Even above the enchanted valley the sun slipped implacably into the west.

•   •   •

They made their camp in a sheltered dell beneath the roots of the tree. The sun set, and velvet shadows welled from ground and sky to fill the valley. It was a living darkness, molding itself into shapes that gestured soothingly in the corner of the eye and then vanished. It was, Danica thought, like the blurred softness that surrounds an infant, the gentle movements blended of its own awareness and that of its mother, the peace that cradles it before its senses awaken to desire and pain.

Bellasteros struck a spark from the flint and watched bemusedly as the tinder caught. A tiny red flame licked upward, throwing the planes and angles of his face into sharp relief. There was no answering flame in the darkness of his eyes.

They set aside their armor to wash—separately—and they shared their ration of dried meat and bread. They plucked the rich golden fruit from the tree, feeding it in small morsels each to the other. The juice ran down their chins and they laughed like children. The stream that welled from the roots of the tree leapt and danced among the rocks at the edge of the campsite, droplets glinting like quicksilver in the light of the fire. The water was cold, slightly effervescent. "A fountain of youth?" Bellasteros hazarded.

"Perhaps," replied Danica. "Perhaps not."

He glanced at her with a wry sideways crumple of his mouth. "You would not even humor my fancy?"

"Why?" she asked, brows tilted teasingly.

"Indeed," he responded with an exaggerated sigh, "why?" He wrapped himself in his cloak and stretched out on the grass, turning his face to the sky.

Above them the tree murmured to itself in the night breeze, and its leaves summoned the stars to hang like tiny lamps among its branches. The sword in its snakeskin sheath rested beside the star-shield, both laid against a great granite boulder that sparked in quick glints of light that were not reflections of the fire. But the weapons themselves were silent.

Danica knew, with that instinct that she had so quickly learned not to question, that there was no need to post a guard. The dangers of the quest were over, and the dangers of the morrow could not penetrate to this place. Here, beyond the end of the world, she lay beside Bellasteros and for a time floated thoughtless on the slow swells of eternity.

"The stars," he said after a time. "The stars are not quite
. . . right. The constellations are altered somehow, the hus-
bandman reaping instead of sowing and the hunter turning to
face the boar."

She pulled her mind back into her body, testing the boundaries of her own life. Its simplicity was gone, but still she
would ask for no other. She glanced over at him. He lay with
one arm flung back, cradling his head; the other rested on his
chest. His fingers, long, strong, powerful fingers that held the
destiny of the world, were as lightly curled as the hand of an
infant clasped against its mother's breast.

She smiled. Strange how her thoughts kept turning to infants. "And the moon is waning, somewhere," she said.
"Here there is no moon, I think. Ashtar's eye closed in sleep—
closed in worship. . . ." If Ashtar holds Harus lovingly on her
arm, she thought, they must be deities of equal power. They
must be . . . one. And yet men fight in their names. . . . Again
the concept slipped through her mind like water through her
fingers, and again she lost it. She remembered only that pierc-
ingly sweet note of harmony.

"Harus." Bellasteros sighed, as if his thoughts, too, stumbled across uncertain ground.

The fire burned down to glowing embers and they made no
move to replenish it; the night was warm, held suspended in a
memory of summer. The tree rustled, tiny nameless insects
chirped and skreeked to themselves, a dove cooed a sleepy
duet with its mate and then fell silent.

"Marcos," Danica said quietly, tasting his name as a liquor
on her tongue.

His solemn aquiline profile did not turn toward her, but at
her voice it softened, its sharpness blunted.

"Marcos," she said again.

Then he did turn, his dark eyes holding a pool of the night
and a distant gleam of starlight, withdrawing from some depth
of the sky to take her in a perceptible embrace. "Danica," he
said.

Her senses quivered, plucked by his look into a deep resonant chord. His stillness, she realized, was deceptive. His body
was tautly coiled, its energy barely suppressed, held ready for
her word, her movement.

She smiled, marveling at how well she had learned to read

him. How well, obviously, he had learned to read her. They were alike, intensity matched by intensity, the same song sung to different melodies.

In spite of herself she reached out and laid her forefinger along the curve of his chin and throat. The quickened beat of his pulse reverberated through her hand. No, she would not goad him; the time for that was long past. She touched him because the touching was a joy. The skin of his throat was a smooth, tight bronze, the pulse bared so vulnerably to her fingertips.

Danica leaned forward, pressing her lips to the hollow in his throat, breathing in the faint salt-tanged, spiced taste of his flesh. And his scent flooded her memory. She seemed to have no will of her own, no strength to resist; she was drawn to his shielded flame like a moth to a candle. She lay against him, absorbing his essence in one long shuddering breath.

And yet it was her will, her strength, to so lose herself in this man, to seek from him a nourishment more essential than food or water. . . . Mother! But that pulse deep in her mind that was the goddess was beating in the same rhythm as his heart.

Bellasteros's arms came around her, not claiming her as a prize, but hesitantly, giving her every chance to pull away. He did not try to raise her face; he waited, until inevitably she looked up. And only then did he set his lips on hers. His body trembled, his breath rasped in his chest, but still he held himself checked. She kissed him greedily, aching for the warmth of his flesh against hers, knowing even as she felt the desire that it would be unfulfilled. The kiss in itself would be enough, an intimacy as deep as any sexual coupling.

At last she withdrew, slowly, reluctantly. He made a quick movement as if to follow, then halted himself, eyes slitted in a grimace. Instead he caught her hand and held it on his face. Her image was reflected in his pupils, as his image was in hers. The words were unspoken. You have ravished my heart, you have stolen my soul. Somehow, with repetition, the words became much easier to bear.

That power she bore hummed in her veins, inseparable from her desire. Ashtar, she sighed deep in the recesses of her mind, Ashtar, this is what you destined for me, for Sabazel. . . .

His eyes stopped her breath in her throat, but he only touched her hand. "There is no moon here," he said. His voice caught, choked, and he shook himself. "There is no moon here, it seems. How can you tell the turning of the year when summer blossoms in midwinter? What if it is, now, here, an eternal solstice?"

"Or what if the year turns not at all?" she responded gravely, "and this land is never blessed with solstices or equinoxes?"

"In this timeless place, beyond the circles of the moon and the sun, where the stars shift themselves from their appointed patterns and the seasons merge—where you, I think, could shift the year at will . . ."

"Yes?"

His voice grew, if possible, even huskier. "Would it break your laws . . ." He turned his face into her hand and kissed her palm. His mouth branded her skin.

"But the rites can be celebrated only within the borders of Sabazel." Her voice, too, was choked, and she tightened her jaw. It was useless, though; he could sense her yearning as easily as she sensed his.

"Is this place not Sabazel? We carry Sabazel with us, Danica."

She inhaled deeply, calming herself, and eyed him with brows raised until at last the intensity of his expression melted into a rueful grin. How attractive, she thought, was that broad smile on his face. Doubly attractive, because it was so seldom seen. "So the warrior," she said, "does not take what he wants but becomes a sophist, and seeks to reason his prey into submission?"

"My sophistry is weak, it seems, since it does not move you. And I could never think you my prey."

"You would not try to force me?"

"Why? It is not your flesh that I crave but the woman who dwells within it. You will only give that woman freely; she cannot be taken."

"And if I submitted meekly, like those women trained to serve your pleasure . . . what then?"

He shook his head. "Then you would not be Danica."

"Ah," she said quietly. Her fingers stroked the clean line of his cheek and jaw, soothing the troubled flame within. "Have I earned your respect, my king?"

"Indeed. As I have earned yours, I think."

Yes, he deserved that. . . . They looked at each other,

searching, questioning. At last she sighed and released him,
lying back amid the folds of her cloak. It seemed as if the stars
had shifted again, dancing about the tree in yet another pattern. The stars, it seemed, were the whirling impulses of her
own mind. "Yes," she whispered. "Marcos Bellasteros has
earned my respect. And I would give him a gift; not an amulet
to bind him, but knowledge of my weakness. Never have I
been tempted by any man save him."

He nodded soberly. "My thanks, my queen, for such a gift.
I shall honor your confidence."

"And Bellasteros is a man of honor," she added. A quick
smile tickled the corner of her mouth and she hesitated only a
moment before releasing it.

He fell into his cloak, laughing. "Once I thought I knew the
meaning of such a word. Now—I learn at your knee, like a
child. And there you have my weakness."

"Is learning a weakness, my king? Would you choose ignorance?"

"Would you?"

But she had no answer. For a time they lay silent, watching
the slow yet perceptible spinning of the stars across the depths
of the sky as if years passed before their eyes, bearing them
away from the nets that held them trapped in the present of
their lives.

"Do you suppose," Bellasteros murmured, "that we shall
return to find the Empire fallen of its own weight, Ilanit ruling
Sabazel, our names only legends told around the winter
fires?"

A wind stirred the night, an urgent breath that bore with it
the faint suggestion of the stench of the battlefield, horses,
men, blood; Danica tensed, opening her senses—no words
formed in her mind. But that second heartbeat drummed on,
and she knew that the nets waited open. Soon she and
Bellasteros would once again be ensnared, not quite enemies,
no longer friends; this moment of peace would soon run its
course and be forever lost.

So grasp it, then, she told herself. Grasp fate, instead of
waiting for it to be presented to you, by the gods, by men—
now, reach out. . . .

"Marcos," she said again.

He raised on one elbow to look at her, inclining his head
with an extravagant courtesy.

Wordlessly she took his hand and brought it through a fold in her cloak to rest on her belly. She was a tall woman, and well-knit, but she was now well past the midpoint of her pregnancy and her abdomen stood up as taut and hard as a melon.

She forced herself to look at his face, watching as his slightly affable, slightly mocking expression faded into puzzlement. And then the child moved, thrusting itself upward against the barrier of time and flesh that kept it from its father's touch. Danica winced at the blow, and at the expression on Bellasteros's face as it darkened with comprehension.

He jerked his hand away, turned, sat up with his back toward her. The child stretched again, desperately, kicking Danica's breath from her lungs. But even as she gasped and retrieved that breath, and reached to pat the curve of her belly soothingly, the child quieted, fluttering into stillness, coiling into its warm nest beneath her heart.

She set her teeth deep into her lip, waiting for Bellasteros to speak. Perhaps she had been a fool, to break that moment of peace, to remind him that the world outside crouched like a great hunting beast, waiting. But she would have been more foolish not to tell him the truth, to let his enemies discover it first and fill his ears with lies.

"My child," Bellasteros stated, brittle.

"Ours," she replied. "Ashtar's gift."

"Indeed?"

Nettled, she went on. "Did you think only of the spending of our passion, and not of the consequences that might well follow? Did you not once wonder what you left behind in Sabazel?"

His shoulders were shaking. With anger, she thought, and she groped for the will to hate him again.

"Did I not once wonder how much of myself I left behind?" he choked. "Of course. Of course, it would have to be, such a fruit from such a passion. And yet I had thought to wake and find it a dream."

He was laughing, laughing in a black humor very close to despair. She frowned, cautious, her will to hate escaping her grasp once more. "Marcos," she tried, but he was still speaking.

"All the women I have known, that I have had; the women who knelt before me, asking for my favor, and the women I have bedded to secure the land of Sardis, and the women I sought for a moment's pleasure—what I thought then to be pleasure—but it is you who would bear my heir. . . ." He turned back as abruptly as he had turned away. "Is it male, do you think?"

"Perhaps." In his present mood she could no longer read him; if she could not hate him, she could at least guard her tongue.

But still he shook his head, his laughter quieting itself to a wry chuckle. "Gods! I am a toy, an object of jest, a piece on a game board. Every time I think I have checked my opponent I discover that it is you, Danica, you who have checked me."

"I am not your opponent. I am also a piece on the board."

He at last regained his breath and his sobriety. His hand rose tentatively, moved to her cloak, opened it so that the curve of her belly was a smooth mound rounded by the starlight. His fingertips barely brushed the fabric of her clothing, stroking her, patting her like a sculptor shaping his creation. And the child moved again to his touch, gently now, flexing its tiny body as if drawing strength from its father's care.

"Gods," Bellasteros muttered. His gaze moved upward to Danica's face. "No, you are not my opponent. But such an ally . . . I am indeed a child, thinking that a shining toy of a weapon will end the game, not realizing that the game goes on and on."

She was tired. She was sustained only by the power of the goddess that sang in her veins. How much more? she wondered. How much more desire and pain, fear and love? She closed her eyes and sighed. "We are caught. We have the favor of the gods, but it is ourselves who must play out the game. And Marcos . . ."

Her lashes parted. His face was close to hers, his breath a caress on her cheek. His expression was not, after all, unreadable. "Yes," he said, when she did not speak.

"It is a game that cannot be won. Compromise, only compromise."

He lay beside her, spreading his cloak over them both. His hand still cradled the child. She let him settle her head on his shoulder in a protective gesture that only a few hours ago they would both have thought ludicrous. His face in the last red glow of the fire was suddenly gaunt and tight, careworn, but the humor still flared deep in his eyes. "This child," he murmured, "like his father of uncertain lineage. Poor bastard. . . ."

She smiled, closing her eyes again; sleep ebbed around her, and she let herself float away on its swell. She did not have to will herself to love him, she thought. She had only to keep herself from speaking. The morning would come soon; there had been compromises enough for one night. But no bitterness lingered in her mouth, and his warmth against her was an inexpressible solace. He shared her pain. It was a tiny shred of victory, but it would suffice.

For a time Bellasteros lay awake, watching the night turn above the valley, watching Danica as she slept so trustingly in his arms. His face was bewildered, almost hurt; he touched her lips with his fingertips as if she were some exotic artifact.

Then his expression smoothed, and his mouth set itself with courage, and he, too, slept.

The morning came soon. They sat munching a tasteless meal, regarding the ashes of the fire, not each other. The tree sighed, rippling in sorrow beneath a sky misted with steel-gray. Already the enchanted valley turned them away.

"You will ride with me against the Empire?" Bellasteros asked.

"I will throw my Companions onto the board," replied Danica, "for Sabazel, not for Sardis."

"Although I am Sardis?"

"Are you indeed? How much Sardian blood, then, flows in your veins?"

He glanced at her reprovingly. "Not a fair blow, my lady."

"No. Forgive me." She tried to smile at him, but the smile withered.

After a time Bellasteros said, "It would be better if you waited a day or so to follow me to the main encampment. And I would not think it wise to set up your own camp within my walls. . . ."

"No," said Danica. "Not wise at all."

They cleared away the camp, armed themselves, and allowed themselves one moment's look, one moment to wonder if the night's affection lingered into the chill light of morning. Yes, it did, but it was a furtive, frightened affection, trammeled by the demands of the living world. Quickly they looked away.

They bore their weapons back over the rim of the world. No creatures, living or dead, impeded them. They walked stubbornly forward, side by side, but they might as well have been on opposite sides of the Great Sea. And yet there remained the memory of trust; a few times, a very few times, they recognized each other's presence and exchanged a brief nod. Meager reassurance, but enough.

They returned through a cold, empty land to the ruined village and the separate armed camps of their followers.

Atalia was the first to see them. She rode out to meet them, casting at Bellasteros a stern look that she obviously wished had been a javelin. She pried Danica from his side and set her upon her own horse. "So much for that," she said, and led her queen away.

Danica, drooping over the horse's neck in a weariness she could not conceal, had time for one last glance at Bellasteros. This man, she told herself, held her fate in his hands. He held her death, and she trusted him. She was a weak and foolish mortal, suffering some delirious dream of godlike power.

He drew Solifrax, thrusting it upward in a flash of captured sunlight, saluting her, hail and farewell. Then his own soldiers came rushing to his side, clamoring to see the sword, standing open-mouthed in awe of it, and smoothly he directed the salute to them.

She turned away. Tears stung her eyes and she strangled them.

The stocky soldier Hern led his king to his tent, brought food and water, removed his boots. He then took up his post before the doorway, his suspicious eyes never leaving the distant shapes of the Sabazian camp.

The fair soldier Aveyron crouched at Bellasteros's feet, warily watching a quiescent Solifrax while the king looked through the accumulated dispatches from the main encampment by the Royal Road. The legionaries toiled at make-work tasks, awaiting their king's return. The scouts of the two armies skirmished bloodily. A raiding party was repulsed, and a caravan of supplies was reported close at hand. . . .

At last Aveyron reached into his tunic and pulled out one more scrap of parchment. Bellasteros, recognizing Patros's handwriting, took the letter quickly. "To be delivered into my hand only?" he asked. The young man nodded.

The message was a terse, hurried one:

Mardoc and Adrastes Falco correspond secretly; the priest arrives here with the supply train in two days.

"By the blood of the falcon," Bellasteros spat between his teeth. "I had expected something of this. No more do I choose my enemies; they name themselves." He tossed the paper into the embers of a nearby brazier. The sudden flame was only a feeble reflection of the flame in his eyes.

Danica was fed, bathed, massaged by Shandir's gentle hands. She thought no longer but submitted meekly to the weariness lapping her mind. Ilanit sat by her bed and burnished the star-shield, round and round, until sparks snapped in the dimness of the tent. The sparks were the droplets of the stream, the seeds of the fruit they had shared, blossoms in midwinter, in mind-winter. . . . Danica fell into dreamless sleep, knowing nothing, her senses still.

Atalia stood guard outside, her eyes never leaving the distant shapes of the Sardian camp.

Chapter Ten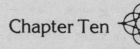

THE WORD WAS passed, from scout to sentry to page, up the flagstone curves of the Royal Road to the hilltop encampment of the Sardians. Patros received the message just as he unrolled yet another untrustworthy imperial map; he released it with an exasperated gesture and the parchment, with many protesting crackles, rolled back up. For a few minutes he cursed, calling on half the deities of the known world and a good proportion of the devils, but he took care to curse under his breath. Then he straightened his back and threw his cloak ceremonially over one shoulder.

Patros found Mardoc organizing an honor guard of soldiers just beyond the gate in the embankment that encircled the camp. The general's seamed face was set tightly in a grimace he probably took to be a smile. It had been a long time since he had smiled; perhaps he had forgotten how. Patros bowed respectfully and Mardoc acknowledged his presence with a curt nod. The young man stationed himself a pace behind the general.

The horses and ox-pulled carts of the caravan appeared one by one, inexorably, on the horizon where the road crested a low ridge. They plodded down the near side, a thin pall of dust wavering about them, and passed the stark mud-brick walls of an abandoned caravanserai that now supported a tattered collection of huts. Curious faces peered from the ragged doorways. Beyond the ridge the eastern sky filled with hillocks of leaden cloud whose darkness was in no way lightened by the rays of the westering sun.

"Look," Patros said loudly. "Some of the outriders are dressed in the livery of the temple!"

"We are honored by a visit from His Eminence the grand inquisitor," said Mardoc from the corner of his mouth.

"You knew this, and the king did not?" Mardoc's back stiffened. Patros lowered his voice, leaned forward, spoke clearly through his teeth. "I should take care what secret correspondence I conduct. Its purpose could be . . . misinterpreted."

"Mind your manners," Mardoc growled, and Patros contented himself with rolling his eyes at the back of the general's head.

A roll of hoofbeats, the panting breaths of the oxen, the creaking of the fabric-covered carts as they lurched off the Road marked the caravan's arrival at the far side of the ditch surrounding the embankment; as it halted a herald stepped forward. "Your permission, General Mardoc, to enter the king's encampment."

"You are welcome," the general returned. At his gesture the soldiers of the honor guard drew their swords and clashed them, raggedly, against their shields.

From the leading cart stepped Adrastes Falco, the talon of Harus. His traveling cloak was brown, woven like a cascade of feathers; the winged breastplate glinted darkly from its opening. His hair and beard were as clean and glossy as if he had just stepped from his bath; his eyes glittered, sly and sharp, raking the group of men before him. "Greetings, General," he said.

Mardoc bowed. "We are honored by your visit, Your Eminence. Please, enter. . . ."

Adrastes walked in stately tread forward, his booted feet barely pressing the ground. "Is my lord well?" he asked.

"The king has yet to return from the quest you directed, Your Eminence," replied Mardoc, "but a messenger only this morning brought word that he has indeed found the sword Solifrax."

"The oracle speaks the truth," Adrastes stated. He lifted his arms, spreading his hands in a liturgical gesture, and declaimed, "Surely Harus smiles upon his son and his devoted followers."

A roar of approval came from the assembled soldiers. "In

the name of the god," Mardoc said. Adrastes lowered his hands.

"The king will be pleasantly surprised by Your Eminence's arrival," said Patros. Whether the legionaries were more pleased by the arrival of the priest or of fresh supplies was hard to tell.

Adrastes snapped around and speared the young man with his gaze. But Patros was bent in a gracious bow, and his expression was hidden. "Yes, yes indeed," the priest said, committing himself to nothing. He turned his back on Patros and took Mardoc's arm, guiding him into his own encampment.

Patros nodded and smiled and sidled away, murmuring something about seeing to Adrastes's entourage. The priest did not look around at Patros's words but flicked his free hand in the gesture of dismissal due a servant. His rings, onyx and topaz, caught a low ray of the sun and sparked.

The black-clad outriders swarmed after Adrastes; the drivers plied their whips across the broad backs of the oxen, urging them into the encampment. Patros rolled his eyes again and slipped ahead to the open space set aside for the priest's tents.

The dark clouds bulged halfway across the sky now, and the sun, admitting defeat, retreated into an early twilight. A guttural rumble of thunder rolled across the torn and wasted lands surrounding the encampment; a chill breeze fluttered the scarlet and purple pennons streaming from the peak of the gold pavilion.

Patros walked among Adrastes's guards and servants, giving directions. A shimmer of lightning caught his eye and he looked upward at the sudden darkness, regarding the approaching storm with the weary resignation of a soldier.

Then his eye fell. He stopped dead, causing the bustling attendants to eddy around him. That cart, there—the livery of the palace, and a hooded figure handed down by an acolyte of the temple . . .

"By all the gods," he muttered under his breath, and he leaped forward, his cloak flying in the wind.

"My thanks," he heard Chryse say to the acolyte.

The priest bowed. "I must attend to His Eminence's quarters, but if you have need . . ."

"My lady!" Patros shouted. "Chryse, how come you here?"

Chryse's hand darted upward to secure her fluttering cowl around her face. Her wide, guileless eyes, rimmed with the dark smudges of exhaustion, blinked out of shadow. "Why, Patros," she said, as if he were the last person she'd expected to see. And, "I shall call, Declan."

Declan disappeared like a wisp of smoke into the hurrying throng. Torches flared around the camp. Patros offered his arm to Chryse and she took it gratefully, leaning almost her whole weight on him, stumbling as he guided her to Bellasteros's own tent. "You may rest here," he told her, "while your attendants prepare your quarters."

"Oh," she said when she saw the table littered with maps, the narrow camp bed, the chests of armor and booty. "Oh, I would not intrude on my lord."

"He is not here," Patros told her. He set her on a chair close to the warm brazier and sent a pageboy scurrying for wine. "He brings the sword Solifrax to battle."

Chryse let the cowl fall from her head; she patted at the crumpled coils of her hair. Her soft mouth tightened. "He rides with her, the witch-queen?"

The wine arrived. Patros poured a goblet full and watched her while she drank deeply. Her cheeks flushed. "He is with the witch-queen?" she insisted.

Patros exhaled. "She guided him to the sword. Perhaps she can be persuaded to bring her warriors here."

"Here? Why?"

"As allies in the coming battle," he explained patiently. "To gain the Empire."

Chryse sighed and folded her hands in her lap. "I understand nothing of military tactics. I know only to fear for my lord."

"As do we all," Patros returned. He lit a lamp and busied himself again with the maps. "Did you have an easy journey?"

"His Eminence assures me that it was not difficult. But"— her voice grew as faint and wistful as a tired child's—"it was so long, Patros, so many leagues; it is cold here, and Sardis is so far behind us. . . ."

Thunder shook the mound of the encampment, and a few raindrops thudded like arrows against the fabric of the tent. Chryse started and squeaked like a small animal when the trap closes around it. Patros threw down the maps, bent over her, offered some gentle and soothing words. "And why," he went on, just as gently, "did His Eminence tear you from the palace?"

"For the same reason he tore himself from the temple. We are here to ease my lord's burdens."

Patros winced. "Indeed," he said dryly. "Or he thought to use you for his own purposes."

"Use me? But I am only—"

The tent flap parted, admitting a gust of wet wind and a glimpse of lightning. Mardoc strode in, removing his damp cloak. "Chryse!" he said heartily, and he advanced toward the woman with arms outstretched.

"Oh, Father," she returned, throwing herself at him. The relief in her voice was plain; here was one who could answer all uncertainties. She emerged from a rough embrace telling him about the journey. ". . . and the settlers at Farsahn have raised a temple to Harus—"

Mardoc pulled her cowl back over her face, cutting her off, and shoved her toward the doorway where a serving-woman waited. "Your quarters are ready. Go rest, my dear."

"Yes, Father," she said. And, glancing back at Patros, "Thank you—" Mardoc dropped the tent flap in her face.

Patros swallowed his farewell as Mardoc also shoved at him. "I need to consult with His Eminence," the general said. "Surely you have duties elsewhere."

"I can make some," said Patros. And added, "Such a pleasant surprise, is it not, to see your daughter here? The first wife of the king, come so unexpectedly to his side. . . ."

Mardoc was opening the maps. He glanced up from under his brows. "What of it?"

"Nothing, sir, nothing at all." Patros turned with a grimace and peered outside. The rain poured down, making of the encampment a dim tapestry picked with the bright threads of lightning bolts. A dark shape followed by attendants was splashing toward the tent.

The young man vanished into the night. Mardoc groaned, as if seized by a sudden tiredness. "You never used to be such an insolent puppy, Patros. Why, why now?"

Adrastes burst into the tent, closed the flap behind him, shook rivulets of water from his cloak. "Well, my general," he began, "you seem to have the situation well in hand. He has the sword, you say?"

Mardoc shook off his weariness and bowed. "Thank you, Your Eminence. And yes, he does. He should return on the morrow."

Adrastes seated himself, picked up Chryse's abandoned goblet, sniffed at it, and drank. "As I told you in my last letter, Mardoc, I am concerned about the king's dealings with this witch-queen. You have met her?"

"A sly one, Your Eminence. A most unwomanly woman."

"Now that we have used her to secure the sword, we must dispose of her and her people. Surely a handful of women warriors cannot make any difference in the battle plan."

Mardoc snorted in derision.

"We must purge Bellasteros of her influence and return him to the embrace of his father the falcon. He must prove his devotion to Harus and repudiate the taint of . . . Ashtar."

"Yes, yes, of course. How else can we bring the name of the god to the Empire and stamp out their pernicious worship of the lesser deities?"

Adrastes nodded. His brows closed like wings over the glitter of his eyes; his eyes searched the interior of the tent as if they could see within each chest and through the hangings of the bed, as if they could see the very thoughts and dreams of the head that had rested there. He toyed with the onyx ring on his finger, drawing it off and replacing it. "It was rumored once," he said, his voice laden with sorrow and regret, "that Viridis, Gerlac's last wife and the mother of the king, was dedicated to Ashtar. And there were worse rumors."

"Spite," scoffed Mardoc. "Jealousy of such a prince as Bellasteros. His mother was indeed a princess of the Empire, tainted with their strange gods, and her death was . . . timely. It was with pleasure that I razed the temple of Ashtar and put her whores to the sword. It is said, true, that Gerlac was not the father of the king. But if he was not, then Harus himself was. I will believe nothing else."

"Of course not. But you must admit that Bellasteros has all his life been touched by this heresy of Ashtar's. I would not have him bewitched by Ashtar's minions." Adrastes allowed himself a delicate shiver. "Surely such has not happened?"

"He is as courteous as becomes a king," Mardoc replied. "And his temper remains as fine and free as ever. But bewitched—I know not. I am troubled, at times, that he would not agree to defeat Sabazel; but then, why turn aside from our course for such a place?''

"Yes. . . .'' The priest removed the ring again and turned it thoughtfully in his fingers. It winked in the lamplight. The pounding rain grew lighter, but a slow leak started in one of the seams of the tent and Mardoc, with a curse, pulled the map table away.

Adrastes laid the ring on the table and stood, stretching. "I must go conduct the evening worship,'' he said. "Declan is a good lad, and serves well as the lady Chryse's chaplain, but he has yet to achieve a certain . . . dedication. Are you coming?''

"With pleasure.'' Mardoc stepped forward to raise the tent flap. A few bedraggled figures, the waiting attendants, flocked around.

"We shall bring this army victory,'' stated Adrastes. "We shall win a victory for the god.''

Mardoc smiled. "The king will be pleased by your devotion to him.''

They trudged off into the darkness. The lamp guttered out behind them as if blown by beating wings. Under the edge of a pen box the onyx ring gleamed, blood-tinted by the embers in the brazier, blood-tinted by some internal light.

The storm blew itself out during the night, and the sun rose into a sky that was a taut, transparent blue membrane arching smoothly from horizon to horizon. A cold clean wind rang through the vault of heaven.

Bellasteros came at midmorning. A shout went up from the sentries; an answering shout reverberated through the encampment, gathering force, becoming an avalanche of sound.

The great warhorse was well ahead of the others. It pranced across the road and up the path to the gate, its hooves throwing clods of mud into the air as if distributing gold coins to the peasantry. It curvetted to a stop, jingling its harness. Bellasteros stilled it with a quiet word.

His eyes were bright chips of adamant, his mouth was crimped in an arrogant smile. His look fell on the troops that lined the embankment, the knot of men before the gate, the peering squatters by the caravanserai, and all voices ceased. The harsh cry of a raven echoed down the wind.

In one fluid movement Bellasteros pulled the sword Solifrax

from its scabbard and thrust it into the air. It flared with an almost audible crack of lightning, brighter than the sun. The warhorse reared, its forefeet pawing the air. As one the Sardians cheered, the squatters fell prostrate, and the imperial officers made the deep formal obeisances due not only an emperor, but a god. Surely some of those same officers would report the king's new power to Bogazkar.

Patros rushed forward to take the reins of the horse, grinning. "Well done, my lord," he said.

Bellasteros slipped the sword back into its sheath and leaped from the horse. "And you, too, well done," he said. "My thanks for the warning. Adrastes tried to kill Danica; sorcery, Patros, of the blackest hue." Patros's brows shot up; hastily he smoothed his expression. Bellasteros strode forward, crimson plume and crimson cloak streaming behind him.

Mardoc's eyes and mouth hung open, set in awestruck worship. With a start he remembered to bow. "Welcome, my lord," he stuttered. "Welcome indeed."

So you are impressed with my new toy, Bellasteros said silently. Aloud he said, "My thanks, General. I am pleased to return."

And there, an eddy in the wind, the tall dark figure of Adrastes Falco. Those glittering eyes cut deep, too deep; play it well. . . . Bellasteros feigned astonishment. "Your Eminence! What brings you here to the edge of the world?"

The priest inclined his head. "I come only to serve my king in his hour of triumph."

"Very good! Come, I will explain our strategy." Bellasteros swept by, returning the nod, deflecting the stare, leaving Adrastes to scuttle hurriedly, like an awkward lackey, in his wake.

Patros turned the horse over to a page and slipped through the crowd to Bellasteros's side. "My friend," the king exclaimed, clapping him on the shoulder, "I have seen some strange places since we last met. Surely Haras holds his wings outspread over me."

"Surely," said Patros.

Mardoc shook himself, shouted a few inconsequential orders to the rest of Bellasteros's company, and strode with as much dignity as he could muster after the others. The gathered soldiers drifted away, oddly silent, as if returning from a solemn religious rite. The squatters crept forward to pry bits of dirt from the king's footprints.

From the corner of his eye Bellasteros saw Mardoc join the entourage. He saw Mardoc and Adrastes exchange a covert glance. So they are in league, he thought. But they are not yet against me. Mardoc, you used to be a father to me . . . and yet it is not you who have changed.

He continued his monologue. "The land is laid waste; the Royal Road was once a flourishing trade route, but it now passes through country left to the lion and the jackal. It is time to conclude our conquest, establish our protection over the Empire, bring peace to the weary."

"Surely," Patros said again.

"Have the poor outside the gate been fed from the new supplies?"

"As well as possible, with our own numbers swelling. . . ." Patros glanced around meaningfully.

Bellasteros nodded. A knot of petitioners was gathered before the gold pavilion and he stopped to chat briefly with each one. He genuflected before the falcon standards, then turned aside for his own tent. There he paused in the doorway, glancing keenly upward at the scarlet and purple pennons whipping in the wind; the wind chimed, the music of Ashtar's voice, but he knew that only he heard it.

He handed Patros the sword; Patros grinned, took it gingerly, stood mesmerized by the play of light across the scabbard as Bellasteros peeled off his armor and threw himself down in a chair. "Gentlemen," he said to Mardoc and Adrastes as they stood before him. "We move against Bogazkar. Iksandarun is perhaps ten days' march along the Road, perhaps fourteen. . . . We shall be there by the winter solstice."

"Good," said Mardoc. "Let the satrap turn at bay at last."

Adrastes remained impassive, his brows angled slightly upward, alert to every fleeting expression on his king's face.

"I have bought allies for us," continued Bellasteros. He reached out his hand and Patros, starting, laid the sword in it. "The queen of Sabazel and her Companions will ride with us."

Mardoc scoffed, "What good can a handful of women do?"

"They took Azervinah for us, did they not? And the high priest commended their queen to me."

"To gain the sword," protested Mardoc. "Surely she has served her purpose."

Bellasteros's voice did not rise, but its intensity easily overrode Mardoc's. "She serves Sardis. As for her purpose, let the gods decide."

Adrastes's brows arched even higher. Quietly, silkily, he said, "You would allow a heretic to ride under the falcon standard? You are generous, my lord."

Bellasteros drew Solifrax. Even in the dimness of the tent its crystalline blade shimmered. He ran his thumbnail up its edge, shedding a spray of sparks. "Better to have her here, under the gaze of the falcon, than plotting against me in Sabazel. Do you not agree?"

The sparks were reflected in Mardoc's eyes. He opened his mouth, said nothing, closed it. Adrastes smiled. "How well you learn the ways of statecraft, my lord. Indeed, better to have her here. And who better to watch this heretic than the talon of Harus, the inquisitor of Sardis?"

"So watch her, then," Bellasteros said. For a moment his gaze locked with Adrastes's, and it was the priest who looked away first. An indefinable air, a god-touched certainty, hung like a numinous cloak about the king.

"I am pleased, lord," Adrastes purred, "that I may serve you."

Bellasteros waved him away with an imperial gesture even as his mind counseled caution. I challenge him; how will he respond? But Adrastes, ever cool and courteous, took his leave, and Mardoc bowed and followed.

But I need you, Bellasteros thought angrily; no matter how we fence and parry, we are still caught together in this game, in games within games. . . .

For a long count of ten neither Patros nor Bellasteros spoke. Solifrax glimmered, humming with a latent power. The general's shouts, the answering shouts of the centurions, and the quickening pace of the camp filtered through the fabric of the tent.

At last Bellasteros exhaled, slumping in his chair. His cavalier manner melted, his arrogance slipped away. "Ah, Patros," he said. "For a moment even Mardoc and Adrastes sensed my divinity. . . ." He laughed quietly, a laugh that had little humor in it. "Have I raised their suspicions?"

"I think not. Not yet. Not until the Sabazians come."

"Until the Sabazians come, and the high priest seeks to assert his power. Over them and over me." Bellasteros seized the sheath and slipped the sword into it, concealing its light. "The world changes, Patros. It shifts and takes new forms before our very eyes. Those like Mardoc and Adrastes . . ."

"Yes?" Patros said encouragingly. His face glowed, reflecting his king's subtle illumination.

But Bellasteros could only lean back, closing his eyes, shaking his head. It hurts, he thought. The learning hurts. Learning that of all the women I could have I want only the one I cannot have, the woman who holds my life and death in her hands, in her belly, the woman I trust. . . . It would be so much easier to cling, blind and unquestioning, to a tarnished doctrine; it would be so much easier not to choose. And yet, he thought, and yet I have seen the falcon sitting on Ashtar's arm.

"Marcos," Patros said warningly. "Someone . . . is here."

Bellasteros lazily opened one eye. His stomach plunged into some dizzying depth and he leaped to his feet. "Chryse! How in the name of the god did you come here?"

She hesitated in the doorway, her cheeks flushed pink, her eyes huge and glistening. "My lord, if I am not intruding . . ."

"Of—of course not," Bellasteros gulped. He turned questioningly to Patros, who could reply only with an eloquent shrug. "Please," he said, grasping the tatters of courtesy, "sit here, rest yourself. Patros . . ."

Patros was already gone. Chryse tiptoed across the tent, keeping far away from the length of Solifrax; she sat on the edge of the chair, her hands folded in her lap, her eyes downcast. Even she was awed by the power of the sword, by his own power. . . . Bellasteros brushed a couple of maps aside and laid it across the table. An onyx ring rolled from behind a pen box and fell to the floor; odd, he thought . . . but Chryse was speaking and he turned to her.

"My lord, I had hoped you would be pleased to see me."

"I am surprised, and pleased as well." Gallantly he knelt before her, took her hand, pressed it to his lips. "You came with His Eminence?"

"Yes."

So Adrastes would use you, too, a gentle sparrow to break

the bond of the star-shield. . . . She looked up at him in open adoration, hoping only for some sign of affection. "Our daughter is well?" he asked.

Her face glowed with a smile. "Yes, well indeed; my father would have her wedded soon."

"Wedded? At her age?" He cast his mind back to that flying visit in the spring, and he saw only a girl-child.

"She is almost twelve, my lord."

Gods! So the child was that old, the plump, quiet babe, the fruit of his impetuous youth. But it was Danica who carried his heir, carried the rest of his life in her grave green eyes. "Whatever you think best, my lady," he said. He kissed her hand again, released it, stood. The sword lay across the maps and he reached out to stroke it. It thrilled to his touch, but still a yawn caught him unaware.

Immediately Chryse was on her feet, fussing over him, urging him toward the bed. "You should sleep, my lord. Your duties are many, and many are those who depend on you."

Too many, he thought, but he let her push him down and brush the tendrils of dark hair from his forehead. "If you require anything, my lord . . ." She blushed and her lashes fluttered over her eyes.

"Thank you," he said with a crooked smile. No, the falcon has no wish to fall upon the sparrow—your meek submission would be a mockery, and it would shame me to rend you. Gently, he told himself; she deserves respect. He took her soft, rounded chin between thumb and forefinger and lifted it to his gaze. "I ask only your contentment, Chryse."

"I am the first wife of the king, of the emperor; how could I not be content? Only to serve you, lord. . . ." Her lips tightened; she knelt at the side of the bed and rested her head on the coverlet, hiding her face again.

And it hurts, he thought, learning that I injure those who love me. Chryse, Mardoc—it is I who change, I who choose to change. . . .

He wondered suddenly how many people watched him—his wife, his general, his priest, certainly; those spies who would be his friends were more dangerous than any sent by Bogazkar.

The Sabazians camped on an easily defended hilltop an hour's ride from the Sardian encampment. Atalia, with many cautionary words, set extra sentries; she feared not only Bogazkar's soldiers but the Sardians themselves.

It was at sunset, at the dark of the moon, that she brought the messengers to Danica's tent.

The queen looked up from the map she sketched and laid down her pen. Lyris set down the lamp she held and stepped away, into her usual position at Danica's back. The visitor was young, beautiful, ebony ringlets cascading down her back and full breasts thrusting forward her cloak. "Theara," Danica stated.

The courtesan fell to her knees. "I am honored to be in your presence at last, my queen. All my life have I bowed to Ashtar in her temple in Farsahn, a bastard daughter, surely, but . . ."

"A true one," Danica finished for her. She smiled a welcome. "Please, rise. You did us all great service by attaching yourself to the Sardians when they took your city."

"Indeed," stated Atalia. She glanced over her shoulder. "A Sardian soldier waits outside. . . ."

"He is Aveyron." Theara rose and brushed off her silk-clad knees. "He was with the king in Sabazel and so was not afraid to escort me here; he is not overly fond of Harus since the high priest had his mother burned for heresy."

"Ashtar!" Danica exclaimed.

"Not this time," said Theara. "It was a provincial deity, I believe. Now the poor lad would believe in nothing."

"I shall find some food for him," Atalia said, and she left. Lyris's gaunt face, washed by guttering shadow, tightened.

"Is it safe for you to come here?" Danica asked Theara.

The courtesan chuckled richly, deep in her throat. "Bellasteros has long since realized which god I served. Now Patros seizes the moment to send me here; it was I who intercepted the secret messages between Mardoc and Adrastes Falco, the grand inquisitor, and now that Adrastes has arrived in the camp Patros asks in the king's name your protection for me."

"Gladly, gladly," said Danica.

"He asks that you take care; Adrastes thinks you a witch, and he will be watching you. And Mardoc is not your friend."

"Are Mardoc and Adrastes plotting against the king, do you think, or only against me?"

"As yet, only against you, my lady. They meant for

Adrastes to take Bellasteros by surprise, but that plan failed. The priest brought the king's wife Chryse with him, though, and no one expected that. Perhaps not even Mardoc . . . but I was unable to discern that.''

"Chryse," Danica said with a sigh. Was she the one Bellasteros had named a placid cow? A waste, a shameful waste. . . . Theara and Lyris both were watching her. "Theara," she said, "I thank you. I would be pleased to have you with us here; ask Atalia to lead you to Shandir, our healer.''

"I am pleased to be in Sabazel at last," Theara murmured, and turned to the doorway. As she passed through she glanced back over her shoulder. "Your image has been much before me, lady. . . .'' She was gone.

Danica grimaced. So she was that much on the conqueror's mind? How many more knew? Patros, probably; Mardoc? Adrastes? She turned to Lyris; the woman was so stiff she trembled. "Well?" she asked softly.

"Let me go to her," Lyris spat. "Let me show her what she has done to me, and to her precious husband. Let me show the high priest for the beast he is.''

"And would anyone believe you? No, Lyris; the priest used Chryse as surely as he used you. Leave her be. Leave your memories behind, and ride proudly at my side.''

Lyris bent her head obediently, but still her shoulders trembled. Danica reached again for her pen.

Mother, she sighed, are we all pawns on your game board? Did you plan this all, long before our births, setting the Sardian oracle into play, and Viridis and Gerlac and Kallidar and my own fleshly mother? Or do you, like we mortals, scramble from fortified position to fortified position, playing as best you can with the pieces you have? Is it truly my own will? . . .

That was not a question she dared to consider. The lines of the map wavered before her, and the breeze that touched her back was cold.

Declan listened attentively as Chryse told him of her visit to her husband. "Truly," she concluded, "I know not why His Eminence brought me here. My lord is polite—always he is polite—but his desire is for his sword, and for battle, and for . . .'' She bit her lip so hard that it bruised.

Declan waited, but she did not complete her sentence. She

raised her hands toward a tiny gilt statue of the falcon. "If I can serve my lord, I am content. . . ."

He joined her in her prayer. But his eyes again and again strayed beyond the image of the deity toward the great gold pavilion of the king, and on his face doubt and thought were mingled.

Chapter Eleven

THE SARDIANS HAD their orders; the next day they would move. The encampment hummed with anticipatory talk. Bellasteros the conqueror, the emperor, king of kings—he bore the sword Solifrax into battle. So confident was he of victory that he brought his first wife to his side. And the talon of Harus walked among the centuries, Sardian and formerly imperial alike, his long, thin hands holding a blessing for all who would bow to the name of the god.

The arrival of the Sabazians added piquancy to the occasion.

Danica left the packhorses, Shandir and Theara, and a guard on the far side of a rocky outcropping, out of sight of the sentries on the embankment but close enough to be counted by Bogazkar's scouts as part of the main armed body. She rode, with Atalia and Ilanit on either side and Lyris just behind, among her hundred picked Companions through the gate of the encampment.

Here there was no woodland, no squawking seabirds, and the sun was a watery gleam in a winter sky. But the main avenue of the encampment stretched here, as it had last summer by the sea, to the shadow of the gold pavilion; it was an avenue lined with curious men, filled with the scent of men and with men's voices. Their suggestions were, as before, unimaginatively explicit. And yet their voices were now tinted with humor; they would mock the daughters of Ashtar, but they no longer hated them.

Have we earned that much? Danica asked herself. She glanced behind her; Lyris was pale and hollow-eyed, her cheekbones as sharp as cutting edges. She looked straight ahead, seeing nothing. Perhaps it had not, after all, been wise to bring her here. The names of Chryse and Adrastes had reopened her wounds. . . . Danica raised her chin even higher, set her shoulders more squarely. It is my decision now, she thought, wise or foolish. My choice, how to finish this game that cannot be won, this game that leaves scars like epitaphs across our faces. . . . I must be strong. Her shield lay against her, burnished with starshine. The pavilion was before her.

This time the pages stood back respectfully; the guards by the falcon standards barely woke from their boredom. But the gold-encompassed dimness stirred with a current of danger, words unspoken, and secret compromises.

Again Danica strode to the foot of the dais, Atalia and Ilanit at her back. Again she braced one foot on the step, removed her helmet, and shook free her golden hair. But this time she kept her cloak draped loosely about her body.

He sat, lazily arrogant, in his chair beneath the tapestry, the outspread wings of Harus protecting him. Harus, who had preened himself in Ashtar's embrace. . . .

"Greeting," Danica said. "You are well?"

"Greeting," said Bellasteros. "Well enough, thank you." Their eyes met, snapped, passed on in feigned indifference.

Patros stood at the king's right hand, holding Solifrax. His knuckles were white on the snakeskin sheath, his eyes staring just beyond Danica's shoulder—Ilanit, yes. His face was very carefully set with no expression at all. Let him look, Danica thought. A look is little enough.

Bellasteros spoke again, cool, controlled. "Patros, lead our allies to my tent and instruct them in the morrow's strategy."

"Yes, my lord." Patros plunged off the dais.

Bellasteros waved his hand in casual dismissal. Danica turned in casual disdain. Atalia's and Ilanit's steps kept close behind her, in unison. The conqueror's dark eyes burned into her back, their look like fingertips stroking her flesh, drawing it into quivering tautness. She inhaled, stilling her importunate thoughts. Please, she thought, let no one read our thoughts.

She noted the Companions ranged in good order before the pavilion, alone, the Sardians having wearied of their sport and gone back to work. A centurion hovered just beyond the periphery of their circle, no doubt detailed to guard them. They ignored him.

Danica was ducking into the tent when she realized that Lyris had not been with the others. Her nerves pricked cold, sending gooseflesh over her body—foolish, to bring her here —but she could do nothing. To her astonishment Atalia greeted the young soldier stationed beside the doorway; Aveyron, she realized, who had brought Theara to her the night before.

The sudden dimness of the tent swirled around her, hissing. Mardoc stood waiting by a table spread with maps. He did not bow.

Danica regarded him evenly, and evenly she greeted him. He was already her enemy; mocking him would serve no point.

Patros bustled around the table, still holding the sword, his eyes downcast. Ilanit looked eagerly at everything in the tent but Patros's face. Mardoc and Atalia eyed each other like rival panthers, circling, searching for a weak point, preparing to strike.

Then Bellasteros threw back the tent flap. He paused, letting his eyes adjust, taking in the exact placement of everyone in the chamber like a player assessing the game board. He extended his hand, and Patros laid the sword in it. He drew Solifrax, a rush of flame tearing the dimness, lighting his eyes, and turned the shining blade admiringly. "My thanks for your aid," he said to Danica.

The star-shield rang gently in response and she willed it to silence. "You are welcome," she replied. She pulled from her cloak a rolled parchment and handed it to Bellasteros. "A map of the approaches to Iksandarun. I was there some time ago, but I remember it well. See if this agrees with those maps provided by your imperial allies."

Atalia growled deep in her throat, also remembering—the surprise attack on the Sabazian embassy, the queen, Danica's mother, dead. . . . You would bear your arms in my presence, Kallidar had said at Azervinah, before she killed him. Her vengeance? Ashtar's? Or part of the game that would place the world in Bellasteros's strong hands?

"My thanks." He sheathed the sword and passed the map to Mardoc, who took it as one would take a poisonous viper. "Here," he said, unrolling another parchment, "the southern plains and the great river Jorniyeh. Here Iksandarun and here the pass leading to its plateau. A few days' journey, if Bogazkar will wait to meet us there."

"My scouts say that he is here," Danica said, placing a forefinger on the paper.

"Your scouts?" asked Bellasteros. A glint from the corner of his eye reached her; yes, she thought, scouts like the one I had here, in your camp, in your very arms, I daresay. . . .

"Yes," he said, clearing his throat. "Just where we thought. And no doubt Bogazkar's spies in this camp have told him that we ready ourselves to meet him; we must be doubly cautious whom we trust. Mardoc?"

The general's baleful glare asked if the Sabazians could be trusted. His eye turned to Patros and darkened further; the young man toyed with an onyx ring, elaborately, his body held with that careful poise of one being watched. But it was Ilanit's eye he courted, not Mardoc's. Danica glanced around to see her daughter transfixed with open hunger, just as Atalia was transfixed with open distaste.

The moment's oppressive silence stretched on into infinity; the tension spun itself out, tighter, tighter— I cannot bear this, Danica thought suddenly. I shall laugh at the absurdity of it, this game the gods play with us—or surely I shall cry. She dared to look at Bellasteros, dared to let one corner of her mouth twitch in a rueful black humor.

He caught her look, returned it. He laid the gleaming blade of Solifrax across the table, slowly, carefully, not crushing even one rolled parchment and yet drawing every eye in the chamber to himself. "In the name of the god," he declaimed, calling no god by name, "do we have the stomach for battle or do we not!"

Bellasteros's child leaped within Danica's womb. Patros tossed the ring aside; Mardoc bent hastily to the maps. Atalia favored Ilanit with a withering look, and the girl withered.

"Iksandarun," Bellasteros continued, unperturbed. But someone was shouting. Shouts reverberated through the encampment, and running feet passed the tent. Aveyron ripped open the flap, revealing a panting centurion at his side. "My lord," he called. "His Eminence has uncovered a traitor in our midst. . . ."

That did not take long, Danica thought resignedly. She lifted the shield once again. I have no choice; it will be played to the end, and there is little humor in it. Mercy, Mother, please, on us all.

Bellasteros scowled. With an oath he plunged from the tent, and the others followed. Danica paused only to beckon to the Companions. The gold pavilion was oddly pale in the thin sunlight; the sky, though cloudless, was a faint steel-gray, and the wind pealed raw and cold from its depths.

Lyris hung by her wrists from a pole in the center of the encampment, circled by soldiers hooting away their uncertainty. They had already stripped her of her armor, and her poor wasted limbs glinted through rents torn in her shirt and trousers. Her head lolled to the side and a trickle of blood snaked its way down her face from her temple. The wind plucked at the loose tendrils of her hair as if seeking to free her.

Atalia, swearing, lunged forward. Danica plucked her back again. Her anger, at Lyris, at herself, at the Sardians, welled over and burst in a spray of venom from her lips. "What is this?" she demanded of Bellasteros, even though she knew it was hardly his doing. "This is one of my Companions; how dare . . ."

But his eyes were focused behind her, their flame suddenly guarded.

It was a carrion bird, talons extended, beak honed to slice flesh from bone. She spun around. No, not a bird; a man, feathered cloak, breastplate like spread wings, hair and beard and eyes the color of a moonless night. Eyes of glittering jet, cutting deep, deep . . .

The power this man emanated crashed against her like a physical blow. She reeled backward, lifting her shield; it hissed on her arm.

He smiled, the smile of a hunter who has successfully cornered his prey. "Danica, queen of Sabazel," he said.

Her lips were numb, her head swam, her limbs trembled with a sudden terrifying weakness. She would fall to her knees, here, before him—Ashtar, no! I must be strong! She embraced the tiny pulse in her mind, sending blood like a strong elixir singing through her veins. "Adrastes Falco," she said, stepping forward, holding the star-sheen of the shield so that the angles of his face glinted with it.

It was only then that she noticed the cloaked and veiled figure of a woman at the priest's side; only her eyes could be seen, the wide, frightened eyes of a rabbit in a trap. Chryse— she, too, was prey. A young priest stood hesitantly, even fearfully, nearby.

Bellasteros interposed, smooth, rational, tautly controlled. "What is this, Your Eminence?"

"This woman is a traitor to Sardis. She was once a serving-woman of your first wife, but now she rides at this—queen's—side."

"But the queen of Sabazel is my ally and my guest. How then do you spell this treason?"

"She is a traitor to Harus; our women do not worship Ashtar."

"But we respect the gods of our allies."

Danica bit her lip to keep from speaking. She sensed the rage in Bellasteros, sensed what it cost him to keep that rage curtained. Behind her Atalia scowled, Ilanit and Patros exchanged a wary glance, Mardoc moved into position at Adrastes's side. The watching soldiers, the Companions, murmured.

"This woman is a thief, my lord," the priest continued, as if his argument were the most logical of constructs. "She stole the necklace you gave your first wife and sought to hide her crime among the Sabazians, who shielded her."

"How did you discover this?" demanded Bellasteros.

"She came to the lady Chryse in her quarters, holding the necklace, speaking nonsense—she was once a devoted follower of the god, but Ashtar's black sorcery has bewitched her, sent her into madness—"

"Watch your tongue, priest," Danica spat. "Surely it will shrivel in your mouth, speaking such lies."

Chryse quailed back. Mardoc and Adrastes between them grasped her arms. "A shame," said Bellasteros, "that the prisoner so suffers from your arrest that she cannot speak. I would like to know why a thief attempts to return her booty, why she returns herself to danger when she has achieved safety."

"Why question her, my lord?" asked Adrastes. "She is a traitor to you."

Atalia again lunged forward. "This woman's only crime was to try to murder the queen, and for that she cannot be held accountable; she was possessed. . . ."

Danica silenced her with a gesture. Wait, wait. No one will believe our words here—except he who cannot act on them.

Bellasteros's eyes narrowed and Solifrax flamed. But still his words were velvet smooth. "What of this charge, Your Eminence?"

Adrastes frowned. He looked from Bellasteros to Danica and back again, piercing them both with his gaze, gauging them. And his eye fell upon the trembling figure of Chryse. A sorrowful comprehension dawned in his expression. "My lady," he said, gently, "your devotion to your lord is indeed commendable. But to pay your serving-woman with your necklace to injure his ally . . . Your necklace, your lord's gift! You must make penance for such petty jealousy, my child."

"Chryse!" said Mardoc, looking at his daughter in horror and approval mingled. Horror that she had had the initiative to do anything, Danica thought. Approval of what she had supposedly done. Regicide was only a crime when the ruler was male. . . .

Chryse fell forward, crumpled to her knees, and clutched at Bellasteros's shining greaves. "My lord, forgive me, I did not—I mean, I intended no . . ."

"Chryse?" Bellasteros croaked, for once at a loss for words; the magnitude of Adrastes's lie astounded even him. His outrage, his frustration, seething like acid, impossible to release—they were Danica's own. Her eyes burned with green fire and the shield hummed. Hear my power, Danica said silently to Adrastes. I will have your blood in the end. . . .

As if he heard her words he turned to her. A smile touched his lips, blandly malignant. You see my power, harlot. Whatever I name truth is truth, and no one dares gainsay me. Check, harlot. Check.

Danica spun away from him, knowing that in another moment she would kill him. The gathered Sardian soldiers parted before her wrath. With one great, ringing blow of her sword she cut Lyris free. "Take her to Shandir," she ordered, and Atalia and several Companions rushed forward.

Quietly, quietly—she swallowed her fury with such effort that her stomach heaved within her. She sheathed her sword. She retrieved her helmet from Ilanit, put it on, and from its shelter looked; the drama continued, reduced to a domestic squabble.

Bellasteros had somehow achieved regal composure, expressionless, the sword Solifrax a gleaming scepter in his hand. Chryse still knelt before him, her veil wet with tears. Adrastes made soothing gestures over her, a kindly avuncular prelate, and Mardoc stood shaking his head in paternal despair.

Petty jealousy indeed, Danica thought; the priest was jealous of his own power. Pity the woman Chryse, caught among Adrastes, her father, her husband, not realizing what truth was. The last thing she needed now was the queen of Sabazel to defend her. Danica's gaze crossed that of the young priest—uncannily clear, that gaze. . . .

The soldiers pressed forward; some were amused, no doubt, that Bellasteros could be troubled by his wife just as they were. But some were perturbed at this crack in their god-king's armor, and they watched, their faces turned to the flame of sword and shield, seeking reassurance. Patros barked an order and the order was echoed by the centurions; reluctantly, the legionaries turned away.

Ilanit appeared with Danica's horse. She clambered up, advanced a few paces to reach Patros's ear; "We shall confer at some better time. Give my respects to your lord."

Patros was distinctly pale around the jawline. He nodded, and for just a moment his eyes met Danica's. Gods! she thought. Would I not also like to be in the garden of the gods, my lover by my side, in peace. . . .

A sudden jangling gust of wind was like a slap in the face—duty, ever duty. She pulled the horse's head around, sparing one more glance for Bellasteros himself. He sensed her clear green eyes upon him; she knew that from the almost imperceptible twitch of his mouth, the subtle tilt of his head. But he could not turn to her. One look between them, and Adrastes would know which truth Bellasteros believed. Let him be my enemy only, Danica prayed, and she urged her horse rapidly down the avenue.

Her shield was cold on her arm, the child a heavy, heavy weight in her belly. The wind faded.

● ● ●

Evening. A silent darkness crept up the eastern sky, overtook
the pale gleam of the sun, and consumed it. The evening star
was a bright gemstone set in smoked glass. The Sardian camp
lay a great blot of shadow on its hilltop; the Sabazian camp
formed a small smudge behind its hillock.

Chryse knelt, shoulders hunched, before her shrine. "Almighty Harus," she murmured, "you know that I would not
be so forward as to interfere in my lord's plans. But neither
would I dispute the word of His Eminence, your mouthpiece.
And my father . . . Harus, I mean only respect for him." She
inhaled shakily, as if yet one more sob hung in her throat.

Declan, his narrow face knitted with concern, appeared
behind her. "Can I be of service, lady?"

She looked up with a start. Her eyes were red and swollen
and a bruise marred the softness of her cheek. Declan stiffened. "Who would strike you, lady? The king . . ."

Quickly she turned, hiding her face. "No, no," she said
quickly. "My lord is too kind to me, and forgives my trans-
gressions with soft words."

"Who then? Your father the general?"

Her shoulders hunched even more tightly together. "He
heeds the words of His Eminence, as should we all," she whispered. "No blame to him."

"But my lady," protested Declan. "Surely you did not
engage in this—this attack. . . ."

"We should all heed the words of His Eminence," she
repeated. "We must serve him in his wisdom. Even Lyris, my
poor Lyris, has her role." She stared at the gilt statue of the
god, folding her hands in her lap, sighing. "If I cannot believe
in Harus, in what then can I believe?"

"In Harus, yes." Declan nodded. He knelt beside her. "In
his followers. . . ."

Bellasteros sprawled in his chair, a sheathed Solifrax across his
lap, scowling. The luminescence of the solitary lamp sent odd
topaz shadows twisting over his face, reshaping its cleanly
carved planes into a gargoyle's sneer.

Patros looked up from the map he copied. "Shall I light the
brazier?"

Bellasteros did not reply. His hand slapped the sword rhythmically across his lap. The scales on the scabbard flicked in
brief crescents of light.

Patros laid down his pen and regarded the sword narrowly. "Chryse had nothing to do with the attack on Danica, did she?"

"Of course not. It was, as I told you, Adrastes's scheme. A filthy trick to begin with; filthier still to blame it on Chryse. And Mardoc swallowed it all."

"You cannot contradict the grand inquisitor."

"No." The word was an epithet. "He asserts his power. He rubs my nose in his power, testing me with my own household. . . ." Grimly, Bellasteros laughed. Solifrax hissed in its sheath. "Now we know, do we not, that his power is black sorcery, not the beneficent magic of the gods."

Patros's mouth tightened. "At least Theara is safe in the Sabazian camp."

"Adrastes would call her a traitor, no doubt, because she serves Ashtar, because she is loyal to Sabazel. But she has always been loyal to me as well—I know that."

"You know." Patros nodded.

The conqueror's eyes gleamed with light, the banked embers of rage, the faint green-gold shimmer of remembered vision. "Ah, my friend," he murmured, "I have seen Harus and Ashtar together. . . ."

An evening breeze gusted through the encampment, echoing with distant chimes. Solifrax sparked. The onyx ring, forgotten, gleamed darkly beneath the table.

"Is all ready?" Mardoc asked Hern. Coins jingled in the shadows.

"I have picked twenty strong men, sir," the soldier answered, pocketing the money. "They have already broached the barrel; fine and rich, they say."

Mardoc bared his teeth in a vulpine smile. "It is exceptionally rich, I would think, with the herbs so kindly provided by His Eminence."

Adrastes emerged from the tent beside them. He held his hands clasped before him, stroking his topaz ring. His eyes were hooded, thoughtful. "Theara," he said. "Who is she?"

"A whore," replied Mardoc. "A tasty bit for the officers."

"Could she have been corresponding secretly with the witch-queen in Sabazel? Could she have seen our letters?"

The general puzzled for a moment; then comprehension empurpled his face. "Of course; I thought they knew too much! The traitorous bitch. . . ."

Adrastes turned to the eager Hern. "You hear? Theara is a traitor to Harus and to the king. With her you may be especially . . . thorough."

"Yes, of course, Your Eminence." Hern bowed deeply and trotted off.

The two men watched him thread his way through the encampment. The breeze fluttered the priest's robes, the general's cloak. "I hope," said Adrastes, "that you have not been too harsh with your daughter."

"Your Eminence is too generous. As is the king, generous indeed."

"Beyond my . . . expectations." Adrastes nodded cordially, blandly, revealing nothing. "You see how this Sabazian divides us, sowing dissent, using the camp followers and even the lady Chryse to bewitch the king; devious, she is, devious, and we must save him from her spell. Tonight, Mardoc, her penance begins."

Mardoc chuckled. "Yes, yes, and very soon now."

They listened. The encampment was silent. Silent, except for a distant murmur of drunken revelry, swelling, becoming more raucous each moment. . . .

Night. Danica sat on a boulder, contemplating the sky. The slender crescent of a new moon hung above the horizon, the evening star a brilliant gem at its tip. They were silver lamps hanging in the arch of the sky, swaying gently, chiming to Ashtar's breath. . . . It was no good. She could not concentrate. Her blood pricked in her veins, uneasy, as if eyes watched the back of her neck. And yet nothing was behind her but the faintly luminescent fabric of her tent. Shapes moved against the light as Shandir and Theara tended the injured Lyris.

The soldier Aveyron folded his height just outside the periphery guarded by the Companions; he had brought Lyris's armor and a note setting another conference for the dawn and had evidently been told to set a guard post of his own.

Lyris. She had not come willingly to Sabazel, had not given herself willingly into Danica's service—she should not be chastised for her disobedience. Her experience at the hands of the Sardians was chastisement enough.

Bellasteros. His position grew more difficult every day. Would it help if the Sabazians decamped and went home? But no—they were needed here.

Adrastes. What in the name of Ashtar—or of Harus, for that matter—was his game? Did he truly believe himself working for the king?

Her neck prickled and in spite of herself she glanced over her shoulder. Nothing: the shapes of rocks, shadows, the glow of the Sardian encampment. Nothing to fear. But her heart drummed in her chest and the child twisted restlessly in her womb.

Danica leaped up. Footsteps or a pebble shifted by a small animal? A muffled breath or some trick of the wind? But the wind did not trick her.

Aveyron was watching her quizzically. She stared unseeing at him, her nostrils flaring. Wine, herbed wine, and the scent of men—not of the one man before her, but of many men. . . .

The sentry burst across the road, calling a warning. "Atalia!" Danica shouted. "Ilanit! To arms!"

She sprinted into the tent, seizing sword and shield. Theara's hand went to her mouth in fear; Shandir reached for the dagger strapped to her thigh and tested its edge. Lyris pulled herself up, hand reaching for her sword.

Danica blew out the lamp and lifted the star-shield. It chimed at her touch, shedding an aureole of light around her like the glow of a full moon. Theara gasped and fell back. No time for reassurances—Danica spun back out the doorway, followed by Shandir.

Loud voices, heavy bodies crashing through the brush, falling with curses over the rocks . . . men scrambled into the camp. One Companion was seized and borne down; another rushed forward to free her.

Shouts, screams, running feet. The horses neighed and plunged, but their pickets were secure. Someone—a Sardian—plucked an ember from the campfire and tossed it onto a tent; the fabric caught, burning slowly at first, then flaring up in gouts of scarlet flame. Scarlet-tinted shadow danced over knots of grappling bodies. Shandir seized a water-skin and ran to the fire.

Danica intercepted one man who sought to enter the tent

and drove him away with a blow. The men were here to ravish and to pillage, she saw; they were only sparsely armed. But her followers were not cowering village women. Atalia pulled one Sardian soldier from the supine body of a Companion and calmly cut his throat. His blood was dark, a spreading pool of darkness. . . .

Another soldier grabbed for Danica and she kicked him in the groin. As he crumpled she brought the hilt of her sword down on his head and he fell like a slaughtered ox, snorting. Another hand approached her; she spun, blade at the ready—it was Aveyron. His blue eyes flickered orange in the light of the fire. "I would aid you," he cried, shrinking back.

"I think I shall have to aid you," Danica told him. Ilanit came leaping across the ground, her teeth glinting in a smudged face, red-tinted sword in one hand, javelin in the other. She saw Aveyron and raised the javelin, but Danica deflected the blow. "He is with us."

Another attack, this time by soldiers with weapons. They were remarkably clumsy, drunk or drugged; Ilanit sliced one across the arm and he fell back screaming into the tangle of his fellows.

Theara was screaming, inside the tent. . . . Danica stepped heedlessly on the man she had felled as she rushed inside.

Dimness, laced with rosy shadow, shadow swirling into indistinct shapes—a blade flashed like the track of a comet, and the screams stopped. No, they continued, suspended in the air beyond hearing, ululating with terror, ripping Danica's senses into quivering shreds.

The shield burned. Its light defined a man, stocky form, dark face—a staring, gaping mask, bestial madness. He rushed out the other end of the tent and into the night. The image of that face remained branded behind Danica's eyes. Aveyron inhaled sharply at her back but said nothing.

Danica raised the shield like a torch, praying, Mother, no, please no. . . . Theara lay half across Lyris, her manicured hands outspread. Blood welled from a gaping wound in her breast. Her eyes were averted, her lips curled back; death had come upon her an unwelcome lover.

Danica heard her own voice swearing, vicious oaths condemning Adrastes to the nethermost pits of hell. And she was answered; Lyris twitched, heaving weakly at Theara's body.

"I tried to stop him," she croaked, "but he had no eyes for me. Even when I cut him, still he came at her. Why not me, Ashtar? . . ."

"You . . . did well," Danica told her. I did miserably, she thought, not anticipating, not preventing this. And why not me? Because Adrastes does not yet dare to attack me openly. Theara died for me, because of me. . . . I glory in my power, but I am powerless.

The shouts from outside began to take on a certain rhythm, the bellows of centurions calling their troops to order. So the set was over. It was time to count the pieces expended. To be strong again.

Shandir staggered in, her hair singed, her clothing soot-blackened; she began cleaning her dagger on a handful of grass, and then she saw Theara. The dagger fell from her hand; she dropped to her knees beside the body of the courtesan, groping for pulse points. "Monsters," she said. "Foul monsters in the guise of men."

Lyris began crying, her thin body heaving with great, dry sobs. Would it help, Danica asked herself numbly, if I could cry?

A hand ripped away the tent flap. A streak of lightning cut the darkness. Solifrax, and a glowering Bellasteros clad only in a short chiton. His eyes reflected twofold the light of the blade.

Shandir looked up, saw the king, and wordlessly hoisted Lyris up and bore her away. For a moment Danica and Bellasteros were alone, surrounded by thin fabric, flames, and blood. "Are you proud of this work your colleagues have done?" Danica asked. Her shield snapped lightning back to the sword.

"Unfair," he told her. "Unfair. . . ." He lowered the blade and knelt by Theara's body. His exhaled breath became a moan; he arranged an ebony curl on her cheek. "Ashtar," he murmured. "Her crime was in loving you?"

"Of course," said Danica. "Her preventing Adrastes's taking you by surprise is hardly worth her life."

"But it called her to his attention, did it not?" His eyes darted upward, his brows knotted with an incredulous surmise. "I was just speaking of her, of how she was safe here. . . ."

His inference leapt from mind to mind. Instinctively Danica

clutched the star-shield closer to her, absorbing its gleam back into herself. "If the priest is that powerful, Marcos, the game is already forfeit."

"We cannot believe that," he replied. He rose and laid Solifrax across the shield; their individual lights ebbed, becoming one soft, shaded gleam. "We must play it to the end, Danica."

"At least we no longer play alone," she told him. They allowed themselves a moment's tender regard, then turned back to their respective roles.

Bellasteros left Patros in charge of cleaning up the battleground in the Sabazian camp and stalked back to the main encampment. The starlight touched his face, and a cold night breeze rippled moaning through his hair, but his thoughts were blood-red, blood-warm.

He plunged in through the doorway of Adrastes's tent, shedding attendants like drops of water. Mardoc and the priest sat comfortably with cups of wine in their hands. The general started at this apparition of his king, but Adrastes bowed graciously and gestured to a chair. "Please to join us, my lord."

Solifrax hissed like a striking snake. "General Mardoc," Bellasteros growled. Mardoc rose warily to his feet, eyeing the sword. "General, are you or are you not in charge of my army?"

"I am," Mardoc replied.

"Then how do you allow soldiers to become drunk, to abandon the dignity of the men of Sardis? Where were you, when the sounds of battle rose from outside our gates?"

"They are only women, my lord," protested Mardoc.

"They are our allies and deserve respect as such! But no, five of our soldiers are dead, five, who would be alive now if you attended to your duties instead of . . ." Bellasteros grimaced. His body quivered, every muscle straining taut against the skin. "Surely," he said, very quietly, "Bogazkar's scouts speed back to him, laughing at us."

Adrastes turned his cup in his hands; his topaz ring glinted. Bellasteros's eye glinted in return. For this you will let Mardoc take the blame, as you let his daughter take the blame for another of your plots; hypocrite, to do this night what you condemned her for this day. . . .

Adrastes smiled silkily, expression hooded.

But I cannot touch you! Bellasteros shouted to himself. To believe I once thought you the model of righteousness. I once thought you spoke for the god. Surely your pride will turn on you someday. . . . He choked down his rage and forced his attention back to the general. "Mardoc, I am sorely disappointed. Would you seek to take my kingship? Would you rule in my stead?"

"No, my lord." Mardoc's injured air was not assumed but genuine.

Once I could talk to you, Bellasteros groaned silently. Once we understood each other, and our desires were the same. Gods! Why do you trust him now instead of me! But all he said was, "Then stop taking so much on yourself. Save our soldiers for battle."

Adrastes was watching him, still smiling, as slimy as some soft creature pulled from beneath a rock. He said nothing, but Bellasteros had the sick feeling that he heard every nuance, every implication, that he knew how much Bellasteros had changed and that he lay in wait to snare him with it. He complacently believed that he knew the mind of Harus.

The army of Sardis believed it, too. And what was a conqueror without an army?

"Good evening, then, gentlemen," Bellasteros said between his teeth. "I hope to have your cooperation by the time we move out tomorrow." Another flash of the sword and he vanished as abruptly as he had arrived.

Mardoc and Adrastes exchanged a long, thoughtful look. "He has the spirit to rule," the general said. "He carries the sword of Daimion."

"He has been touched by the gods," agreed the priest.

Mardoc sat wearily into his chair and lifted his cup. "By the talons of Harus, Your Eminence, he is in danger. My poor lad. . . ."

"We must save him from himself," Adrastes murmured.

My poor Theara, Bellasteros thought, gaining his tent. I condemned you with my own words—and I cannot even mourn you or ask vengeance for your death, for you were only a woman and said to be of little account in the world.

He slipped Solifrax into its sheath, laid it down, and kicked an ewer viciously across the tent.

Adrastes is powerful indeed, he thought. And my power is

hemmed tightly, tightly . . . I condemned Theara with my own words. Danica, can you avenge her when I condemn you as well? His anger died with a shudder; pale and cold, he grabbed for the ewer and was wrenchingly sick.

Theara's funeral pyre lit the dawn sky, driving away the mid-winter chill. Flames licked insatiably toward the sun; smoke spread in slow whorls down a discordant breeze, shaping itself into ringlets, into draped gowns, into the curves of a woman's body, and then dissipated, gone forever.

The Companions saluted, a triple row of greedy swords offered to the sky.

The Sardians returning from burying their colleagues had the sense to hold their tongues about such barbarous customs. The king sat his warhorse atop the embankment, his eyes as clear and hard as the falcon's.

The fire was hot on Danica's tight, still face. Atalia, Lyris, Ilanit, Shandir shot strained glances from pyre to queen and back again. It was impossible to tell which burned the brighter.

Chapter Twelve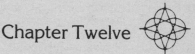

THE ARMY OF SARDIS crept across a damp, stony plain, following the Royal Road. It seemed as if the soldiers, the carts, the animals stayed in the same place and the sky turned above them; the horizon ahead was the same hazy nothingness as the horizon behind. The cold, sharp wind promised rain.

Promised sleet, perhaps, Bellasteros thought. Only I would move south in the winter. He squinted upward. The sun was a ghostly disc behind a shroud of clouds, just large enough to hold in the hand, like the disc Mari had given to Daimion, that he had held as he died. . . . The conqueror shivered. He was small, an insect in a horde of insects, stubbornly moving a handsbreadth across the great expanse of the world.

His senses, questing like an insect's antennae, felt rather than heard the grumbling of his soldiers—a deserted land around them, and Sardis far away. . . . Soldiers always grumbled; it was good for them. Just let them obey.

Patros rode beside him, silent, holding upright one of the falcon standards. The bronze image of the god rode the wind proudly, unblinking. Its talons were ready to seize the world. . . . Bellasteros straightened his back and spurred his horse, moving through his personal guard so that he alone led the army. And the nothingness ahead wavered, growing darker; hills, rocky hills, the road leading through a wide valley.

He gestured, and scouts galloped ahead.

Mardoc rode on the far flank with the cavalry. Adrastes, Chryse, Declan rode in the center of the army in the baggage train. Aveyron walked beside Hern, not commenting on the fresh sword wound across his arm. Bellasteros himself led the infantry that snaked in a crescent of trudging feet from the vanguard, down the opposite flank, to the rear.

And the rearguard was also cavalry, Sabazian cavalry, Danica and her warriors eating the men's dust. Bellasteros did not look back. She had skulked there ever since that night when Theara had died. Lyris, sent defiantly as messenger, asked that he punish the men who had raided her camp. No, he replied. I shall not punish them, and I shall not punish you for killing five of them, as my centurions request; let it go, Danica, let it go.

It was as if he felt Mardoc's baleful glare on the back of his neck. It was as if he felt the piercing eyes of Adrastes cutting away his pretenses. Danica, he cried silently, what can I do?

His thoughts pummeled his mind. Galloping hooves pounded his ears. She was there, followed only by the faithful Atalia, cutting through the ranks of infantry and sending his guard veering aside. "Harus," the conqueror swore.

Patros looked around, his eyes widening, and he deftly turned his horse into Atalia's so that she had to remain with him just out of earshot. He ventured a pleasantry; she returned it as if it were an epithet.

The army plodded on. Danica looked not at Bellasteros but at the valley opening before them. "You refused my request?"

"I had no choice but to refuse."

"You hear what the soldiers are saying? That we lured them to our tents, that we lay with them and killed them for sport?"

"I hear. Women have always endured such lies."

She turned to him with a toss of her head, eyes glinting like cut and polished emeralds. "Then stop it. Show the truth. Punish those who attacked us and punish those who spread such vile lies about us."

"Then I would have to punish Mardoc and Adrastes," he told her. "The men who attacked you were drugged, enspelled to do the deed. Few Sardians are the monsters you think, my lady."

Her reply was short and coarse.

Testily, he went on. "You ask justice, as do I. But justice is a rare and dear commodity. One that I cannot afford—that we cannot afford now. My kingship rests on a sword's edge."

"And if that sword turns, we both perish. True?"

"True. We and our people with us." Bellasteros allowed himself a long look at her stony profile, willing her to bend. "Danica," he said softly, "you feel that you should have prevented the attack, do you not? But Adrastes is strong. If we quarrel over this, will he not gloat? Is he worth it, Danica?"

"You jolly me along like a child," she returned sharply. "You tell me the obvious."

"Then why confront me with demands you know I cannot grant?"

For a time she did not reply. Their horses walked forward, side by side. Her hands clenched and unclenched on the reins. He eyed sideways the careful draping of her cloak, filling in the curve underneath. *I condemn you, too, my son. With my own mouth I condemn you, and I am helpless, helpless. . . .*

"It gnaws me," said Danica. "What good is the power, what good knowing the mind of Ashtar, of Harus, if we remain helpless?"

"You know me too well." He laughed, quietly, from the corner of his mouth. "You hear my thoughts."

"And you mine." She lifted her shield in the briefest of salutes. "Doubt, I think, is another commodity we cannot afford."

Bellasteros touched the hilt of Solifrax in reply and then glanced exaggeratedly behind him. "And neither must our adversary doubt. . . ."

She was quick, so very quick. Her brows tilted, her mouth crumpled. "You name yourself king!" she shouted, jerking her horse away, circling back. "You cannot even control your rabble!"

"If you seek an alliance with me," he bellowed in return, "you will control your own rabble and leave my soldiers alone!"

"By the blue eyes of Ashtar . . ."

"You dare use that name in the presence of the falcon, woman? You will buy this alliance with your respect!"

Danica spurred her horse away, plunging through the ranks of infantry and scattering them like a disturbed covey of partridge. Atalia spun and followed, shooting an evil if somewhat puzzled look at Bellasteros. Patros hastened up; the king was shaking in rage. No, the king was shaking in an attempt to contain his mirth.

"A dangerous game you play, Marcos." Patros said. "The high priest will see through your ploy as easily as we saw through his."

"But the army watches, and the game turns on their strength. Adrastes needs me to play, as I need him. Has it ever been safe?"

"No. But I wonder at times . . ."

Bellasteros regained his breath and arranged his face in stern lines. "Speak your mind, my friend."

"I wonder if you—if we pursue the right course. Perhaps Ashtar mocks us for falling so easily to her snare. She could still betray us."

"Spoken like a true minion of Adrastes Falco."

"But do you not ever doubt?" persisted Patros.

Bellasteros turned a dark, annoyed glance on his colleague. "And do you never dream of the full moon, Sabazel and the peace of Ilanit's embrace?"

Patros flushed. "I spoke too hastily, my lord. I—did not think."

"No, you did think. And I think. Too much, perhaps. We never used to question the wisdom of the gods or of their self-appointed mouthpieces."

The soldiers of Sardis entered the passage of the valley. The thin metallic disc of the sun followed them, but they cast no shadow on the bare branches, the tumbled rocks that surrounded them.

I like not the smell of this place, Bellasteros thought. Acrid, the stale blood of the battlefield.

He grimaced at the importunities of his own mind.

It was late afternoon. One last shaft of sunlight cut between massed clouds, gilding the thin veil of dust that hung over the army. The centurions prepared to make camp.

A distant rumble disturbed the wind—thunder and rain— no, not thunder. A deep cry from the throats of many men. Scouts came pounding across the floor of the valley, leaning low over the necks of their horses, shouting urgently of imperial cavalry and of imminent attack.

The army swirled, glittered with drawn blades. Bellasteros and his guard fell back into the main body of the infantry; messengers went scurrying toward Mardoc, toward Danica. Trumpets blared.

A darkness on the horizon, wavering smoke in the glare of sunlight, gloom spangled with the bright points of weapons—a shimmering mirage of horsemen pouring across the valley floor.

Danica heard the distant shout and rose in her stirrups. Her eye saw as clearly as that of a falcon spiraling high above the valley; two groups of horsemen, one large, one small. Raiding parties only, designed to damage and dishearten. She had given her own orders by the time a messenger reached her.

The Sardian infantry formed a shield wall bristling with spears. The falcon standard fluttered its wings above them. On the far flank Mardoc swore at the cleverness of Bogazkar, attacking from the eye of the sun when the Sardians were at their weariest.

The baggage train circled in on itself, oxen bellowing protests and women shrieking. Chryse looked out, gasped, fell back into her soft carpets. Declan leaped out and grabbed the harness of the lead ox, yanking it around. Adrastes glanced out of his own wagon, pulling a long dagger from his robes.

A shower of arrows, and the imperial horsemen crashed into the shield wall. Their animals plunged, screamed, fell in a tangle of thrashing legs. The riders leaped down and battled the Sardians face-to-face.

Bellasteros's horse reared. He raised Solifrax toward the sun. It shone, clear, blinding—the soldiers of the Empire quailed. With a shout the Sardians drove forward, over the crumpled bodies of horses and men.

And another wave of cavalry broke through the line, throwing men down, trampling them. Bellasteros, his guard, and Patros bearing the falcon leaped into the struggle. Solifrax rose and fell, flaming, blood-red fire licking the astounded faces of the imperial soldiers. The king's warhorse pranced among them, smashing them with its powerful hooves.

And Danica was there, with Lyris and a number of the Companions, cutting a swath through the heaving, struggling bodies of horses and men to the king's side. The crested helmets of the Sabazians caught and held the last brilliant shaft of sunlight. "Well met!" Bellasteros called, grinning, and Danica rang her shield with the hilt of her sword, equally fey.

The baggage train halted, hopelessly entangled with itself. Another body of cavalry plunged into its midst. Fires sprang up, oxen fell butchered in their traces, women were snatched from the ground and thrown like sacks of meal across the imperial saddles. The screams of fighting men, of dying beasts and ravished women, swelled upward and burst against the sky.

Mardoc's cavalry cut through the confusion, following the falcon standard that he bore, charging in a tightly packed mass straight through the stalled carts to join with the infantry on the other flank. Arrows flew after them, but they were under orders to ignore the small imperial contingent that was slaughtering the camp followers. One Sardian, and one only, paused at Mardoc's bellowed word to hoist the hooded form of Adrastes Falco onto his own horse.

"Father!" Chryse screamed. She scrambled out of the cart, her veil thrown heedlessly aside, her face gaunt and pale. "Father, here I am!" Her outstretched hands clutched at the heaving flank of Mardoc's horse; it pounded by, throwing her aside. If the general saw her, he showed no recognition.

Side by side Danica and Bellasteros fought, the falcon's wings fluttering above them both. Their horses danced together in an intricate and deadly step. The star-shield flared, casting fleeting shadows about it. Solifrax rose and fell as quickly as a serpent's tongue. The Companions wetted their swords in the service of Sardis—and of Sabazel.

One of Chryse's serving-women was seized by an imperial soldier and thrown down in the dirt behind the cart. Chryse's screams were as loud as the woman's. She shrank back, her hands covering her face, and a man's hands touched her from behind. Spinning, she screamed again. It was Declan.

Without formal preamble he grabbed her arm and jerked her into a run. An imperial trooper bore down on them, spear raised, harness jangling. Declan dodged, Chryse stumbling behind him, and they fell into a tiny shelter behind the boxes and bags spilling from an overturned cart.

"He picked up . . ." Chryse gasped. "He s-stopped for him but not for . . ."

Another mounted trooper grabbed a baby from a woman's arms and dashed it against an ox's yoke. The woman, howling, clawed at the man's legs. He kicked her away with taunts and jeers.

Chryse screamed again and Declan set his hand firmly over her mouth. Her eyes rolled, the whites glinting; she subsided into a trembling huddle.

Imperial horsemen made another breach in the shield wall and mangled Sardians beneath their hooves. They drove straight for the red plume and the gleaming blade, the unmistakable signatures of the conqueror himself. Bellasteros and Danica and their guards with them gave way, drawing the enemy deeper into the deadly embrace of the infantry. More than one Sardian soldier risked flailing hooves to stab upward, felling horse and rider into a shrieking, crashing tangle. Those imperial troopers who could be unhorsed did not rise again.

Mardoc's standard appeared beyond the far flank of the enemy, cutting into them from the side, throwing them back in confusion. More than a few of the imperial soldiers jerked their horses about and ran; others had no chance.

Solifrax rose and fell, hissing. The star-shield snapped in reply. Patros raised the falcon standard to salute the last gleam of the sun, and then the sun was gone. But still a light hung about the battlefield, a lingering red twilight as if the clouds themselves were wounded, as if blood ran down the sky.

Three imperial troopers leaped down from their horses to drag Declan and Chryse from their hiding places. One dealt the young man a glancing blow with the flat of his sword, knocking him sprawling, blood soaking through his dark hair and staining his face.

The other troopers seized Chryse, tore at the fine fabric of her cloak, ripped at her necklaces. She was too terrified even to scream; she could only squeak and clutch futilely at her garments.

A streak of light in the gathering gloom, and one of the soldiers reeled backward, a javelin protruding from his side. The other turned, raising his sword; he received a javelin in the throat and crashed heavily down, eyes still open and surprised, hand still clenched on his weapon.

Chryse stood swaying, staring out between her spread fingers, as Atalia and Ilanit ran to her side. "Are you mad, woman?" Ilanit exclaimed. "Would you just stand there and let them use you?"

Chryse said nothing, did nothing but look from face to face as if the two Sabazians were imperial soldiers in yet another guise.

"She is not mad," said Atalia. "Her mind has been cut and dried by her men, giving all, daring to ask nothing." She turned, set her foot against the ribs of the first soldier, yanked the javelin from his side. A gout of blood splattered Chryse's cloak. The trooper expired. Chryse fainted.

Cursing, Ilanit and Atalia threw Chryse over a stray horse. The girl led the burdened animal away; Atalia turned to supervise the rest of the Companions. Their swords and spears were wreaking havoc among the plundering imperial soldiers, sending them to their deaths with their booty and their women still in their hands.

Atalia threw her head back, laughing, letting the paean thrill from her lips. The song rose high and clear above the battle, and the wind repeated it.

Danica heard. Her throat filled with the sound. The shield sang in her hands, bearing her forward. Bellasteros was at her side, urging his horse to longer strides; Patros carried the falcon at her other side. The guard, Lyris, and the Companions rallied behind.

Their charge scattered the remaining imperial horsemen. The infantry broke the shield wall at last and followed, hooting with delight. Mardoc's troops chased the enemy far into the scarlet-shadowed tints of the lowering night.

One remaining imperial officer saw the falcon, the shield, the scarlet plume. His bloodstained face twisted in rage. He wheeled his horse, set his lance, and drove straight for Bellasteros.

Patros glanced around, his mouth shaped to comment on the apparent victory. He saw the charging horseman and emitted instead some garbled warning cry. Even as Bellasteros and Danica whirled about, Patros jerked so abruptly at his reins that his horse reared, falling sideways into the path of the imperial officer.

The horse scrambled, regaining its balance. The officer screamed an epithet. But it was too late to redirect his blow.

The lance hit the edge of Patros's cuirass, glanced off, bit deeply into his abdomen.

Patros's face went stark white. He dropped his sword, grasped the lance, and with a superhuman effort pulled it from his side. The officer, still clinging to the other end, was toppled from his horse. He scrambled upright.

"God's beak!" Bellasteros cried. He reached out. Solifrax swept in a glittering arc through the dusk. The imperial officer's head parted cleanly from his neck, bounced onto the churned and bloody dirt, and was trampled instantly into fragments. His body stood upright for one long moment and then collapsed like a deflated bladder.

Patros swayed in his saddle, his breath rasping through clenched teeth, blood streaming over his thighs. The falcon standard wobbled and began to fall. Danica's heart wrenched. No, such loyalty deserves a better end than this—Harus deserves more. Marcos, he is your brother and therefore mine. . . . The shield glinted, streaming light, an aureole of starshine reaching out to the wounded man. It lifted him, holding him on the back of the plunging horse; it carried the gilded form of the god from his hand to Danica's.

She grasped the pole with her left hand, holding it above the glowing shield, her face set almost in surprise at what she found herself so assiduously protecting.

The Sardian Aveyron appeared from nowhere, his long arms easing Patros from the back of his beast. Bellasteros leaped down and knelt beside him, shouting for compresses, for wine, for the surgeon. With his own cloak he staunched the flow of blood, leaving Solifrax for a moment abandoned in the dirt. The sword gleamed in crystalline purity, unstained, although Bellasteros's hands and arms and thighs, and the shining bronze of his armor, were splashed and spotted with rusty crimson.

Danica watched, silent, leaning down from her horse. The shield faded, becoming dull and featureless, just as the light waned from her eyes. The paean, she realized, had scraped her throat raw, and her arms and shoulders ached under the weight of shield and sword. The form of Harus gazed down at her calculatingly. Test me not, she told it. It is Ashtar who would plumb my strength to its bitter dregs.

Ghosts shifted around her in the dimness, shrieking, lamenting. Then torches sprang up, and she saw that the ghosts were men, living their pain. Attendants bore away the twitching form of Patros; Bellasteros picked the streak of pale phosphorescence that was Solifrax from the ground and stood contemplating it.

Mardoc and Adrastes materialized from fire-streaked shadow, leading their horses by their foam-flecked bridles. The beasts stumbled, wheezing, exactly like the infantrymen they passed.

"Well done, my lord," said Mardoc. His eye lifted to Danica, shied away, returned to Bellasteros. "Your ally fought well."

"Tell her that," Bellasteros ordered. He sheathed his sword and rubbed his hand wearily over his face, as if he could not quite tell if the features were still there.

"My . . . compliments," Mardoc said grudgingly to Danica.

She nodded politely. Adrastes was looking at her, narrow-eyed; "This," she said, holding out the falcon standard, "I believe is yours."

The priest stepped forward and snatched it from her hands, inspecting it closely to see if it had been contaminated by her touch.

"That is the standard Patros carried," Mardoc blurted. "Where . . . ?"

"Wounded," replied Bellasteros. "Wounded in my place."

"A brave lad," Adrastes said. He lifted the standard regally, like a scepter, beginning a prayer. The bronze falcon remained mute and still on its perch.

Mardoc bowed his head, Bellasteros shifted restlessly, but Danica turned to beckon to Lyris. Atalia was there, with some of the Companions. Gods! Danica thought. I am losing my touch, I did not hear her coming. . . .

"General Mardoc," Atalia said, with some relish at interrupting the prayer, "I am pleased to report that your daughter Chryse, the first wife of the king, has been saved from a . . . nasty fate."

Mardoc's mouth opened, hung open, and then closed. "Ah," he said faintly, as if the name at first meant nothing to him, "my thanks."

Bellasteros glanced up, looking from Danica to Mardoc and Adrastes and back again, following the import of Atalia's statement. "And mine," he said at last.

Adrastes pounded the pole of the standard against the ground, a chamberlain trying to attract the attention of a busy court. But Bellasteros had already turned back to his horse. "If you will offer a service of thanksgiving, Your Eminence," he said. "Later."

"A sacrifice," stated Adrastes, gathering his robes about him and following.

Bellasteros's eye met Danica's. Sacrifice enough for one day, she thought. Forgive us, Mother, for our pleasure in it.

The Sardians went one way, toward the ravaged baggage train; the Sabazians turned the other and slipped quietly into the torch-gutted night.

The torches and the campfires burned sullenly that night, the air of the valley thick and stale. The dead imperial horsemen were dragged to a nearby ravine, tossed like garbage into it, covered with rocks and brush. The howling of jackals soon began to waver down a discordant wind.

Bellasteros spent the night moving sleeplessly from burial squad to baggage train to hospital tent—where surgeons often completed the butchery already begun on the hapless wounded. Everywhere he had an encouraging word, a compliment for brave deeds performed. Solifrax rested, murmuring just beyond hearing, at his side.

More than a hundred dead Sardians were buried in tidy ranks, their families, massacred in the skirmish, laid like afterthoughts at their feet. A great mound was built over them, set with broken spears and swords. At dawn Adrastes raised the falcon standards and with his own hand cut the throats of three imperial prisoners, draining their blood in offering to the falcon god.

Declan held the knives and the bowls. His flesh seemed almost green in the thin morning light, as if he fought to keep his stomach down. Surely it was his wound that so nauseated him.

Bellasteros was also there; he stood to attention, his features stretched taut over his skull, deathly quiet, deathly reserved. Mardoc shifted uneasily beside him. Why should the king seem to force himself to this ceremony, so stiff, so still? The king had become a stranger to him.

Danica and her Companions turned their backs on the Sardians and raised a pyre for four of their number. The flames were slow to burn, hissing and crackling above the dead faces, reluctant to consume them. These my friends, sacrificed for Sabazel, Danica thought; Ashtar, please that we may soon end this game. Please that we may soon begin a gentler one. . . .

The fire sputtered. Dawn came, with only a slight easing of the darkness. Thick gray clouds hid the sky, lidding the valley and trapping the various smokes and smells within. Brief sprays of sleet raked the camp, the huddled soldiers, the hunched backs of the horses. The amy would move no farther that day.

Bellasteros sent to Danica asking for scouts to join his; she dispatched three Companions. And he sent asking for Shandir's help with a dying Patros. Danica could not refuse Ilanit's desperate plea to go as well.

At least Patros rated his own tent, Danica thought. The fabric shelter had been hastily raised during the night and now drooped in lopsided disarray. Aveyron stood guard outside the door; Hern slipped quickly away when he saw the Sabazians.

Bellasteros stood at his friend's bedside, hollow-eyed, stooped like an old man over the hilt of Solifrax. He was still flecked with the dirty stains of old blood, caked with dust and sweat; he straightened only slightly when the three women stepped in. His pain was a palpable current in the tent and Danica ached in response.

Ilanit moaned in dismay at the sight of Patros's still form. "If only I had been by his side. But I was rescuing that . . ." Danica's hand fell on her shoulder, hushing her.

Shandir immediately knelt by the narrow bed. "How did he pass the night?" she asked the surgeon who sat helplessly by.

"Feverish at first, tossing and calling . . . strange names. Then, just before dawn, he quieted, began to sink."

And indeed the young man's face was sunken, his cheekbones standing like mountain ridges above cavernous cheeks. Pale, too pale, and his breathing a shallow flutter. Shandir quickly called for warm water, peeled the bloodstained bandages from his wound, and began to apply an herb poultice. The rich scent rose upward, enveloping the tent, easing the harsh lines on Bellasteros's face.

Mardoc, with an unveiled Chryse on his arm, entered, followed by Declan. To Mardoc Danica said, silently, Will you thank us for saving your daughter from the fate you wished on us?

". . . I understand," Chryse was saying. "I know so little of strategy. Thank you for explaining, Father."

Mardoc bowed slightly to Bellasteros. "She was . . . perturbed that I could not stop for her as I hastened to your side."

Bellasteros winced, imperceptibly, but Danica saw. "The general arrived in the nick of time," he said, by rote, to no one in particular. "His courage and decision are to be commended."

Ilanit looked balefully at Chryse. Chryse looked at Patros and her eyes filled with tears. Mardoc muttered something and vanished; Declan stepped forward to take Chryse's arm in his place. "His Eminence sends his prayers," he said. His voice was thin, as if it had been through a beer strainer. A bandage was stark against the tangled tendrils of his hair.

Chryse drew herself up with a sniff and turned to Danica. "My . . . Your . . . Danica . . . " She paused. Danica nodded encouragingly. "I thank you for your rescue of me. I . . . am grieved to cause such difficulty, but I have never been beyond the bounds of Sardis, and battle terrifies me. . . ."

"As it does us all," Danica said graciously. Pitiful woman, dragged from her peaceful nest—but she is not a placid cow, Bellasteros.

Bellasteros, oblivious, watched as Shandir's long fingers probed Patros's abdomen. He moaned. Ilanit forgot Chryse and stepped closer to the bed, biting her lip.

"It is time to bleed him again," the Sardian surgeon announced.

"He lost enough blood on the field," scoffed Shandir.

The surgeon turned protestingly to Bellasteros. "My lord . . ."

"You have done your best," Bellasteros informed him. "He dies. This lady cannot hurt him."

"But my lord . . ."

Bellasteros's dark eyes lit, pinpoints of flame. His hand rose from the hilt of Solifrax and gestured peremptorily. The surgeon scuttled away.

Shandir sat back with a sigh. "His internal organs are not damaged. But the wound is deep, and still his blood flows. I cannot heal him. Only the favor of—'' She stopped, glanced over her shoulder at Chryse and Declan, continued, "Only the favor of the gods will save him now."

Ilanit emitted a shaky breath. "If only I had been with him. . . ."

"Then you would have been skewered as well," Danica told her.

She stepped forward and knelt beside Shandir, laying her hand on the damp skin of Patros's brow. Her fingertips burned with the heat. If she could use the heat in his body, if she could mold his flesh together . . . His courage deserved the attempt. His courage, and his love for Ilanit.

"Then we shall beg that favor," Danica said to Shandir. "We must tap his strength." She looked back at Ilanit. "Take his hand and call his name."

The girl fell to her knees, seized Patros's limp fingers, pressed them with her own. Her voice caressed him and he stirred, his breath quickening. His eyelids twitched. Ilanit spoke again and his lips formed her name.

Danica lifted her shield. For just a moment she let her look linger on Bellasteros; he started up with a furtive hope. "Mother, please," he whispered under his breath, so that none but she could hear.

Declan raised his hands, shaping wings above the prostrate form, and Chryse joined him in murmured prayer.

Sabazel, Danica thought. The hollow in the mountainside, the basin, the light of the moon on Cylandra's ice field. The star-shield gleamed, drawing the light of the lamps and the brazier, drawing the faint filtered sunlight to itself. It gleamed, a slow, pale fire, a luminescent mist. Moonlight on a cloudless night, the sharp brilliance of the stars. . . . The emblazoned star keened with one high, sustained note of power.

And star motes showered over Patros, hissing where they touched his skin. His eyes opened, wavered unfocused, fell on Ilanit's intent face. Feebly he smiled. Feebly his hand lifted, touched the golden waves of her hair.

Danica trembled, straining, shaping her will. The child in her belly twisted, as if it would leap from her body as her strength poured from her mind. Patros! she commanded silently, and his eyes shifted to her, widened, cleared.

A pain tore at her, a lance cutting deep into her abdomen

The child! But no, it was his agony, not her own; she caught it, tightened her teeth on it, molded it to her will. And she directed his own pain back into his body, directing every quivering inch of flesh to still itself, to join with those next to it, to seamlessly bind itself together. His strength, the vitality of his young body, encompassed her.

His blood steamed in her mind, scalding her thoughts—a scarlet cloak flowing behind her eyes. . . . She jerked with the last expulsive thrust of her spell, and the babe leaped inside her. Patros gasped, arching back against the linens; the bones in Ilanit's hand creaked.

And the blood was gone, the scarlet cloak only stained fabric crumpled at the bedside. Patros lay panting, watching her with eyes both fearful and pleased. "My lady, what . . . ?" he murmured.

With shaking hands Shandir lifted the poultices. The taut flesh of Patros's belly shone in the light of the shield, marred only by a long pink scar.

Chryse fell to her knees, her hands to her mouth, amazed. Declan looked quickly from face to face, seeking reassurance that he could indeed believe his eyes. Bellasteros bowed weak with relief over his sword.

Ilanit bent her forehead against Patros's hand and again he touched her hair, laughing in quiet pleasure. She beamed at him. His chest rose and fell, even, deep breaths, and he stretched as if waking from sleep.

Chryse watched their mingled smiles in meek, hopeless envy.

The shield sheen ebbed and went out. Danica leaned over the metal rim, exhausted, hardly able to control her dizzying thoughts. Foolish, she told herself, to expend so much for a man. Foolish, to entangle my daughter in my spell. Foolish and doubly foolish to do it before a priest of Harus—but Harus sits in majesty on majestic Ashtar's arm. It is Adrastes who is our enemy.

She looked up, the perspiration glimmering on her forehead. The midnight darkness of Bellasteros's eyes were fixed on her, his thought written as plainly on his face as on parchment: My thanks, Danica, for your favor; my love, Danica, for your compassion. . . . How wise is Ashtar, to share her power with you.

Numbly she returned his look, pleading, I am so weary, I

shall betray myself, please, do not ask this now. . . . She pulled herself to her feet and accepted Shandir's arm, swaying against her as if the ground heaved beneath her feet. "Come," she told Ilanit, and the girl reluctantly stood, flexing her fingers.

Chryse rose in her path, her eyes filled with tears of relief, of pain, of awe. "May I . . ." she squeaked. Her plump white hand touched the shield; its answering chime was audible only to Danica's ears.

"If you will excuse us," Shandir said.

Declan leaped to raise the tent flap, bowing in respect, and the three Sabazians exited into the dim light of day.

Bellasteros, also swaying, leaning on his sword, paced to Patros's side. Patros sat up slowly, testing his body. "I . . . had a nightmare," he said. "An imperial officer . . . a lance . . . blood . . ."

"It was true," Bellasteros told him. He laid his hand on Patros's shoulder, also testing, questioning if his friend remained normal flesh. "She saved your life, Patros."

"Indeed."

Declan bowed before the king, struggling to speak calmly. "Such an ally, my lord. Such an ally. We are fortunate."

"Are we?" replied Bellasteros, somewhat dazed.

Chryse whispered, "How can she be a witch?" She looked desperately upward, seeking guidance, seeking comfort.

Declan led her away. "We shall discuss the matter," he said firmly.

"And for a moment I dreamed," Patros went on, talking to himself, "that I was a woman, carrying a child in my belly. . . ." Suddenly he looked up, catching his king's eye; his king's eye, the quirk of his brow and the rueful crimp of his mouth, confirmed the unspoken sentence. Patros exhaled between pursed lips.

Bellasteros looked at the doorway, as if he could see through the fabric and across the camp to where Danica, supported by Ilanit and Shandir, carried her shield back into her own temporary borders and joined the huddle of wounded Companions.

Even as she sat wearily down, slipped the shield from her arm and propped it against her knees; even as she accepted a hot cup of barley broth from Atalia's hand, leaned back, and tried to empty her mind of all thought, one thought remained.

It was sent from Bellasteros, as straight and direct as the flight of an arrow. This, then, is the good of the power. This, and you will never be helpless. Stand with me, Danica, I beg you. . . .

She smiled into her cup. Yes, my lord, my king, yes. . . .

The day wore on, bleak and cold, but she slept and dreamed of a golden tree and a warm embrace. Her hands cradled the silent child in her womb. This, then, is destined for me; death and the healing after. The curving edge of the sword, a crescent moon, and my shield the evening star at its tip.

Chapter Thirteen

THE ARMY MOVED on the next dawn, passing out of the tainted valley, leaving the jackals and ravens to their feast. The storm clouds followed them with wind, sleet, and rain. Many provisions had been lost in the imperial attack, and Bellasteros had to send raiding parties to despoil the countryside.

Beside the Royal Road appeared another caravanserai, another dilapidated pile of mud-brick surrounded by withered tamarind trees. Several children, bellies distended, pitiful limbs barely covered by rags, played desultorily around a well.

Bellasteros spoke an order, the waiting pages relayed it to a quartermaster; the army took water and left some of its own meager stores with an aged crone crouching inside the smoke-scummed building. The children stared at the passing procession, unblinking, until their wasted forms seemed to fade into the walls of the caravanserai, and the caravanserai disappeared over the edge of the world.

"Like a swarm of locusts we come," Bellasteros said to Patros, who rode again beside him. "Sardian army, imperial army—the countryside is desolate. This land is long overdue for peace. Children with ancient eyes. . . ."

Patros, muffled to his eyebrows against the gale, cast a wary look at his king. "Mardoc would say you have lost your stomach for battle."

"Would he? Then Mardoc misses the point of battle."

"As we did once, I think."

With a sigh of agreement Bellasteros looked up at the sky. The moon, sliced cleanly into light and dark as if by the blade of Solifrax itself, seemed to dance among tumbling clouds. A pale, spectral moon, competing with the sun for power. Bellasteros frowned up at it. No, the moon would be the mate of the sun, if only they could meet across the invisible borders that bound them. . . .

Danica eyed the same moon from her place far back in the marching column. If only they could meet across those borders, she thought. . . .

"We should be at Iksandarun by the full," said Atalia.

"Midwinter's moon comes late this year," Danica replied. "And the rites will be but a shadow, without us there."

"Next year in Sabazel," Atalia stated, with more hope than confidence.

Danica sighed. I want to be there, in Cylandra's embrace; I want to rest in the womb of Ashtar, eating the figs from my garden, listening to the girl-children playing in the streets. . . .

"Next year," she said.

The army struggled on, ever deeper into the southern provinces of the Empire.

"She did what?" Adrastes demanded.

Declan laid down the tray with the high priest's evening ration. "She healed Patros of his wound. The legions buzz with the miracle. Did you not see him today, Your Eminence, riding at the side of the king?"

"I remained in my cart today, repeating the catechism in thanks for our victory."

"Yes, of course." Declan dodged a page bearing sumptuous carpets, pillows, furs, and bowed before the jeweled shrine and the gold image of the god.

Adrastes tucked a napkin under his chin and contemplated with distaste the stringy meat of some unidentified beast and the stale bread. "My personal stores were lost in the raid?"

"Yes, Your Eminence."

Adrastes shook his head. "A pity." Delicately he placed a crumb on his tongue. "And the witch-queen—the king made her heal his companion?"

"I would say, Your Eminence, that she did it because she wished to."

Adrastes snorted. "Because she wishes him alive for some

plot of her own, you mean. She would enspell him, too."

"A powerful spell, then," ventured Declan. The bandage he wore helped to conceal his expression, and he stood behind Adrastes, just beyond the circle of lamplight; but something in his voice made the high priest turn and stab him with a black, forbidding stare.

"Take care, Declan. Devious, she is, very devious, all lies and mockery; she seeks to cast down the throne of Bellasteros and drag the name of the god in the dust. We are the sons of righteousness. She and her whores—evil, Declan, evil. We must defend the god from vile Sabazel." His lips were moist, Declan saw, and he savored his words as he had savored the sacrifice of the prisoners.

"Yes, of course, Your Eminence," Declan said with a bow. "Do you require anything else?"

"Where is my wine? Surely that, too, did not perish?"

"No. I shall bring it." Declan backed away, turned, and vanished into the gathering dusk. His brows were drawn down, his mouth tight with thought.

I should not be here, Danica told herself even as she ducked, alone, out of the winter night into Bellasteros's tent. The feeble light of lamp and brazier assaulted her eyes; she stopped and blinked.

In that moment when her eyesight failed, her other senses leaped awake. Something small and black and glittering, something hidden and dangerous—her eyes cleared. Bellasteros stood beside his table, watching her. His gaze was dark, rich, and warm. And this winter had chilled her to the bone. She laid her shield against a chest and went to him.

They embraced. Danica set her cheek against his and allowed herself for just a moment to taste his scent, to dwell on the memories that taste evoked. He was tired, she thought—they were both tired. Too tired, too tense to rest, suspended tautly in their words and deeds, intertwined.

"I become a small soft creature, protected by a shell," Danica told him. "I make that shell thicker, stronger, fearing what I feel—fearing to feel at all, until I cannot feel. Forgive me. . . ."

Bellasteros's fingertip stroked her face, her chin, her throat. "Too much to say. Too much that can never be said. Forgive me."

She let her lips brush his and she turned away. Her shield glimmered in odd discordant swirls, responding to something. . . .

"My thanks again for your compassion," said Bellasteros. "Patros, Chryse—I should have prevented the attack on the baggage train."

"And I should have prevented the attack on my camp," Danica returned.

Bellasteros sighed. "Mardoc turned their flank and routed them. Of course he could not stop to save Chryse. . . ."

"He did not have to save Adrastes, either."

"True. Very true." They touched again, hand to hand, glance to glance, seeking reassurance. "The power is hard to bear," he murmured. "We are mortal, but we know too much for mortals. We know our fates rest in the hands of others—friends and enemies alike. We have the power to see our own vulnerability."

"So then, you sense it, too," said Danica. "But is it a blessing, or a curse?"

His mouth softened. "At this moment, a blessing." He laid his hand against the mound of her belly; the child twitched, restless, as torn with difficulty as its parents. "Of all my weaknesses, this little one here is the greatest—its mother rides hard, she fights hard, she spends her strength in my behalf, in Harus's, and in Ashtar's."

Danica smiled against his cheek. "The same?"

"Ah . . . perhaps."

"We shared the fruit beyond the end of the world, you and I."

"My sister," Bellasteros whispered. "My spouse. You of all women to carry my heir and plumb the depths of my weakness."

"You," she began, "of all men . . ." A thorn in her mind, pricking her; she started from his arms. Her eye fell on the sparking shield. "What?" she asked, stepping toward it. A wave of nausea swept over her and she staggered dizzily, as if she fell from a great height into waiting nets, nets spread open and ready, black as jet, sharp as flint, pitiless. . . .

In two strides she was by the shield. She lifted it, set it on her arm, flung open the chest on which it had leaned. There, beneath oddments of silk and ivory, a black onyx ring. She touched it. It was so cold it burned her finger.

Bellasteros leaned over her shoulder. "It was in my tent when I returned with Solifrax," he said. "I knew it not."

"And your pages packed it away when we moved." Danica lifted the ring. Heavy, heavy and cold, it was an icy pulse driving the blood from her hand. With a curse she tossed it into the center of the tent.

Bellasteros seized Solifrax from the table and whipped it from its sheath. It spat fire, ripping the shadows. With the razor-sharp point he plucked the ring from the floor and held it aloft. "Notice," he said, in a dry ironic rage, "that the band is cast like the encompassing wings of a falcon."

"A pretty bauble, surely," growled Danica, "and yet no one has complained of its loss."

"Then I did condemn Theara from my own mouth!" Bellasteros exclaimed. "Stupid fool that I was, not to have realized what this meant. . . ." They eyed each other, remembering what they had said in the last few moments, blanching in one mingled agony of fear, anger, and exasperated weariness.

"So declare yourself my enemy, Adrastes!" Bellasteros cast the ring into the embers of the brazier. It seemed at first to attract all the heat from the fire, growing larger, blacker, denser, blotting out the flame. Then, with a resounding crack, it exploded.

Both Danica and Bellasteros ducked, warding off the flying, needlelike shards, sword and shield ringing. The brazier was filled with a hissing scarlet fire, leaping upward, snapping at the braces of the tent—then it was gone. The brazier toppled onto its side, spewing cinders over the rug.

Bellasteros reached warily out, stirred the cinders with the point of the sword, then bent and touched them. They were ice cold. "And he accuses you of sorcery," the conqueror said at last. His breath trembled.

"I am not sure," said Danica, "whether to be angrier at his spying on you or at his interrupting the moment. . . ."

Bellasteros rose and stood slapping Solifrax against his leg. "Perhaps I should escort you back to your encampment, my lady. The morrow, I think, will soon be at our throats."

They did not touch again as they exited the tent. Their weapons dulled and fell silent, numb. The wind screamed as it scored the camp with tiny spicules of ice. Side by side the king and the queen walked, wrapped in individual cloaks, wrapped in individual disgust. They did not notice the cloaked figure that stepped from behind Bellasteros's tent and followed them.

I should not have come, Danica thought. Mother! Given one moment of peace and I reveal everything. . . .

"I let my guard fall for one moment of peace," Bellasteros muttered, "and I reveal everything. . . ."

They paused in the lee of another tent. Patros's tent, Danica noted idly. "So we thicken our shells," she said to Bellasteros.

He sighed, his face concealed by the murk, eyes shuttered.

Someone else sighed. A long, quavering sigh of pleasure and of satiety. A chill tightened Danica's back that had nothing to do with the sleet lashing her face. Patros's tent, and Ilanit's hand drawing him from death . . . It was no happenstance, then, that had drawn her here, from Bellasteros's quarters, with Bellasteros at her side. It was her accursed sixth sense. No, she moaned to herself. Not this as well. Mother, please, I cannot.

A gentle laugh, a murmured endearment, rustling linen. Even Bellasteros heard this time; the soft resonances penetrated the gale. He turned, seized Danica's arm. "No, let it go."

Desperate, the ground swaying beneath her, her heart wrenching unevenly in her chest—she set her jaw so firmly that it ached. "If I wink at her law-breaking, what then would I have left?" she demanded hoarsely. "What then?"

Her voice stung him. He dropped her arm and stepped back.

Danica almost wished he could stop her. She turned and ripped open the flap of the tent. No light but the gentle rosy glow of the brazier, shadows softly draped about enlaced limbs, a garden of joy blooming in midwinter, in mind-winter. . . . It was too beautiful to be wrong; surely the borders of Sabazel enclosed this place, surely the winter solstice was already here—no!

The horror in the lovers' eyes as they saw her cut her to the quick. She hated them for making her do what she had to do, hurting them, hurting herself.

Strike, before I fail! She lunged forward, drew her sword, knitted her fingers in Patros's hair and yanked him upward, away from Ilanit's supine body. Her blade indented the throbbing pulse in his throat. He wilted visibly. "So," she said, acidly, "you are recovered from your wound."

His eyes glinted in the glow of Danica's shield, but he said nothing, pleaded nothing, retained his dignity. The salt scent of his body, so like Bellasteros's, made her dizzy. And Bellasteros himself stood just behind her, tensely silent.

Ilanit sat up, knowing better than to grasp her mother's sword arm, assaulting Danica instead with her great shining eyes and the quavering strength of her voice. "It is I who should atone; I came here of my own free will. Mother, please, spare him."

And my will that brought me to Bellasteros tonight—strike! Danica's sword traced a thin red line down Patros's body, past the scar on his abdomen, down to the inside of his thigh. And this time he did gasp, the cold metal nicking the root of his manhood.

"Danica," Bellasteros said. Only one word, but his meaning was clear: Remember where you are, what this would signify to the army of Sardis.

Ilanit rolled off the bed and threw herself at Danica's feet. "In the name of Ashtar, Mother, it is I who should pay, not him, the fault is not his. . . ."

"No," Patros croaked, "I enticed her here; if I must pay, I will. . . ." He closed his eyes. The blood drained from his face; the perspiration stood in great amber beads across his brow. But he made no struggle, no protest.

"By all the gods, by starfire and moonglow, may the sky-demons damn me for my weakness. . . ." Danica was almost sobbing with frustration, Patros's courage too great, Ilanit's honesty too painful, Bellasteros's restraint too noble. Her wrist turned and her sword flicked, leaving a red furrow in the fold where Patros's leg met his groin. And she released him.

He collapsed on the narrow camp bed, inhaling as deeply and shakily as if he had not taken a single breath since Danica had entered the tent. Bellasteros wobbled, started to step forward and thought better of it.

Danica whipped around and grasped Ilanit's hair, jerking her upward so roughly that her knees left the ground, jerking her head forward and baring the back of her neck. "If you admit your complicity, then you shall indeed pay," Danica said between her teeth. She hated the sound of her own voice. How can you do this to me? she thought. How, my love, my daughter, how can you make me do this?

Ilanit gasped at the pain, stiffening, but she did not struggle. My child, Danica screamed silently, I love you as my life. . . . Her sword rose for the blow. The star-shield flamed, washing the girl's naked body in fire.

"No!" both Patros and Bellasteros cried. The king lunged, grasping Danica's arm in a steel-hard grip, holding the sword upraised.

Danica stopped, looking from horror-stricken face to horror-stricken face. And she realized what it was they thought she was doing. She wanted to laugh in despair. She wanted to cry.

"Leave me be," she snapped at Bellasteros. "Only Sardians murder their daughters."

He flinched, stepped back, turned aside. She remembered then, too late, that his own infant daughter, his and Chryse's younger child, had been exposed by Mardoc simply for being a girl. Ah, Mother, Danica sighed to herself, I lash about me blindly, striking everyone, hurting those I love—forgive me most of all, forgive me.

Her eyes glistened in the glow of her shield. Her sword moved in delicate strokes, cutting Ilanit's hair from her head; the finespun gold cascaded from Danica's hand. When Ilanit appeared shorn among the Companions they would know why and would taunt her for her frailty.

Danica sheathed her sword and set down her shield. Her anger drained away like blood from an open wound; she seemed to be upheld in a thin, clear bubble of light, observing herself and the others from a great distance, carved figures moving painfully across a game board of light and shadow.

Patros huddled on the bed, hands covering his face, shoulders shaking, heedless of the blood smearing his thigh. Bellasteros swayed against a tent brace, eyes closed, mouth slack. Ilanit reached for her strewn clothing and dressed shyly, quietly, avoiding Danica's gaze. But Danica's gaze was as soft as the short curls now covering her daughter's head. "My poor shorn lamb," she murmured, and she gathered the girl into her embrace.

Danica, one arm clasping Ilanit securely to her side, laid the handful of hair across the glowing embers in the brazier. Patros and Bellasteros looked up. Each strand caught fire, flaming up into the image of a net, interlaced filaments of brilliant gold. Inside the net a luminescence gathered, crimson fire, yellow sun, silver moon. The light grew, flowing upward, brushing the top of the tent with tiny bursting sparks. It wavered as if breathing, and two points of blue, distant glimpses of a clear sky, shaped themselves like eyes at its top.

Danica and Ilanit fell to their knees. Their upturned faces shone, cleansed of anguish; tears left trails of molten fire down their cheeks. Patros and Bellasteros exchanged one glance, then they, too, knelt.

The light formed the suggestion of a woman, seen more by the mind than by the eye. Wise eyes saw frailty and accepted it, raised arms offered absolution. A cold, fresh wind, the pure breath of ice-crowned Cylandra, sang through the tent and through the bodies of the people within, lifting them, bearing them away to some bright haven. . . .

Then there was nothing but blackened strands matting the embers and a faint stench of burning hair. But the exaltation lingered.

Danica was strong enough to rise, calm enough to lay her hand against Bellasteros's face and turn it to her own. "What, then, do we have?" she asked.

"Everything," he replied. He turned his lips into her palm.

Patros bent to kiss Ilanit's hand. He gave Danica her sword and shield and escorted them to the tent flap as if he showed them from the audience hall of the emperor's palace.

The sleet was over. Stars raced among scudding clouds, dancing with a waxing moon. The wind sang across the depths of the sky, its melody a hymn of winter's promise.

"Good night," Danica said to Bellasteros. "Until the morrow, and the destiny thereof."

"Until the morrow." He bowed to both women; his dark pellucid eyes rested on Danica. "And the morrow after that, until the end of the game."

She walked with Ilanit close by her side into the rushing shadows of the night. A moment's peace after all, she thought. One blessed moment. "Was it worth it?" she asked her daughter wryly.

Ilanit returned, equally wry, "I think . . . yes."

And Danica could not help but laugh.

Bellasteros turned back into Patros's tent, finding his friend collapsed once more on the bed. "Never again," he said, "accuse me of playing a dangerous game."

"No, my lord," Patros groaned.

But Bellasteros was smiling. Ruefully, but smiling nonetheless.

The hooded figure stumbled away from a tiny gash in the seam of the tent. A safe distance away it stopped. Declan's narrow face turned upward to the fitful starlight as if he had never before seen stars, as if they were new molded of ice and fire for his own private audience.

"Ashtar?" he queried tentatively. The wind caressed him, filling his ears with distant, barely discernible chimes.

Adrastes and Mardoc sat opposite each other, empty wine cups dangling from their hands. The high priest's ring finger was seared red, his face glistened with a pale sweat; his topaz ring, crushed and blackened, lay before him on a patch of rug burned to ash. In sepulchral if somewhat shaky tones Adrastes said, "He has fallen. You heard, my friend; the witch-queen holds him in the palm of her hand, and the evil light of her shield blinds him."

Mardoc's face grew even longer. "My poor lad. If only I had killed her then, after Azervinah, before she drew you to her in . . . Sabazel. . . ."

"But he has always been obdurate, has he not, insisting on dealing with her?"

"She is an ally, he says, and she does fight well. If only . . ."

Adrastes tightened his jaw, leaned forward, and rapped Mardoc smartly on the knee. "Stop it," he said. "Stop moaning over might-have-beens. Recognize the situation now."

Mardoc stirred and stared with red-rimmed eyes at the priest. Adrastes stared back, glittering nodules of jet pinioning the general to his chair.

"He has fallen," repeated Mardoc, unblinking. "The witch-queen holds him in the palm of her hand. She carries his heir and he preens himself, pleased. He would not listen to my warnings and he is lost."

"Yes," Adrastes hissed. He leaped to his feet, speaking urgently to himself as he paced across the tent, leaving Mardoc squinting at the empty chair. "Yes. I tested him by sending Gerlac's shade to kill the witch. But he would not accept my word that it was Chryse's deed; he already knew of it, he said, and it angered him. Therefore he has fallen to the witch's guile. He knew his concubine Theara was tainted with goddess worship, and yet he did not correct her, leaving that task to me.''

Mardoc shook himself and peered into his cup. The name of Chryse had penetrated his fog. ''She gave him only daughters,'' he said belligerently. ''The demon-woman promises him a son. She must die, and the child she carries with her. Only then can Sardis be saved.''

Adrastes nodded. ''He is strong and clever, but he cannot hide the truth. He fears me, as well he should, but he does not fear me enough.''

''Truth?'' Mardoc asked. ''The Sabazian has enspelled him. Her alliance is useless and she must be destroyed. That is the truth.''

But Adrastes continued. ''No, a greater truth than that. The rumors of his birth . . .'' He scowled, his beard coiling venomously. ''He has Gerlac's temper, Gerlac's courage—he has the spirit of a god. How could he have hidden, all these years . . . No. If it is true, he did not realize it himself. Not until the witch-queen bound him to the service of the goddess. He is no god, but a devil.''

Mardoc's face flushed with comprehension. He hauled himself from the chair. ''Could it really be true, that that chit Viridis was consecrated to Ashtar, that Bellasteros was conceived not in Gerlac's marriage bed but in . . .'' He could not say it.

Adrastes could, and with relish. ''Sabazel. Think—he was born two moons early, but a lusty babe. He could have been conceived at the barbarous rites of Sabazel, a bastard with no Sardian blood, a heretic.''

''Gerlac always suspected. . . . Forgive me, Your Eminence, but I thought it was the madness of age and care, lies planted in his overtaxed mind by those jealous of such a prince—'' Mardoc's voice broke. ''Such a prince. A son to me, taking his first sword from my hands, returning my staff of office to me first, of all his officers, when he became king. . . .''

Adrastes set his hands on the general's shoulders, fixing the other man's eyes with the force of his gaze. ''Enough of this maudlin memory. Do you know what I recall? That Gerlac and I heard the girl Viridis praying to Ashtar, singing some spell over the babe; fortunate, that she was still weak from the birth and Gerlac's hands so strong. Bellasteros was spared the taint of Sabazel then, and nurtured under the wings of Harus. Even I believed him the son of Gerlac, of the god. Until now. Now the witch-queen calls him and he obeys. He obeys, Mardoc!''

"He obeys," repeated the general. Adrastes released him and again he blinked around him, shaking himself. "Proof," he said, as if seeking for some remaining shred of his honor. "Show me proof, please, Your Eminence, that I may believe."

"And that I may believe," said Adrastes, frowning in a brief uncertainty. "A heretic king—a serious charge. We must be sure, so that being sure we can move."

"Move?" Mardoc muttered. "Two days' march from Iksandarun, and the army eager to see Solifrax drawn in battle . . ."

But Adrastes was not listening. He blew out all the lamps except for the two before the altar of Harus. They guttered, flickering madly, casting gouts of shadow over the image of the god. The gold falcon seemed to move uneasily, its feathers fluffing, its bright eye fixed in guarded interest on the movements of the priest.

The tent flap shivered and Declan crept inside. "You!" Adrastes ordered. "My knives, my bowls—quickly."

Declan scurried away, returned with the tools, set himself in the darkest, dimmest corner of the tent. Only his eyes reflected the twin flame on the altar, slowly filling with a terrible conviction.

"The dead know the answer," said Adrastes, "let the dead respond."

"Sorcery?" hazarded Mardoc, but the priest's glittering eyes pierced him and he shut his mouth.

"Even Gerlac did not know," said Adrastes. "He suspected, on good evidence, but he did not know. And his shade has been shamefully cast into darkness by the goddess and her minions, beyond reach, beyond hope. . . ."

Adrastes lifted a large cloth-shrouded jar from behind the altar, wincing as his finger touched it; he pulled the cloth away and a thick scent of spices and natron flooded the tent. Delicately he dipped inside, grasped something, pulled—the severed head of one of the imperial prisoners appeared, flesh sloughing from bone, eyes glazed, dripping vinegar and decay.

Even battle-hardened Mardoc gulped several times in succession and dropped quickly onto his chair. In the corner Declan was surreptitiously sick.

Adrastes, chuckling with pleasure, set the grotesque object on the altar of Harus. He raised his knife, held the bowl ready, began the incantation. The lamps guttered again, whipping away from the severed head; then the flames leaped up steady and blood-red.

The entire interior of the tent flushed scarlet, as if bathed in blood. Only Adrastes's breastplate did not reflect the light; it remained dark, a void on his chest. The image of the god shimmered rosily, somehow clean, pure as a sunrise, and a quick rustle of hunting wings sounded in the shadows.

Mardoc's eyes danced red and gold, awestruck. He slid from his chair to his knees. Declan huddled farther back, looking out between his fingers as if hardly daring to see.

The incantation grew louder, commanding. The knives did their work, filling the bowls with gore; the skull beneath the skin was florid, the eye sockets filled with flaming motes, the teeth clenched in a rictus grin.

The tent flapped suddenly, billowing as if admitting some presence. The incantation stopped between one syllable and the next. "Speak," ordered Adrastes.

And the skull spoke. It was hesitant and slurred, but it was speech. "Who calls—breaking the bonds of the otherworld. Who dares . . ."

"The talon of Harus, the grand inquisitor of Sardis, Adrastes Falco. I call, offering flesh, offering fire; answer me."

"Answer . . ." The voice trailed off, a sigh, a moan.

"Who are you?"

At first silence, and then, distantly, "I was serving-woman to the princess Viridis, and nurse to her son. I fed him and bathed him and guided his first steps, until he was taken from me. The king, Gerlac, the demon murderer . . ."

Adrastes's knife flicked. Liquid from the bowls sprayed the face of the skull, leaving steaming pockmarks. The bone cracked. The unearthly voice stopped, mumbled disjointedly, moaned again.

"The child," asked the priest. "Where was he conceived? Not born, woman; conceived."

The lamps sprayed sparks upward, golden flecks of light raining on the image of the god, on the grisly skull, on Adrastes himself. "Fathered in Sabazel, under the eye of the goddess Ashtar. Fathered according to her rites and consecrated to her name. . . ."

"Then may he be damned to all eternity!" Adrastes raised the knife and drove it deep into the skull. The voice shrieked, not loudly, but high, keening, a blade of sound. And the skull shriveled into black gobbets of stinking muck, fouling the altar so that it reeked like a charnel house. "So perish all heretics," declaimed Adrastes. He panted, his eyes flashed, his mouth opened on sharp teeth. An orgasmic shudder rippled through his body. "So perish them all!"

The fires of the lamps guttered again as wildly beating wings swept through the tent. Then there was silence. The lamps were only tiny clear flames, the shadows simply shadows.

Adrastes inhaled deeply, calming himself. "Declan," he ordered. "Clear this away." And to Mardoc, "So our questions are answered, General. We have waked from our dream and find our duty clear before us."

Mardoc looked not like one wakened from sleep, but like one cast into the depths of a nightmare, incapable of escape. "He was a son to me," he croaked. "I loved him. But he betrays me, he betrays Sardis, he betrays the god—he chooses the witch-queen to bear his son. . . ." Suddenly he turned to Adrastes, grasping his arm. His eyes almost started from their sockets. "No one must know this, no one. Not here, not before the gates of Iksandarun. He must take the Empire for Sardis. . . ."

"Indeed," said Adrastes. He eased Mardoc into the chair and laid a soothing hand on his shoulder. "Fear not for Sardis. It will prevail; the falcon's wings will protect it, grateful for this cleansing."

Mardoc lay back in the chair, looked up at the roof of the tent, and wept.

With an impatient snort Adrastes turned away. He inspected his burned, gore-stained finger. Shrugging, he began to suck on it. "Declan," he said thickly. "Do your ears no longer function! Clean up the altar!"

The young priest drew himself up slowly, as if he had aged fifty years in the last few moments. He stepped forward, avoiding even the hem of Adrastes's robe. "I doubt," he whispered, "if such befoulment can ever be cleaned." He reached out in supplication to the falcon, and the falcon, briefly but perceptibly, nodded.

Danica lay awake on her bedroll. Through a slit in the tent flap she could see the clearing night. Her body seemed to float a handsbreadth above the blankets, buoyed by the wind, the starlight, the setting rays of the moon. Tired, so tired, and yet for a moment the tension was gone, the grim awareness abandoned; her thoughts drifted like snowflakes down Cylandra's clear, cold wind.

She was growing accustomed to the cleft in her dialogue with the goddess. She spoke in monologue now, answering her own questions—could it be that even the goddess had to answer only as best she could?

Ilanit is to me as I am to you, Mother, she thought. Both of us, bound by an implacable mercy; you ask much, but you give much in return.

If I bear the power, she thought, am I, too, a god? Do the gods hate the power they bear, hurting themselves, hurting others? Do the gods seek the purification of desire, the peace that comes beyond desire?

And she thought, The gods move slowly, subtly; entire lifetimes are to them but a brief movement on the gameboard. Mother, do you not know the end of the game? Is this why you withdrew, leaving me alone, with only the power to sustain me—could it be that you are as much like me as I am like you, that we are both gods, that we are all our own gods and the power comes from our meeting, our hating, our loving? . . .

Do even the gods remain, in the end, vulnerable?

A soft melody fell on her ears and she pulled in her thoughts, binding them together, tucking them firmly into the back of her mind. I shall never know. Not in this life, at any rate.

Lyris sang softly as she stood guard outside Danica's tent—a Sabazian lullaby, to soothe a baby into sleep. Danica smiled. Like as not the woman sang only what came first to her mind.

Danica joined the song, humming to herself. She had sung to Ilanit, and to her two sons before they began their journeys across the borders of Sabazel. And to this baby, too, she would sing. . . .

A trailing tendril of consciousness was Bellasteros, dreaming the same lullaby, stirring in some fearsome infant memory connected with that lullaby. She touched him lightly, consoling him.

Danica floated in the night's gentle wind, rocking herself and her love to sleep. If she heard, distantly, a keening shriek, a blade through the mind, she gathered that in, too, and sheltered it from abuse.

Tomorrow, and the destiny thereof. Tonight she would claim peace.

Chapter Fourteen

THE MORROW AND its destiny came all too soon. The army of
Sardis was hardly moving again, striding forward through the
cold light of day, when scouts came riding in with reports of
another raiding party, and another behind that.

The skirmishes went on all day, brief, bloody, inconclusive.
By day's end the Sardians had won to within sight of the pass
leading to Iksandarun. The legionaries, though tired, were
heartened by that distant shadow on the horizon, the rock
walls of the plateau. An occasional glint from the top showed
the position of imperial sentries.

Just before sunset an embassy came from Bogazkar, a priest
and two soldiers riding weaponless from the gathering dusk.
Quickly the gold pavilion was raised, and quickly the Sardian
officers arranged themselves before the dais where Bellasteros
waited. The terms were brief and to the point. A pitched battle, to be fought at the pass tomorrow, to determine the fate of
the Empire.

Graciously Bellasteros bowed and promised to consider the
matter. Graciously he presented gifts to the imperial soldiers
and sent them on their way. The Sardian troops murmured
among themselves, eager for a conclusion to their endless
quest.

The king called his advisors, old Sardian colleagues, new
imperial allies, the Sabazians, together in his tent. Finally, Bellasteros thought, I need no longer fear Bogazkar's spies. . . .

185

"Well done," he said privately to Patros as they waited for Mardoc. "This day you have not stopped my heart with your antics."

Patros returned an eloquent stare and Bellasteros allowed one eyelid to shiver in a wink. His own good humor surprised him. Open battle and an end to the endless skirmishing with enemies both avowed and hidden; action, and the end of the game. He had dreamed of a song, a gentle melody haunting some deep, almost forgotten corner of his mind; the music brought dread, but it brought peace.

The sword Solifrax hummed, hot at his side, and Danica, queen of Sabazel, stood holding her humming shield an arm's length away.

He nodded gravely to her, aware of the eyes of his officers on him; she nodded gravely back. But the officers seemed not to question her presence at his side. How quickly had the confused night of the attack on her camp been forgotten, how quickly had legends sprung up of the sword and the shield wielded as one in battle, as one for Sardis.

Behind him Patros spoke quietly to Danica. "Has Ilanit suffered this day?"

"Less than she deserves," she replied. "Her friends would not mock her overmuch in the presence of the Sardians."

"Ah," said Patros. "That pleases me."

Danica favored him with the thinnest, subtlest smile. Beyond her Atalia muttered, "And you, young stallion, less than you deserve."

The tent flap opened and Mardoc strode in. Mardoc, eyes blood-streaked, jowls hanging loose, was a man walking in nightmare, hurt and turning that hurt outward into hatred. Bellasteros remembered the onyx ring, the loving words overheard. His good humor shattered into spinning pellets of ice that cut into the back of his neck and drew it tight, alert, wary. We might yet lose this game, he thought. Enemies before us, enemies behind; no wonder my queen stands so pale and still, hemmed in by failure—her failure, and mine.

Bellasteros sighed. This is indeed the end of the game, whether for good or ill. He raised his sword, drawing every eye in the room to himself. Grave green eyes, strengthening his will. . . . With a flourish he unrolled the map of the pass and Iksandarun. "Here," he said. "We have come to the end of our journey. The imperial army turns at bay, as they did before Farsahn. Tomorrow the Empire will be ours, and Sardis will rule the world.''

Sardis. Mardoc stirred, repeating the name under his breath. But his sullen gaze was still locked on his king, as if waiting for him to be transformed into some slavering beast.

Thank Harus that I have not seen Adrastes this day, Bellasteros thought. He hides his evil face from me, as well he should. . . . The conqueror drew himself up. ''Bogazkar meets us below the pass, willingly baring his throat to Solifrax. I mistrust only one thing.''

''A force above the pass,'' intoned Mardoc, ''would take us by surprise after a feigned retreat draws us in. Such treachery would I expect from Bogazkar. . . .'' He paled and looked down at his feet.

Mardoc, Bellasteros cried silently, we have waited years for this moment! Why let Adrastes so poison your mind as to take the pleasure from it? Why? But his speaking voice continued, sleek, calm, leading the discussion, and Danica's voice was a cool counterpoint to his.

''So it is decided,'' he concluded at last. ''Our scouts will range far this night, guarding against treachery. The Sabazian force will climb the plateau beside the pass tomorrow and guide our best archers to outflank the enemy.''

''A good plan, my lord,'' Mardoc said, and he meant it. But there was a flicker in his reddened eyes that Bellasteros did not like.

''Patros,'' said the king, ''write the message. The battle will be joined soon after dawn, just below the pass. Mardoc, designate messengers—that young priest, my wife's chaplain; I like his face. Two soldiers.''

''Yes, my lord,'' the general said. He slipped out of the tent.

Bellasteros thanked his advisors and escorted them into the evening. He dispatched Declan and the soldiers—Aveyron was the name of the fair one, he thought—with a salute of gleaming Solifrax. ''For Sardis!'' he called. ''In the name of the god!''

Danica beside him was frowning. ''What?'' he asked her.

''That one,'' she replied. ''Not Aveyron, the other, with the cheekpieces of his helmet close about his face . . . No, I know not.''

He could not ask her to explain; Mardoc was approaching. Declan, Aveyron, and Hern clattered out of the temporary encampment and up the Royal Road to Iksandarun, the plump, waxing moon at their backs. The priest was not a horseman, and his clumsiness drew some amused comments from the watching soldiers. No one saw Hern place a piece of parchment inside his cuirass. Not the official message— Declan carried that. Hern bore a private letter from Adrastes and Mardoc to Bogazkar. The paper might well have burned his flesh; it carried death written large upon it.

"May I speak with you, my lord?" Mardoc asked. "And with . . . her?" He jerked his head toward Danica but did not look at her.

Carefully exchanging only the most casual of glances, Bellasteros and Danica left Patros and Atalia outside in the twilight. The inside of the tent was dark; Bellasteros shooed away a pageboy who was fumbling with firebox and tinder and lit the lamp himself. The small yellow flame leaped up, lighting Mardoc's haggard face; he was staring at his young king, pleading somehow—pleading for something I cannot give, Bellasteros told himself. His sorrow was keen. "Yes, my general," he said with a smile. "How may I serve you?"

Mardoc inhaled, as if steeling himself to an unwelcome task. Swiftly he turned and ripped Danica's cloak from her body. The pin holding it did not give way; the material tore instead, leaving a shred in his clawing fingers. She started back, hand on sword, shield raised. "Who are you, to lay hands on me! . . ."

Too late. Her mail corselet glimmered, bright crescents of lamplight curving over her breasts and curving further over her belly. "That," Mardoc said harshly. "You would tell my king that is his child?"

Bellasteros intervened. "Our child," he told Mardoc. "So you admit to spying on my privacy? I would have thought you more courteous, my general."

The general snorted, not to be turned aside from his purpose. "You believe her, my lord? She is no better than a whore, sleeping with any man who comes to her. She tells you the child is yours only to use your power. . . ."

"Mind your tongue," Danica said slowly, "or you will find it suddenly shorter." Her sword was halfway from its scabbard; the shield gathered the lamplight to itself, the star pulsed in its center.

"If you think that, Mardoc," said Bellasteros, still polite, still wary, "then you know little of Sabazian customs. I doubt not the truth."

"Truth!" spat Mardoc, as if the word burned his mouth. "Yes, there is a truth, is there not. . . ." He shuddered, went on more quietly, "You would claim this bastard as your heir? Then you are surely bewitched. Marcos, repudiate this spawn of Ashtar, repudiate this child of evil."

Danica stepped forward, swinging the shield up, and her sword flicked at the ready. But Bellasteros thrust a sheathed Solifrax before her, stopping her. "Danica," he said. Just the one word.

With an aggrieved look at him she retreated. Elaborately, eyeing Mardoc with a look like a thrown javelin, she replaced her sword, calmed her shield, turned her back, and pretended to study the maps. Her back, Bellasteros noted, was as straight and taut as a flag borne outward by the wind.

He turned with a sigh to Mardoc and met his general's eyes. His stomach plummeted at what he saw there—unreasoning anger, unreasoning hatred, and a sly secrecy that reminded him too strongly of Adrastes. "Mardoc," he said, placing his hand on the older man's arm. "You were once a father to me. I took my first sword from your hands, and I returned your staff of office to you—"

"Maudlin memories. I speak of now, and your . . . obstinacy. Will you drag the name of Sardis, the holy name of Harus, in the mud?"

Gods! Mardoc, I am trying to placate you, I need your skills as I once needed your paternal love. . . . Bellasteros retrieved his hand. "How can you speak this way? Tomorrow I shall win the Empire for Sardis, and Harus will spread his wings over us. Do you doubt this?"

The two men struggled eye to eye, and it was Mardoc's eye that fell at last. "No, I cannot doubt that. I . . . only want to warn you—barbarian gods . . ." He sputtered out. He cast one last frown at Danica's back and plunged out of the tent as if fleeing from contaminated air.

Bellasteros stood, hands clenched before him, teeth set, trembling. I have driven him mad. No, Adrastes has driven him mad. . . . He will not change, he will spend his life taking the Empire, but he will not see that such an undertaking demands change. Ah, Mardoc, my only father . . .

Danica was beside him, her hand gentle on his shoulder. "If

we could choose our destiny," she said, "would we not include those we love in it? But we cannot choose, and it is upon us."

He nodded. He loosened his fists, his jaw. He shook the icy shiver away from his neck. "And have you wondered if Sardis, if the Empire, would accept your child as my heir?"

"It is the custom of Sabazel to relinquish male children. Who better to take this one, the only child of Ashtar to have a father, than its father himself?"

"Ah, yes," said Bellasteros, and for a moment he dwelled on that pleasing prospect. Then he touched her hand where it rested on his shoulder and reluctantly put it away. "But the battle comes first. Everything rides on our victory; even Mardoc, even that accursed priest have to admit to that."

"Indeed," Danica said. And with a tight smile and a salute she was gone. He gazed after her, letting her seep from his senses. *Without you, my love, I would have no destiny. . . .* He shook himself.

Mardoc is as subtle as a rampaging bull, Bellasteros thought. *But he hides something from me, some knowledge. . . .* His neck twitched again, cold black eyes gazing pitilessly at him. *Stop it, you have no time for this!* "Patros!" he bellowed, and when his friend appeared, "Come. Let us show Solifrax through the legions, consecrating ourselves to tomorrow's task."

Adrastes sat pensively in his tent, hands folded together, as patient as a spider waiting for its prey to enter its web. When Mardoc came in he barely looked up. "Our message is dispatched with the others?"

"Yes, Your Eminence. Bogazkar has been told where the Sabazians will be tomorrow. He can exterminate them at his leisure. As they deserve, whores and witches all. The commander of the archers has been instructed to stay back."

"Good. Now, as for the queen herself . . ." Adrastes's lips twitched in anticipation. "It would be best if she did not survive until tomorrow. She is strong, and she might escape the imperial levies."

"Hern will be back by the middle of the night. He has proved trustworthy, has he not?"

"We shall sweeten his trustworthiness with more coins. Perhaps he can at least damage her shield."

Mardoc nodded. His eyes burned, two bright red spots seared his cheeks, his forehead glistened—but the fever from which he suffered was not a bodily one. "And the king?" he asked, lowering his voice. "He must lead us into battle or we shall have no victory."

"Let him then have his victory. And afterward—a cooling cup of wine, or a spiced sweetmeat; you have seen the potency of my herbs, General."

"Yes, Your Eminence." Mardoc closed his eyes and rubbed them with his fingertips. He discovered he still held the shred of wool from Danica's cloak. With a grimace he threw it down.

"Mardoc," Adrastes said softly. The general looked up and was transfixed by the priest's glittering black gaze. "Mardoc, who shall rule after the king is dead?"

"Who better to bind the wounds of Sardis," mumbled Mardoc obediently, "than the high priest of Harus? Who better to cleanse both Sardis and the Empire of the taint of barbarian gods than the wise and holy talon of Harus?"

The black eyes were bottomless pits into which one could fall forever, lost and unlamented. "Yes," hissed Adrastes. "Who better? And according to Sardian law, he who weds the first wife, the widow of a sonless king, establishes his right to the throne."

"We are at your service, Your Eminence, my daughter and I."

Adrastes dropped his gaze and Mardoc swayed, almost falling. "She is still young," the priest said to himself. "She will bear me many sons—I shall make sure of that. Emperor, king of kings, god-king, a dynasty. . . ." His tongue flicked between his lips, wetting them. "You may go, General," he said with an imperial gesture of dismissal; Mardoc turned as if sleepwalking, and sleepwalking went into the night.

Adrastes bent, picked up the scrap of wool, and considered it, smiling.

Declan and the soldiers returned from their mission well before the middle of the night. Hern was immediately called to Mardoc; he went, his chin high—witness my importance! Aveyron trudged off toward his own quarters with many a troubled backward glance.

Declan found Chryse still awake, stitching briskly at a piece of embroidery while a serving-woman held a lamp for her. "May I speak with you, my lady?" the young priest asked.

Chryse eyed him wonderingly. He was weary, of course, from his journey, but his weariness seemed much deeper; it seemed the exhaustion of a mind that traces a convoluted path, over and over, hoping each time to find a different answer and each time failing. And yet he concealed his weariness behind a quiet dignity, a decision made, a decision accepted.

Chryse, concerned, started to send the serving-woman for food and drink, but Declan shook his head politely. "I wish simply to speak with you," he said, and the servant vanished.

Declan paused a moment, frowning slightly, as if pondering how to begin. Chryse waited, her head to one side like an inquisitive sparrow.

At last the young priest sighed. "My lady, do you remember the prophecy of a falcon held on Ashtar's arm?"

"Yes, yes I do. We hope to prevent—"

Declan raised his hand warningly. "Do you suppose, my lady, that we have misinterpreted that prophecy? We assume so quickly that Ashtar means to imprison Harus. Perhaps he comes to her freely, trustingly. Perhaps he is trying to ease the enmity that men are quick to assume among themselves, naming that enmity god-given."

Chryse's eye grew round, shocked. She glanced over at the gilded falcon of her shrine as if she expected it to rise into the air and attack Declan for impiety. "How, how can you say such a thing?" she breathed.

"My lady, you know me. You know my devotion to Harus."

She shook herself. "I see many strange things. I doubt—I must not doubt."

"Perhaps some doubt is healthy. Think—you saw the queen of Sabazel heal Patros. You saw what it cost her. You saw—I beg your pardon, my lady—you saw the respect with which the king regarded her, and she him."

"Yes." It was a faint whisper, but enough to make the lamp gutter and the shadows dance. Wings, hovering wings . . . "She does not seem evil, but compassionate, caring for Patros and Lyris and me; yet His Eminence denounces her."

Declan leaned closer to Chryse and dropped his voice to a

low mutter. "His Eminence spies on the king, plotting with Mardoc against him. Last night I saw His Eminence making black sorcery; I saw blood on his hands. I heard . . ."

Chryse had to almost touch him to hear him. She listened, started back, clasped her hands over her breast as if protecting herself. Her cheeks went pale. "That old lie? How, how can it be true?"

"Is our lord a demon? Has he done ill for Sardis? Has he showed any less than the utmost respect for us his people and for the god Harus?"

"No, but . . ."

Declan kept on talking, not loudly, but with an intensity that had Chryse thrust tight against the back of her chair. "Would you repudiate your lord for the fact of his birth? He could not help his birth; indeed, he is stronger for it. Surely he is more than noble, to live his life caught between man and god and yet to live it so well."

"True, true. . . ."

Declan grimaced, as if finding his own words distasteful. "The queen of Sabazel, my lady, bears the king a child."

"Oh," said Chryse, pierced through the heart. Her eyes filled with tears and she covered her face with her hands, trying to block out his voice.

But he continued, kindly, insistently. "Hear me, lady. Tomorrow Sardis and the Empire will be joined, bringing an end to war. Is not this child also a symbol of peace, binding Sabazel to Sardis, joining the gods themselves and cleansing the evil done by such as—"

"Do not say it," Chryse ordered. She looked up, tears streaking the softness of her cheeks. Heedlessly she took her embroidery and dabbed at her face. "Declan, I am only a woman, I do not understand the will of the gods. I do not know what to think. My own father, a traitor. . . . Why burden me with this?"

"We are not animals. We must know what forces govern our lives. And the king has need of us at this moment, for the forces of his life close on him like circling wolves."

She waited cautiously, but he said nothing more. He leaned back in his chair and allowed his head to loll wearily, his eyes to close.

"I shall think on it," Chryse said after a time. She sniffed, raising her chin, tightening her mouth. "I wish only to serve my lord, and if His Eminence wishes instead to hurt him, if my respected father turns against him . . ."

Declan watched her, a small pained smile on his lips.

Chryse exhaled, deflating. "I will think on it."

"My thanks, my lady. Such is all I ask." Declan stood, bowing over her hand.

The tent flap opened. The serving-woman bobbed in the doorway. "His Eminence, the talon of Harus, to see you, my lady."

Chryse squeaked, turning terror-filled eyes to Declan. He cast a furtive glance over his shoulder and set his finger against his lips. "Be strong, my lady," he whispered. "I go now to the king." He slipped away.

She gulped, folded her hands in her lap, looked appealingly at the shrine. The falcon's eyes gazed at her, adamant, yet not without understanding.

Adrastes entered the tent, a swagger in his walk that had not been there before. "My lady Chryse," he said, sweeping his cloak into a bow.

"Your Eminence," she returned, and swallowed again, gathering her wits.

"You are upset, my lady," he said softly, as if chiding her for feeling. "What is the matter?"

Chryse told the first lie she had ever told. "I—I am concerned about the battle tomorrow." Then, truthfully, "I am concerned for my lord's safety."

"Charming," said Adrastes, seating himself and taking one of her hands. "Your devotion to your lord is an inspiration to us all."

"My thanks," she said politely, even as she drew away from him. His robes emanated an odd scent, musky herbs and stale blood. "If you will excuse me, please, Your Eminence, I am weary. . . ."

"Of course. I wished only to pay you my respects." His talonlike hand caressed hers, his eyes probed her eyes as intimately as if they were exploring fingertips on her body. No longer the kindly avuncular prelate—with an effort she reclaimed her hand.

"Good night, then." Another bow, another stare, and the tent flap dangled listlessly behind him.

Chryse stumbled from her chair to the shrine, fell to her knees, and sobbed out her dilemma. The falcon listened.

At last she fell asleep, a tired child, on the carpet before the shrine. The lamp continued burning, a pinprick of light in the eyes of the image, a blush on Chryse's cheeks. Outside the tent the wind sang a wordless song, and somewhere in her troubled dreams she heard.

Danica and Bellasteros stood side by side, just outside the encampment, gazing toward the horizon. The rim of the plateau was a dark knife-edge against the stars. The moon was almost round, flattened a little on one side; its silvery light spilled over the camp, blending each tent, each horse, each sentry into a pale unity.

"Listen to the wind," said Danica. "Look at the sky."

Bellasteros lifted his eyes. The starlight touched them, polishing them into rich, dark gems. "I hear, I see . . . peace to come, and these abandoned fields flourishing again. The gods contented, and men no longer killing men—and women—in their names."

"May your dreams be prophetic," Danica told him. But even as she spoke a shiver caught her neck. Foolish, she thought, to glance around as if eyes watched me. . . . She looked around. The young priest Declan hesitated a few steps away, trading polite salutations with Lyris.

Bellasteros turned to see what she was looking at. "Declan?" he called. "The message was received, I hear; the terms agreed on. Surely you can rest this night, after such service."

At Danica's nod Lyris let him pass. He joined the king and queen on the slight prominence where they stood, and he, too, lifted his eyes to the sky, opened his ears to the wind. "I have yet another service to give you, my lord—and lady. And a confession to make."

Danica's brows arched up her forehead and she glanced at Bellasteros. He shrugged imperceptibly. "Speak."

"I listened through the fabric of your tent, my lord, last night. I watched through a rent in Patros's tent. I heard, I saw, everything."

Bellasteros vented a short laugh. "I had thought," he said to Danica, "that we were figures on a game board. Now it seems as if we are also actors in a play.''

''One written by a major tragedian, at the least,'' she responded.

''My apologies, my lord, my lady. I meant no harm. I had to know . . . the truth.''

''And which truth is that?'' asked Bellasteros.

Declan frowned a moment, glancing from face to face, choosing his words carefully. But neither face held more than a fey amusement. Inhaling, he said, ''The truth that there is no battle between Ashtar and Harus. That . . . some people are too quick to hate, when your—forgive me—when your love and your compassion are what the gods intend.''

''I shall surely be damned,'' said Danica in amazement. ''A man who would not condemn for who I am?''

''No, my lady. I have come to admire you and your goddess as well. But there is one who works evil against you, and who would like to see you damned.''

''You need name no names,'' said Bellasteros quickly.

''No, my lord. I wish only to warn you. He, who will be nameless, but whose pride is limitless, he and your general last night worked the blackest of sorcery, calling the spirit of your old nurse.''

A gasp in Bellasteros's throat, pain and dismay. ''And she thought that she would have nothing to fear after death.''

''I sensed her lost spirit,'' said Danica. ''The goddess protects her own; fear not for her soul. But for you . . .''

''They know?'' Bellasteros croaked. His cheeks paled, and he stiffened as if he expected Declan, with this admission, to turn on him.

''They know. As do I. They condemn you for it. I do not. I—would serve you, my lord, and not them.''

Bellasteros said nothing, turning away, gazing intently into the darkness. His fate come upon him at last. Oh, my love, Danica thought, aching for him, but she managed to summon a smile for Declan. ''Our thanks,'' she said. ''We shall need such courage in our service.'' And, with a sidelong glance at the conqueror, ''Go now. Pray to Harus for our victory.''

Declan bowed. With one tentative hand he touched the star-shield. It murmured gently—remote, muffled chimes. ''I brought this matter to the lady Chryse,'' he said. ''Just . . . to let you know.''

No placid cow, she—this should be most interesting. "My thanks," Danica said again. Declan hurried away, disappearing among the ghostly shapes of the tents. Danica turned to Bellasteros. "So that was Mardoc's game this evening. Pitiful man; his deepest certainties betrayed, and his love for you turned to hate."

"Adrastes has much to pay for," murmured Bellasteros. "The day after the morrow, when I have a moment to deal with him. When I shall no longer need him."

"We might all be dead by then, and so it will no longer matter."

"You cannot cheer me that easily, my lady."

They stood in silence for a few moments, not looking at each other, sharing their private thoughts without words. The camp was so quiet that a passing sentry's footsteps sounded like a cavalry charge. At last Bellasteros stirred, drawing himself up. But he was still pale. "So it has happened, that which has hung over me for so long, that which I feared when I first fell under your spell. . . ."

He was jesting, releasing a grim humor, and she did not bridle; she touched him.

"But it was your spell that delivered me from fear." He smiled tightly. "I must be strong. I must feel not dismay but relief. That accursed priest has made his discovery too late; he cannot denounce me now, the day before the battle. If he moves against me, we can move against him, for his word will no longer be credited."

"Indeed," Danica said. "Let his own pride destroy him." The shield whirled in quick motes of light. "But we must watch our backs, my lord. Such as Adrastes do not fight honorably."

Bellasteros's reply was direct, explicit. Danica had to nod agreement. They shared a long look, denying their fear; then they turned and walked down the gentle slope into the camp. Lyris followed, her usual few paces behind. "Declan," Bellasteros said thoughtfully. "I thought I liked his face."

Danica did not quite hear him. Eyes on the back of her neck—really, this was becoming tiresome. She raised her shield. It swirled again, growing brighter.

Bellasteros watched her. "A cup of wine, a stirrup cup?" he asked.

"Unwatered Sardian wine?" she responded.

He cleared his throat. "Perhaps, then, no stirrup cup. Sleep."

"And gentle dreams. Good night, my lord."

"Good night, my lady."

Their fingertips touched. So quickly, she thought, do you become my friend. She let her smile linger on his back as he directed his steps to his own tent.

The moonlight cast strange, distorted shadows on the ground, and it was hard to tell where shadow ended and substance began. Her smile faded, her shoulder blades crawled. Nothing, nothing but the unease. . . .

Bellasteros walked hesitantly, looking back again and again to where she still stood, soft-silvered by the moon, her shield a luminescent glow at her side. Uneasy. . . .

A solitary figure leaped from the shadows at her back, sword upraised and glinting with cold light. Bellasteros shouted, spun about, ran. Danica whirled and the sword stroke landed with a peal of sound on the shield's rim.

Danica, her footing unsure, staggered back. Her assailant's sword fell again, slicing her cloak and glancing off the chain mail beneath. Solifrax lit the night, lightning called from heaven, and the attacker quailed.

But Lyris was there first. Her attack was clumsy, but her heart was in it. She beat the dim figure away from Danica, stroke after stroke falling so quickly that the assailant could barely fend them off. Danica recovered herself; her slender blade turned and cut, and the man fell hamstrung into the dirt.

Bellasteros threw himself on the man, his knee grinding into his back, his hand tearing the sword from the other's grasp. "Are you injured?" the king asked. The corners of his eyes cast upward in a frenzy of anger and dread.

Danica caught her breath and leaned easily on her sword. "I am uninjured, but my cloak will surely not survive this night." She exaggerated; a shining streak across her corselet showed the force of the blow, and her ribs still shivered. But the noise had waked several Sardian soldiers, including Patros, from their sleep; now they gathered about the scene with lamps held high. On their heels came Atalia, Ilanit, and Shandir, weapons drawn.

"Are you injured?" Atalia asked.

Danica waved away Shandir's inspection. "No, thanks to

Lyris, and to your training of her, my weapons master.''

Atalia beamed on Lyris, and the woman looked down at her feet in confusion. ''This much I owe you all. Would that I had killed the wretch.''

''No,'' said Bellasteros, hauling the miscreant to his feet and shaking him like a lion shakes its prey. ''No, I have a question or two for him.''

And in the gathered light of lamp, of shield and sword, Danica for the first time saw her attacker's face. ''You!'' she exclaimed, and then she bit her tongue. The dark face of the man who had killed Theara, sullen now, underlip outthrust, but bestial still. Mardoc and Adrastes were behind this—she dared not speak.

Bellasteros read her hesitation well. ''Patros!'' he ordered. ''Have the centurions form up these men at the edge of the camp.'' And, spying Aveyron hovering uncertainly at the back of the crowd, ''You! Take the prisoner.''

Aveyron looked right and left, as if for an escape; with a deep sigh he seized the other man's arms. Atalia, too, stepped forward to guard him. The lamps disappeared, one by one, as the soldiers moved away, and again moonlight bathed the camp in cool anonymity.

''Hern,'' Shandir said, naming the attacker to Bellasteros and Danica both. And, under her breath, ''Mardoc's spy in Sabazel this autumn.''

''The man who killed Theara,'' said Danica. ''See, the half-healed wound where Lyris cut him.''

Bellasteros bent, picking up several coins scattered on the ground where Hern had lain. ''Who was meant to kill you. Paid well for his efforts, I see. By whom?'' His jaw twitched, his eyes burned brighter than Solifrax itself.

''My lord,'' said Aveyron suddenly, as if ridding himself of some distasteful potion. Hern looked around at him, struggled, and spat curses. Atalia's sword brushed the stubble on his chin, silencing him.

''Yes, soldier?''

''I—I saw him, too,'' Aveyron grimaced, ''leading the attack on the Sabazian camp . . .'' That was not all he had meant to say; Danica glanced, one brow arched, at Bellasteros, and his nod agreed with her intuition. If he knows more, she thought, his knowledge terrifies him. Not that I blame him. No use questioning him, tracking such an elusive scent;

they would only frighten him further.

"Who paid you?" Bellasteros demanded of Hern.

Hern saw his fate in the king's eye; he set his jaw and remained silent.

"By all the gods!" exclaimed Bellasteros, out of patience. "I shall not stand for this! Take him, there, before the troops." Atalia lowered her sword; Aveyron dragged Hern beyond the ring of tents.

"Treachery," Danica said, in a chill resignation.

Bellasteros shuddered with fury. "I fear—Harus alone knows my fear. I cannot name it. It seems as if we must walk into the trap, Danica; we shall not know what it is until it is sprung."

"Yes." She sheathed her sword and turned a brief smile to Ilanit's worried frown. "It will be good to know, at last. . . ."

"Indeed." Bellasteros jingled the coins in his hand and turned decisively toward the edge of the camp. "You will come?"

"No. Let Sardis take its vengeance. I shall sleep; and hope more than ever for gentle dreams."

"Then sleep, my lady. . . ." He was gone, Solifrax a glimmer of gold beside him.

The shield sighed into quiescence. "Come," Danica said, leading her warriors toward their own camp. She sensed, with one brief quiver of her consciousness, that Mardoc watched silently from a distant shadow. You strike, but your aim is bad, she thought. And now one whom you have corrupted dies in your stead. . . . Shameful, Mardoc, a shameful coil for Sardis's great general.

Behind them Bellasteros's voice, caught by a fitful breeze, rang out: ". . . such lawlessness—murder—disgrace to the honor of a Sardian . . ."

Patros's voice, equally intent.

"No, I would not sully Solifrax with his blood. Centurion . . ."

A cry, short and sharp, rending the sky. And the wind, pouring in great waves from the vault of night, cleansing starlight and moonlight of the acrid scent of death.

Adrastes was unperturbed. "So Bellasteros has killed the only man who knows of our message to Bogazkar. How subtly the gods work."

"But the witch-queen yet lives."

The priest regarded Mardoc's florid face impatiently. "So, a minor setback. Let her enjoy her few remaining hours of life. Tomorrow I shall pit my powers against hers."

"Yes, Your Eminence," said the general grudgingly. And, as he turned from the tent, "Tomorrow, then, death." His face was hollow-eyed and thin-lipped, the bones of cheek and jaw standing out in great shadowed ridges.

Adrastes chuckled quietly. "An honor, Mardoc, to die in the name of Harus. An honor indeed." But whether he spoke of Danica or of Mardoc himself was hard to tell.

Atalia stood guard over Danica as she tossed and mumbled in the grip of one nightmare after another. Atalia prayed, affirming her devotion to Ashtar, affirming her devotion to Danica, sending the agony of her faith skyward like the smoke of a burnt offering. "Your will, Mother, not my will but yours, and the life of this your daughter. . . ."

At last Danica's furrowed brow smoothed, and she slept, dreaming of peace and a world where peace was possible.

Chapter Fifteen

A HAND TOUCHED HIM, and Bellasteros struggled up from a fathomless well of sleep. Thin gray night shading to dawn—the battle fixed, and this day the fulfillment of destiny. . . .

"Forgive me," said Chryse. "I told Patros I would wake you."

He roused himself, leaned on one arm, took the hand she proffered. Her face was thinner, her eyes sunk deep. "What is it?" he asked.

"I—I know of your birth, my lord."

He winced. "Yes, my fate is upon me. Perhaps we should have the herald declare it to the camp."

His jest escaped her. "Oh, no, no; I shall not betray you. I spent the night thinking, praying, dreaming of strange places and strange gods. . . ."

"As do many of us, these days."

Her hand tightened on his, demanding his attention. "Marcos, I respect you too deeply, I love you too deeply, to believe that you could have turned heretic. So it must be that our definition of heresy is wrong. That . . . His Eminence is wrong. It is you who are in the right, and the queen of Sabazel with you—that must be."

"That is," he replied. "How you must have struggled with such thoughts, Chryse. I am pleased."

"Are you?"

Some men, Bellasteros thought, would have beaten her for daring to think at all. He lifted her hand to his lips; I have wronged you, Chryse, down these many years, over and over. And I need you, too; reassure me. . . .

"His Eminence frightens me," she continued, frowning, seeking comfort in his strength. "At times you frighten me, but never in the same way. He—he came to me, he touched me. . . ."

"He dares even to set himself in my place?" Bellasteros exclaimed. "Evil has taken him, Chryse."

"Yes. I believe so." She bent to kiss her husband lightly on the cheek. In all the years they had been together she had never once been that forward.

Bellasteros returned her kiss, as gently as he could. "What do you wish, my lady?"

For a moment she hesitated, her teeth set into her lower lip. Then, gulping, she met his eyes. "I wish a son for you and Danica. An heir, to the Empire you have won. Peace for men and for the gods."

"If it is a son, then you will have him as your own. You are my first wife, and will remain so."

She smiled. Her eyes glistened. "My thanks that you should think so highly of me. . . ." She pulled herself away and stood. "Victory, my lord. Victory, and the Empire at your feet."

"My thanks to you." He lay back after she left, staring up at the fabric above his head, listening to the shouts of the centurions beyond. So Adrastes dares to court my wife even before I am dead—dead at his hand, no doubt, in the flush of victory. I was helpless to move against him, until he moved first; but now . . . He will strike first, he has already struck, at Danica.

Bellasteros sat up and with a decisive movement threw the covers from his body. "You have much to pay for, Adrastes Falco," he said aloud, and he reached for his armor, his helmet, his sword.

Danica caught her breath sharply. "Forgive me," Shandir said. She bound the last bandage around her queen's bruised ribs with a touch as light as the fall of an eyelash.

"No, no," said Danica. "You did not hurt me; the baby kicked me."

"Strong as his father?"

"Indeed." Danica slipped on her shirt and corselet. "Shandir, is it a boy?"

"Judging by the way it lies within you, yes. But it would be just like a child of Bellasteros's to go its own way, shattering our expectations."

Danica shot a searching glance at her friend. Shandir was smiling, her eyes dancing. "If he has changed," the queen said, "then so have we all. If you had told me at last midwinter's moon where I would be, what I would be doing and thinking at this one . . . I would surely have thought you mad."

"It is just as well, then, that I cannot foresee the future." The healer began rolling up the remaining bandages and stowing them away.

"Shandir"—Danica sighed—"my friend, my shield . . . I have sadly neglected you of late."

"As you said; we have all changed."

Softly, "And you do not condemn me for it?"

"No. Your destiny is with him, beyond the borders of Sabazel. Who am I to condemn the will of the gods—particularly when you are gods yourselves."

"Ah, Shandir," Danica said. And there were no more words; an embrace, a kiss, and the queen once more turned to her armor and her weapons.

Lyris knelt at Chryse's feet. "Forgive me, lady, for the grief I have brought you."

"Lyris, no. I have brought you grief far beyond any nightmare. . . ." She shivered and looked over her shoulder, but no one was there save a serving-woman packing away the shrine. "Here, this, as a token of my sorrow."

Lyris looked in dismay at the gold chain she held. "My lady . . . I shall never return to Sardis—I cannot. . . ."

Chryse hushed the woman as she would her own daughter, raised her to her feet, and embraced her. "Guard the lady of Sabazel, Lyris. She needs you more than I."

Declan helped to load the lush appointments of Adrastes's wagon. The high priest stood nearby, a dim shape in the darkness, talking to Mardoc, quietly, urgently, as if he were giving orders to the general of Bellasteros's army.

Mardoc made a smart about-face and strode away. He

passed so close to Declan that he could have touched the young priest but did not see him. His eyes were pyres of madness.

Declan leaned his forehead against the closed doors of the jeweled shrine, touching in thought the gold image inside. "Harus, protect your own, I beg you; intercede with your lady Ashtar for us. . . ."

Adrastes raised his hands, molding the mist before him into the shape of a woman. And with a gloating smile he crushed the small form into nothingness.

A dawn for binding up relationships as raw wounds are bound, carefully but firmly. . . . Danica came up behind Atalia as the woman saddled her horse.

"Would you betray me if my birth were proved to be under Harus's wing?" she asked quietly.

Atalia looked at her in surprise. "You are Ashtar's daughter. My loyalty cannot be swayed. Do you not believe that, Danica?"

"I meant only . . . a supposition. . . ." But no. Atalia burned with a love and a faith as intense as death itself. "I am honored to have you by my side," Danica told her, and with a grave kiss turned away.

It was that uncertain hour between dark and dawn. In the east a faint blush rose up the sky, licking at the stars. A light mist hung tattered over the army as it prepared to move out; each man looked uneasily at the phantom shape of the man next to him, wondering if before the day was out that mortal form would indeed be nothing but phantom memory.

Atalia glowered grudging acceptance at the falcon standards, one held by Aveyron at Bellasteros's side, the other held by Mardoc himself in one last, desperate pledge of faith. The bronzed images rode upon the mist, swooping and circling, seeking their prey.

Danica watched the red plume and the red cloak, muted now in the feeble light, neither sun nor moon nor stars, that presaged the dawn. Bellasteros spoke quietly with Patros and laid a smile like a benediction upon Ilanit's tousled head. And there, too, she thought, a love that hurts like a battle wound. . . .

Ilanit returned to her place with the Sabazians, her eyes

downcast. Patros and Bellasteros went to the front of the column. For one moment the conqueror's eyes sought and found Danica's; they were calm and confident beyond faith, confident with certain knowledge. And I, too, have seen the gods, Danica thought to him. Strength, my love, for the ordeal ahead.

His mouth softened, twitched, firmed again. We shall meet again before Iksandarun or in paradise. . . . He raised Solifrax, she lifted the star-shield, and with a salute they parted.

The army moved forward. The chill gloom echoed with footsteps, hoofbeats, the creaking of the carts in the baggage train as it laboriously followed. Shandir rode there, and Chryse and Declan, and Adrastes in his luxurious wagon. Its wheels stirred Hern's unmarked grave.

A darkness loomed in the mist, a hint of the edge of the plateau. Bellasteros, Patros, Mardoc splashed across a thin stream, through a stand of stunted poplars, and with one last glint of the falcon standards disappeared. Swiftly Danica and her Companions dismounted, consigning their beasts to the care of Bellasteros's horse master. Their path and that of the archers diverged from the army's, leading instead along the course of the stream to where, the scouts reported, it fell from the top of the plateau down a narrow defile.

It was a walk of less than an hour, away from the low reverberation of the army, through spiky, knee-high grass. The strands of mist were like lethenderum, Danica thought, the crushed grass an intriguing scent of sage. Marcos Bellasteros, the name a caress. . . . She shook her head and settled her mended cloak more securely about the telltale curves of her body.

The plateau rose before them. "Not as steep as the cliff of Azervinah," Atalia announced, peering up into tumbled blotches and streaks of shadow.

And there was the defile, twisting upward, blotted with mist, its top lost in darkness against a dark sky. It was steep and rocky, but it could be climbed; it was filled with thornbushes, dwarf oak, and hazel, an occasional tamarisk anchored to solid stone—perfect cover.

At Danica's nod Atalia stepped light-footed through the trickle of stream and across the loose rock at the mouth of the defile. She eased around one large boulder, used an overhanging branch to hoist herself into shadow.

Danica gestured at the archers, but their commander waved them back. "You are to go first, my lady," he said politely, "clearing the way for us. We are not accustomed to such climbing."

True enough—but she had to ask. "Whose orders?"

"General Mardoc's."

Every fiber of her body jerked itself into singing tautness and she felt her face flush. She cast a glance at the archer so keen that he stepped back, confused. But no, this man did only as he was told, not a traitor but an innocent dupe. "Very well," she said. "I shall expect you to guard our backs."

"Of course," he said. He patted the bow arching over his shoulder, full of his own ability.

Atalia was poised between two boulders, looking back curiously. Danica could not quite see her face in the gloom. Suspicious? Resigned? "Up," Danica ordered Ilanit, and, taking Lyris aside, "Stay with my daughter, I beg you."

"What?"

"I cannot explain. Please." Puzzled, Lyris turned and followed Ilanit. For a moment Danica watched them clambering upward behind Atalia, and the other Companions behind them. I took the shield from my mother's dead hands before Iksandarun, she thought with a grim precision. Ilanit is young, too young—but she must live to take the shield from me, live to hear the goddess's words stir her mind, if Ashtar so wills it.

Danica started her climb. The boulder, the branch, one foot in a cleft—the shield was heavy, her mail was heavy, the child lay a still, heavy weight in her belly. But on the plateau of Iksandarun the game would end, for good or for ill.

A light fell on her, a hint of warmth, and she started. Clinging to a root she turned and looked back. The sun rose, a flare of red along the horizon washing away the stars, and then the blazing disc itself burned a hole in the sky. The mist thinned and vanished. The plains lay before her, dim shapes and smudges solidified into hills and fields. And the Sardian army moved into battle, weapons glittering, trumpets singing high and sweet, banners fluttering.

The pieces move onto the game board, Danica thought. The conqueror comes to claim his victory. She rode at his side, her hand and his together on the hilt of shining Solifrax, his arm and hers together bearing the weight of the shield. . . . She blinked, returned to her precarious position in the ravine. The archers were looking at her, waiting for her to move on.

She moved up into lingering curls of mist and damp, earth-scented air.

The mist thinned and vanished. Fitful puffs of breeze stirred the flags.

Patros emitted a shaky breath. "Look."

Bellasteros looked. The imperial army might have shrunk considerably since the days of Kallidar's glory, but it was still imposing. Cavalry in sparkling armor, archers, their bows bent, rows of infantry with their shields high, reflecting the morning sun. Elephants, tusks banded with gold. Chariots, each wheel armed with the sharp blade of a scythe.

Bellasteros shouted his orders; the centurions wheeled, right and left, forming their soldiers into the phalanx, an impenetrable wall of shields, spears, and swords held by the youngest soldiers with the veterans just behind. Mardoc and his standard led the cavalry to the far flank.

The two armies watched each other in silence. For a moment Bellasteros sensed the enclosing walls of a rocky defile, damp, earth-scented air around him. Danica, the name a caress. . . . Would the army turn against me now, he wondered, if they knew of my birth? But no, by Harus, that nightmare has lost its power to wound.

The sun was at his back. A falcon coasted across the sky before him, shrieking a battle cry; the Sardians greeted this omen with a great shout. Bellasteros laughed. "In the name of the god!" he called, carefully calling no god by name; he drew Solifrax and thrust it upward. It caught the sunlight and flared, a pure crystalline flame before the army of Sardis.

The officers of the imperial army drew their swords and with them beat their reluctant levies into position. The elephants, goaded, screamed.

Solifrax spat lightning. The army of Sardis lunged forward. The falcon images seemed to screech and flutter on their poles.

With a rumble the chariots began to move. The imperial archers strung their bows and let fly.

"In your name, Harus," Bellasteros cried. "In your name, Ashtar!" But his soldiers were also shouting, a great wave of sound that by itself deflected the rain of arrows, and no one heeded his strange words.

•   •   •

A distant shout flooded the still morning air. The wagon stopped. Adrastes did not even look up from the small clay figure he had shaped. Two green beads for eyes. A long strand of yellow flax for hair. A scrap of wool for a cloak. The figure's breasts and belly swelled grotesquely.

Adrastes pressed a lead pellet into the clay, and another, and another. He muttered over the tiny flame that burned before him, and it sparked.

The still morning air filled with the shouts of many voices. The distant cry of one voice echoed in Danica's mind. In your name, Ashtar. . . . So the battle was joined. But she had no attention to spare for it. She was as clumsy, she chided herself, as she had been the night before when Hern had attacked her; she moved like some lumbering elephant. Atalia dropped back to aid her, grasping her hand and pulling her bodily up a steep slope.

"Forgive me," gasped Danica, clinging to a tamarisk root and wiping the sweat from her eyes.

"You bear too much weight," Atalia said laconically.

"True. . . ." She looked up. Pale blue sky glinted between the bare branches of the trees. The stream burbled happily, oblivious of the many feet disturbing its course. Ilanit and Lyris clambered from rock to branch to rock like cats, almost at the top; the other Companions were close behind.

She looked down. The archers had fallen back, huffing and puffing indignantly.

There was not the faintest hint of a breeze in the defile; the air was moribund. Danica's senses pricked, sending gooseflesh flowing over her body. She cast a tendril of her mind into the shield and it rippled in a quick luminescence.

Her body grew even heavier and she slumped against the root. It was as if a great hand pressed her into the ground. "Mother!" she murmured. "Please . . ."

Sorcery. Adrastes practiced sorcery against her—he was strong, and her strength was spread thinly. . . . A most effective spell, she thought with acid admiration, playing upon her weakest point.

A shout from the top of the rock, the flash of weapons, a scream. Ilanit came sliding back down in a flurry of dirt, matted leaves, pebbles; Lyris scrabbled at her heels. "Ambush!" Ilanit cried. "They are waiting for us!"

She did not need to speak. Imperial soldiers crashed down into the ravine, swords raised. Two Companions sprang forward, drawing their weapons, and were slaughtered before they found their footing.

Lyris and Atalia turned to Danica. "Up!" said the older woman, and began to push her queen straight up the side of the defile.

Danica shoved her away, trying to pluck her sword from its scabbard. The shield wavered with a watery light but her hand was leaden, not moving. . . . "Up!" Atalia said again.

Another Companion leaped forward and fell. The Sardian archers, to their credit, were taking cover and firing. But their arrows were worse than useless in these tight confines. "Stop!" Danica shouted at them as one flying shaft nicked Lyris's breastplate and embedded itself in a tree trunk.

They stopped. Ilanit and Lyris seized Danica's arms and pulled at her; she seemed rooted to the ground. Atalia turned, plunging upward to intercept the soldiers. She struck one down, and another; a third, an officer, leaped by her, heading as straight for Danica as if he had been given a description of her. Atalia threw herself after him. They fell together into the stream, armor crashing, water splashing in prismatic droplets around them.

Ilanit jumped to the rescue. The officer raised his sword. Atalia seized it, heedless of its deep bite into her hand, trying to turn it. . . . He held a dagger in his other hand, and he drove it through her throat.

"Atalia!" Danica screamed, but her voice was only a sick wail. She could not move, she was slipping backward, the shield was falling from her arm, its light winking out. . . .

The low sound of Adrastes's incantation lay heavy on the air, sinking like a heavy cloak around Declan and Chryse as they whispered together beside his wagon. "No one will think it odd that you are here," he said.

"I . . . will try," she breathed.

"You can do it," Declan assured her. And, thrusting his head between the hangings, he called, "Your Eminence, a message from General Mardoc!"

The incantation stopped. A flurry of breeze flicked the hangings as Adrastes emerged. "Where?" he demanded.

Declan pointed to where most of the waiting folk had

gathered on a low hill, watching the light-mottled shapes of the battling armies. "A page said the messenger is over there; come, I will guide you."

The high priest stalked off, his robes fluttering behind him, the pectoral dark on his chest. Declan cast one wide-eyed glance at where Chryse huddled and followed.

Chryse threw herself frantically around the corner and at the tailboard of the wagon, climbed in, slipped and fell, blew out the lamp, and grasped the figurine in a trembling hand. She peered out; Declan had lost Adrastes in the throng and was circling back. "Here!" she hissed as soon as he drew close. "Take the accursed thing!"

Declan took it, groaned, and helped Chryse climb down.

A few moments later, before the gilded shrine in Chryse's cart, Shandir removed the lead pellets, picked out the beads, the flax, the shred of wool, and molded the soft clay into a small round disc. With the point of her dagger she incised a many pointed star upon it.

Chryse and Declan, using two embroidery needles, pried a flake of gold leaf from the shrine. Shandir pressed it onto the shape of the star. She laid the miniature shield before the image of the god.

She looked up at her fellow conspirators with a sigh. "Now we pray," she said.

Declan took one of the women's hands in each of his hands. "Harus," he began, "Ashtar, we beseech you; as you love your son and your daughter, they need you now; obviate this evil spell. . . ."

Shandir and Chryse closed their eyes and bowed their heads. A tear sparkled on the Sardian woman's cheek.

The glided image of Harus shifted, its feathers ruffling themselves. And the tiny star flared with a clear radiance.

"Mother!" Danica gasped. She summoned her strength, letting it pour, hot, stinging, through her body. And like a sodden cloak lifted from her shoulders, the spell vanished. She was still clumsy; she still bore a heavy weight. But she could move. "Atalia!" she cried, but the woman lay unmoving. The officer scrambled over her body, trying to reach the queen. Too late; Ilanit was on him, and Lyris with her; cursing him they struck, one after the other, and the water in the stream flowed suddenly crimson.

Danica leaped from her perch and leaned over Atalia; the woman's sightless eyes gazed toward the sky, her faith at last united with her god.

Danica settled her shield on her arm, set her teeth together. I shall avenge you, my mentor, I shall make them pay, Adrastes and Mardoc both. . . . She stood, calling the remaining Companions. The shield flamed, a clear radiance driving the shadows of root and branch rushing upward, driving the dawn gloom to shatter against daylight. And the light of the sun spilled over the crest of the plateau, flooding the ravine with brilliance.

The imperial soldiers quailed, looking about them, hesitating.

Danica called again, and a breeze came from nowhere, whistling up the defile, gathering dirt and leaves into tiny, angry spouts of spinning wind. The Sabazians drove forward, their swords flickering red. The astonished Sardians gathered up their arrows and followed. The star-shield sang, one high, sustained note of power.

The surviving imperial soldiers scrambled over the rim of the defile and fled. Danica designated two Companions and a Sardian to gather up the dead and wounded; she refused to count how many Sabazians lay dead, but they were many. I cannot mourn you now, my friends, she thought. Later, your shades will be laid to rest, I promise you. She hesitated just below the brink of the ravine and with a weeping Ilanit looked back to Atalia's still form. She, too, died for me—Ashtar! Give me the strength to avenge them all!

A falcon fluttered down from the sky and perched on a branch overhanging Atalia's body. The shield snapped. "Harus is also with us." Danica sighed, oddly comforted; Ilanit swallowed her tears and saluted the messenger of the god. Stained with mud and blood, the Sabazians clambered out of the ravine and stood upon the crest of the plateau.

A distant blue-green shimmer on the horizon, the gleaming spread tail of a peacock—Iksandarun. A smudge against the sky beyond—the sheltering mountains.

An archer stumbled, and Danica turned to glare at him. "This way," she said. "Follow me."

The imperial chariots made one deadly sweep through the Sardians and then spun back into the pass. The imperial archers loosed one more volley and faded into the infantry. The elephants stamped and bellowed, shaking their tusks, but they, too, soon turned back.

"Just as we thought," Bellasteros said to Patros. "They feign a retreat through the pass."

"The real battle will be above. Where Bogazkar waits, I wager."

The conqueror shouted orders, sending pages scurrying. His horse reared and pranced and Solifrax magnified the sunlight tenfold. The Sardians moved forward, marching in good order. The imperial army sucked itself through the pass, leaving a few outriders who were soon overrun by the advancing troops.

Mardoc watched from beneath his standard, his eyes shifting again and again to the side, down the rocky slopes of the plateau to where the ravine was lost in a haze of dust and sunlight. His seamed face split into a smile, but his eyes still burned.

Adrastes struck Declan down into the dirt and kicked him where he lay. "You turned your back for an instant! You took your eyes from my wagon! You fool, you damned moronic jackass! . . ."

Declan crouched, unmoving. A woman's robes swirled near his eyes. Chryse's voice, thin, quavering, and yet tautly intense, spoke. "Your Eminence. I called him to my side. If I did wrong, forgive me. . . ."

Disgusted, Adrastes abandoned the crumpled form of the priest. "No, you did no wrong. I beg your pardon, my lady. . . ." He was gone.

Shandir hurried from concealment to lift Declan's head into her lap. "He will be all right," she assured Chryse.

Chryse glanced tensely over her shoulder, watching for the feathered robes of the high priest, watching for some message from the battlefield.

The reserve imperial troops waited, hidden in the ruined fortress atop the pass. They peered through whatever cracks they could find in the shattered stones, watching their army stream from the pass and re-form on the plateau. They did not notice the Sardian archers climbing up behind them.

The Sabazians waited outside the tumbled gates of the fort

to pick off whatever imperial troops escaped the bowmen. Danica climbed up the stump of a watchtower, finding toe and handholds between the great weathered stones. At the top she stopped, muted the shield, caught her breath.

The view was magnificent, even without her extended senses. With them, casting her thought over the battlefield like a circling falcon, she saw the exact lie of the armies. There, to her right, the imperial army filled the fields of winter wheat and barley that stretched to Iksandarun. Bogazkar himself was there, wearing the gold diadem of the emperor over the long black curls of his hair. His beard, too, curled long and shining black. An attendant held an embroidered parasol over his head, protecting him from the sun, and his charioteer held taut the reins of two white horses.

"Ah," Danica said. She turned. Ahead of her were the Sardians, just breasting the top of the pass. Bellasteros and his warhorse were in the lead, the red plume streaming in the wind, the wings of the falcon standard outspread. Solifrax emitted a light of its own, a solitary flame brighter than any other weapon. Her shield rang in response.

"Ah," she said again.

Bogazkar signaled. An officer close to the fort turned, raising his hand, drawing in his breath—the Sardian commander spoke first, and the officer fell pierced with an arrow.

Arrows rained into the fort and the imperial troops ran shrieking for the gates, only to be driven back by the waiting Sabazians. Danica clambered down and joined in, her sword dancing in the forefront of the fray. It was a savage pleasure, killing and killing again, knowing that each man who fell was one less to come in conquest over the borders of Sabazel.

The archers began to shoot fire arrows, directing them skillfully to the splintered and broken braces supporting the walls of the old fort. Flames leaped up, chasing a thick black smoke into the sky.

The Sardians drove forward, into the hesitating imperial army. Bogazkar signaled the chariots and the elephants forward; the huge feet rose and fell, the sharp tusks tossed, the gleaming scythes turned round and round, harvesting bloody death among the Sardian infantry.

But Danica saw, and she summoned the commander of the archers. At her instructions he grinned broadly. Within moments he and his best men had climbed the watchtower and sent their last arrows ripping into the great bodies of the elephants.

The animals shrieked, throwing off their drivers, dashing them into shreds in frantic pain. They seized the charioteers with their trunks, throwing them down among the battered bodies of their other victims; they crushed the chariots with their mighty feet and, cut by the scythes, raged off across the field to send the infantry howling for safety.

And there, Danica thought in grim satisfaction. And there, Bellasteros, blood enough even for you—she was dizzy, her thoughts spinning, hard to grasp—blood and death and destruction now . . . healing after, after. . . .

For a moment her knees trembled, a prickling cold chill flowing down her back, across her abdomen, through her legs. The child leaped and was pressed back as her muscles went into a quick, involuntary spasm.

Then the Sardian horse master was there, leading the Sabazian beasts safely through the battle. He said something, some compliment, perhaps—Danica did not hear it. Now, she thought, flinging away the chill, now to his side, the gates of Iksandarun and the end. I come, Bellasteros, I come, Mother. . . .

She jerked her mare's head around, pressed her knees into its side, and raced down the slope from the burning fort, plummeting into the battle so swiftly that Ilanit and Lyris and the Companions had to spur their beasts to keep up. They laughed and sang in a fell delight; the Sardians looked up at their voices, saluting them with smiles and comradely jests and upraised scarlet swords.

Except for Mardoc. From far across the field he saw the gleam of the star-shield, he heard the voices of the Sabazians. And his fever burned away, evaporating into the sunlight; his face drained of color, his eyes glazed, gray and frozen, the creases in his cheeks deepened themselves into icebound crevasses. "Death," he cried. "For Sardis and for Harus, death. . . ."

Imperial soldiers issued from the ruined fort on the side of the pass opposite the one that burned. Mardoc spun his troop of cavalry about so suddenly that his horse stumbled, its hooves seeking purchase in the stubble of the field. He waved the standard and the image of the falcon circled against the sky; he led his horsemen against the enemy soldiers as they sought to outflank the Sardians. The imperial soldiers fell beneath the falcon's wings and were trampled into the churned and bloody ground, for Mardoc had ordered no quarter be given.

"Well met!" Bellasteros shouted to Danica. "Well done, indeed, my lady!"

Aveyron hoisted his standard. Patros saluted Ilanit with a grin. The horses of the king and queen met and curvetted about one another. Danica wiped the soot and blood and sweat from her face and cried in an incandescent fury, "We were betrayed! The enemy waited for us—they knew even to look for me. I was enspelled, but Atalia saved me. Atalia is dead, my king. . . ." Her voice choked in her throat and she struck out blindly with her sword.

Bellasteros heard. His dark eyes, already burning with the fierce joy of battle, sparked into an even greater flame—rage, violent and implacable. "So they would murder you and all your warriors with vile treachery? So they would even imperil our victory?"

"Mardoc told the archers to stay back," Darcia said. "He knew, he knew, Bellasteros!"

Bellasteros screamed, the cry of a falcon falling upon its prey. Solifrax sliced the air into sparkling tatters. "Harus! Harus, attend me. . . ."

"Ashtar!" shrieked Danica. "Take me, now. . . ." And the power filled her to overflowing, melding her body and her shield into one blinding, gemlike flame.

Solifrax dipped and turned. Its point touched the shield. A star exploded upon the battlefield, and a wind pealed down from the azure dome of the sky. The bronzed falcon, ensorcelled, launched itself from its standard and shot upward, shrieking through the smoke, the stench, the screams of battle. It turned its blazing eyes toward the sun, and the sun flared.

As one, berserk, Bellasteros and Danica drove straight for the center of the imperial line. The Sabazians came behind them, their voices ringing in the paean. The Sardians flowed in a deadly wave across the field.

Bogazkar spun and fled, his parasol abandoned; it was crushed beneath the running feet of his soldiers as they fled behind him. And the ringing wind carried the Sabazian song of victory even to the walls of Iksandarun.

Chapter Sixteen

THE WESTERING SUN lingered above the battlements of Iksandarun, bathing them in light; their enameled bricks shone blue, green, gold, as if they were freshly painted, not scratched and faded with years of neglect.

The gates stood open; a delegation of imperial generals awaited. Their battered weapons lay in the dirt before them. And something else lay there: the bloodied form of Bogazkar, black curls matted, embroidered robes torn and stained.

"So," said Bellasteros. "His own officers killed him." He looked to his right, to the gray and shrunken figure of Mardoc, and to his left, to the hooded, malignant form of Adrastes.

Mardoc said nothing. Indeed, it seemed as if he did not even hear his king's words. His cold eyes rested on Danica as she stood just behind Bellasteros, and one corner of his lip rippled in a growl.

But Adrastes heard; he favored Bellasteros with a low bow and a bland smile. "So it seems, my lord. My emperor."

Declan stood behind him, his face swollen and bruised, escorting a veiled Chryse. Shandir followed, on the periphery of the knot of Sabazians; she glanced at Lyris, at Ilanit and Danica, searching for one more face, and at Danica's solemn shake of the head she groaned.

Mother, Danica prayed, just a little more strength, I beg you; sustain me a few more moments, it is not yet over. . . .

The shield hummed. The wind licked at the walls of the city, purring, settling around them like a great hunting cat. The wind kissed Danica's smeared and dirty face, cleansing it.

She was the wind, it seemed, coasting above the crowd, the victorious army and the defeated people; everything was focused in uncanny clarity, each face defined, each object painted with light. The blue and green of the gate, the red of Bellasteros's plume, the bronze of both falcon standards—each color shimmered before her eyes. Her sinews sang, taught, still angry but no longer berserk. Now she waited, ignoring the brief tremble that stroked her limbs.

And neither was Bellasteros's anger abated; it was only banked. She saw its embers burning hot in his eyes, in the set of his jaw and the line of his mouth, ready to be fanned again into flame at the first opportunity.

An imperial officer walked forward. He held in his hands the gold diadem of the emperor. "Mighty Bellasteros," he said with a deep obeisance, "please accept this, the symbol of the Empire."

Bellasteros did not move. The dark fire in his eyes held the man impaled for a long, breathless moment. A vast silence settled over field and city; even the lathered horses, held in a group to one side, and the distant shapes of the exhausted elephants stilled their cries. Only the wind spoke.

Bellasteros removed his helmet and handed it to Aveyron. He gestured. Patros took the diadem. Kneeling, he offered it to the king.

But the king gestured again. Yes, my lord, Danica said to herself. Let us make it clear, for all to see. . . . It was she who took the crown from Patros's hand and set it on Bellasteros's crisp dark hair. The gold gleamed on his brow, catching the light of his eyes. Ah, she thought, how well it suits you. She inclined her head, a brief movement of respect, but she said quietly, "You have won your Empire. Now you must rule it."

"I will," he returned with a quick smile. "I will."

As one the people of the Empire made obeisance to the new emperor, king of kings, god-king. And many of the Sardians bowed as well. But not Mardoc. Adrastes's bow was perfunctory; he never removed his eyes from the diadem. Their black glitter did not reflect the light of the crown, they swallowed it.

Bellasteros drew Solifrax, flourished it in a graceful arc against the sky. The falcons on their standards preened themselves. "Thanks be to the gods who brought this day," he said. "Harus, the patron of Sardis; Ashtar, the patron of Sabazel, our ally."

Adrastes glared at Bellasteros, realized the hardness of his look, blinked. Mardoc's breath caught in his chest.

A low murmur went through the Sardian army; the emperor, in his wisdom and courtesy, dares to name Ashtar; the emperor, in his glory, is favored of all gods and may name any one he likes.

Patros ordered a couple of soldiers forward to remove the body of Bogazkar. "An honorable funeral," Bellasteros said, "according to the rites of his own god."

The mass of imperial people sighed.

"Centurions!" called Bellasteros. "Any man of my army, Sardian, or other, who takes any object, who damages any property, who forces himself on any woman, will be punished. Rewards will come soon enough; now we are to uphold the honor of Sardis."

The centurions nodded. The army grumbled a moment in good-natured resignation. The mass of imperial people sighed again, in relief.

"Come," said Bellasteros to the imperial officer. "Walk by my side into the city."

Danica elbowed Adrastes aside and followed closely, a half pace behind. Not that the high priest would suddenly leap forward, dagger in hand . . . His evil glare struck her, and she turned it. You grow weak, she thought, your power wanes. As does mine. Her shield seemed now to float on her arm, buoyed up by its own faint luminescence; the child in her womb, concealed by her carefully pinned cloak, shifted restlessly, settling lower into her body, weighing more and more as each moment passed.

Aveyron and Mardoc bore the falcons behind the emperor, and the Sardians and Sabazians followed through the streets. If the people of Iksandarun did not cheer, they at least accepted their new ruler with the equanimity born of long misrule. The buildings the victors passed were ill kept, mortar flaking from between bricks, paint peeling; the public squares held only stunted fruit trees and dry fountains. Many houses seemed to be empty, their shutters banging on blank windows like the staring eyes of the dead.

Danica shivered. The city was, if possible, even more

decayed then when she made her disastrous visit over a decade ago. And yet she could sense some ghost of its former glory; columns and carvings on the public buildings, tangled gardens spilling sere, withered vines over intricate brickwork. Bellasteros would restore it; he had energy even for that. He had drawn the wind with him into the city and it played with the short-cropped tendrils of his hair.

The baby shifted again, pressing on the nerve that branched into Danica's right leg; a sharp pain shot down her thigh and her step faltered. Bellasteros glanced back at her, even as he continued expounding to the imperial officer about some point of law.

She smoothed her grimace, waving away his concern. The wind—the wind, a playful cat, its purr growing louder, jangling . . . That chill in the back of her neck, and her shoulders tightening.

They passed the brightly enameled walls of the palace, the only building in the city the recent emperors had cared to maintain. Guard posts were spaced at intervals along the walls, and the gates were those of a fortress. Obviously Bogazkar, and Kallidar before him, kept treasures inside that were well worth protecting. Bellasteros's own personal guard took over the posts.

The imperial officer led the company up a series of steps to the gates of the temple precinct. Several priests and priestesses—none of whom seemed to serve any particular deity—bowed a welcome. Bellasteros bowed in return, whispered an order to the officer, passed inside.

The officer stationed himself at the gates, allowing only a few people, Sardian and Sabazian, to follow the emperor. Then it is to be here, Danica thought. As much privacy as can be found at this moment. . . .

It was an ancient holy place, stirring with the ghosts of forgotten gods. Various stone and mud-brick temples were jumbled together around an irregular open space, few seeming in better repair than any other; the Empire had always been fickle in its allegiance, choosing whichever deity the moment made expedient. It was no accident, Danica told herself, that the shrine of Harus was freshly swept and garlanded. The image of the god, though only carved wood, gleamed with paint so fresh it was still wet.

Bellasteros bowed gravely before Harus and allowed Solifrax to lie for a moment on the great slab of an altar. The stone glistened, still damp from its cleaning, but no amount of scrubbing could remove the rusty stains that seemed bound inseparably to the ageless rock.

Danica turned aside, gathering her own people, and walked across the uneven pavement to the house of Ashtar. Its doors had not been opened since her mother's hand had shut them years before; Kallidar's seals still clung, weathered and faded, to the latch.

Danica drew her sword and sliced the seals cleanly in two. With the shield she shoved at the doors; creaking, they opened. The interior, a tiny columned chamber, a cobwebbed atrium, rustled with shadow. Ah, Mother, she sighed, not knowing if she called upon the goddess or her own mortal parent. The shield flared and the shadows for a moment fled.

A shout echoed from across the courtyard. A breeze whispered through the abandoned temple, stirring dust and dried leaves into almost discernible shapes. Danica pulled the doors shut again and turned. Her nerves snapped, plucked like the shortest string of a lyre. The unease dissipated into certainty.

Mardoc confronted Bellasteros, Adrastes at his side, speaking low and urgently. Patros ran across the bricks. "My lady, the emperor's respects, and would you please come? . . ."

A plump red sun hung low over the flat roofs of the city. The temple courtyard was filled with light like thick, fluid amber. Danica seemed to swim, slowly, painfully, toward Bellasteros where he stood on a dais with Declan and Chryse at his back. Aveyron held both standards now; the bronze falcons seemed to sit stolidly on their perches, waiting for what was to happen.

Danica halted, Lyris and Ilanit just behind her, Shandir to the side. A few other Companions stood with a handful of Sardian officers just inside the gates. "I am here," Danica said to Bellasteros.

The diadem was a row of flame across his brow, his eyes twin brands burning in a pale, stern face. Danica, said his thought, I would have prevented this; forgive me for laying this burden upon you. . . . His clear voice said, "Danica, queen of Sabazel, you stand accused of treason."

So we play the game to the end. She let her eyes widen in amused surprise. "I am Sabazel; how could I betray it?"

"Not Sabazel, lady; Sardis."

"And if you are Sardis, lord, I stand accused of betraying you?"

"You said it." Bellasteros's mouth crimped and straightened. "General Mardoc testifies that you bargained with Bogazkar to aid the troops flanking the pass. Is this true?"

She turned, swinging her gaze and her shield toward Mardoc. She might as well have confronted an ice-rimmed stone. "Those troops I was to aid," she said acidly, "killed my weapons master and others of my Companions. This general himself told the archers following me to stay back, knowing we would be ambushed; it is he who commits treason."

"You return the charge," stated Bellasteros, flat. "According to Sardian law, opposing charges must be settled with a trial by combat. To the death."

Adrastes stepped forward with swirl of his cloak. "You would listen to her, a heretic, a witch?"

"My bravest ally," Bellasteros told him. "Yes, I would listen to her."

Adrastes turned his glittering eyes on the emperor. The emperor did not blink. Not a muscle in his face tightened, but the high priest dropped his eyes, turning, drawing his cloak around himself like a shield.

Danica wanted to shout, to laugh, to cry. Every sinew in her body tensed; she considered the bricks where she stood, what kind of footing they offered. But her voice, calm, cool, said, "I am Sabazian. I am not bound by Sardian law. Only out of respect to you, lord, do I accede."

"And you?" Bellasteros said to Mardoc.

The general drew his sword and pointed at Danica with it. "She may not use her shield," he said hoarsely. "The shield carries sorcery, she may not use it in trial."

Gods! Danica turned an outraged glance on Bellasteros. He winced. "If she cannot use her shield," he said, "then your master Adrastes may not use his sorcery."

Adrastes drew himself up indignantly and turned a black look on Declan.

Declan returned his look evenly. "If you had not committed black sorcery, you would have no reason to fear its exposure."

Very good, Danica thought. She flexed her knees, rotated her shoulders.

Again Adrastes turned to Bellasteros. He opened his mouth, but the king forestalled him. "Declan is the model of righteousness. You should be grooming him as your successor, Your Eminence.''

Adrastes shut his mouth with a snap. He stalked away to stand in regal aloofness at the side of the dais. Patros, not at all unobtrusively, went to stand beside him, his hand resting on the hilt of his sword.

Wearily Danica slipped the shield from her arm and handed it to Ilanit. "I shall hold it gladly," the girl hissed under her breath, "but I shall not take it as you did from your mother; if he downs you, we shall strike."

"No," returned Danica. "Let it be played to the end. Let the emperor decide." Ilanit lifted the shield to her own arm, glanced from Danica's smoldering eyes to their reflection in Bellasteros's face, finally nodded and stepped aside.

The gathered officers muttered among themselves. Aveyron closed his eyes as if in pain, the knuckles of his hands standing white and sharp against the poles of the standards. Chryse turned away, hiding her face. "My own father," she breathed. "Dishonor to his name, to the name of the god." Declan set his hand firmly on her shoulder; his lips moved in prayer. The sunlight flickered, rippled like the surface of a pond by the wind.

Bellasteros wore the wind and the light like a numinous garment. He raised Solifrax, pure gold in the sunset, and formally, stiffly, he saluted Danica. But his thought was an impassioned cry: Mardoc, my mentor, no. . . . My queen, my strength is yours, I am yours, you shall not lose this trial. . . . He did not look at the general, abandoning him to his fate.

Mardoc, with a desperate curse, leaped from the dais.

Danica surprised herself with the cool clarity of her thought. She was remote, above the scene, watching herself like an impersonal participant in some exotic tableau. This place, an ancient place of sacrifice, bloodthirsty gods demanding payment for the gift of the Empire—for just a moment she faltered, knowing with a godlike certainty that Mardoc's death alone would not be enough, that Adrastes's coming fate would not be sufficient. . . . Then I shall fight the gods themselves!

Mardoc sliced at her and she danced back, spinning to the side, carrying her bulk as lightly as she could. But she was clumsy, oddly lopsided without her shield, and the pavement beneath her feet was rough—their blades met with a clang.

Their eyes met, her fiery green gaze striking him. He spat at her.

Danica thrust his sword away and spun again. He was slightly taller, she thought; his reach was slightly longer. But he carried a short Sardian stabbing sword, and she a saber. And he was old and mad and weary of his madness, and she bore the brightness of the emperor's eyes like a golden luminescence flowing through her body.

Mardoc struck, too fast, leaving little time between thrusts to gauge his moves. Danica beat back his attack, looking for an opening—there! She drew him to her left with a feint, leaped, struck. Her blade glanced down his cuirass and bit into his abdomen just below the edge of the metal.

A minor wound—her hand was weak, she told herself scornfully. He hardly even hesitated but pressed his attack. And his sword traced a bloody path down her left arm, slicing shirt and skin alike.

Danica saw rather than felt the wound. Counting on a shield that is not there, she thought. Encumbered by this damned cloak. I can do better. . . .

The courtyard spun around her, Ilanit's flushed face, Adrastes jostling Patros aside. Declan's cool stare bent on his superior—Bellasteros, unmoving, unblinking, glowing perceptibly with sunlight and majesty and anguish.

Again she feinted, boldly to the right this time, and again he followed. She ducked, danced—clumsy! her nerves shrieked as she realized she had not moved quickly enough. But Mardoc's wound was beginning to slow him; it must be deeper than she had thought—blood stained his tunic and flowed in scarlet runnels down his leg. . . . Even as she felt his sword puncture the side of her corselet, driving the mail through her shirt and into her flesh, her own sword stabbed through the seam of his cuirass, stabbed between his ribs, and buried itself to half its length in his body.

With a gasp she wrenched her weapon free and spun away. But he was not pursuing her. He crumpled to his knees beside the great stone of Harus's altar, amazement on his face, his eyes melting, running in great tears down his gray-stubbled cheeks.

Danica stood upright. Another muscle spasm gripped her abdomen. Her arm burned, as if her blood were searing hot, and each metal crescent of mail seemed branded on her side.

She could not quite catch her breath, and she trembled—Adrastes's eyes were on her. . . . She knew without seeing that Ilanit raised the shield before the high priest's gaze and blocked it. He retreated and bumped into Patros. He stepped to the side, and Chryse edged away from him.

"Whore," Mardoc said, quite calmly. "Kill me, whore."

She looked at him, for a moment not quite remembering who he was. Theara, Atalia dead, the borders of Sabazel—the world fluttered around her, and a numbing weakness crept up her limbs.

"Kill me!" Ah, yes. . . . She gathered her strength, stepped forward, ripped his helmet from his head, and sent it bouncing across the bricks; she seized his hair in her fingers and set her blade at his throat.

The sunlight poured across her, red, amber, gold. Bellasteros watched, creases of pain setting themselves deep into his face. His thought struck her: Mercy, I beg of you; leave him some dignity. . . .

She lowered her sword, turned her back on the general, paced across the bricks to stand at Ilanit's side. "Why?" the girl asked, but Danica hushed her.

Mardoc grasped the edge of the altar and raised himself to his feet. "Marcos," he gasped, "you are bewitched, turning away from me. . . ." A bloody froth spilled from his lips.

"It is you who are bewitched," Bellasteros returned, his voice grating his throat. "You who would not see."

Mardoc stood to attention, pulling the shreds of his honor about him. With a shaky hand he raised his sword in a salute. "My respect, my emperor." Solifrax glinted in reply.

"Father," Chryse moaned, her hand pressing her veil into her mouth.

Mardoc reversed his sword, setting the hilt against the edge of the altar. For a long, silent moment he did not move, and no one in the gathered company drew breath. Then, "Harus!" he cried, and threw his body against the blade. Slowly, his body unbending even in its final throes, he toppled across the stone; his face smoothed, his eyes closed peacefully, and he lay dead in the ancient place of sacrifice. His blood flowed over the rusty stains, obliterating them, pooling on the weathered bricks beneath.

A murmur passed through the Sardians, not of protest but of sorrow. Bellasteros bowed his head and shuddered so violently his armor creaked. Chryse bent against Declan, weeping. Danica drew a quavering breath against a wave of nausea. No, it is not yet over; Mother, leave me the power a few more moments, I beg of you. . . .

The sun touched the horizon and cast flares of crimson across the sky. The air was thick with motes of gold dust, stirred in slow circles by the wind. A faint gleam rose up the eastern sky. An imperial official opened the gates and ushered in several servants bearing great brass trays filled with cups and bowls. He saw Mardoc's body, started, quickly recovered himself, and bowed, smiling, before Bellasteros.

Bellasteros straightened, seizing his composure. He hardly seemed to see the man, waving him away casually; the official began to distribute the cups. "My lord," said Aveyron, jerking his own voice from his throat. Bellasteros's eye fell on him, lighting with thought; he beckoned the young soldier forward.

Adrastes's eyes flicked to every face in the courtyard, black flies disturbed from the carrion on which they fed. When they fell on Bellasteros they swirled, opening onto black nothingness. He reached into his robe and pulled out a tiny vial. Chryse, Declan, Patros took cups, leaving two on the tray. The vial snicked against the rim of one, and Adrastes lifted the other.

Danica winced as Shandir ripped her shirt and tied it tightly around her upper arm. But the pain was not from that; something struck her, fluttering blackly across her vision, pricking at her consciousness. . . . Aveyron conferred with Bellasteros; he was quivering with terror, but each quiet, precise word of the emperor's drew a responding word from him.

The official passed the remaining cup to Bellasteros; the emperor hardly noticed it in his hand as he continued to speak to Aveyron. Chryse swallowed her tears and sipped at her wine. Declan gulped. Lyris and Ilanit burnished the shield with their cloaks, and it hissed, spitting rays of quicksilver into the dusk.

Gods, does his corruption have no limit! Danica shoved Shandir away and reached for the shield. Adrastes emanated an evil purpose; a dark miasma gathered about him as he leaned over to offer a mockery of comfort to Chryse. . . . Chryse shrank away from him with a faint cry.

Bellasteros dismissed Aveyron. He turned. His face was livid, his eyes burned, the diadem glittered across his brow. "Your Eminence," he said, his voice vibrating as tautly as the fibers of his body.

The sun set, drawing the light of day with it. A cool breeze sifted the twilight, laying translucent shadow over the precinct. But Solifrax, and Bellasteros's eyes, still held the light of the sun.

Adrastes drew folds of hauteur about him. "May I serve you, my lord?"

"Tell my councillors how you corrupted my general. Tell them how you and he sent a message to Bogazkar, revealing the disposition of the Sardian army."

The gathered officers gasped.

"What?" demanded the priest, as if his ears deceived him. "How can you say such a thing, my lord?"

"This soldier," said Bellasteros, "heard the boasts of your messenger. The man showed him the parchment, sealed with your seal and Mardoc's."

Adrastes snapped about like a snake, and the force of his gaze sent Aveyron reeling backward. The falcons staggered in midair. "You," he hissed. "You lie, your tongue should shrivel and you should burn—"

"You condemn yourself, priest," scowled the emperor. At last he was revealing his fury, searing the air around him with his rage.

Danica stepped forward, into the luminescence shed by his form. She lifted the untouched cup from Bellasteros's fingers and held it out to Adrastes. "Drink. Your sorcery has made you thirsty; drink."

The star-shield flared, leaving Adrastes standing alone in a pool of pale light. The color drained from his skin and beard, as if they were the decayed remnants of mortality on a week-old corpse. But his eyes still lived, black, pitiless, rejecting the light. He struck out and dashed the cup from Danica's hand. The wine splashed across the bricks, each drop leaving a sizzling scar.

The Sardian officers muttered angrily and moved forward. The official's sharp intake of breath was louder. "I gave it to you, forgive me, my lord. . . ."

Chryse choked, coughing, and threw her own cup away.

"He knew," Bellasteros growled, "that I would accept

nothing from his hand." He stepped off the dais and stood an arm's length from Adrastes, at Danica's side. Solifrax shed sparks onto the pavement, and the shield sang in reply. "But you would not murder my first wife, would you? You would take her, and my diadem, and the Empire I have won—you would steal them from my dead hands."

The priest retreated a pace. "You, too," he cried, "a spawn of Sabazel. You, too, born of the goddess. Bastard, unfit to rule Sardis. . . ."

"Go on," said Bellasteros between his teeth. "Spew out your poison. Your powers wane, and you will enspell no one else."

True enough; the faces around Adrastes reflected only shocked disbelief.

"Bastard!" the priest screamed. He pointed a clawlike finger at the emperor. "Heretic! You should burn, shrivel to nothingness for your deeds!"

Bellasteros laughed, and the power in that laugh froze the priest's expression in gaping madness. Solifrax rose; its tip brushed Adrastes's throat, passed down his chest, settled on the winged pectoral. Delicately, the emperor lifted the symbol of office and removed it. "Declan," he called.

The young priest ran forward, knelt.

"You are hereby appointed the talon of Harus. The office of grand inquisitor is abolished, due to the treachery of he who last held it."

Declan caught the pectoral as it slid from the blade. In his hands the metal swirled, beginning to glisten, reflecting the light of shield and sword. "My thanks, my lord," he said, genuinely surprised.

"You shall restore honor to the name of Harus," said the emperor. The images of the god seemed to flutter in satisfaction as he turned again to Adrastes.

Quicksilver spilled across the courtyard. Every eye turned to the east; the full moon rose above the horizon, a caldron of light. Pale light, tinted with the faintest blush of red.

Adrastes screamed as if the light seared him. He shrank back, turning to run. With a beatific smile Lyris thrust out her foot and tripped him. He fell headlong at the foot of the altar, and Mardoc's drying blood mottled his face and his robes with dark carnelian.

He crouched on the pavement, a cornered, wounded basilisk. And yet he bore some remnant of his power, and his pride was limitless—he raised his hands, beginning an incantation, and darkness gathered at his fingertips. The darkness swelled, streaming outward, seeking its prey. . . .

As one, deliberately, Danica and Bellasteros stepped forward. The shield reflecting the moonlight, gathering it, pouring it like molten silver over the shadow and dissipating it—the sword, holding the golden gleam of the sun, making of the light itself a crystalline-bladed weapon that sliced the gathering darkness into tattered smoke.

Awed silence fell upon the courtyard; more than one spectator shrank back, covering his eyes. But not Patros or Lyris, Declan or Chryse. They watched, their faces as taut as the pale light they beheld.

And the shadow turned, enveloping Adrastes himself, sucking the color from his clothing and drawing the darkness of his eyes from their sockets. He screamed, crawling across the bricks, but could not escape. His tongue shriveled in his mouth, his eyes burst and melted down his face, his skin peeled away, revealing the black blood underneath.

The shadow winked out. But still Adrastes writhed, his robes burning in the clear white flame of shield and sword, fire and light consuming him until at last only a charred simulacrum of a human form lay before the altar. It whimpered, the cinders of its limbs twitching feebly. Bellasteros stepped into the luminescence of the shield, drawing it about him, and with Solifrax cut the life from the pitiful remains.

For a long moment the scent of burning flesh hung heavy on the air. Then a wind poured down the sky, bringing the cold cleanness of an ice-crowned mountain. The gathered people seemed to inhale in one great sigh.

Bellasteros stood silent in the moonlight and its reflection from the shield, letting it cleanse his sword, letting it purify him; his face was gray with the ashes of his anger. He turned to Danica, whispering, "Your forgiveness, Mother. . . ."

Danica heard again the note of harmony, the strand of melody straining at her consciousness, that they had heard in the garden of the gods. He heard it, too—his dark eyes glistened with it; for one eternal moment they stood together, filled with the light of the sun and moon, filled with the music of the gods.

"We are forgiven." Danica sighed. The absolution was

sweet, sweet. . . . The melody was gone, burst like a pricked bubble. The shield muted itself and another wave of nausea drained the blood from her face.

Voices rose clamoring into the night. Bellasteros was suddenly surrounded by his officers, by Declan, Chryse, Aveyron, and Patros, declaring their fealty; the priests and priestesses crept forward in awe to touch the hem of his tunic and the rim of Danica's shield. The falcon standards seemed to murmur contentedly, the god freed at last. No one went near Mardoc's cold form or the cinders that had been Adrastes.

Danica looked at Ilanit and Lyris, and Shandir's smooth face, as if she had never seen them before. She was falling, plummeting down from a great height; her remote, celestial viewpoint evaporated and drifted like silvered mist down the wind. Her power drained from her body, ebbing perceptibly from her mind, leaving her aching and hollow. Mortality and pain, the end of the game. . . .

She leaned against Shandir, her knees suddenly too weak to hold her. "Take me away," she said. "Alone." Her ears buzzed, her head swam, all the blood in her body drained into her abdomen and twisted, tighter, tighter, into a cramp that took her breath away. "No." she gasped. "No, not now, Mother. . . ."

Shandir, horrified, took Danica's shield and gave it to Ilanit, took her sword and helmet and passed them to Lyris. "Come," she said.

Bellasteros looked over the heads of the people around him, sensing something amiss. "Patros," he ordered, "escort the queen of Sabazel to a place of rest befitting her rank." Patros hurried to take Danica's other arm, and Chryse, her brow furrowed with concern, followed.

She walked from the courtyard, placing one foot before the other; I shall not fall here, not before all these folk—Marcos! Bellasteros's eyes rested on her back, offering his own strength, accompanying her. . . . Imperial officials and his own people mingled raised him up and bore him away.

The gate, steps, a street, and the gates of the palace; torchlit hallways flowed through her mind; a large shadowed bedchamber. Another cramp, wringing her entire body with its force—a rush of warmth down her legs as the waters holding the child burst from her body.

And no more thoughts, only sensation, only the consciousness of her own muscles straining rhythmically. Marcos! she wailed, even as she despised her own weakness, her own helplessness; but he was not there.

Chapter Seventeen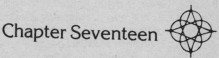

BELLASTEROS WALKED IN A DREAM. The night undulated like a serpent around him, eyes flaring with lamps and torches and the great round glow of the moon. He slipped Solifrax hissing into its sheath and tried to focus on at least one face before him. . . . Sardian officers, requesting food, requesting medicines. Imperial officers swearing fealty. Palace officials and servants bearing gifts of wine, gold, spices. People touching him, wanting to share some shred of his power.

The throne room. Someone had brought the great tapestry, and the outspread wings of Sardian Harus stretched between lotus-capped columns. The embroidered battle it overlooked was won; the threads shifted, weaving themselves into a new scene—Farsahn, Iksandarun, and the Empire, prospering under the rule of Bellasteros. On the opposite wall, a fresco of Daimion with Mari at his side, their painted faces regarding him in cool challenge.

King of kings, god-king, emperor—the diadem was warm, sitting lightly on his hair, whispering of power. Bellasteros mounted the steps and seated himself gingerly on the imperial throne. Mother-of-pearl and lapis lazuli, garnet and gold; the throne was an ornately carved peacock's tail, and he felt as if his dirty, sweaty, bloody armor befouled it.

Thousands lay dead this night, sacrificed to his ambition— Mardoc, Atalia, Bogazkar—the legions, imperial and Sardian alike, decimated. . . . The challenge, he thought, is to build.

His subjects, new and old, bowed before him. No longer would he have to worry who was faithful, who a spy. Aveyron, smiling, held the falcon standards at his side. Make the lad a centurion, he told himself. On a gallery above the room women watched him, exchanging pleased asides; the harem, one of the officials had whispered. Now his.

Danica, he thought. Where was she, what was happening, had she been wounded with some foul lingering poison of Adrastes? A pulse beat in the back of his mind, urgent, desperate. He peered through the glitter of the room, searching for Patros, but Patros was not there.

More petitioners, more decisions—and here an official came with a young girl, hardly older than his own daughter. Roushangka, said the man, Kallidar's only surviving child.

She was his own cousin, come to think of it, a relative of his mother. But Roushangka was fair, unlike Sardian-dark Viridis. The child watched him with great gray eyes, her painted mouth tight with fear, the blond curls that streamed down her back trembling like poplar leaves in a breeze. In sixteen days, the astrologers said, a propitious time for marriage, the binding of a new ruler to the Empire.

"Yes, I would be honored," said Bellasteros, abstracted. Blond, like Danica—Danica. . . .

Roushangka was gone, carried away into the crowd. Someone produced wine, watered wine—he sipped, and his head cleared somewhat.

A group of Sabazians approached him, led by the thin one —Lyris—requesting a funeral pyre, games in honor of dead Atalia. "Yes, yes, of course," he returned, and designated an officer to assist. "Lyris!" he called.

Pale, shuttered eyes, reserving emotion, reserving thought. "Yes, my lord?"

"Please, give me news of your queen. Is she well?"

A slight crumple of her mouth, then a polite inclination of her head, enough to conceal her face. "She will send messages when she is ready, my lord."

"My thanks," Bellasteros said dryly. But the pulse hammered on. Something was wrong, something had gone terribly awry. Gods! he thought. Have you not had your sacrifice for this day—forever? . . .

Patros appeared at his side, his helmet carried under his arm, his face set carefully so as to reveal little to the watching crowd. "Marcos," he said under his breath, "your lady is caught in the travail of birth; she is tired and weak, and Shandir fears for her life—" His voice cracked and he hastily cleared his throat.

Bellasteros tried to speak and could not. Birth? Now? The room spun around him, torches elongating into fiery banners, voices quickening into one blended clamor, the heavy buzzing of insects on a hot summer's afternoon. . . . Perspiration streamed down his back as he fell into reality.

"You must excuse me," he said to whatever faces were closest. "I have urgent business elsewhere—I shall return as soon as possible."

The people parted before him, bowing, reaching out to touch his sacred person. Then he was in a cool marble hallway, past a courtyard where the bare branches of orange and almond trees rattled in a jangling breeze, before a door guarded by a Sardian and a Sabazian, into a large bedchamber lit by braziers. Shadowed silk hangings, shutters open to the moon—the moon, held in a taut membrane of imperial purple, picked with diamonds. . . . The light streamed across the floor, cool, impersonal, blotting out the scarlet luminescence of the fires.

Chryse, wringing out a cloth in herb-scented water; Shandir, kneeling at the foot of the bed; Ilanit, wiping gleaming rivulets of sweat from her mother's naked body—Danica! he thought, her name wrenched from his heart. She was propped up by thick pillows in the center of the bed, knees bent, hands trembling over the oddly flattened mound of her belly. Her face deathly pale and drawn, her hair tangled across the coverlet. . . .

"Danica?" he said aloud, and hesitantly stepped to her side.

Tired, so tired—Danica was buffeted by the waves of pain, drowning in them, not coasting with a fierce glee down their slopes, as she should have been. Never like this before, one part of her mind insisted. Wrong, all wrong—too soon. Oh, my poor child, I have failed you. . . .

Her eyes cleared, and for one lucid moment she saw the moonlight streaming across the floor, lapping at the foot of the bed. The shield gleamed in its corner, humming discordantly. I shall climb up the moonpath, climb up Cylandra to the peak, throw myself into the sky—cool, clean, quiet. . . . Chryse poured a drop of wine between her lips and she swallowed. Her mouth was foul, her body streaked with dirt and blood—the moonpath, clean and cool. . . .

Again the tightening, twisting, wringing, deeper and deeper until her eyes bulged from her face. The bandage on her arm reddened. She heard her own breath escape in a moan—Marcos . . . Weak, that tiny shred of coherence told her. Weak, to call upon a man now; none of a man's business, this.

Danica's eyes cleared. She was hallucinating. Bellasteros bent over her, his fingertips touching her face lightly, so lightly. . . . "Danica?" She was even hearing his voice. He was pale, frowning—the diadem muted and forgotten on his brow, Solifrax sheathed and forgotten by his side.

He was there, sitting uncertainly on the edge of the bed. She reached for his hand and grasped it convulsively in her own. "And my strength, my lady. . . ." he whispered. Or perhaps he only thought it.

Danica's muscles strained into one great expulsive thrust. She rose from the pillows, sitting almost upright. "Shandir," she gasped, "now, the time has come."

"What?" Bellasteros asked.

"Have you never witnessed a birth?" asked Shandir. She probed gently, announced, "It is lying correctly, Danica. But small, very small."

"A birth?" Bellasteros replied. "No, of course not; women's work. . . ."

"But with materials you provided," Shandir said tartly.

"Indeed," he returned. His voice shivered and he steadied it.

"Bellasteros breaks all the rules," said Danica. "He breaks them, and he builds new and better ones. . . ." Her voice spun itself out and shattered in a sharp exhalation. Tired, so tired—she could hardly hold her head erect, her hands shook, her legs were only strands of flesh connected to her body—her body worked without conscious direction, wringing itself inside out.

"Prop her up," said Shandir's distant voice, and Bellasteros obeyed, placing his arm behind Danica's shoulders and lifting her forward.

A moment later she fell back, spent. Chryse quickly forced another drop of wine between her lips. Chryse, the first wife of the emperor, Danica thought with detached amusement. Our child it is, hers more than mine. . . . The Sardian woman's face reflected a passionate hope, an agony almost equal to Danica's own.

Bellasteros's dark eyes glistened damply. Ilanit's touch trembled. The shape in the corner—Patros, forgotten, unable to leave.

Again the thrust. Surely her body would rip itself apart, seared into two pieces, tattered flesh. . . . "I can see its head," Shandir said quietly. "Dark hair, a proper little Sardian."

Perhaps she attempted a jest; Danica could not tell, did not care. She fell back, exhausted, no more strength, no more consciousness. Bellasteros's arm was tight behind her, his hand still held hers. Draw from me, take whatever you need, my lady, my love. . . .

Strength—with an effort she inhaled deeply, let his strength seep into her—and up, clenched with effort. . . . Danica heard her own voice cry out, a wordless shriek of pain so intense it was ecstatic. And Shandir bent forward, pulled gently, held a tiny baby in her hands.

Danica collapsed, sliding down the far side of a great wave, faster and faster—the moonpath retreating across the floor, drawing her with it, out into the star-pricked sky and Ashtar's arms. . . .

Ah, my daughter, a game well played, indeed.

So the voice, the presence returned—returned to take her. . . .

Bellasteros still held her. He was silent. Everyone was silent. She grasped the last strand of her consciousness and pulled herself from her dream. With an effort she cleared her head, opened her eyes.

Shandir held the baby gently. A boy. Heir to the Empire. Eyes closed, dark lashes crescents on his cheeks. Blue cheeks, flaccid limbs, little chest unmoving—tiny azure fingers limp on Shandir's wrist.

The healer looked up, met Danica's eyes, shook her head in a slow, reluctant grief.

Chryse gulped and turned aside. Ilanit dropped the delicate cotton wrappings she held, covering her face.

Bellasteros said, very quietly, "No. Have we not had death enough, this day, this year—these past years? This innocent will not pay. . . ."

In a paroxysm of denial Danica started up. She took the baby from Shandir's hands. Small, too small—she felt as if she held a doll. The umbilical cord still coiled from his body into hers, not taut but slack. "No," she said, low, fervent, "I shall not accept his death, too. Mother! Hear me—" Blood gushed from her body, splashing Shandir, and the healer bent hurriedly to her work.

Danica hardly noticed. Her gaze was fixed on some infinite horizon, beyond this room and the path of the moonlight. "Mother!" she cried. "Hear me!" The shield seethed with quicksilver.

The winter king, daughter. The winter king, sacrificed that the summer king might live, and living, secure Sabazel. . . . The game is over.

"Sacrificed to my ambition?" asked Bellasteros. "No! You no longer demand sacrifice, Mother. . . ."

"And the game will not end like this!" Danica bled. Shandir grew pale, redoubling her efforts. Chryse and Ilanit stood helplessly, clutching at each other.

"Death," Danica said. "Pain, and after pain healing, or what is the purpose, Mother!"

Sorrow, for a game that cannot be won.

"Compromise, only compromise—Harus himself upon your arm. . . . What is this child but compromise!"

The baby lay cold and still against her breast. The goddess was silent. "We sustain you," Danica cried, "as you sustain us; will you betray us, Ashtar? If we cannot believe in you, then we can believe in nothing, nothing. . . ." Another gout of blood burst from her, pattering like rain onto the marble floor. A chill shook her, the room wavered, moon-glowing mist shading her eyes. "I die, Ashtar," moaned Danica, falling back against the pillows, clutching the baby. "Take me, too; kill me with your betrayal. . . ."

"Ashtar," Bellasteros said, his face creased with pain, "I have bowed to you, I have given myself to you, have we not had betrayal enough? . . . Compromise, Mother; life for death." He held Danica closely, his body cradling hers, his mind cradling her mind—strength, purpose, and power—her power, feeble tendrils of power coursing through her veins. Her bleeding slowed and stopped.

Ah, my daughter, my love for you is great; my son, my love, my child. . . .

Danica summoned the last remnants of her power, gathered it, refined it, poured it through her body; the umbilical cord tautened, the baby drew breath, coughed, emitted a tiny wail. His skin flushed a rosy pink.

For a long moment no one spoke, no one moved; the presence of the goddess filled the room, swelling outward in the infant's cry: "I am! I am!"

Then Chryse fell swooning into a nearby chair. Shandir, beaming despite the tears in her eyes, tied off the cord and cut it with a flourish. Ilanit turned to Patros, opening her arms to him; "Well," he said, his voice squeaking uncontrollably, "such a mite to rule the world. . . ."

Danica lay back against Bellasteros, weary, spent with effort; they watched in perfect unity as the baby's chest rose and fell, as its eyes opened and stared up at them. Dark eyes, flickering with the smallest, most distant flame, reflecting the gleam of shield and sword and imperial diadem. Thank you, Mother, thank you.

"Andrion," Bellasteros murmured, naming him. "Beloved of the gods. We shall see if he comes to deserve the surname Bellasteros. . . ."

Andrion's little fist waggled up into the air, thrashed about uncertainly, fell back. His face split into a yawn, obliterating nose and chin.

"In time," whispered Danica. "In time." She floated in some eddy of time and space; this, then, and nothing more. . . . Gently she turned Andrion's face to her breast, guiding him; his hands grasped at her and his cheeks inflated as he sucked. The pleasure of it, the warm mouth drawing the last drops of power from her. She sighed and turned with a smile to Bellasteros.

He tried to smile in return, but his lips crumpled. Trembling, Bellasteros laid his face against Danica's shoulder and wept.

The moon reached its zenith; the night wind swept away its path.

Chapter Eighteen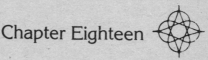

DANICA CURSED HERSELF for her weakness. Her limbs wobbled like those of a newborn colt and the marble buckled beneath her feet. She fell against Chryse, and from her other side Shandir laughed at her. "Do not try to move so fast. It will take time to regain your strength."

"Time," said Danica, "is something that for once I have."

Shandir eased her down in a chair by the window; Chryse opened the shutter a little farther. Thin winter sunlight lay on the city, picking subtle glints and gleams from battlement, building, courtyard. The mound of the temple precinct stood up on the right, the different shrines dozing in a midday torpor. To the left, from beyond the city walls, rose a thick plume of smoke.

Danica rested her forearms on the windowsill and sighed deeply. Atalia, laid in honor among her fallen comrades, and the emperor himself to light the pyre; may she go peacefully to her rest. Atalia, if only you could have seen my son. . . .

But, Danica thought wryly, Atalia would have only glanced at the baby and turned to her queen demanding to know why she risked so much for its life—it is only a man-child, after all, and of little account in the scheme of things.

A breeze brushed her face and passed on into the room, stirring the shadows into opalescent glimmers. The hangings over the cradle fluttered in slow, fluid waves. But you, Mother, you know the significance of this child.

Yes; compromise, healing, and the end of the game.

Danica smiled. I was once a god, and the gods no longer awe me. She wondered for a moment if this was her loss or her gain. A tiny cry came from the cradle, and she abandoned her problem as insoluble. She started to rise.

"No, no," said Shandir. "Sit." But before she could reach the cradle Chryse did, picking up the wriggling bundle and rocking it in her arms. The woman's face glowed with pleasure.

My loss, thought Danica, or my gain?

Chryse looked at her. "My thanks, my lady. My thanks for such a child."

Gain, surely. Gain.

Bellasteros stood quietly, the heat of the pyre glowing on his face. Patros waited at his side, with Aveyron and the falcons, with Declan the high priest in attendance. Beyond the pyre, in a fallow field beside the road, was the mound of the dead Sardians. Facing it, the graves of the imperial soldiers. Bogazkar, Mardoc, Adrastes—decomposing slowly to dust, and as dust mingling with the ages.

The pyre of the Sabazians snapped and popped. The heat was too great; Bellasteros stepped back. He turned to the rank of Companions, Ilanit with her mother's shield reflecting a red glare, Lyris, straight and confident, at her side. "My thanks," he said quietly, "for your aid these past days."

Ilanit lifted her chin, tossing her head in a proud gesture worthy of Danica herself. "We have bought Sabazel's safety?"

"I have already issued the proclamation. The borders of Sabazel are inviolate."

Ilanit nodded. "Then we are honored to serve with you." She glanced from the corners of her eyes at Patros, and her mouth crumpled. "Honored indeed. . . ."

The wind pealed down from heaven, gathering up the smoke of the pyre and spreading it across all the lands between Iksandarun and Sabazel, spreading it even to the streets of Sardis. And the fire consumed itself and went out.

Declan, wearing the winged pectoral and a becoming gravity, signaled the massed Sardian and imperial troops to silence. The echoing shouts of the centurions died away. "The blessing of almighty Harus upon this child," he cried. "His spread wings protect this heir to the Empire. In the name of the god. . . ."

Bellasteros, very carefully, held the tiny form of Andrion up to the army. The baby clenched its eyes, screwed up its face, shrieked. The glittering falcon standards seemed to shriek in reply, and the army shouted its approval.

Bellasteros lowered the child and tucked it into the crook of his arm. Here, feeling more secure, Andrion quieted. His eyes, bright little beads, gazed out wonderingly at the width of the world.

The army shouted again, saluting with a crash of swords against armor. Bellasteros lifted Solifrax in reply.

Andrion's eyes fixed on the gleam of the sword, unblinking. "Not yet," Bellasteros said quietly to him. "Not yet."

Chryse and Danica sat side by side in a window, overlooking the ceremony. They turned to each other with indulgent smiles. "At least this Sardian ruler knows his father," Danica said.

"Most people will think him mine," returned Chryse. "The king was, after all, in Sardis in the spring. And these robes . . ." She patted her flat stomach with a chuckle. "Those who know the truth, Danica, will know its importance—Andrion, beloved of the gods. . . ."

"And of his mothers," Danica said.

The moon diminished, died, and then came again, a silver paring clinging to the sun's path.

The wedding ceremony was held according to imperial custom, with several priests and priestesses in attendance, with bells ringing and tapers glowing, with jewels and silks and incense. Declan said a special blessing over Bellasteros's bowed head and that of Roushangka beside him; then he turned to bless the Sardian officers, Patros and the others now wedded to the younger members of the imperial harem.

The festivities went on most of the night—singing, dancing, feasting. From her room Danica heard the lilting strains of the music, and she sang softly over Andrion's dark head. For a time Ilanit pouted, envisioning Patros in another woman's arms; soon, though, she heeded the soft Sabazian songs her mother murmured, and her expression smoothed.

Bellasteros was led to the door of Roushangka's chamber by

a group of imperial officers bearing torches and wine goblets. There they left him and with many ribald jests returned to the party. He had not drunk much—strange, how his taste for wine had decreased since one eventful evening in the gold pavilion—and he entered the room quietly, with a certain wry resignation.

A few oil lamps barely shifted the shadows. Somewhere, behind the hangings of the great bed, the child was waiting—the child he was expected to violate for the Empire. He made a mental note to halt the marriage of his own daughter until such time as she made her own choice.

There was Roushangka, draped in darkness, the coverlet held high in her two clenched hands. Her eyes were huge wells of fear—he imagined he could hear her teeth chattering. And why not? He came to her stained with the blood of her relatives—with the blood of his own mother. . . .

He eased himself down beside her, talked to her of the world and the wondrous things it held, of the garden of the gods and the sword Solifrax wrapped by a serpent, of the moon rising over Cylandra. And slowly she let the covers fall from her face.

With one delicate fingertip he touched her cheeks, her lips, the hollow of her throat. She was scented with some rich fragrance, not at all like Danica—but then, her hair was blond. . . . He stroked her body, lightly, until she smiled and opened her embrace to him.

The Empire secured, he rose and left her pink and tumbled, asleep. Roushangka, he thought, may you find some purpose to your life; I cannot be it. He dressed, picked up the diadem, sought Danica's chamber.

She lay with Andrion tucked against her side, holding him with her arm as he nursed. "Ah," she said drowsily. "Another bloody deed done for the Empire?"

"Unfair, Danica. Unfair."

"Forgive me." She sighed. "I would be surprised to see you here, but Patros has already come seeking Ilanit."

"We know our minds." Bellasteros smiled. He bent to touch one tiny hand splayed out against Danica's breast. He could, he thought, pass the baby's entire body through the diadem. "You are my lady. I would sleep with you on my marriage night." He lay down behind her, enfolding her in his arms.

"You are scented with an exotic fragrance," Danica said, laughing. "Did they drench her with an aphrodisiac?"

"Probably. She is a child, after all, and it is a woman I love. I prefer the scent of asphodel."

"And the queen of Sabazel, frail enough to love a man. . . . My strength returns, Marcos; soon I must go back."

The words pierced him, arrows in his mind. But they were not unexpected. "I know," he said after a moment. He laid his face against her hair. "I shall come in the spring."

"We shall be expecting you, the goddess and I." She turned slightly and met his lips in a gentle kiss. Andrion continued feeding, oblivious.

The moon swelled again, passed its ripeness, and decreased. Danica did not count the days. She slept as much as the baby slept; she lay by his side in the noon sunlight and tickled his little waving feet. He grew, slowly but perceptibly, his wizened arms and legs filling out, his body becoming plump.

I, too, shall become plump, Danica chided herself; Bellasteros had ordered the palace cooks to tempt her appetite with succulent lamb basted in lemon juice, dates, pomegranates, delicate pastries flavored with honey and pistachios. She pulled herself from the bed, stretching and bending, and her body returned to its sleek firmness.

One day she was appalled to notice that the star-shield had gathered a veil of dust. Frowning, she cleaned it, drawing gentle sparks from its surface; it was dented and scarred with its many battles. It was time, she thought, to return it to the basin of light, to mend it. She thought of Sabazel, the mountain, the little town, the wind in her garden . . . For a moment she was dizzy with the memory of it.

The next day she dressed again in helmet and corselet, the mail flapping loosely over her waist. She lifted the shield into its accustomed place on her arm, drew her sword, thrust and parried across the floor.

Chryse stood at the window, absorbed in the vista of the city, in the quiet song of a hoopoe. She held Andrion on her shoulder and his dark eyes boggled at Danica as she exercised.

Laughing, she saluted him. With a purposeful grimace he lifted his head, held it upright for a slow count of five, then let it fall again. His nose hit Chryse's collarbone and he howled indignantly.

Chryse shook herself from her reverie and soothed him. She saw Danica in her armor and her face struggled to find an appropriate expression.

"It is time for me to go." Danica said.

Chryse flushed. "Please do not think that I—"

"But he is to be your child. You have already found a nurse for him."

"Yes, but—"

"And I should leave you with your husband. He is your husband, Chryse, not mine."

Chryse flushed even more deeply. "He . . . looks at me in a new way. That I owe to you, my lady."

"No, you owe it to your own efforts. Shandir told me how you saved me from Adrastes's sorcery. I thank you, Chryse."

"What else could I do?"

'You could have done nothing, as was expected of you."

The door opened and Ilanit came cat-footed into the room. Indeed, Danica thought, the girl looked like a cat, preened and petted, her lengthening hair held back by a thin fillet. "And you?" she asked.

"Pardon?" Ilanit replied.

"You are ready to return to Sabazel?"

"Ah," said the girl with a sigh, "I had thought to die, leaving him—but I am Sabazian, after all; Ashtar calls me home, and . . ."

Danica drew Ilanit to her side. "And?"

"I think I am with child," she said shyly.

Life after death, and compromise at the end. . . . "Have you told him?"

"No. He will learn soon enough. But then, only one child of Ashtar has a father." She stepped away from Danica to take her mite of a brother from Chryse. He stared up at her, and his face crumpled into a wide, toothless smile.

"Patros will not hear it from my lips," Chryse assured Ilanit.

"My thanks," returned the girl. "His new wife is much like you, lady."

Danica flexed her sword again before her. The shield glimmered faintly, drawing a slow stirring of air through the window. And what if peace, she thought, is a greater danger to us than the enmity of our neighbors? Creeping contentment, and our guard lowered; a new game, Mother? Not all men learn as readily as Bellasteros.

Vigilance, my daughter; vigilance, now more than ever.

Then we shall be wary, Danica thought. And she tucked the thought away, to examine it at some later time, in some more suitable place within the borders of Sabazel.

She set down her weapons, removed her helmet, stripped off her corselet. "Bring me my son," she said to Ilanit. "Already I ache with the thought of leaving him." We give away our sons, to be cherished by our neighbors—cherished indeed, she told herself. Loved by the gods, as is his father, as is the woman who bore him but who could not be his mother. . . .

She took the warm, wiggling little bundle and clasped it to her. Andrion rooted at her breast, then looked up, cooing and smiling. His eyes, the eyes of the king, dark and rich. . . . He began to suck.

Tears clogged her throat and she swallowed them. Vigilance, she thought. And she thought, It is not Ashtar who is implacable. It is I.

Declan bowed in respect. "I am pleased that you like it."

Ashtar's shrine had been scrubbed, painted, garlanded with vines and early spring flowers. "It is worthy of the goddess," Danica told him. "My thanks." She raised the shield toward the atrium and the cool morning sunshine; a quick swirl of light emanated from the emblazoned star. Moonlight, drawing her home to Sabazel.

Light reflected in Declan's pectoral. "The honor of the god restored," he murmured, and she nodded agreement. Hard, to take leave of even this priest. . . . She bowed before the shrine of Harus and walked out of the temple precinct.

Bellasteros waited by a small troop of horsemen. His hair was beginning to wave over the back of his neck and across his brow, a gleaming sable bed for the diadem; his cheeks and chin were shaded by a soft beard in the fashion of the Empire. It becomes you, she thought, but she could say nothing.

Shandir spoke with the centurion Aveyron. ". . . welcome in the spring." Ilanit stood somberly by a somber Patros, their farewells made. At a high window Chryse held sleeping Andrion, her unveiled face damp with the tears no one else would shed.

Danica's breasts tingled and a warm trickle of milk wetted her shirt. A small discomfort, she assured herself. Just as the look in Bellasteros's eyes was only a small discomfort. Too much to say. Too much that could never be said.

Silently she mounted her horse and led the depleted group of Sabazians, seventy strong, out of the city. Lyris turned and waved to Chryse; the gold chain glinted at her throat, and she wore it as a badge of honor. But Danica would not look back.

Sabazel, sighed the goddess. *Sabazel secured, my daughter*.

A game that cannot be won, Danica replied. But she had thought that so many times that it had at last lost its power to wound her.

Bellasteros and Patros, a ceremonial guard, and a falcon standard rode with them to the pass. Peasants tilled the fields beside the road and built farmsteads of mud-brick and brush. Soldiers worked rebuilding the walls and the forts. "And who would attack you?" Danica asked the emperor as they rode ahead of the rest.

"Vigilance," Bellasteros returned. They looked at each other, looked away quickly. "Danica," he murmured, and a purling wind plucked the name from his lips and bore it away. "Danica, have we come full circle, back to where we began?"

"No. We began as enemies, clinging to the narrowness of our sight. Now . . ."

"Now?" He turned to her again, letting the full force of his gaze rest on her.

Her arm moved to raise the shield against that look, but she forced it down again. "We know that the world has no edge, no ending. . . . Come to me in the spring, Marcos, and we shall celebrate the rites of Ashtar, together in joy—" Her voice broke and she turned her horse, turned away from the dark eyes and the distant flame they held. Ilanit extended her hand; Patros reached out, touched it. And they, too, parted. The Sabazians saluted the falcon standard before they moved alone down the pass and across the rolling lands. At the stream they paused. Danica allowed herself one deliberate backward look.

A streak of crystalline fire in the throat of the pass—Solifrax, claiming the sunlight, making of it a salute. The gods had surely intended that sword for his hand. . . .

She lifted the shield, and it flared in reply.

Ilanit sighed and settled herself more firmly on her horse.

Danica exchanged a glance with Shandir. And she looked ahead, to the expanse of the world, turning her back on Iksandarun, on Sardis and the Empire. She led her people northwestward, to Sabazel and spring.

A crescent moon pierced the blue arch of the sky—the goddess's smile, shaded by the open wings of a falcon. . . .

Danica thought, I come home, Sabazel. She, too, smiled.

Stories
⊱ of ⊰
Swords and Sorcery